THE KINGDOM OF FLAMES AND ASH

Jen L. Grey

THE
KINGDOM
OF FLAMES AND
ASH

JEN L. GREY

ANYA

Anya
An Imprint of Meredith Wild LLC

This is a work of fiction. Names, characters, places, and incidents either are the product of the author's imagination or are used fictitiously, and any resemblance to actual persons, living or dead, business establishments, events, or locales is entirely coincidental. The publisher does not assume any responsibility for third-party websites or their content.

The author acknowledges the trademarked status and trademark owners of various products referenced in this work, which have been used without permission. The publication/use of these trademarks is not authorized, associated with, or sponsored by the trademark owners.

Copyright © 2024 Grey Valor Publishing LLC
Cover Design by Covers By Christian

All Rights Reserved.
No part of this book may be reproduced, scanned, or distributed in any printed or electronic format without permission. Please do not participate in or encourage piracy of copyrighted materials in violation of the author's rights. Purchase only authorized editions.

Paperback ISBN: 979-8-88953-100-5

Name Pronunciation

Lira (LEE-rah)
Tavish (TAH-vish)
Eiric (AY-rik)
Faelan (FAY-lan)
Finnian (FIN-ee-an)
Caelan (KAY-lan)
Eldrin (EL-drin)
Lorne (LORN)
Moira (MOHR-ee-ah)
Torcall (TOR-kahl)
Finola (fi-NO-lah)
Rona (ROH-nah)
Dougal (DOO-gal)
Malikor (MAL-ih-kor)
Moor (MOOR)
Struan (STROO-an)
Pyralis (pie-RAL-is)

General Glossary

Ardanos (ard-AN-ohss) – Realm Name
Aetherglen (AY-thur-glen) – Unseelie and Seelie joined kingdom
Cuil Dorcha (COOL DOR-kha) - Unseelie Kingdom
Dunscaith (DOON-skah) – Unseelie Castle
Gleann Solas (GLYAN SO-las) – Seelie Kingdom
Caisteal Solais (KASH-tul SO-lash) – Seelie Castle
Aelwen – (A-el-wen) - River in Seelie Kingdom
Tìr na Dràgon (CHEER na DRAY-gon) – Dragon Kingdom
Cù-sìth (koo-shee) – Wolf-like Unseelie creature
Sunscorched – Seelie Fae derogatory term
Night fiends – Unseelie Fae derogatory term
Wilding – Bastard
Blasted – Fucking for Unseelie
Blazing – Fucking for Seelie
Blighted Abyss – Bloody hell
Thornling – Pain in the ass
Ashbreath – Dragon
Thornclutched – Manhandled
Cailleach-sgath – Bitch
Gauntlet – Prison Games

Chapter One

Tavish

Watching the gigantic, crimson-colored dragon flapping past the last of the dilapidated Unseelie village toward the sea at the end of the ruined island, with Lira dangling from his talons, obliterated my heart. She was angled toward us, her long, blonde hair blowing in her face, hiding the cobalt-blue eyes I knew better than my own. The dragon had bound her arms and sparkling sea-green wings so she wouldn't have a chance to escape.

The blasted ashbreath.

Eldrin, my cousin and former father figure, straddled me on the stone ground at the bottom of the Unseelie castle stairs with the tip of his sword pressing into the skin over my heart.

"If you'd just *listened* to me, none of this would have had to happen," he spat, his white eyes almost a faint gray similar to mine, barely contrasting with his pale skin. "You're the reason we've come to this, and it's only proper for you to die knowing that you couldn't keep your *fated mate* safe."

Lira, I'm coming, I connected, using our fated-mate link, determination like I'd never experienced before flashing through me. Eldrin had betrayed me in so many ways. He didn't get the luxury of feeling as if he'd accomplished anything when it came to me.

I was the blasting King of Nightmares, Frost and Darkness,

and I refused to lie here like a victim, especially when Lira needed me the most.

With strength that I hadn't been aware I possessed, I bucked my hips, causing Eldrin to fall forward and over my head. The tip of his blade sliced up my chest with a burning sting, but the wound wasn't deep. Ignoring it, I jumped to my feet and stepped on Eldrin's dark wings, pinning him to the ground.

"I never listened to you because you weren't my king. I was yours, and I did what I believed was right," I gritted out. I pushed the sword into Eldrin's back, ready to end his life. I'd wanted to make his death slow and painful, but not at Lira's expense.

I don't need you to come for me; I need you to go after my sister, Lira responded. Her fear and desperation thickened in our bond.

Averting my gaze for a moment, I spotted Eiric about twenty yards away, running with the giant cù-sìth Nightbane toward me. Her emerald eyes shone with fear, and I didn't understand why she wasn't flying after Lira. *Your sister is fine. I'm staring at her right now. You're my concern.*

"Now you won't be a threat to any of us any longer." I needed to end Eldrin and get to my mate.

"Stop. Wait," Eldrin cried. "I know a way to get Lira out of her agreement with the dragon prince. A way other than killing him, and it's simple. Let me live, and I'll tell you."

I didn't have time for games, but the import of his words couldn't be ignored. Right now, the only option I had was killing Prince Pyralis, and that feat alone would be damn near impossible with our weak and shaky guards, thanks to Eldrin's attempt to dethrone me.

"Watch him, and don't kill him yet," I called to Finnian and Caelan. I hated that, once again, Eldrin had something to hold over me, but I didn't have time to be rational... not with Lira getting farther from me every minute. "I need to go after Lira." My voice broke.

"You aren't going alone." Finnian bent down, his blue wings blocking my view of my cousin, but his fist struck, the hilt of his sword going first. There was a thud, and then Finnian straightened. "There. Problem solved, though I would've preferred to kill the wildling. Now, let's save Lira from the ashbreath."

Black blood seeped from the back of Eldrin's skull, mixing in with his white hair. From the way he didn't move, it was clear that he was unconscious and would be out for a while.

Caelan fought another Unseelie on the ground because Eldrin had injured one of his wings minutes before. He was fighting against some of the townspeople who were unaware that Eldrin had lost. I shouted, "Eldrin has fallen. The fighting stops now. Caelan, take him inside the prison and watch over him to ensure no one lets him out." Under normal circumstances, I'd want Caelan to come with us, but he couldn't fly, and I needed someone I trusted to oversee Eldrin's capture once again. Last time, he'd managed to escape.

I stood and sheathed my sword as my leathery onyx wings flapped, lifting me from the floor. Lorne had proved his loyalty to Lira once again, flying after the dragon prince alone.

Pyralis spun around and expelled flames at him, and Lorne screamed in agony and dropped into the water below.

Taking to the sky, Finnian remained at my side. My magic was dangerously low, but I could try to use my nightmare illusion magic on the dragon while Finnian used his frost. His magic wasn't half as strong as mine, but it would still counteract the flames.

Tavish, be safe, Lira linked, her concern slamming into me. *I wish I could fly to help you.*

My heart squeezed. I hadn't considered how much agony Lira had to be in with the dragon holding down her injured wings. The fact that I couldn't feel her pain told me she was trying to protect me from it.

I pumped my wings harder, racing toward Pyralis, who was now at least one hundred yards ahead of us. He flew a little slower, clearly believing that we were preoccupied and wouldn't give chase. Still, I needed to move quicker because I wasn't certain I was strong enough to fly a long way with Lira in my arms.

Don't fret. I'll reach you soon. I won't let him get away with this. The dragon had come onto what was now our land and killed some of our own before kidnapping my mate. I wasn't sure how he'd known she was here, but that was a separate problem we would contend with later.

"What's the strategy?" Finnian's pale-blue eyes homed in on me. His ash-blond hair blew back as his forehead lined with worry. "I mean, besides attacking the ashbreath, I'd like more specifics. Though, personally, for me, I'd aim to remove his testicles so he can't produce any heirs, in case—"

"Stop right there." I bit back rage, feeling as if I might burn alive. The mere suggestion of the dragon prince forcing Lira to conceive a child with him made me more bloodthirsty than I'd been in my entire life. No one mistreated my mate... including me. I still had eternity to grovel and make up for what I'd done when I first brought her back here. "Or I will kill you for suggesting it." The only positive thing that came out of him speaking was that I flew faster, even more desperate to reach her.

Finnian flinched. "I didn't mean with her... although she is betrothed to him, so I could understand how it'd be implied."

"She is *mine.*" I pounded a hand against my chest, ignoring the warm liquid it landed against. The wound burned, but it wasn't deep. The injury would heal within a day or two, but not my heart if I couldn't get her back. This was worse than when the Seelie had taken her... at least then, she'd been returned to her people and parents. The ashbreath knew about our fated-mate connection, and he still wanted to force the chains of marriage on her.

My chest constricted to the point where it felt as if I couldn't even breathe. All I could focus on was getting Lira back.

Finnian sighed. "I know she's yours. I'm not arguing that fact. I'll make the plan then. I'll distract him while you free her from his grasp."

"Fine." I curled my free hand into a fist, ready to do whatever it took to save her from him.

We were closing in on them, and Lira's eyes met mine, her fear pushing me harder.

I raised my right hand, preparing to cut off his talons to free her as Finnian pushed forward, his wings moving so fast they blurred.

I tugged at the darkness magic that sat heavy in my chest. If I could blanket the dragon in horrible illusions, it would allow both Finnian and me to get closer. However, each time that I yanked, the inky magic flared faintly and fizzled out.

I'd drained myself by arriving here and using my magic to reinforce that I was the true leader and rightful heir to the Unseelie throne. If only I could go back in time and not be so flamboyant.

Prince Pyralis's wings stiffened, and he turned his head, focusing his amber eyes right on me. Smoke trickled from his nostrils as he called his flames.

"Finnian," I warned, but before I could say more, red-hot flames shot toward us.

Finnian lifted his free hand and shot frost from his palm.

The flames cut through the frost as if he hadn't done

anything at all.

I gripped Finnian's ankle, dragging him down with me out of the flame's path.

"Blighted abyss!" he grunted but shifted his wings to fly down quickly, keeping pace with me.

The flames followed us, the ashbreath turning so he could chase us with his fire.

Tavish, Lira connected, her terror choking me and adding to my own.

The two of us barreled toward the ocean, and I took a deep breath a half second before I dove under the surface. The water heated as the flames hit it, causing my body to warm even more than it did in the Seelie land. I stalled my wings and kicked my arms and feet to move quicker under the water.

Once we outpaced the flames, I swam in that direction and flew out directly under the beast. Luckily, the ashbreath must have expected us to give up and was already facing Tìr na Dràgon, the dragon kingdom.

I shot upward, trying not to make a noise as Finnian soared out in front of the dragon prince.

A lump formed in my throat. Finnian had said he'd serve as a distraction, which meant that I couldn't take my time. I had to hurry before he got killed.

As quickly as possible, I flew upward, seeing the belly of the dragon extend as he readied to engulf Finnian in flames once again.

I reached toward his talons, coming within touching distance of Lira, whose eyes widened.

Everything will be okay. Trust me, I linked, wanting to reassure her despite my own racing pulse.

Be quick, Lira replied. *Please. I don't want any of you to get hurt.*

Flames were expelled, and I lifted my sword. *Be still. Don't move.* Then I swung, the movement making a *swoosh*ing noise.

Lira gasped and jerked back as my sword hit the end of one of Pyralis's talons, cutting in about an inch. Red blood squirted from it, hitting me in the face as the ashbreath's fire quit for a moment and he turned his attention toward us. I readied to swing again.

He spun around, and I grabbed Lira's leg, anchoring myself to her.

But the strangest thing happened.

The buzzing of our fated-mate connection didn't spring to life between us.

That had never occurred before, even when I'd been chained and held prisoner by the Seelie. Something had to be extremely wrong, and before I realized what I was doing, I let go.

The dragon prince twisted and hit me with his tail, propelling me back in the direction of the ruined land. I tried to open my wings, but the pressure of the wind crashed into them, causing a bone-deep ache.

Tavish, no, Lira cried through our bond.

Just as I got traction to head back for her, Pyralis doused Finnian in flames. Finnian dropped like Lorne had, then hit the water and sank.

No. I had to save him, but Lira was being taken. I was torn.

Save Finnian, Lira shouted. *Otherwise, he could die. Struan and a few other guards you trust are coming to help you.*

My chest tightened, and the dragon prince flew quicker now, getting away.

I'd failed Lira.

Again.

But at least I could rescue Finnian before he died. Then, I'd regroup with the guards who were loyal to me and bring my mate back home.

THE KINGDOM OF FLAMES AND ASH

I was able to catch air and rush back to the spot where Finnian went under. My wings ached, but I managed to reach the site just as four others caught up.

Inhaling deeply, I dove back in, searching for Finnian. The water was clear and easy to see through, but Finnian was nowhere in sight.

I turned toward the shoreline, hoping he was swimming back that way, but all I saw were fish swimming in the opposite direction, trying to get away from me.

And then I looked down and spotted Finnian halfway to the bottom.

My lungs were already aching, but I didn't have time to resurface for a quick breath. Not with him being submerged as long as he'd been. I pushed myself to swim faster.

Pressure built in my ears, and my lungs screamed, but I finally reached him. His face was charred along with his clothes, which were blackened and stuck as if molded to his skin. There wasn't a healed place for me to touch, so I wrapped an arm around his waist and kicked my feet and wings upward.

Thankfully, more guards were already swimming toward me.

Struan took one side of Finnian while one of the female guards took the other, and I relinquished my hold, needing to get above water. They'd be able to bring Finnian to the surface quicker than I could. And I needed to ensure the fighting had stopped so we could get Finnian to his bedchamber as quickly as possible.

Please tell me you're okay, Lira asked, her worry flowing into mine.

You're gone, I answered. *Of course I'm not okay.* I freed myself from the water and darted back to the ruined land. I wasn't sure what I'd see, given my people were fighting one another. My wings ached, my heart hurt, and fury still thrummed inside me from losing Lira.

Thorn, I haven't gone anywhere.

Communicating through our fated-mate connection wasn't the same as having Lira in my arms and at my side. However, I didn't want to burden her further. And I refused to let him keep her for long.

If Eldrin had a way to free her before it was too late, then I'd allow him to breathe.

I made it back to the kingdom to find the fighting had stopped. Dead bodies lay everywhere, but Caelan had managed to remove Eldrin from the street.

I had to speak to the people and make them see, once and for all, that I was their king. Then throw everyone who'd risen against me into prison, though I didn't relish the thought. Still, it had to be done because they'd proven their allegiance to Eldrin.

Which meant there were fewer people to help me fight the dragons to get Lira back.

Eiric and Nightbane stood with Isla by the double doors of the castle. My heart grew heavy, knowing Eiric would blame me for Lira's capture and be desperate to get her back.

Eiric's dark-brown curls blew in the breeze as she placed a hand on her chest. "Tavish," she said brokenly.

I landed before her, ready to appease her and ask for her help, when she ran forward and buried herself in my arms.

My body buzzed against hers, causing me to step back in surprise. Even though the contact felt right, she wasn't the woman I loved.

What the blast had Eldrin done?

Chapter Two

Lira

When Tavish wrinkled his nose in disgust and his forehead lined with confusion, my heart shattered. His eyes darkened to slate, the very shade I'd seen in my nightmares during my time on Earth.

He held out both hands so I couldn't step closer and rasped, "What the blast?" His dark hair dripped past the bottom of his ears, contrasting with his pale skin.

Nightbane growled, coming to my side. The cù-sìth resembled a wolf but was the size of a horse. The green-tinged tips of his dark fur rose, and he was clearly ready to intervene.

I threaded my fingers through his fur, wanting to calm him as my bottom lip trembled after Tavish's rejection.

Watching Eiric be abducted by Prince Pyralis, Tavish try so desperately to save her, and then Finnian and Lorne get injured by the ashbreath had been awful. The only reprieve had been Tavish returning, but it had resulted in *this,* the most agonizing torment I'd ever experienced in my life.

"Your Majesty, what's bothering you?" Isla asked from her spot next to me in front of the dark Unseelie castle. Her crystal-blue eyes glanced from me to him. Her light-blue hair appeared gray in the darkness. "You triumphed over Eldrin."

I placed a hand on my chest, trying to steady the pain flaring inside. I wanted to figure out what was going on with Tavish but didn't want the girl to feel ignored. "Sometimes, winning doesn't actually feel like a victory. Sometimes, important things get taken from us that make it still feel like losing."

"Oh, Lira. Right." She winced. "I forgot about their connection."

I had no clue what she was talking about, but I needed to focus on Tavish, whose face had twisted into despair. "Did I do something wrong?"

Maybe he was angry with me for pressuring him so much to save Eiric. One of his best friends and solid guards had gotten severely injured because of my request.

"No, but Eldrin must have done something to me." He frowned, scanning me. "If this is what he meant about not needing to kill the dragon prince, I'll slit his throat and enjoy watching him bleed out."

"What?" My brain felt foggy, and intense pain from my injuries made my wings ache. "What did Eldrin say and do?" I took a step toward him but paused, unable to handle his rejection once again.

"You don't feel the connection between us? Maybe it's an illusion he somehow pushed onto me, and I need to find the magic to release its hold." His terror and anger intensified.

"Tavish, did you hit your head or something?" A chill ran down my spine. Something was truly wrong. I squinted and looked him over, searching for some kind of injury. "We've had this connection since you took me from Earth."

His eyes widened. "I didn't bring you here. I brought Lira."

But I am Lira. I looked downward, noting my tan complexion, which was several shades lighter than my sister's. I didn't understand what was going on until realization washed over me and relief flooded through our bond. I faced Isla again, remembering her strange comment from moments ago. "Who am I?"

Isla's nose wrinkled as she glanced at Tavish and me and answered, "Eiric."

My heart seized, and then I felt the faint hum of Seelie magic covering me. *Son of a bitch.* "She glamoured us." *Of course she did.* "And took my spot. That's why Pyralis didn't hesitate to grab her. I thought that was odd." Since she'd glamoured us both at the same time, I hadn't seen myself as the others had. She'd known what she was doing when she did this to us.

Now that I could sense her magic, I removed the glamour with my own. Glamour used passive magic, so it didn't take more than a thought to remove it now that I'd realized it was there.

As soon as it dropped, Tavish sagged with relief. He stumbled to me, pulled me into his arms, and buried his face in my hair. The buzzing between us sprang up once again, and this time, he relished the embrace and didn't pull away.

I could feel Nightbane ease at my side.

I thought I'd lost you again.. He kissed the shell of my ear, and my body tingled. *I should be pissed that Eiric put us through that, but I'm glad she did.*

In my mate's arms, it was hard not to agree with him. There was no place I'd rather be, but I couldn't enjoy the moment. "What happens when he realizes it's her?" My stomach dropped, and cold tendrils of fear clutched my heart.

"He won't harm her... not if he believes that she's important to you." Tavish exhaled. "He'll decide to begin a chess match and use her as a pawn."

And there was no doubt I'd hand myself over to him to save my sister. I'd do it without a moment's hesitation.

Concern flooded our connection as Tavish leaned back. *You giving yourself to him isn't an option. We'll find a way to get her back without you sacrificing your own freedom.*

I nodded, choosing to believe his words. Before I could ask

him about Eldrin, Struan and a female guard with silver hair flew over to us, holding an unconscious Finnian. Parts of his fair skin looked charred.

My wings had to feel better than what he'd experienced.

Two other guards flew behind them, carrying Lorne, who was in a similar state. Even the ends of his pale-blue hair were tinged black from the dragon's fire.

"Take them to their bedchambers." Tavish stepped away, intertwining our fingers. "Then have someone wash their skin gently to remove anything that could irritate it as it heals."

"Yes, Your Majesty." Struan bobbed his head, his light-green hair spilling into his face. "Isla, come with me. Let's get you behind the castle walls."

Isla pouted. "But what if the king and Lira need protection?" She unsheathed the knife from her side. "I should remain here to help guard them."

The corners of my mouth tipped upward. I understood, especially with my memories returned, that Fate was a little more cutthroat than humans. But this ten-year-old girl had everyone I knew beat, and when she grew up, I had no doubt she'd be in charge of the guards, even over her father.

"She can remain with us." Tavish forced a smile, though it didn't meet his eyes. "I'm addressing the people now to reinforce that the fighting is over. There's no need for alarm."

Tavish sounded way more confident than I felt, but as I finally paid attention to the village and the people on the stoned pathway, I noted that the fighting had stopped. Dead bodies littered the area.

Since being forced to relocate to this decimated island, about seven thousand of Tavish's people had perished due to the harsh living conditions and lack of food. Now, the remaining three thousand had been reduced by a hundred, if not more.

Not wasting any additional time, the guards carried off

Finnian and Lorne as Tavish led me to the top of the stairs and spread out his dark wings behind us, Nightbane flanking my other side.

"I, the true and rightful king, have proven once again that I'm the strongest Unseelie and will lead my people." His voice boomed, echoing against the village walls. "The revolt against me is over, and the ones who turned on me—"

Don't make them prisoners, Tavish. I didn't want to tell him how to lead, but at least a quarter of the Unseelie had aligned with Eldrin, and the others had remained quiet, giving in to peer pressure, afraid to speak out for what they wanted. *Show them that you're better than Eldrin. Make them see the difference. After all, haven't you made a similar mistake, siding with others when you didn't want to or remaining silent even when you felt like it was wrong?* I didn't like bringing up how he'd treated me, but this was a unique circumstance. He had to see how hypocritical he was being when I'd forgiven him. *If they abuse your trust again, that's a different story.*

Silence hung heavy since Tavish had cut off midsentence in order to listen to what I had to say. Proof that the two of us had come far in a short amount of time.

"Your Majesty." A man with hair the color of charcoal bent to one knee and bowed. "You are the rightful king, and I should have stood strong beside you. Punish me as you wish, for I deserve it for my betrayal."

Murmurs of agreement filtered through the village as fae after fae kneeled, including children, leaving a handful of Unseelie standing before they dropped as well.

Those have to be Eldrin's loyalists. Tavish's hand tightened. *The blasting wildlings who assisted in getting everyone to turn on me.*

But now we know, and we can let them believe they got away with it without being noticed. I understood that, eventually, some of these people would need to be dealt with. *We can have the guards you trust closely monitor the holdouts to see if they attempt to free Eldrin or something else.*

Unfortunately, though they weren't the majority, Eldrin's followers numbered more than we'd anticipated. Still, the ones who'd cried out against Tavish had given us more information than we'd known before, and we might not have learned of their disloyalty if Tavish hadn't paused to consider what to do next.

You're right, but there is one person who won't be given that grace. Tavish lifted his chin, looking ever more the royal that he was. Even with his injuries and weakened magic, he appeared stronger than any man I'd known.

My chest expanded to the point that it felt as if it might explode from how proud I was of him and how much I loved him.

"I understand that, under the circumstances, it was easy for you all to doubt me. I did allow you to believe that I'd perished, and I left the land to save the Seelie princess. But I never intended to abandon you. I had to rescue my fated mate, who was taken away from me against her will." He lifted the sleeves of his black tunic, showing them part of the intricate fated-mate tattoo of delicate vines and leaves interconnected with thorns that spread across both our chests, down our arms, and continued to our left hands, circling our ring fingers.

Following his lead, I pulled the sleeves of my dress toward my elbow and allowed the crowd to see that I had the same markings.

A few people gasped, and one of the women muttered, "Impossible. There hasn't been a fated-mate pairing in centuries."

"Well, the tattoos are proof, and he spoke the words." Isla appeared on the other side of Nightbane and wrinkled her nose. "I'm a child, and even I know better than to question that."

I planned to hug the girl as soon as I was able.

"As soon as Lira and I found a way back here to you, we didn't hesitate to return." Tavish paused, allowing his words to sink in. "And though I'm willing to give all of you a second chance, there is one person standing out here who won't be allowed that fate."

Completely human, I might have interjected and tried to convince Tavish to change his mind, but I knew of whom he spoke and understood that the person had purposely harmed me, and worse, she had a weapon that we needed to learn how she'd gained access to. There would be no talking him out of it.

"Princess Lira," Tavish said tenderly but firmly. "Please turn around so the people know what will *never* be tolerated."

My heart hammered as my emotions clashed. A part of me did want justice for what had been done, but I feared Tavish's choice would be death.

Obliging him, I did as he requested and spread my wings just as the breeze picked up, causing them to ripple. The injury I'd sustained near the base of my wings from an Unseelie woman's arrow throbbed. The arrow had been made of true Unseelie wood from their original kingdom and some sort of special stone, and while I'd healed my wings partly with my magic, they hadn't fully healed. Plus, the wounds had reopened during battle.

Nightbane growled at the sight, and Tavish let out a low snarl that could've passed as an animal's.

"This was done to my fated mate, your future *queen*, when she wasn't threatening anyone," Tavish said and patted his chest where blood smeared from a cut that I hadn't noticed until now.

I sucked in a breath. He'd proclaimed I was to be their queen. Even though I wanted to be with him in every way, for some reason, being queen hadn't actually crossed my mind. And in that moment, I realized it was because I suspected that the Unseelie would never acknowledge me that way. Yet Tavish stood here, emphasizing exactly what he saw my future role to be.

He placed an arm over my shoulder and turned me, wrapping his wings around me affectionately.

He continued, unfazed, "I cast the illusion magic, but only on the traitors. If an arrow was shot, it should have been aimed at me. That would've been wiser than attacking my beloved."

Whispers shot throughout the village as everyone turned, searching for the person who would face the wrath of their king.

"The woman who is responsible, come forward now or face a more painful punishment." Tavish quieted, letting the echo of his voice resound.

But there was silence.

Can you pick the woman out? Tavish asked.

I could, but I can't fly to search for her. The village wasn't large, but walking it on foot would take significant time. If I could fly, it would be easier, but my wings were too damaged to chance that.

"If someone doesn't point the woman out or she doesn't come forward herself, the entire kingdom will be punished." Tavish clenched his jaw, making sure he slowly scanned the entire crowd so the people all felt like he was looking right at them. "Attacking Lira will always be a punishable offense."

"I know who it was." A man flew upward from the center of the village. "I can bring her to you." He turned, racing toward the sea near where I'd been shot, which added credibility to his claim.

The next few minutes felt like an eternity, and then three men dragged the woman who had attacked me toward us.

Is that her? Tavish linked.

I nodded. *But we should question her before doing anything rash. Find the stash of weapons that Eldrin hid to use against us.*

They're still out there and need to be recovered before someone else is injured.

The woman tried to yank free from the men holding tightly to her wrists. A woman flew behind her, holding a dagger in case she tried to escape us once more.

Finally, they landed on the first step in front of us. The lady scowled at us, showing no fear.

"Do you feel remorse for what you've done to my mate?" Tavish arched a brow, watching her every move and expression.

"She's a Seelie wildling. I don't feel anything but hatred toward her!" The woman spat at my feet.

Tavish removed his sword from his sheath and stabbed her in the side. "Your punishment is death, but not until you've felt more pain than Lira has endured tonight." He gestured to the windows. "Take her to a different cell from Eldrin. The two of them shouldn't share with anyone else if it comes to grouping people together. I want to enjoy breaking her, and then I'll return to assist in taking care of this." He gestured to the dead bodies on the ground.

I glanced at each person who'd died in vain, especially the seven the dragon prince had burned without any hesitation before grabbing my sister and flying away. My breathing grew shallow.

Finnian's and Lorne's charred faces surged into my mind. And Caelan, hauling Eldrin into the castle with his injured wing so that Tavish could go after Eiric—er, me. So many people that I cared about could perish, and I couldn't access my healing magic. I needed to do something, even if it was only to help give them water.

Let's get you tended to, Tavish connected tenderly. *Blood is still dripping from your wings. It's one reason that you're weak and struggling.*

He wanted me to take care of myself, and the benefit of

doing that was that I could help the others. Caelan and Finnian already knew my secret, so there was no increased risk in healing them.

As I readied to follow my mate's instructions, the Unseelie began to shout, "Fates, no" and "Blighted abyss" and, "Princess Lira, please protect us."

My stomach dropped. Had Pyralis returned to get me?

However, when I spun around, I saw something that made me even more heartsick.

Chapter Three

Lira

Out of every possibility, of course this was when the Seelie would arrive.

Two people flew in front, leading the massive army. In the darkness, their golden armor and appearance looked comparable to the Unseelie guard, further proof that we were similar fae who merely held different sorts of magic.

I had no doubt that the two in front were Mom and Dad, but from this far away, their features weren't easily distinguishable.

The Unseelie grabbed their weapons from their sides once more.

My limbs grew heavy with dread. The way I'd helped Tavish and Finnian escape and run from my people plagued me. I hadn't relished betraying my parents—both biological and adoptive—but they hadn't given me much choice. They had bound my fated mate and friend, even starved them. And with an army this size, I wasn't sure what they might be trying to accomplish.

Tavish froze, his wings tensing as he stared at the newcomers. *They know our numbers are small. Why would they bring so many guards with them?*

Good question. *I don't know, but whatever they do to the Unseelie, they'll be forced to do the same to me.* Now that Tavish had proclaimed me his people's future queen, I wouldn't stand being treated any other way, even if I had to attack the guards alongside him. *But, thorn, the Unseelie are primed to attack. I don't think that's wise.* I wanted to reassure him that Mom and Dad wouldn't attack him, knowing the bond he and I shared, but ultimately, the guards would obey their royals. *There's no way we'll come out unscathed, especially after what we've endured. They need to put down their weapons to show they don't intend to fight.*

Displeasure surged through the bond, and Tavish's breathing turned ragged. *Lira, that goes against every natural instinct we have. Your parents killed mine and relocated us here by force. Asking them to put down their weapons is like asking them to stand in a dragon's flame, and look how injured Finnian and Lorne are.*

My head and heart were in conflict because I understood everything Tavish was saying, but a part of me remembered loving and caring parents, even though I hadn't seen much of that side of them since returning to Gleann Solas. The best course of action would be to speak with Mom and Dad before they reached us, but I couldn't fly—not with my injury.

A scream built in my chest, but releasing it would only worsen an already volatile situation.

Still, I had to try.

I flapped my wings, sharp pain shooting through them and down my back. The woman who'd injured me had hit a vital spot in both wings. Still, I needed to head off the Seelie and see what their intentions were.

Lira, you're injured. Tavish's concern jolted through me as he turned my way.

Something snapped inside me, causing my sarcasm to come out swinging. *Oh, right. I was wondering why moving my wings hurt!* They'd been throbbing the whole time, and now it felt as if my wings were going to fall off.

His brows lifted as shock filtered in.

Immediately, guilt assailed me. I didn't care if I shouldn't apologize to him. *I'm sorry. It's been a long... well, month, and I have no idea why the Seelie came in force. I need to speak with them before they reach us.* The last twenty-four hours had been awful, and the pressure was getting to me. Add in Eiric being taken, the deaths, and the injuries along with my own pain. I could've sworn I hadn't slept in days.

You never need to apologize to me. Tavish caught me in his arms and continued, *You could speak to me in that manner for the rest of eternity, and I'd still be indebted to you for what I did and allowed to happen to you when I forced you to come here with me.* He flapped his wings, lifting us from the ground.

A deep ache pulsed in the bond, proving that flying caused him discomfort too. *You're uncomfortable with my weight.*

It's nothing I can't handle. He flew a little higher across the stoned path over his people's heads.

"Your Majesty," a guard yelled. "You should hide in the castle. We'll protect you with our lives."

I lifted my head to take note of the guard, who had salt-and-pepper hair. His offer to protect Tavish made me favor him, hoping he was one Unseelie we could count on to be on our side and not Eldrin's.

"Everyone, remain calm." Tavish's voice echoed the way only a royal's could, as if it were some sort of magic. "Princess Lira and I will meet with the Seelie and determine if they're a threat to us or not."

"They're Seelie." A man lifted his sword in the air. "Of course they mean harm."

"I didn't." I couldn't remain silent while others amped everyone up, preparing to attack my people. At this point, I didn't identify as Seelie or Unseelie any longer. From here on out, I would be fae—because that's what we all truly were.

"Maybe they aren't coming here to attack or do anything untoward. And if they are, I'll fight alongside you."

A woman gasped. "Against your own people?"

"You are my people now, too. Your well-being means just as much to me as theirs." I shifted in Tavish's arms, trying to see everyone better. In the process, the edge of my wing got stuck on Tavish's arm, causing me to nearly double over in pain.

Tavish's breath caught like he felt my misery through the bond. I still wasn't great at hiding physical sensations.

His arms tightened around me so I couldn't lift the wing as easily again, and he cleared his throat. "Stay calm. If we need to fight, I'll give you a signal."

Not waiting for his people to respond, he pushed his wings harder, heading toward the Seelie guards, who were only about a hundred and fifty yards from the start of our land.

I can fly, I offered, trying not to flinch. The thought of forcing my wings to do anything but dangle made tears burn my eyes.

Don't you dare. He pushed harder, picking up speed to face the Seelie. *Your wings are still bleeding.*

Not only that, but the breeze from flying made my vision blur. There wasn't a point in fighting him, especially when he was right.

I slipped my arms around his neck, wanting to anchor my body more securely to his and feel the buzz of our bond everywhere we could touch. As we got closer to the Seelie, I tasted bitterness. What if I'd been wrong about reaching out and meeting them before they arrived? What if my parents did try to take me from Tavish again and deliver me to Pyralis? All my doubts swirled inside me, but I bit my tongue.

My instinct told me to do this, and I had to trust that it was right.

As I expected, Mom and Dad were leading the guards. The

THE KINGDOM OF FLAMES AND ASH

tips of Dad's dark-blue hair stuck out from under his armor, and his dark skin made it possible to notice the gold in it. His amber eyes widened.

Mom's brows furrowed. She tilted her head, her curly mahogany hair blowing behind her as her dark-brown eyes scanned me.

Mom raised a fist, causing the guards behind them to halt and hover in place.

The two of them looked at each other then nodded. They weren't fated mates, but they'd always been able to understand each other without a word, even on Earth.

"Lira," Mom rasped. "Why are you being car—" She noticed my wings and stopped short. "Who did this to you?" Her gaze shot straight at Tavish. "Was it *him*?"

My head jerked back. "It wasn't him."

"Then who was it?" she seethed, her hand going to her hip, where I noticed a dark stone hilt.

She had Tavish's sword.

"We can discuss that later, but at the moment, I need to understand why you've brought what appears to be your entire guard to the land you banished us to." Tavish lifted his chin. "And I'd like my sword back."

"Let's not get ahead of ourselves." Mom lifted her hands and flew a few feet back. "That's not what's important."

Dad edged in front of Mom. "It's not the whole guard. We brought half because the king and queen demanded to travel with us. The threat of the dragons is imminent since we forced Pyralis to leave Gleann Solas."

I swallowed. Mother and Father were here. They never traveled outside of Gleann Solas. "Why are they here?" Maybe this *was* a formal attack.

"Because their daughter, the Seelie heir, helped the Unseelie king and his friend escape and left with them." Mom's

28

wings fluttered behind her, resembling flames. "They're upset and wanted to try to resolve things here."

"Attacking the Unseelie isn't the way." I didn't want to be on opposite sides of either set of parents, but my place was beside Tavish, and they didn't respect that.

"We aren't here to attack." Dad lifted both hands, emphasizing he had no weapon in them. "We're here to check on you and Eiric and to make sure the dragons don't try to capture you before the agreed-upon date that you are to wed the prince."

Tavish's jaw clenched, causing its bones to pop. He gritted, "She will *never* be his. She is *mine*."

"Now isn't the time to get into that." Dad rubbed his hands together. "Because, at the moment, we're all on the same team— we all want to keep Lira away from him."

"Team?" Tavish parroted. "I'm not sure what that means."

Sometimes, I forgot that he hadn't spent time on Earth and didn't understand the vernacular. "That they have the same goal as you."

"At least temporarily." Tavish huffed but relaxed marginally.

Wanting to make sure their intent was clear, I asked, "So, you won't attack while you're here, even if the king and queen demand it?"

"Those are the orders." Dad licked his lips. "Do not attack unless one of our kind is threatened."

Threatened is subjective. Tavish's nostrils flared, and the strain on his wings made his discomfort even worse.

We needed to land before he couldn't fly anymore.

It is, but if they decide to attack, staying with them won't prevent it. I didn't know what the right answer was, but either way, the Unseelie were at a disadvantage. *So it's best if we trust them until there's a reason not to.*

Trust the people who killed my parents? His disgust trickled

THE KINGDOM OF FLAMES AND ASH

through the fated-mate bond.

My chest constricted from his emotions, and I hated that I couldn't reassure him. That was exactly what I'd asked him to do, and I understood that trusting the Seelie was the last thing he'd ever want. *If you can't—*

You're right, and I'm willing to allow them into our land. But I can't trust them.

My heartbeat quickened, knowing that he was doing this for me. If I weren't here now, the Unseelie would've attacked the Seelie without blinking. *That's more than fair, and you're a better man than you give yourself credit for.*

No, I'm not. I'm only able to do this because you're with me. Otherwise, I have no doubt my hatred would take control. He straightened his shoulders despite holding me and said, "We won't attack you unless we feel threatened."

Mom and Dad looked at each other and nodded.

Unease floated through our bond—Tavish's discomfort from turning his back to his enemy. My skin crawled from the sensation, adding more stress to my own. He took off back toward the castle, with the Seelie following right behind us.

Everywhere Tavish and I turned, we couldn't catch a break. I could only hope that Eldrin did have a way to get my parents out of the contract with the dragons, or I feared that, for the rest of our lives, Tavish and I would be facing threat after threat. The thought of being with anyone else made me sick to my stomach. He was it for me, and I didn't want a life without him by my side.

Sprite, I won't allow them to do anything to you. Tavish kissed the top of my head. *I'll protect you to the end.*

He thought I feared what the Seelie might do to me, and I didn't want to correct him. We needed to face one adversary at a time, and I needed to decipher my parents' intentions and inform them that Eiric had been taken.

A sharp ache pierced my heart, making it feel as if it might shatter. If something happened to Eiric, it would have a huge missing piece. A sob built in my chest, and I tried to push it away. Maybe if we worked together, we could uncover an effective way to get Eiric back with minimal bloodshed without having to hand myself over.

The Unseelie men and women stood in the streets. The handful of children who had been outside were no longer in sight.

"The Seelie have vowed to let us be as long as we don't attack them." Tavish spoke slowly and clearly, making sure that everyone could hear each word. "We shall honor that request and retaliate only if they betray us once again."

The two thousand people who had to be standing in the pathway between the two rows of homes lowered their weapons but kept hold of the hilts, ready to wield them at a moment's notice.

I couldn't blame them.

Tavish continued to fly overhead, leading the Seelie guards to the castle. Nightbane remained at the stairs where I'd left him, his glowing lime eyes keeping watch.

The silence was deafening as both sides sized each other up, determining the threat. When we reached the top of the stairs, Tavish landed, placing me gently back onto my feet.

Wanting to comfort Nightbane, I threaded my fingers through his fur. His body uncoiled ever so slightly at my touch.

"Open the doors," Tavish commanded his guards.

A second later, the doors creaked and opened. Struan and several guards he seemed to trust stood in the center of the massive, dark hallway. Lanterns hung on the walls, flickering only dim light that limited vision.

The way Tavish had preferred to keep the castle when I'd first arrived here.

THE KINGDOM OF FLAMES AND ASH

We stood in the center with the dark wall at our backs as Struan took up a position to the left of Tavish and a woman guard moved to the right of Nightbane, with me in the center.

Most of the Seelie guards stopped outside, hovering above the people while they created a hole in the center where Mother and Father would fly down, heavily protected on all sides.

Mom and Dad landed a few feet before us, scanning the guards.

"Lira doesn't need protection from us." Mom snorted and wrinkled her nose as if the thought were insulting. "We mean her no harm."

"But you do us?" Tavish countered, tilting his head and interlacing our fingers.

"As we said, we mean you no harm." Dad cut his eyes at Mom and sighed. "Lira is our daughter, and we love her. That's all that she meant."

Normally, Mom was the one smoothing out Dad's words, but Eiric and my leaving the way we had must have rattled her more than I'd realized. My shoulders sagged. I hadn't meant to cause her that much distress, but of course, our actions would have impacted her. Both daughters gone in one breath.

A commotion sounded outside, and I looked over their heads to see Father and Mother almost at the stairs, Father wearing his golden tunic with black pants and Mother in a matching golden gown. The Unseelie grumbled, and a few spat on the ground.

I winced, but they weren't attacking... just expressing their disgust, which was fair.

My father, King Erdan, didn't appear fazed.

When Mother's emerald-eyed gaze landed on me, she let out a shaky breath and soared toward me. "Lira," she exclaimed in both relief and frustration.

A tone damn close to resembling a threat.

32

Nightbane snarled and moved in front of me. He hunkered down, and before I could reach him, he jerked forward to attack.

Chapter Four

Lira

I jumped forward, my heart lurching into my throat, trying to stop Nightbane in time.

Sprite, Tavish connected, his concern slamming into me just as Mother exclaimed, "Lira, don't!"

My arms caught Nightbane's waist, his momentum jerking my body. The injury in my wings spread misery through my back as I tangled my fingers into his fur. "Nightbane, stop," I gritted out, tugging back but trying not to do it hard enough to hurt him.

I wished that I could tap into my healing magic since that seemed to calm him, but it hadn't yet sparked back inside me.

Thankfully, he stopped a few feet shy of my parents, but his snarls became more vicious, and his body shook with anger.

I'm beginning to suspect that you're trying to test whether I'm truly immortal. Tavish scowled as he landed in front of Nightbane, blocking my parents. *My heart has never beat so frantically as it has since you came back into my life.*

If I wasn't suffering, I probably would've smiled, but not now; holding the tears back so I didn't look weak was the priority. *Father would be a huge pain in the ass about the beast if he hurt Mother. We don't need anything else working against us.*

"Put that dangerous animal away." Father's voice boomed and echoed against the dark walls of the barren room. "And save my daughter before it attacks her."

I grunted, unable to keep the noise contained as I went to my knees on the ground, the tattered ends of my gray dress protecting my skin from the chill of the floor. I straightened but made sure to keep my hand on Nightbane. "He won't harm me."

As I shifted my attention back to them, I saw Mom flanking Father and Dad protecting Mother. The two guards on their outsides had their swords in hand, waiting for Nightbane to attack again.

Father's normally tamed chestnut-brown hair was disheveled from travel, and it was a tad disconcerting to stare into cobalt eyes that appeared nearly identical to mine. "But he tried to attack us, and you're Seelie."

He always came back to the divide between the two magics, not seeing anything beyond the type that flowed in our blood.

"He'll attack anyone he believes is a threat to Lira." Tavish lifted his chin. "Lira, it would be better if the command came from you instead of me."

Once again, Tavish was giving me the opportunity to prove myself, not only to my parents but to his people. The only guard I truly had on my side was Lorne. Struan and the others served the king, which included the relationships he had with other people.

Running a hand over Nightbane's fur, I noticed Mother's flush gilding her normally fair skin and freckles, and her sparkly blue wings fluttered, causing her light-blonde waves to lift haphazardly over her shoulders.

My parents usually presented themselves as very put together, but in this moment, both royals looked untidy and clearly didn't feel comfortable, especially with Nightbane's presence.

Turning my back to them, I slid between Tavish and Nightbane. The cù-sìth remained crouched so I cupped his face and pressed my forehead to his. I needed him to see that I didn't feel threatened by my parents' presence. "Don't attack them. *Please.*"

Nightbane was displeased, but his snarls eased into impatient huffs.

Like Tavish, the more time I spent with the animal, the more he endeared himself to me.

Knowing we had a blast ton of information we needed to discuss with both sets of my parents, I rose to stand next to Tavish. Nightbane eased forward, guarding my other side, and pressed against me. The heat he emitted kept a shiver from running down my spine.

"Isn't that a rare Unseelie animal?" Father's forehead creased, and his sun-kissed complexion turned several shades lighter. "Why would it be so partial to Lira?"

"I'm not sure how you haven't noticed, but your daughter is quite exceptional." Tavish's face was filled with adoration as he kissed me on my forehead. "Even some of the Unseelie fae are partial to her and not me."

My face burned, but I refused to hide because I wasn't ashamed. Just uncomfortable with the attention. "As much as I'd love to beat around the bush, we should get straight to business."

"Beat around the bush?" Father scanned the room. "We said we wouldn't fight unless forced to, and I don't see a bush nearby. And what is this 'business'? Is that some location on this horrid island?"

"Your Majesty." Mom lowered her sword but kept it at her side. "She is speaking as humans do on Earth. She wants to discuss the matters at hand, like her freeing the nightfiends and having Eiric go along with the plan. Speaking of which, where is my daughter?"

I tightened my fingers in Nightbane's fur, trying not to

mouth off. Even though she and Dad had been great parents on Earth, whenever Eiric had gotten into trouble, Mom had always blamed me. Granted, most of the time, I'd deserved it.

The realization that Eiric was gone damn near ripped me in half again. I needed them all to know where she was. "She's—"

"I'm good with having a direct conversation, especially when my daughter is standing here *injured.*" Father's face grew haggard. "This is why we wanted to keep you away from him. The Unseelie are nothing but trouble."

Disgust oozed into our bond as Tavish's hand clenched mine tighter. He said, "If you hadn't kidnapped your daughter and imprisoned me, then what happened here would have been avoided. Because of your meddling, my cousin tried to overthrow me."

"*Kidnapped* my *daughter?* How is that possible when she's Seelie? And if you were truly a strong leader, you would have nothing to prove to your people, and your cousin wouldn't have dared risk betraying you." Father wrinkled his nose like Tavish was beneath him.

"Whoa." I lifted my hands, needing to stop this pissing match between two kings. I should've known this would happen. "Everyone, take a deep breath. Tossing insults at each other isn't going to make things better." I placed my hands on my hips, trying to ignore the way my back muscles protested. I wanted to hunch over. "Father, the only reason Eldrin even believed he had a chance of stealing the crown was due to the horrible conditions forced upon the Unseelie fae."

"Because of what *his father* did to the realm." Mother placed a hand on her chest. "You make it sound like we are the villains. We did what needed to be done to ensure that the Seelie magic remained strong. Our magic requires both the sun and the moon. It cannot work cloaked in complete darkness."

THE KINGDOM OF FLAMES AND ASH

"Forgive me if I believe that coming onto our land, killing my parents, taking me while I was injured and unable to protect myself, and throwing me into a holding cell makes you the villains in my mind." The heartbreak that haunted Tavish daily came back to the forefront.

I couldn't imagine waking up to find my parents murdered.

Father sucked in a breath, his brown wings tensing. "Why would you accuse us of killing your parents? You know better. You were there when it all happened."

My mouth dried, and the walls closed in on me. I couldn't believe that my father would try to wordsmith and dance around the fact that our people had killed them. "Father, this isn't something to be political about. Tavish woke up with the Seelie guards standing over him."

"One of the guards was me, Lira." Mom ran a hand over her outfit. "No Seelie killed them. Our orders were to take the king alive."

Tavish shook his head. "I don't understand how you can say that. That's a lie. I was there, and you were standing over them with blood on your sword."

"Unseelie guards attacked us, and we fought them off. That's where the blood came from." Mom blinked and then winced, recalling the memory. "We had to fight our way into the royal chambers. You must have been knocked unconscious during the scuffle. Our intent was to capture both your mother and father, not for them to die. One of our guards captured Queen Morven, and we tried to use her to capture King Dunach without more bloodshed. Your father only pretended he was going to surrender. Then, when he got close to us, he stabbed the queen in the heart before shoving the blade through his stomach, ending both their lives. It was chaotic, and the Unseelie retaliated with a vengeance. When you regained consciousness, you screamed, and I noticed a pool of blood underneath you.

I knew I needed to get you away from the battle, so I carried you back to Seelie. We couldn't risk the true heir dying and the magic becoming unbalanced."

A strange emotion I couldn't read crashed through the bond to me. Tavish's shoulders sagged as if his understanding of his entire world had just crumbled. He spun around, addressing his guards. "How did we not know this?"

A guard with mustard-colored hair cleared his throat. "Your Majesty, as you know, we locked all four of the royals in the king's chambers. The Seelie weren't able to come through the windows since they were sealed, so they fought their way to you. Torcall and Lorne stayed behind to guard the door, but when the Seelie breached the bedchambers, they were both injured in the battle."

"Four?" My lungs seized. I suspected I knew who the fourth person was, but I needed confirmation.

"The king, the queen, Prince Tavish, and Eldrin. The four remaining members of the royal family. The king had taken Eldrin in when he was a small boy and raised him like his own until Tavish came along, but even then, they remained close. Tavish's father demanded that Eldrin be included in the family's protection," the guard explained.

Understanding slammed into me. Eldrin felt that he was the firstborn and entitled to lead. My stomach revolted. "Was he injured?"

Tavish shook his head. "He hid under the bed. Dad tried to get me to do the same, but I didn't want to look weak. I stayed out there beside them."

My brows furrowed. "Why didn't the three of you hide too?" I didn't mention his hidden bunker because I already knew why they couldn't reach it. We might need to use it again one day if we couldn't determine a way to break the contract my parents had made with the dragons and I might have to turn myself over to Pyralis to save my sister.

Tavish pinched the bridge of his nose. "The Seelie wouldn't leave until we'd been located, and Father refused to be a coward."

That one day had set Tavish's and my lives on a whole different course than we'd expected. He wound up alone, trying to rule and trusting his one remaining family member, who tried to take the throne from him. Whereas I'd been promised to a dragon and sent to Earth to live with no memories of my childhood. It was a mess, and now my sister was the one paying the price. She hadn't done a damn thing wrong and was an innocent.

"A coward cloaks the sky in darkness while remaining in his castle in his kingdom," Father spat. "And forces us to ally with dragons in order to survive."

Tavish braced, but I'd had enough. We were dwelling on facts that couldn't be changed, and at least now, we understood that the Seelie hadn't killed his parents.

"We need to deal with the past, but right now, there's a more important threat." I karate chopped the air, needing them to focus on me. "Prince Pyralis came here and killed some Unseelie before attempting to kidnap me." I was beginning to see a theme.

"Thank Fate he didn't get you." Mother's wings lowered.

"Only because of Eiric." I licked my lips, preparing for my next words. I wasn't sure how they'd react to the news, but we needed their help to get her back.

Dad grinned proudly. "That's my girl. Where is she?"

I swallowed, and Tavish stepped closer to me, our arms brushing. Our proximity eased his turmoil but emphasized that my emotions were a strangled mess. Because of that, I understood something I hadn't realized until now.

I didn't want to see their disappointment and anger at me

when they found out it was my fault Eiric was taken. I should've done better. "When Prince Pyralis appeared, she glamoured us both. I didn't realize she had. The dragon prince took her instead of me." A tear trickled down my cheek, but I couldn't stop talking. "Tavish, Finnian, and Lorne went after the dragon, but they all got hurt. Tavish was hit by the dragon's tail, and Finnian and Lorne...they're charred from the flames."

"Blighted abyss." Mom's chest heaved.

"He *took* her?" Dad's voice cracked.

Father ran a hand down his face. "How did the dragon even know you were here?"

Good question. One that I hadn't fully considered since we hadn't had a moment to collect our thoughts.

"We didn't inform the dragons you left for Unseelie territory." Mother bit her bottom lip.

The moment stretched taut between us until Tavish's emotions narrowed to one.

Rage.

It pulsed from him, increasing the temperature of my own blood in response.

"I believe I know how." Tavish grimaced. "My blasted cousin. He spoke to the dragon like he was annoyed that he'd come here, but he didn't seem surprised."

His words were a kick in my gut. Eldrin had told Pyralis that he needed more time, and then the dragon prince had burned seven Unseelie guards to death just moments before he'd taken Eiric. "We should visit him *now*."

Tavish nodded. "I need to talk with Caelan anyway."

"I want to speak with Eldrin as well." Dad was seething.

A scream came from outside the castle. The sound was raw, full of anger, and followed by an explosion.

The walls shook as the floor rolled underneath our feet.

"No! Guards, to the prison. *Immediately*." Tavish took

THE KINGDOM OF FLAMES AND ASH

flight, rushing off in the direction of the prison. *He'd better not be attempting to escape again. Caelan is too injured to fight alone.*

With my injured wings, I couldn't keep up, but I took off at a steady run. Each step jolted my wings, but I pushed through the pain, desperate to fight alongside Tavish.

"Lira, stay here with us," Father shouted. "Brenin and Hestia can go with them. The Unseelie could try to kill us at any time."

"I'm going with Tavish." I pumped my arms, moving as fast as I could, when Dad swooped down and picked me up.

"You don't need to make your injuries worse," he said, and I allowed him to carry me. "Besides, we need you to give us directions."

I didn't like feeling weak, but this would get me to Tavish more quickly and make sure Eldrin didn't escape. I led them through the turns, and just as we flew by the night chambers, I sensed Tavish's confusion as another explosion came from outside.

What's going on? It didn't feel as if someone was trying to get into the castle.

Eldrin is locked up and not at risk of escaping, Tavish replied.

I heard beating wings that had to be him and Struan coming back in this direction.

Dad passed by a window, and I said, "Wait."

He obliged. Mom landed beside us, and the three of us looked outside.

Immediately, I wished the commotion *had* been caused by Eldrin trying to escape. That would be far better than what I saw happening out there.

42

Chapter Five

Tavish

Despite the deep ache in my wings, I pushed myself to return to Lira as quickly as possible. When the first blast of the volcanic rock had shaken the castle, I'd been certain Eldrin's loyalists were attempting to free him once again.

But when I arrived at his cell, I found Eldrin leaning against the wall with a frown. Given the absence of his usual arrogance, I'd understood that, whatever this was, he wasn't behind it.

I had just left Caelan behind in the prison with a group of guards he trusted, making sure that we didn't leave Eldrin unguarded when a second explosion happened.

I had to get back to Lira. For all we knew, the dragons were coming back for her, or my own people were trying to capture her to use against me since she was my one *true* weakness.

I couldn't survive without her.

Apart from a handful of people, I wasn't sure who in my kingdom I could trust anymore. All the loyalty I'd thought they had shown me for the past twelve years had merely been them feeling as if they didn't have a choice.

Lira had been right all along. I hadn't fostered respect but fear, and the first chance they'd had to dethrone me, they hadn't hesitated.

My icy chest could shatter at any moment. Everything I'd

believed to be fact had been shredded before my eyes in less than twelve hours. Not only had my people turned on me, but the Seelie hadn't murdered my parents. My father had taken both my mother's and his own life.

I would never have believed it possible, but Lira's adoptive mom hadn't minced words or tried to be vague to make us assume anything. She'd been direct and had spoken with something haunting in her eyes.

When I made the turn that would lead me back to the castle entrance, I smelled Lira's wild rose, mist, and vanilla scent, and my heart thawed. It was like coming home.

I should've known that she'd find a way to follow me, but I hadn't expected her to catch up so quickly with her injured wings.

When my gaze landed on her standing between her mom and dad, I realized one of them must have carried her. The concern and fear swirling from her had me flying up behind her.

Fates, no.

The Unseelie weren't trying to free Eldrin. A group of about twenty of them were hovering over the jagged mountaintop, firing arrows with volcanic rock arrowheads and slinging pieces at the Seelie guards.

Then, the Unseelie nearby were using their frost and illusions magic against the "enemy" guards. Even though my own magic was low, I could sense it around them.

The Seelie fae had clearly been caught off guard, a few lying still on the damaged stone streets, golden blood pooling underneath them.

"We have to do something," Hestia rasped, darting out the window to join the fight.

"Mom," Lira shouted, but her dad blew out the window, following his wife. "Dammit." Her terror sank its claws into our bond, making my chest even tighter.

"We must stop them." I turned to Struan and the three guards who always seemed to be with him. "Our people attacked when I told them not to."

Struan nodded. "Uaine, go alert the other guards. The three of us will detain the twenty on the mountaintop while the rest of the guards stop our people from fighting in the streets."

"Yes, sir." Uaine spun toward the prison area once again with his silver wings beating so fast it could pass for one movement.

"You two follow me." Struan flew down the hall in the direction of the insurgent Unseelie with the two guards close on his wings.

A part of me wanted to stay here and protect Lira, but she wasn't the one in peril... at least, not this second. "The Unseelie are focused on the guards who organized our journey to this ruined place after my parents died."

One thing I'd learned from Lira's actions was that I couldn't expect my people to do something that I wouldn't do myself, so I followed Struan and linked to Lira, *Go to our bedchamber, lock the door, and stay there until I tell you it's safe to exit once again.*

As I flew out the last window, a bitter laugh sounded behind me, and I didn't have to turn around to know it came from her. I waited for her to threaten or yell at me, but when our bond remained silent, a shiver ran down my spine.

I glanced back where she'd been standing, but she was gone.

She had to be up to something. Something she wouldn't inform me of, which meant I had to resolve the situation quickly.

The ten Unseelie, who had bows and arrows, nocked in tandem and released. The arrows shot toward the base of the castle stairs where most of the higher-ranking Seelie guards

THE KINGDOM OF FLAMES AND ASH

were protecting the king and the queen. A few of the Seelie guards lifted their hands, directing the wind, and the weapons hit behind the village. Still, a few arrows made impact, and two different blasts rocked the castle, the village around it, and even the area behind the village close to the cave where we grew mushrooms.

Blast, no.

Several Seelie screamed, but the ones in the back where the attack hadn't been aimed had made it to the center of the village, using their powers and weapons to fight my kind.

This had to stop now before more perished. I couldn't fathom how my people could be so asinine as to target our enemy when we were at our weakest and fighting among ourselves, let alone against an army that had about the same number of guards here as there were Unseelie alive.

I connected to the trickle of magic I had to amplify my voice and commanded, "Put down your weapons *now*. The Seelie aren't here to threaten us."

Half my people obeyed, stepping back to the edges of the stone path. The others didn't seem to register that I'd said a blasted thing. They didn't pause in their fighting, including the ones with the volcanic rock that was devastating the village below.

Wind continued to pick up, causing my aching wings to sway in the breeze while fire sprouted from Seelie hands, burning the feet of my people. The earth shook, forcing some of them to fall.

If we didn't stop the fighting, a lot of my people would die. Our magic was weaker because we hadn't had access to our true land for so long.

I removed the unfamiliar sword I wore at my hip, ready to kill any of my people who didn't obey, if that was my only choice. My wings throbbed, indicating that I wouldn't be able to keep pushing them like this much longer. Between being starved while a prisoner in Seelie and then the brutal battle and injuries here, I wasn't sure how much longer I'd have any strength.

The clanging of swords signaled that the battle had intensified. As if the combatants were attempting to get in a last bit of fighting.

When Struan reached a dark-haired man who'd positioned himself closest to the castle, he stabbed the man in the arm so he couldn't string his bow effectively again. The other two guards followed suit, but the group of rebels removed their daggers and prepared to fight against their own kind.

I went for the one farthest from the prison, flying over the heads of others who didn't pay me any attention, prepared to make my point. When I reached the man who seemed like the leader of the group, he spun around with his bow but paused when he realized who was there.

At least he had some respect for my position and title, but that wasn't enough. "You didn't obey." I swung my blade, slicing through his neck.

I spun to attack the woman beside him, but she dropped her sling and raised her hands. "We were only trying to avenge the people who were taken from us by *them*. The exact vow you've made every day since we arrived on this blasted island."

My heart cracked, realizing that, while my intent had been to give my people hope and the will to survive; instead, I'd made them reckless. I didn't care if the Seelie perished, but the person who meant the most to me in the entire realm did. If it weren't for her, I would, without a doubt, be fighting alongside them—even if my father had killed my mother, the Seelie chose to bring us here where so many of my people had starved to death. That decision had caused a lot of suffering and loss for us. "I know, but right now, we have a bigger enemy to face."

Her bottom lip trembled. "The dragons?"

They would've seen Prince Pyralis come and kill seven of us without even blinking before flying away with his hostage.

At my nod, she shook her head. "But we might never get another chance."

The fighting continued, but when I heard the creak of the double doors, I had no doubt who it was. *Lira, please tell me you're in our bedchamber.*

You're not my father, thorn. I don't have to listen to you.

I glanced over my shoulder and watched her step onto the stairs just above the fighting. Several of the Seelie guards flew toward her, prepared to protect her.

She didn't wait for them. Instead, she put her fingers into her mouth and made the strangest noise I'd ever heard. It was loud and piercing, making my eardrums want to burst.

The noise cut through the battle, causing the fighters to pause and search for the new threat.

"Does everyone want to die now?" Lira arched a brow and placed her hands on her hips. "Or do some of you want to live for eternity like you planned?"

Needing to be there to protect her, I flew toward her. The *whoosh* of my wings was the only noise besides her voice. *Sprite, please go inside. It's not safe for you out here.*

Nor is it for you. She lifted her chin higher and continued, "We are all fae, and we shouldn't be fighting against one another. Each one of us has been a victim of the other, and we're going to continue that cycle if we don't reach peace now."

The Seelie guards landed in front of her, spreading their wings to protect her from the crowd, but my mate pushed through so the Unseelie could see her.

Blighted abyss. Get back inside the castle!

"Of course you want to protect them. They are your people!" a man shouted, raising his sword in the air.

My stomach churned. The man was trying to keep our people upset so they would fight once again.

"You are, too." She straightened, and discomfort from her wings pulsed through the bond. "And the Seelie could easily kill all the Unseelie. They only need Tavish alive in order for magic to remain stabilized. Is that the choice you want to give them?" She arched a brow, scanning the crowd. "Despite every one of you wanting me to die during the gauntlet, I'm doing this now because I care about you and the future we'll share with each other."

The Seelie kept their swords lifted in case the Unseelie attacked again. I recognized that, at the moment, the Unseelie were the problem, and I hated it. The Seelie were here only because Lira's parents cared about her. They could've barged in, launching a war to retrieve her.

As I approached, the Seelie guards tensed, but Lira lifted a hand and said, "He's my mate. He's always welcome to stand beside me."

My heart stuttered, making me wonder once again if having her near meant that I wasn't immortal anymore. Immortals didn't have health issues, but when it came to Lira, the mere smell of her left me feeling strange... and I wouldn't change it for all of Ardanos.

I landed beside her, and she took my hand, once again emphasizing that the two of us were one. We would fight to be with one another.

"We need to learn to trust one another. I understand it will take time, but maybe we can be the stronger species and put down our weapons first, then work to bridge the gap between us."

To my surprise, more Unseelie dropped their swords, and I glanced around to find that Struan and the other two guards had confiscated the weapons of the nineteen Unseelie who had launched the attack.

The Seelie guards managed to position themselves so that if my people started to fight once more, it would be futile between their weapons and strong magic. Lira hadn't intended it, but the Unseelie, who still had their weapons, glared at her and the guards with distrust and hate.

Lira's parents strolled out of the castle and joined us on the other side of Lira. King Erdan expanded his brown wings and commanded, "Take their weapons now. They can't be trusted."

"Father," Lira gasped. Her shock and frustration slammed into me. "They just stopped fighting."

"Because of the noise you made. If it hadn't been for that, they'd still be at it, and we can't take more losses. Not with the threat of war with the dragons. I need every guard we have." The king gestured to the twenty dead Seelie at the bottom of the stairs, and his shoulders sagged. His voice broke as he said, "This should've *never* happened. These were needless deaths on both sides, and I refuse to let this happen once more."

Despite not wanting to hand our weapons over to the Seelie, I couldn't be sure this wouldn't happen again if my people kept them. There was too much loss of life on both ends, and I hated that my hatred might have helped prompt the attack. More deaths I was responsible for, and I refused to allow my people to act recklessly once more. "I'll give the command and agree as long as my guards are able to retain their weapons."

"Absolutely not." The king scowled. "They—"

"Helped end the fight," Lira cut in. "That counts for something, Father. You did command them to come to a place where seven thousand Unseelie perished because of the lack of food and living space."

King Erdan's eyes bulged, but Queen Sylphia looped her arm through his and said, "Our daughter is right. King Tavish agreed to have most of his weapons confiscated. We must begin rebuilding together somehow."

The king's eyes turned steely as if he were about to argue when the queen said, "Remember what we talked about. Besides, we need to focus on how to get Eiric back."

"Fine. The Unseelie guards may retain their weapons, but all other weapons must be confiscated and placed under guard." The king huffed and folded his wings behind his back. His jaw clenched, indicating he wasn't thrilled with the decision.

Neither was I, but both groups were unsettled, and I needed to process what I'd learned about my parents. Now wasn't the time. We had too much at stake, and Lira needed to rest so she could help herself, Lorne, and Finnian.

Discomfort and concern swirled from Lira as she turned toward me and linked, *If you aren't comfortable—*

I didn't want her to feel more responsible for burdens that weren't hers to carry. She had a knack for that. *I'm not thrilled, but if your parents want to try to create some sort of harmony, then I won't fight it, especially since I don't know who I can trust. Eldrin still has loyalists who will do anything to see me fail, and taking the weapons allows me to reduce the potential threats while I try to determine who is and isn't loyal to me.* I squeezed her hand reassuringly. *As long as you trust that your parents are being sincere.*

She swallowed, contemplating the question. *They are people of their word.*

The fact that she'd considered it instead of immediately defending them reinforced how lucky I was to have her. *Then that's enough for me.* I kissed her forehead then turned my attention back to the masses, expecting their dissent. "Since we did attack the Seelie, I'm in agreement that any person who isn't a guard must hand over their weapons to be locked in the castle."

The armed village people sneered and booed. I noted each

THE KINGDOM OF FLAMES AND ASH

one because we needed to keep them under more scrutiny.

"This will be temporary, but with the stress everyone is under, it's best for everyone here. Our guards will keep an eye on the weapons as well as the perimeter of the island." I took a step forward and lifted the sword in my right hand, black blood still on the blade. "Anyone who goes against my wishes again will meet the same fate as the person who launched the attack."

The insinuation was clear. I sheathed my blade.

The four of us stood side by side as the Seelie guards began confiscating weapons. The stares between the groups were strained, but no one started fighting again. After perhaps thirty minutes, the weapons had been gathered, and Struan supervised placing them in the castle armory.

Brenin and Hestia separated from the others and rejoined us in the large room.

Brenin cleared his throat. "Your Majesty, I understand that we have a lot to handle, but the longer Eiric stays with the dragons, the greater her chances of being harmed. We need to develop a strategy for retrieving her."

Even though I agreed because my mate needed to save her sister, I didn't want to rush into anything. "If we attack now, the dragons will demand that Lira is handed over in her place." I shook my head. "That's not an acceptable risk. We must find a way to recover her without risking my mate."

"Lira will eventually be handed over to the dragons," King Erdan rasped. "We gave them our vow. If we do not uphold it, all of the Seelie will lose their magic."

"Over my dead body," I snarled. The thought of Lira with Prince Pyralis had the edges of my vision turning black again.

Lira stepped between us. "Calm down. Father, you said I wasn't even supposed to be handed over until I was twenty-five, so why argue about this now? And Tavish, there is someone who swears there's a way to get me out of the contract without

52

the Seelie losing their magic. If we learn what that is, then there won't be a reason not to leave and get E right now."

Blast. She was right. What were we doing standing here sniping over it? I had a cousin to torture to finally get some answers.

"Then the interrogation begins now." I turned, heading into the castle.

However, when I stepped inside, I froze.

Chapter Six

Lira

The strong jolt of surprise that pulsed through Tavish and me had my heart racing. Knowing that Tavish wasn't far off from my own injured state, thanks to the continued use of his wings, had me hurrying forward to prepare to face the adversary together... as we should do.

I ducked under his wing, ready to claw someone's eyes out, when my attention landed on Finola.

My breath caught, and I realized that I hadn't seen her since the day I'd been captured and taken back to Seelie.

Her normally light-tan complexion was a few shades paler, and there were dark circles under her deep-set eyes. She wore a prison outfit—a light-gray tunic and holey leather pants—which hung off her, and her fine, straight black hair was unkempt and greasy.

The strong guard who had protected me and taken care of me countless times while I'd been a prisoner appeared almost unrecognizable.

The icky feeling of disgust slugged through our bond, but that didn't stop my feet from propelling me forward. I hurried to Finola and wrapped my arms around her. Moving my back muscles caused my wings to throb, but I didn't blazing care. "Thank Fate you're okay. I didn't see you when Eldrin put us all in the cell."

Finola stiffened slightly before returning my embrace. "He placed us in the back near the doors to the arena."

The stench of feces and urine hit my nose, confirming that she'd been kept in the worst part of the prison. But that wasn't what had me relaxing my hold on her. It was how frail she felt... like she'd been starved. Like my parents had done to Tavish.

"Finola, I should've known you'd been taken hostage." Tavish patted her arm and continued, "I'll do whatever is necessary to ensure you get justice."

Unease prickled the base of my neck at seeing him touch another woman. I ignored the sensation because he was concerned about the guard, as he should be. I couldn't let the craze of the fated-mate bond turn me into someone I wasn't. I had no doubt that Tavish had no interest in anyone but me. And if he did, I'd happily cut his dick off.

He dropped his hand awkwardly, and his discomfort seeped through the bond, making my irrational possessiveness ease a bit.

A tingle along my spine made me realize we were being watched, and I turned to see Mother, Father, Mom, and Dad standing in front of the now-closed double doors. Father's forehead was lined with confusion while Mother tilted her head, examining the three of us.

"I merely want Eldrin to receive the punishment he deserves for everything he's done to the Unseelie." Finola bowed, taking time to acknowledge both of us.

"The future is set for him. Don't fret." Tavish's disgust returned in full force. "Someone come in here and take Finola from this cell so she can get cleaned up."

I had no doubt seeing Finola in this state would haunt Tavish, especially knowing that Eldrin had been planning to betray him all along. I could only imagine how I'd feel believing that someone had saved my life and protected me when they'd been plotting to dethrone me the entire time.

Father cleared his throat, and all three of us turned in his direction. Once he had the audience he wanted, he rubbed his hands together. "I understand that we're all emotional, but the disagreement outside solidified that everyone in Unseelie needs rest, including the three of you."

I placed my hands on my hips, ready to argue with Father. He'd just taken the Unseelies' weapons away, and Eiric had been captured. We didn't have time to rest. We needed to find a way to get my sister back before the dragons injured her. "Father—" I started, wanting to remind him that he wasn't king here.

He lifted a hand. "Lira, just let me finish. Please?" His words softened in the end. "I know I was hard on you back in Gleann Solas and didn't listen to your wants or needs. It took you freeing two people I'd claimed as prisoners and leaving with them to realize that I wasn't completely right. We did decide to send you to Earth, though it was out of love. However, I expected my little girl to return. And you're not a little girl anymore. All I'd like to do is offer a suggestion." His cobalt eyes lightened as sincerity shone through them. "I'd like to try again, and if we can see a way to free you from being betrothed to that ashbreath, then I'd like to help."

The thick walls around my heart that I'd constructed while with the Seelie began to shake. Father reminded me of the man I remembered through childlike eyes—a parent who'd cared for his daughter and wanted the best for her.

Tavish wrapped an arm around my waist, pulling me to his side. He nodded. "I'd like to listen to what you have to say."

Tears burned my eyes. Tavish was trying to bridge the gap between them as well.

Father's brows lifted, but then he pressed his lips together. "Your cousin clearly desires to feel significant and in control. Even though we ignored you during your imprisonment with us, you didn't react as expected." He winced a little but continued, "However, I suspect that your cousin would react predictably."

Thumb rubbing my side, Tavish took a deep breath and said, "So, you're suggesting that we ignore him. Make him believe we aren't interested in hearing what he wants to say."

Displeasure oozed through the bond at that suggestion, but Tavish didn't react. Instead, he seemed to mull over the words.

Even though I agreed with Father's plan, I was more desperate than ever to save my sister. "There's too much at stake."

"You mean Eiric?" Mother asked.

"Of course." The walls seemed to close in on me. "I don't know what they'll do to her once they realize that she's not *me*." As much as I loved Eiric and what she was willing to do to keep me safe, I feared I might hit her for putting herself in danger like that if we managed to get her back safely. "She's *just* as important as me."

She absolutely isn't, Tavish connected, his hands tightening on my waist. *If you were with the dragon prince, I wouldn't be standing here now. Eldrin could've had the Unseelie as long as I didn't lose you.*

My chest warmed from his affection, and I replied, *I would feel the same way if the situation were reversed, but Tavish, Eiric means the world to me. If something happens to her because—* Pressure built tight in my chest from a sob that wanted to release.

"King Erdan is right." Dad closed his eyes momentarily. "We all need rest, or the dragons will beat us. They won't hurt Eiric. Not yet. They know she's the only leverage they have against the fae, and the dragons are aware that you lived with us on Earth. They'll know Eiric means something to you."

Mom gasped, her jaw dropping in shock. "Brenin, you can't be serious. That's one of our babies. We need to retrieve her." She grasped the hilt of Tavish's sword—which was still sheathed at her side—while holding hers in her right hand. "Time is of the essence."

"If I thought she was in trouble, I wouldn't say this. You know me better than that, Hestia." Dad's head jerked back, and he clenched his teeth. "If we try anything now, the dragons will demand Lira, and Eldrin needs to believe that we aren't desperate for his answers. We must be wise, or we could lose *both* girls."

Mom's chest heaved, but she eventually nodded.

The two of them never had a disagreement, so I didn't expect to see them on opposing sides. But this was their daughter's life on the line.

Father and Dad were right. All of us were tired, stressed, and heartbroken from the significant losses and injuries we'd endured over the past several hours. We needed rest as much as we needed answers.

What do you want to do, sprite? Tavish asked. *Your opinion matters more than anyone else's. If you want to go after Eiric, we will. No questions asked.*

That's what I want *to do, but we need the Unseelie more settled, and Father is right. I say we get some rest and let me rejuvenate so I can heal Finnian and Lorne while you get answers from Eldrin.* At the thought of rest, exhaustion hit me, and the deep ache in my wings got worse. I sagged into Tavish's side, almost unable to stand.

He scanned my face. *I do agree. Eldrin always told me that I lost to him in chess because I'm not patient. He'll expect me to barge in and demand answers. I believe it's best if we wait a day or two so I don't make the move he anticipates.* His attention went back to my father. "Lira and I agree. We'll rest and strategize.

Worst-case scenario, if we can locate a map of the new island, then a small team could attempt to infiltrate and retrieve Eiric. Or we could send some guards to keep watch and alert us if anything drastic changes."

"Very well. Brenin, send four Seelie now to keep watch and report back in the morning. We may be able to discover where they're keeping Eiric since she arrived so recently," Father said and patted Dad's shoulder comfortingly.

"In the meantime, I'd appreciate my sword back." Tavish's eyes landed on Mom.

"We were just attacked, and Eiric is gone." Mom lifted her chin. "I think I should hold on to it for a little longer, especially since you already have a sword."

"With your people not obeying your commands, it might be best if we keep it until we're sure your cousin stays detained and can't get access to the royal weapon." Father nodded, his mouth pressing into a line.

I could feel the rage snaking from Tavish, but I understood pushing Father too hard now would only cause more resentment. *Let me handle this. I can get it back for you. It'll be better coming from me.*

Tavish scoffed inwardly. *This proves how much I love you.*

The double doors opened as the guards carried in the confiscated weapons. When Struan entered, Tavish said, "Struan, get someone to show King Erdan and Queen Sylphia to a bedchamber. Lira's wings are bleeding, and she needs to rest immediately."

"Yes, Your Majesty. I'll make sure someone attends to their needs." Struan flew out the door.

"Anything you need, let one of the guards know, and they'll take care of it." Tavish bent down and lifted me into his arms.

"Just take care of our daugh—" Mom's words cut off. "Our princess."

THE KINGDOM OF FLAMES AND ASH

Tavish took off toward our bedchamber. He didn't fly, but his pace was brisk. I leaned my head against his chest, hearing the rhythm of his heart and noting that it was in sync with mine. Somehow, that felt right... Like it made sense.

Soon, he stalked into his bedroom. The moon shone, and the stars twinkled brightly through the glass-top ceiling over the huge king bed. He carried me to it and placed me down gently.

Dirty, I connected, but even then, my eyes were closing.

We'll have our sheets changed tomorrow, sprite. Just get some rest. He kissed my forehead and slid in beside me.

Before I realized what was happening, I fell fast asleep.

Light and warmth blanketed me, and I woke up to the sun shining through the glass ceiling. For a moment, I feared I was back in Gleann Solas. I sat upright, taking note of the dark room around me.

I was still in Cuil Dorcha.

Tavish wasn't in the room with me, but Nightbane lay at my feet. The beast was still out cold after being locked in prison and tortured.

My chest clenched. Had something happened and Tavish hadn't woken me? But then I heard the sound of water.

He must be taking a bath.

I stretched my wings, finding they felt marginally better. They still ached, but it didn't feel as if they might split in two, and I could feel a faint eddy of my magic returning. The improvement was better than nothing, and joining him in the round, clear tub sounded like the perfect plan.

Getting up slowly so as not to bother Nightbane, I tossed off the navy sheets and tiptoed to the door across from the bed. I turned the knob, wondering if it was locked, but it opened up easily.

As I shut the door behind me, my attention homed in on my mate. I took in the curves of his body in the clear tub with the frosted bottom that was elevated on a wooden floor.

If Eldrin hadn't been behind bars, I'd have been wary of the shadows on the wall directly in front of me, which looked as if a dark forest lay behind them. But I wasn't now, and especially not with Tavish near.

"I won't lie." Tavish beamed, his eyes turning the light gray they did only around me. "I was hoping you might join me, but only if you're not hurting." He sprawled in the tub, and through the clear glass, I could see every inch of him. My body heated.

"I'm still not fully healed, but I'm thinking your body might make me feel all better." I grinned and slowly removed my shirt, careful not to jar my wings and back, and then removed my pants.

His dick hardened, and a knot of need twisted deep inside me.

"Unless you aren't up for the challenge," I whispered, moving slowly to him. My eyes adjusted to the soft candlelight in the dark room, and I embraced the essence of Tavish's power running throughout the castle. I noticed that he'd laid out two towels and clothes for each of us.

I stepped into the tub and submerged myself in the warm aqua-blue water, soothing my muscles and easing the lingering tension in my limbs.

Tavish's eyes never left me, and his wings wrapped protectively around me. I lay against his chest as our bodies buzzed from our fated-mate connection, and he traced gentle patterns on my arm.

"I'm glad you're feeling better, but if you're hurting, we need to ensure we don't reopen the wounds." He placed a kiss on my forehead. The warmth and tenderness of our embrace made the horribleness of the world vanish from my mind.

The water settled into my limbs, easing the discomfort in my wings and back, but heat flooded my body.

I raised my head and kissed him, swiping my tongue across his mouth, begging for entrance. His hardness pressed into my stomach, informing me that he wanted me as much as I wanted him.

Sprite, he growled. *I'm trying to take care of you here.*

I believe I made clear exactly what I want. I wrapped my hand around his cock and stroked it, and he shuddered.

His mouth opened, allowing me access. Our tongues intertwined as a hand caressed my breast.

I moved my hand slowly, teasing my fingers along the length of him, feeling him harden even more beneath my touch.

He groaned softly, his hands gripping my waist, pulling me farther up so he could capture my nipple in his mouth and forcing me to release him.

I'm too close to finishing, he linked as his teeth gently scraped my skin, leaving a trail of fire. One hand steadied me while the other went between my legs, rubbing ever so slightly.

Heat burned so bright that I feared I might implode as he slipped two fingers inside me.

My heart pounded as his fingers and mouth worked, bringing me closer to the edge. His musk-and-amber scent covered me, and I lost myself in him completely. Friction began to build deep within me.

Just as I was on the brink of pleasure, I gripped his hand and removed his fingers from within me.

What are you— he started, but when I slid down onto him, his breath caught.

My thighs wrapped around his waist, the cold air hitting the top half of my body. He sat more upright, completely filling me. My hands gripped his shoulders, digging in as he began to move within me.

If I hurt you, I need to know. He gently placed his hands on my hips, anchoring me to him.

I'll be fine. I need this connection with you. I leaned forward, kissing down his neck and scraping my teeth against his skin as my head spun with the need for release... to feel our souls merge... especially after how close we'd come to losing one another.

My breath hitched as I struggled to keep pace with him. The world around us melted away, allowing us a moment of peace.

His hands cupped my face, and then one tangled in my hair, pulling me closer to him. He tugged slightly, and I moaned louder.

Blast, sprite. He tilted his head back. *You're going to kill me.*

The friction peaked, and I orgasmed as his body shuddered underneath mine. Our connection opened, our pleasure blending together as the ecstasy increased.

We rode our pleasure for minutes—or hours—I wasn't sure. All I knew was, at this moment, I felt complete.

He kissed my lips gently and connected, *I love you so blasting much.*

I smirked and leaned back, cupping his face. *I love you too.*

A scratch came on the door, followed by a whimper.

Nightbane.

We must have woken him up.

I stiffened. I hated that I hadn't given the cù-sìth much attention since I'd gotten back here.

"Let's get cleaned up so you can spend time with the beast." Tavish winked, knowing exactly what I was thinking.

Of course he did. He could feel my emotions and knew me better than anybody. "With you too, right?" I wanted the two of them to get past their rough history.

"Sure." He kissed me again. "Just for you."

The two of us quickly bathed, dried, and dressed.

I'd just slipped on the silver gown he'd brought for me as he dressed in a black tunic and pants when there was a loud pounding on the door.

"King Tavish," Struan yelled so loudly we could hear him from inside the bathroom. "We need both of you, now. It's about the woman who attacked Lira."

CHAPTER SEVEN

LIRA

My heart dropped, and my lungs seized.

Tavish's anger blazed within me, and he rushed to the bathroom door and yanked it open.

A deep, threatening growl came from near the bedroom door, indicating that Nightbane sensed a threat.

I refused to be left behind, so I marched right behind my mate to face whatever the threat was together.

When we reentered the bedchamber, I had to press my lips together, attempting to hold in the laughter.

Struan had the door cracked, and the fur on Nightbane's neck stood up as he readied to attack the guard if he risked opening it further. I jogged over and scratched his neck. "He means us no harm."

Nightbane quieted as Tavish opened the door. "What the blast is going on?"

"There's been an attack." Struan winced.

"What does that mean?" Tavish's wings expanded, and now, I didn't sense any discomfort from him.

Some of the weight on my shoulders lifted. He didn't seem to be in pain anymore, which meant he would be at full strength when handling his people.

Struan's wings went taut. "She's been attacked, and there's no way to prevent her from dying."

THE KINGDOM OF FLAMES AND ASH

"We need answers." Tavish shoved past Struan, flying in the direction of the prison. Terror and anger wound within him like a thunderstorm building between two drastic temperatures in spring in Savannah back on Earth.

I flapped my wings, hoping I could keep up. My healing magic must have started working when I hadn't noticed because they only ached when they moved, instead of causing pure agony. *Tavish, I can't get there as quickly.*

Stay in the bedchamber, and instruct someone you trust to stand guard outside. Something dangerous could happen in the prison, and I need you safe.

My pulse raced, and my breathing quickened. I couldn't believe he'd taken off, thinking I couldn't protect myself.

With my magic regenerating, I could potentially heal the woman enough for her to survive, but I needed to reach her side before she passed. And then, when it was handled, teach Tavish a lesson of his own. "Struan, can you carry me there? My wings still aren't completely better."

He winced. "If Tavish sees me touching you—"

"Then he'll have to get over it quickly," I gritted out. "He left my ass behind, so he doesn't get a say on what happens next."

His brow furrowed. "Not just your... er—ass. But all of you as well." He closed his eyes for a moment. "I'm not sure how I expect that to make you any less determined."

I didn't waste time explaining that wasn't what I'd meant and just leapt into his arms. He grunted, wrapping his arms around my waist and stumbling back. I didn't wrap my legs around his waist and opted for the hug hold because, even if I was pissed, I'd never want my privates touching any other man, even through clothes.

"Blighted abyss," he grumbled. "Since you're determined for me to die today, I expect you to take care of Isla once I'm gone." He took off for the prison.

$\maltese$ 66 $\maltese$

"Agreed." If that was the price I paid to get him to carry me there, it was one that I'd gladly accept. Besides, I liked Isla way too much for that to actually be a burden.

We were several yards behind Tavish, and I could sense the tension rolling off the guard. "If there was a woman guard outside our door, believe me, I would have had her carry me instead of you," I added. "Why *wasn't* there a guard outside the door?" Even though his arms were stiff around my waist and not at all tender, the feel of another man's touch had my skin crawling.

I swallowed, not wanting to make a big deal out of the situation. The more awkward and wrong I felt, the more I wanted to yell at Tavish.

But not now.

We had to get through this first.

Struan coughed, his body jarring mine, and then he suddenly stopped and released me.

I opened my mouth to complain when the stench of feces and urine hit my nose, and I gagged. I hadn't been prepared for the strength of the odor.

"I'm not about to carry you in front of him feeling like that." Struan stepped back as if he'd never been close to me.

About twenty-five feet away, a cell door was open, and I could sense the frustration rippling from Tavish.

"How the blast did this happen?" His voice boomed. "Where were the guards?"

Struan had gotten me more than close enough. My bare feet hit the grimy floor, but I could wash them later. I jogged toward the cell, each step jolting my body and aggravating the ache in my wings. I gritted my teeth, knowing that I needed to get there in a hurry.

"Of course the sunscorched wildling wouldn't be far behind," Eldrin's voice came from the cell to the left of me.

My head jerked in his direction, taking in his disheveled appearance. Even unkempt, he wore a smug expression, and his white eyes seemed sinister.

I hated the chill that ran down my spine at remembering the way he'd seemed to materialize out of the shadows as I'd bathed not long enough ago. I schooled my expression and glanced away, not wanting him to know how much he still impacted me, and pressed forward.

Now the cell was near, and I could see inside. A guard with hair the color of flint was pressed against the bars within the cell as Tavish held the tip of his sword at his throat. The woman who'd injured my wings with the arrow lay at their feet in a puddle of black blood from the slit in her throat, surrounded by Finola, back in her normal guard attire, and the silver-haired guard who accompanied Struan most places.

Whoever had killed the woman had made sure that, even dying, she couldn't speak and let any information slip out.

Tavish's body quivered with rage. "If you answer me, I might spare your life."

"He was the only guard down here. I told him to change out her bucket while I kept watch on Eldrin, and then I heard the woman gurgling." Finola glared at the traitor.

"Did you do this? Or did you allow it to happen?" Tavish spat.

I didn't need to see his face to know the exact expression my mate wore. I wanted to be at his side because even though I was pissed he'd left me behind, I would always stand beside him. Though he'd have a lot to make up for later when we were alone once more.

"The point was to kill her, so you couldn't. Her death was quick and painless so she wouldn't suffer needlessly for rightfully attacking our enemy... the sunscorched princess." The guard's nose wrinkled as he stared at my mate. "Eldrin should be our king, and I proved my loyalty to *him* by—" Tavish's blade slid into the guard's throat, cutting off his words. Black blood trickled down, oozing underneath his dark armor. The man's face twisted in agony, but the sword's blade kept him upright.

"That's for killing one of your own who was also loyal to Eldrin, just so that I didn't get the joy of draining the life from her for the suffering she caused my *fated mate*." Tavish's wings stretched out, blocking the guard's face from my view. Anger emanated from him. I didn't need our connection to sense it.

I stepped inside the cell, and Finola moved toward me as if to stop me from interfering.

Blaze that.

I ducked under Tavish's wing, and his dark-slate irises turned toward me. *Sprite, don't even ask me to spare his life. He did this on behalf of Eldrin so my cousin could take away something else I desperately wanted and prove he still has power even behind bars. That he doesn't need to escape to undermine me.*

Not hesitating, I stepped into Tavish's side so the guard could see me. A tiny part of me knew that I should tell him to stop, that we could use this man for something, but I couldn't make myself say the words. Instead, I said, "I want to make sure the last thing this nightfiend sees is me, seeing as he thinks so highly of the Seelie."

I hated that Eldrin still had people close to him who would obey his commands. We needed to kill him.

Fuck what he claimed to know about the dragons.

Mercy was appropriate at times, such as Tavish's actions yesterday. He'd given the people who hadn't spoken out against Eldrin's supporters one more chance. This was different, and I understood that.

Wrapping his left arm around my waist, he pulled me to his side and connected, *You're making me want to devour you right now, sprite. Those words were the sexiest I've ever heard you say.*

Of course, it would be threats that would get my fated mate going. *Keep it in your pants, thorn. You won't be getting anything from me for a while after what you just pulled back there.*

I won't regret trying to protect you. And I'm comforted by the fact that I was able to kill the man who murdered your attacker. His eyes narrowed as he dug the blade deeper into the guard's throat. *We don't know everyone who's loyal to Eldrin.*

Eldrin wants you as a prisoner so he can be free and rule. For some reason, ever since my memories came back, he doesn't seem as intent on killing me. I hadn't put that together until now. But with Eldrin telling Malikor that he couldn't kill me, just make me bleed for the veil, and then Prince Pyralis showing up, he had to be working with the dragons. That had to be how he knew something about them that we could use to our benefit.

Tavish kissed my forehead, making sure the guard saw the tender moment pass between us. Then he sliced the rest of the way through the guard's neck. Blood spattered Tavish's shirt, blending in with the dark color, and after a moment, the guard crumpled to the ground.

"Clean this up," Tavish barked, glancing at Struan. "Finola, make sure you or Struan are watching Eldrin all the time. Obviously, he's trying to cause unrest among us, and I want only the guards I trust watching him. Once Lorne is healthy enough, he can join the rotation. No one besides you three, do you understand?"

"Yes, Your Majesty," Struan said from his spot outside the cell.

Let's get you out of here. Tavish tightened his arm as we walked down the hallway, with Tavish closest to Eldrin's cell. He continued, *Don't pay Eldrin any attention. That's what he wants, and I refuse to give in to him. We need to continue to make him feel worthless.*

As we passed by his cell, Eldrin shuffled his feet. The two of us didn't even twitch, pretending we hadn't heard a noise.

"Clearly, you haven't learned anything," Eldrin drawled loudly.

Tavish stiffened, so I pushed comfort through our bond, wanting to ease his turmoil. *You didn't expect him to stay silent if we didn't acknowledge him, did you?* In reality, Eldrin had a hard time remaining quiet. He liked hearing himself talk way too much.

That doesn't mean I want to kill him any less. Tavish's nostrils flared, but he didn't move back.

"If you keep ignoring me, I'll be forced to take more drastic measures. Maybe even have someone attack the Seelie princess."

Before I could say or do anything, Tavish snapped. He released me, spun around, and headed back to the prison cell. His chest heaved, and his wings spread out, blocking Eldrin's view of me. He snarled, "Do not threaten Lira again, or I'll remove your tongue myself."

"You speaking to me was all that I wanted, Tavish." Eldrin chuckled. "If you'd just come last night or even first thing this morning, then maybe I wouldn't have been forced to get you down here."

I refused to be cut out of this conversation, especially since Eldrin had gotten exactly what he wanted. I stepped into the unlocked cell next to him so I could see the vile man once more.

"I've always suspected you were a toddler demanding attention." I smirked, tilting my head, wanting him to see that I wouldn't hide behind Tavish. I never had and wouldn't begin now, even if that was what my mate wanted. "Does your bucket need emptying? Is that the issue?"

Eldrin scowled. "This is between my cousin and myself. I

won't waste time speaking to someone so inconsequential."

"Yet, I'm not the one in a prison cell vying for your king's attention." I batted my eyes, wanting to push him the way he tried to goad Tavish. "If it helps, no one has asked about you or your well-being. In fact, I doubt anyone cares about your existence."

"You stupid wildling." Eldrin's hands clenched at his sides. "I have more allies than you'll ever know."

Tavish snapped, "Unlock Eldrin's cell. There's no reason to keep him alive."

"That would be foolish." Eldrin straightened. "I haven't yet told you how Lira can get out of the agreement with the dragon prince. Or is saving her from an eternity with him not worth keeping me alive?"

There it was. The piece of information he'd continue to dangle in front of us. I wanted to watch the bastard bleed to death. Maybe even drain him like he'd wanted to do to me.

"I don't believe you." Tavish stepped back so that Finola could unlock the door. "You're playing with words, trying pathetically to save your life. If you truly know of a way to save Lira from the agreement, tell us now."

Eldrin smirked like this was what he'd wanted all along. "I know things that would most definitely make the vow that the Seelie princess will marry the dragon prince void. I'm the only fae aware of this fact, and if you want a chance to have a future with your sunscorched beloved, then there are certain vows that I need made by both you and the Seelie king and queen."

A sour taste filled my mouth. He'd made sure his words were clear and precise so that Tavish wouldn't dare risk killing him.

Finola had slipped the key into the lock when Tavish said, "Stop. Don't open it."

Of course, that made Eldrin smirk even more. I'd never

experienced the amount of hatred in my life that I held for this man. I wouldn't put it past myself to dance over his dead body once we were relieved of his vile breath.

Stepping back, Finola placed the key back into her pocket and glanced at Struan. A strange expression crossed between them.

"What are your terms?" Tavish lifted his chin, and disgust seeped through our bond.

"No one kills me." Eldrin shrugged like it wasn't a big deal. "I get to live for eternity with the protection of Unseelie guards of my choosing."

Tavish laughed loudly and bitterly. "Like that will blasting happen. Your presence is a disgrace to every fae alive. You don't respect our magic or how the system works."

"It's the only agreement I'm willing to make." Eldrin shrugged. "Kill me now and spend what little bit of time you have left with your *fated mate,* or allow me to live and have her by your side for your time here in Ardanos."

I didn't miss that he didn't mention anything about obeying Tavish. If the pompous ass remained alive, he'd never stop trying to steal Tavish's throne from him and would continue to pit Unseelie against Seelie, keeping the cycle of hate and distrust going.

"You don't even have the king's sword, Tavish." Eldrin wrinkled his nose. "The Seelie are taking everything from us one day at a time."

He was trying to get into Tavish's head. He'd been gaslighting him his entire life. *Tavish, he's manipulating you.*

I know. Tavish smiled, though it didn't meet his eyes. "Well, I've heard enough." He folded his wings into his back and held out his hand to me. "Let's go get breakfast with the Seelie king and queen."

I swallowed my laughter, loving the words he'd tossed out

just for Eldrin's benefit.

Obliging, I strolled away from the cell and took his hand, and the two of us headed back to the main castle.

"Enjoy it, Tavish, while you can," Eldrin called. "Because one day soon, you'll be desperate for this information."

Wrapped in Tavish's arms, I could feel my magic pulsing stronger within me. We had two people who could benefit from the healing that might be enough to help.

The two of us enjoyed the walk, making sure that Eldrin could hear us move farther and farther away. Something he wouldn't be able to do for a long time. Finola followed us, and Struan and the other guard stayed behind to keep watch over Eldrin.

As we passed the bedchamber, I stopped in my tracks, catching Tavish by surprise. I turned to Finola and smiled, thankful to see her a little closer to her normal self. "Do you mind standing guard for a while? I need to be alone with Tavish."

We should eat, but I do believe I can hold off for a few more minutes. Tavish's eyes lightened to the light gray they did when he was alone with me.

I'm glad. I winked, knowing exactly what I planned to do when we got behind closed doors.

"Yes, of course." Finola took her usual spot by the door as the two of us entered.

As soon as the door shut, Tavish pulled me against him, leaning down to kiss me.

Nightbane huffed, making his displeasure known. He wouldn't have to worry about that for long.

I spun Tavish around and shoved him against the wall, letting him feel the frustration and anger boiling inside me, making him realize he'd misread the situation completely. "Because what you did earlier is *not* acceptable."

He winced, preparing for the inevitable.

Chapter Eight

Lira

Maybe I should temper my frustration with him, but I couldn't bring myself to even attempt to do that. Instead, I found myself pressing a finger into his chest and hissing, "You left me behind so you could face a threat alone. What the *hell* was that?"

Nightbane jogged to my side, growling faintly. I could hear the confusion in his voice despite him not saying words. He had accepted my bond with Tavish even if it had been begrudgingly, and he wasn't used to us fighting like this anymore.

He exhaled, his breath hitting my face. "Sprite, I had no doubt Eldrin was behind this when Struan mentioned the woman was dying. I don't want you anywhere near the wretched monster."

"And you think I want you near him?" I dug my finger in a little harder, wanting to make a point in any and every way possible. "I thought we were equals and going to stand beside one another?" My voice cracked as my heart sank.

His face softened. "That isn't what I meant. You're injured, and I almost lost you last night. If Eiric hadn't glamoured herself as you—" His words cut off as agony lined his face. "I... I can't even allow myself to fathom it because the thought alone has me going insane."

"Don't you think I feel the same way?" The double

standard frustrated me more than anything else. "People want to hurt you as well. It isn't *just* me, and if you want the Unseelie to believe that you view me as an equal, then you need to back up your words with actions. I refuse to be left behind while you run into battle. How would you feel if I did the same thing to you?"

"You don't think I know how that feels? Watching someone rush into danger while you get left behind? Remember, I had to watch you come close to dying so often in the gauntlet." His fingers tangled into his dark hair, causing pieces to fall across his forehead. "Something that I never should've pushed upon you, and I never want you to experience anything close to that again. Being with me makes even your wings targets, and an Unseelie took that shot the first chance she got. Every time something happens, you're the one who gets the brunt of the punishment, and I'm so tired of not being able to protect you."

As turmoil and guilt swirled through him, I wanted to give in. But that wouldn't improve our situation. In fact, it would do the opposite and empower him to continue pushing me aside when it mattered the most. I couldn't allow the fated-mate bond to influence me to bend when I needed to stand straighter than ever. "How could you protect me when you left me behind?" I took a step back, removing the temptation to fall into his arms. "That could've been exactly what Eldrin wanted! Then I could have been imprisoned somewhere, so one of his loyalists could drain me of my blood."

He flinched, revealing that he hadn't considered that.

"Furthermore, when have I *ever* asked you to save me?" I patted my chest. "Because I don't believe I ever have. Both my sets of parents ensured that I could defend myself. Even on Earth, Mom and Dad taught Eiric and me how to defend ourselves if we got into trouble. I need you to trust me like I do you—trust that we can fight beside each other. I refuse to play it safe while you stick your neck out."

"Is that more Earth speak?" His brows furrowed. "Because I don't believe I've ever stuck my neck out. It seems like a peculiar thing to do, and I hope you'd inform me if I looked foolish."

I laughed, unable to stop myself in time. I loved how he seemed more perplexed than amused by Earth sayings. Finnian ate the information up, but Tavish seemed to believe each figure of speech was a complex problem he'd rather do without.

"It is Earth speak." I rolled my eyes, trying to force my expression back into indifference. "It means I won't hide in our bedchamber while you put yourself in danger. It's really rather simple."

He smirked. "*Our* bedchamber?"

My pulse froze, and I tilted my head back. I couldn't believe I'd just assumed that his bedroom was ours, but it was too late to yank it back. "*Your* bedchamber. I just meant—"

"You had it right before," he interjected and took my hand. "It is *ours*. It's just the first time I've ever heard you say that, and I really enjoyed it. I know you haven't made any changes to make it feel more like your own, but love, everything that is mine is also yours."

Chest warming, I squeezed his hand. I could feel the truth of his words through our bond, but that wasn't all that I needed. "Then I need that to include our enemies and danger as well. I want it all, Tavish. I want us to be beside each other in all ways. We're stronger together, and though I know when we fight, we tend to get split up, we're still working toward the same goal and can protect each other."

He huffed and leaned his head back against the wall. "I can feel this is important to you, and you're right. If you tried leaving me behind to fight, it wouldn't work. I'd fly after you the same way you did after me this morning. But all I ever want is to keep you safe and happy."

My anger vanished, leaving my shoulders feeling lighter than when Struan had informed us about the issue this morning. "And I want the same for you, but we both have to remember that we aren't each other's parents. We're lovers, friends, and equals who embrace everything, even challenges, together."

"I can agree to that as long as we acknowledge that there might be a situation where the other person must be part of the battle." Tavish cupped my face and leaned forward. "And we need to realize that there are times when it could be best if one of us removed ourselves from the threat, such as if one of us is at significant risk. I don't want to make a vow that can't be broken and gets us both into trouble."

I hadn't considered this a vow, but I could see his point. We were coming to an understanding about how each of us wanted to be treated. "Fine, since you're including yourself in the equation."

He smirked. "I figured I had to in order to get your agreement."

"Then you assumed correctly."

The buzz from his hands on my skin had my annoyance with him fading away.

Nightbane huffed, no longer worried about what was brewing between us, and trotted back to the bed, where he lay down at the foot of the mattress.

"I didn't mean to upset you, but I understand why you were." He kissed my forehead tenderly. "My intent was anything but malicious. You're my entire realm... more important than anything else, including my people. I understand that you can protect yourself. I've seen you overcome the odds way too many times. I just don't want you to have to."

Lifting my head, I kissed him gently. *I know you weren't being mean or thought me incapable. If I believed either of those* was the reason, we wouldn't be having a conversation right now. *I'd be forced to prove myself to you with a sword.*

I'll spar with you any day, Princess. He winked but then frowned. *Which brings up another point. I need to retrieve my sword from your mother—er—mom.*

Even in my mind, he sounded strange using *mom* because, in Ardanos, we called our parents mother and father.

I understood this was important to him, even more so now that Eldrin had made sure everyone knew Tavish no longer had his father's sword. Though I found that part a little silly, I understood that the sword itself was sentimental to my mate. *Why don't we eat some breakfast and find Mom so we can retrieve it? Then we can check on Finnian and Lorne.*

I'd normally try to convince you to return to bed, but we already had a late start, and we need to inform Caelan of what transpired in the prison. Hopefully, he can help discern who is loyal to me and who is still following Eldrin beyond those already imprisoned for speaking out against me. His unease filtered through the bond, and my chest constricted.

We had no clue who was truly an ally or enemy.

My knees weakened, but I didn't want Tavish to realize how much that impacted me. *Then let's go and see if we can find leverage against Eldrin.* The last thing I wanted was for him to get the vows he was so desperate for from Tavish and my parents. Vowing that we wouldn't harm him meant that he could go after both crowns, and we could never eliminate the threat.

That thought sent a shiver running down my spine.

One day, I want us to fly away and find a small island for only the two of us to stay on for a few days. He smiled crookedly, reminding me of the boy I'd once known. *We can swim, make love, and even bask in the sun if that would make you happy.*

Now that sounds like a plan. I kissed him again, fighting

the urge to devour him.

He groaned, taking my hand and pushing away from the wall. He then opened the door, causing Nightbane to leave the mattress once more and hurry to follow us.

The three of us walked in silence, and soon, we entered the dining hall, where a long rectangular table seated sixteen. Five places had been set at the end near the windows overlooking the kingdom, and two servants flanked the window, waiting to serve.

My skin pebbled as I remembered the previous time I'd come here. I'd been a prisoner, and Tavish still believed that he would kill me.

Mother and Father sat on one side of the table with Caelan across from them. Mom and Dad stood by the window between the servants, looking at the kingdom outside as well as scanning for threats within these walls.

Tavish led me to where Caelan sat and pulled out the seat next to him, directly across from my mother, then sat on my other side.

Mother wrinkled her nose as she played with the fish on her plate, though she had only a few bites left of the mushroom. Father had managed to eat about half of each, and I couldn't help but notice that he'd shoved several sizable pieces of fish to the side like he didn't plan on eating them.

Fae didn't enjoy meat but could tolerate fish.

The older servant bowed and went to the kitchen.

"We've just been informed about what transpired this morning." Caelan took a bite of his fish. "We expected you two to be down before now, so we assumed you weren't coming."

"We usually don't wait on each other for the first meal of the day." Tavish slid into his seat. "Why would that change now?"

"In Seelie, we eat all meals together." Father lifted his glass of water and took a large gulp.

Tavish's jaw clenched.

Not wanting him to challenge Father, I leaned back in my seat. "You aren't in your kingdom anymore, or did you forget?" He needed to be reminded that this wasn't his kingdom... even if Seelie were currently guarding it.

Warmth filled Tavish's and my bond as Father stilled.

I braced for an unpleasant response, but he remained silent and ran a hand through his brown beard. "You're right. This isn't our kingdom, so our expectations and rules shouldn't apply here."

Mother smiled but raised a hand to hide it.

"I can imagine it's hard to come to another kingdom and remember that you aren't the ruler in charge." Tavish rolled his shoulders, trying to relax. His words were a little stiff, but they lacked anger. Both men were trying to get along for me.

Not wanting to waste the goodwill between them, I pivoted the conversation to what had happened in the prison cells then let Tavish take over. Father needed to see that Tavish was a worthy ruler, the same as him.

The older servant returned with Tavish's and my food. Someone had taken a bite from each piece of fish and mushroom on our plates. I swallowed, not enjoying the thought of eating the items.

Since we're unsure who is ally or foe, Sine has been taste-testing the food to ensure it's not poisoned. Tavish placed a hand on my thigh and squeezed. *The food is fine, or she wouldn't have served it.*

How do you know we can trust her? I wasn't thrilled about eating after someone, but I knew that was the Earth-raised side of me coming out. The fae didn't care, especially if it served a purpose.

Sine has worked for the royal family her entire life. I trust her, and you know I would never risk your life. He arched a brow and took a bite of his food, proving his point.

If he was wrong, then we'd both be in the same situation. I followed his lead, hating the stringy texture of the fish. I'd gotten spoiled by all the breads, jams, honey, and sweets back in Gleann Solas. There was nothing like that here. Yet more things the Unseelie didn't have due to their forced relocation.

The others continued the conversation around the mishap this morning and the capture of Eiric, and I worked on eating. If I wanted to heal Finnian and Lorne, I needed to be at full strength, even if I didn't feel hungry.

When Tavish informed the table about Eldrin's stipulation for revealing how to free me from the agreement with the dragons, Caelan growled, "Blighted abyss. Do we even believe that he knows something that would help?"

"He was clear that he does, in fact, know of a way to release Lira from the contract." Tavish finished his last bite of mushroom. "And he knows that I won't risk losing her."

"Nor do I want to hand my daughter over to those dragons after the stunt he pulled in Gleann Solas." Father rubbed his temples. "I knew better than to ally with the dragons, but our entire realm had been blanketed in darkness."

"Your Majesty, you did what you felt was right at the time." Dad lifted both hands.

Mom nodded, her left hand resting on Tavish's sword. "I even advised you to make the agreement."

"I still don't understand how Father could cover the realm." Tavish leaned back in his seat. "I'm not strong enough for that, not even when I reconnected with the Unseelie land after we fled Caisteal Solais, so he wouldn't have been either."

As soon as I finished my last bite, I drained my glass of water, wanting to get rid of the taste. "Something must have caused it."

THE KINGDOM OF FLAMES AND ASH

"Then that's what we will determine." Now that we were all finished, Caelan stood. "I'll do some research and see if I can find out how it could happen."

Father and Mother rose as well.

"That sounds like a good strategy." Father pointed at himself, Mother, Mom, and Dad, adding, "The four of us will check in with the Seelie guards in the village to ensure they haven't noticed anything worrisome from the dragons."

Knowing that the request would look better coming from me instead of Tavish, I placed my palms on the table and got to my feet. "Speaking of danger, I see that Mo—Hestia has Tavish's royal sword. Since he's been amenable to having you here and even confiscated his people's weapons, I think he should have his sword back." I hated sounding less than fully confident, but I didn't want to hurt the progress our two peoples had made. The truce still held on by a thread, but it could be severed at any second.

"I think that's a reasonable request," Mother replied, placing a hand on Father's shoulder.

She wanted to bridge the gap too, and I further reconsidered my original position regarding my parents. They needed time to acclimate to me not being who they remembered, the same as I needed to adjust to them now.

"He already has a sword anyway." Father bit his bottom lip as if he was trying not to say more. "Might as well."

Tavish's relief flooded our bond, making me realize how much he wanted the sword back.

He moved around my chair with his hand extended. "The sword is important to me."

Possessing it would give Eldrin one less item to use against him.

Mom unsheathed the sword and held it out so that Tavish could take it by the hilt.

84

But when Tavish reached for it, Mom yanked the sword back and said, "No."

Chapter Nine

Lira

At Mom's strange reaction, I startled back a step while Tavish's wings tensed as if he was prepared to fight her.

Mom flew back out of Tavish's reach, and the hand that held the sword shook.

"Hestia," Dad exclaimed, raising both eyebrows. "Is something wrong?"

Caelan unsheathed his sword, preparing to intervene, while my heart galloped.

I loved Mom, but if she were to attack Tavish, I had no doubt where my loyalty would lie. I'd feel no true guilt either because Tavish hadn't done anything wrong. Even though it hadn't truly been my biological parents' place, they'd still given Mom their blessing to return Tavish's sword. There was no reason for her to deny him.

"I..." Mom chewed on her bottom lip and took a ragged breath. "I don't know. A strange sensation came over me, like I shouldn't give it back to him." She cleared her throat and moved forward, handing the sword to Tavish. "But of course, it's his, especially since the royals agreed upon it."

Something still didn't seem normal with her, but when Tavish took hold of the sword once more, air filled my lungs more easily.

Shock filtered through our fated-mate bond as Tavish

lowered the sword to his side. The hilt was made of smooth dark stone, and the edges of the blade were white as if they'd been dipped in snow.

Does it feel strange having the sword back? I connected.

I didn't expect it to, but I believe so. He lifted the sword slightly, examining it once more. "I'd like my sheath as well." He nodded to the extra belt Mom had around her waist.

As Mom removed the belt, Tavish followed suit and handed the sword he'd been carrying to me.

I froze. Normally, I didn't carry a weapon. Before, I'd been a prisoner, so the option had never been provided outside of the gauntlet. Then, back in the Seelie palace, we'd had guards. I'd never considered asking for one.

After our discussion this morning, I planned on finding you a weapon, but this is easier now that I have my father's sword back. Since we agreed that you'll be by my side, no matter the threat, you need to always be prepared to protect yourself. You should know living here isn't nearly as safe as Gleann Solas, even for me. He tilted his head, watching to see my reaction.

He was right. I needed to be armed, and even in Gleann Solas, it wouldn't have been a horrible decision to carry a weapon. Since coming back to Ardanos, I'd learned that enemies could be anywhere, even in the guise of your closest family member.

I took the sword in its sheath, realizing how silly it'd appear over my gown, but I didn't care. This was about survival, not vanity. Tavish and I both fastened our weapons around ourselves.

"Lira, don't worry about your safety. We can provide guards to protect you if he can't." Father placed a hand on his chest, his forehead lined with concern. "There's no need for you to carry a weapon, and the fact that the night—"

"If you're about to hurl an insult at my fated mate, I'd advise you not to." Tavish's guilt pulsed through the bond, so I had to shut my father up. "Not only is he the person who means the most to me, but you're the one who forced him and his people to these ruined lands. The fact that you stole their homeland is bad enough, but to come here and speak ill of Tavish after all the Unseelie pain and suffering at your hands is more than an insult. It's repulsive and vile."

Nostrils flaring, Father fisted his hands at his sides. Mother laid a hand on his shoulder once again like she constantly needed to provide him comfort.

Warmth spread through our bond as Tavish connected, *You're blasting sexy, especially right now.*

Don't distract me. You can show me how attractive I am later. I didn't want to seem like I crumbled under Father's glare.

"Tavish isn't thrilled with giving me this weapon, believe me. I can feel his trepidation, but unlike you, he respects my wishes and knows that I'm more than capable of protecting myself and wielding a sword." I lifted my chin, wanting Father to truly feel my defiance.

"She's right, dear." Mother turned toward him and continued, "Nothing is lost by her carrying a weapon, or even me for that matter. Besides, she was trained with a sword until she went to Earth."

"And on Earth, we trained for self-defense even when we didn't remember our fae lives." Dad smiled. "She and Eiric were both naturals at it. That's the one thing saving me from going insane while thinking about Eiric with the dragons."

E.

My eyes burned from the threat of tears. We needed to unearth a way to break the contract between Prince Pyralis and me and get my sister back.

It hadn't even been twenty-four hours since we lost her, but it felt like months. Each second that passed made me even more anxious about her remaining with the dragons. "And the dragons already made it clear they feel as if the Seelie insulted them twice. Eiric's trick of glamouring herself as me will make them that much angrier." I would give anything, even my own freedom, for Eiric to be here.

Father stretched out his fingers and wings as if he was trying to release his anger. He took in a steady breath. "We need to get your cousin to tell us how to break the contract so we don't risk Lira."

"Fate, yes." Caelan placed his sword back at his side and rubbed his temples. "Because I suspect I know what the demand will be when the time comes, and if we can't prevent it, my king will lose all sense of rationale like he does anytime it comes to *her*." He glanced at me, but instead of the twisted expression of disgust he usually threw my way, he hung his head as if he'd given up on fighting my place here.

"We have to make Eldrin suffer. Right now, he thinks he's in control," Tavish spat. "He already gloated this morning. We need to break his confidence."

I stretched out my wings, the pain where the woman had shot me still twinging. It was odd. Even when I'd been near death after the gauntlet, my magic had healed me quickly. Now it seemed to be hindered somehow. My magic thrummed a little, but not nearly as strong as normal.

Still, I needed to see Finnian and Lorne and try to heal them both enough to make a difference. "We could pull one of Father's tricks and not feed him or allow him water."

"Tricks?" Father rocked back on his heels. "Withholding food and water isn't a trick at all. It's about making the other person weak. It's common knowledge."

Mom snickered, sounding a little more like herself.

There went my smart-ass comment. It clearly hadn't hit the mark with anyone besides her and Dad.

THE KINGDOM OF FLAMES AND ASH

"I'm all for allowing the thornling to starve." Caelan frowned. "Our food supply is already strained, especially with all the extra mouths to feed, and I haven't heard back from the village fae I sent out to assess the damage to the cave."

I'd forgotten about the blast behind the village. Worse, he was right. The three thousand Unseelie here could eat only twice a day. With the Seelie who joined us doubling our numbers, we would be reduced to once a day, and that was if the cave wasn't damaged.

"Get an update on that, and inform the guards Eldrin is to receive no sustenance." Tavish took my hand and tugged me toward the hallway as he continued, "Lira and I are going to check on Finnian and Lorne. We can all reconvene here in two hours to provide updates, if that works for the Seelie king and queen?" His eyes narrowed, but that was the only sign that he'd forced himself to be respectful of my parents.

"We're agreeable to that." Father puffed out his chest. "Hestia and Brenin will watch over the Seelie weapons and make sure the counts haven't changed."

Now that our tasks had been decided, Tavish and I walked down the hallway in the opposite direction of our bedchamber. As we strolled into the area, the walls seemed to darken, and the floor grew uneven.

We reached a door to the left, and Tavish led me inside. As soon as I entered, my feet dragged like weights were wrapped around my ankles. Finnian lay shirtless in the middle of a king-sized bed, his face, chest, and arms still charred. Frost-blue blankets, almost the shade of his eyes, covered him from the waist down. His chest rose slowly as if his breathing was labored.

I thought he'd be more healed than this. I'd expected him to not be in great condition but at least sitting up and making a jab as soon as we entered.

Dragon fire is hard to heal, so it takes more time. Tavish scowled. *And the dragon prince knew it. It's easy for fae to lose their lives when engulfed by it.*

Dragon magic was different from that of the faes', and before I'd left for Earth, my parents had avoided the dragons and rarely spoken of them. Clearly, that had changed after the alliance.

Entering the room, I noticed it was about half the size of Tavish's, with two large windows that looked out the back side of the village. The room screamed *untidy*; I had to step around various tunics and pants on the floor. That seemed particularly like Finnian, who enjoyed getting lost in the moment.

When I reached his bedside, I sat gently on the mattress, not wanting to cause him more discomfort. I touched the top of his shoulder.

Displeasure spun through the bond as Tavish huffed.

I paused, glancing over my shoulder at him. *What's the matter?*

You're sitting on another man's bed and touching him while he's shirtless. Tavish's expression turned stony. *This isn't easy for me.*

Smirking, I winked. *But you're the only one who gets the pleasure of seeing me naked.*

That may be so, but the memory of walking in and finding you with the bottom of your gown around your waist and Finnian leaning over you on the bed remains in my head, and is not making this moment any easier.

Unable to help it, I laughed. It'd been innocent and had happened while I was a *prisoner* here. Finnian had walked in just after I'd tried to put on a gown over my wet body, and it had gotten stuck. He was trying to help me pull it down, and by the time Tavish got there, we almost had the issue resolved, but it had looked like a compromising position. So much so

THE KINGDOM OF FLAMES AND ASH

that Tavish had tried to harm Finnian, and Finnian had used Tavish's chessboard to protect himself. *That looked way worse than it truly was.*

A faint groan came from Finnian, and then he opened his eyes a bit. They focused on me, and he croaked, "What does a man need to do in order to get some rest around here?" As he spoke, his charred skin cracked a little more, deepening his wounds.

The laughter vanished, and my stomach churned. Finnian wanted to lighten the situation even when it caused him more pain.

My magic pulsed, both the healing and the water, though it wasn't nearly as much as I wanted. Still, a little bit had to be better than nothing.

"I want to try to help you if that's okay," I whispered.

He nodded faintly, but that was enough.

I tugged at the magic inside me, the tingles of the healing magic swirling from the center of my chest near where the fated-mate bond sat, and funneled it toward my hand.

Feet shuffled behind me, and Tavish positioned himself at my side. His frustration vanished, and I could feel the worry he had for his closest friend.

As magic pushed inside him, the lines on Finnian's face smoothed. The chill of his magic mixed with mine, but it wasn't comforting like it was with Tavish. Ignoring the strange sensation, I tried to clear my head so my magic would do what needed to be done.

Finnian's breathing eased, and I wondered if Lorne was also this bad off. I needed to save enough to help him as well. Neither of them deserved this misery.

When my magic dwindled enough that I needed to stop to save some for Lorne, I opened my eyes and saw that Finnian's face was no longer charred, and scabs were healing all over it.

I withdrew my magic from him. "I need to help Lorne as well, or I'd do more."

Finnian's eyes opened a little bit wider. "Of course. I'm overjoyed that the sharp, throbbing torment is gone. I still feel raw but a whole lot better."

"I'm glad. I'll try to do more tomorrow."

"Don't overextend yourself." He winked. "Even if your touch is the best thing I've experienced in my whole lifetime."

"That's it." Tavish moved to the side and placed his hands on his sword. "I'm going to end you."

I dropped my hand and rolled my eyes. "He's goading you. You should know better." I stood and wrapped my arms around Tavish's waist but leveled my gaze at Finnian. "And you should know better than to pester him when you can't even get out of bed. It's like you have a death wish, which is not okay with me after I used so much magic on you."

"Oh." He tilted his head slightly. "So next time, tell you that *before* you use your healing touch?"

Tavish scoffed while I snorted. "Yes. That's exactly what I mean."

The twinkle Finnian's eyes normally held wasn't there, which told me he was putting on a brave face. He didn't like appearing weak, just like the rest of us, and he used humor to deflect.

He needed rest, and I needed to determine what was preventing me from recharging as quickly as I had before so I could help them better.

"Get some rest. We'll come back tomorrow."

Tavish and I left Finnian's room and then went down another two doors to see Lorne. His room was even smaller than Finnian's, with two queen-size beds inside. Lorne lay on the one closest to the door.

A small cloth doll sat in the middle of the other bed, which

THE KINGDOM OF FLAMES AND ASH

was close to the window, and I tilted my head. *Is Lorne married?*

No, I believe Struan and Isla are staying with him since Struan is watching over the guards here. Tavish scanned the room.

Odd slashes marred the walls as if they'd been damaged, and I didn't want to imagine how.

Unlike Finnian, Lorne was wearing a shirt. And though his face and neck were burned, he didn't seem as bad off as Finnian. Still, his charred skin appeared painful.

This time, not wanting to aggravate Tavish, I didn't sit on the bed. Tavish didn't feel nearly as loyal to Lorne as he did his close friend.

I leaned down and touched his shoulder, pushing my magic inside him. Just like Finnian, mixing my magic with Lorne's felt strange, but I powered through it the best I could. When my magic became significantly low, I stopped.

This time, when I straightened, the walls spun around me. I'd pushed my magical limits once again.

Tavish's arm slid around my waist, anchoring me to him. The buzz of our connection sprang to life. I laid my head on his chest and listened to the beating of his heart, which matched my own.

"You did too much, didn't you?" Tavish sighed, not even bothering to scold me.

"You don't seem surprised." I lifted my head and stared into those light-gray eyes that shone like silver.

He kissed my forehead. *I figured you would and want to lecture you, but I know it won't do any good. You're the most stubborn person I know and will do all it takes to help other people, especially the ones you feel loyalty toward.*

I smiled. *Sounds like someone else I know.*

I'm not nearly as good as you, sprite. At the end of the day, if I had to burn the realm down for you, I'd do it without hesitation.

There's nothing more important in this realm than you, not even my people.

I should've chastised him for saying that, but it would do as much good as him asking me not to drain myself while helping our friends. We were who we were, and I loved that he cherished me as I was.

And I'll do the same thing for you if it ever comes to that. I cupped his cheek. *We need them healed so we can retrieve Eiric. We need the people we trust on our team, and that list is short.*

Struan's voice came from outside the door. "Go check on Finola and ensure that she doesn't need anything. I'll keep watch tonight, and I'm going to rest until then."

"Yes, sir," a female responded as the door opened. "I'll let her know."

The door opened, and Struan huffed. As he entered the room, his gaze landed on us, and his mouth dropped open. "Your Majesty." His wide-eyed gaze landed on me as he said, "I didn't want to do it, but I was given no choice."

Suspicion and rage slammed into Tavish, and he tucked me into his side as he drew his sword.

Chapter Ten

Tavish

I should've known that someone I'd decided I could trust would be allied with Eldrin. I'd allowed his young daughter, Isla, to influence me with her words, but he could've said those things to her strategically to have her vouch for him.

I lifted my father's sword high, ready to end the threat before us. The part of me that used to crave bloodshed sparked back to life.

Tavish, it's not what you think. Lira placed a hand on my chest, and some of the bloodlust receded.

Even though I cherished my mate, she had a tendency toward mercy. Something I was incapable of at this moment.

Lifting both hands, Struan pressed himself against the wall. His bottom lip quivered. "I told her no, but what was I supposed to do? She jumped into my arms, and if I hadn't caught her, she would've been hurt, and that would've angered you more."

My mind stopped. I'd expected him to explain his loyalty to Eldrin, not... My blood turned to ice as realization settled deep within my bones. In all the chaos, I hadn't considered how Lira had managed to get to the prison cells so quickly. Her wings were still injured. She couldn't have flown, yet she'd arrived there mere minutes after me.

My vision darkened, thinking of his hands touching my

mate. "You're not allowed to touch her. I made that clear the day I brought her back here, yet you *carried* her to me?"

"Because you left me behind," Lira said, blocking me from the thornling traitor. "I didn't give him a choice. I threw myself on him, knowing he wouldn't let me fall."

The image of her legs wrapped around Struan while his arms held her body tight against his had my chest heaving. "You did *what*?"

Struan swallowed loudly. "Should I have let her fall instead? Just so I know what is expected of me next—"

"There won't be a blasting next time." I flew over Lira's head, about to stab the wildling in the throat.

My mate grabbed my boot and yanked me back down to the floor. Pain flashed through the bond, reminding me of her injury, and I bit back a snarl, not liking her protecting him.

Before I could move toward him once more, she cupped my face with her hands.

"Tavish, stop. I hung on to his shoulders, and he just held my waist, trying not to touch me. Nothing nefarious happened, and the contact was as minimal as possible." The normal warmth in her eyes vanished, making the color turn navy. "It wouldn't have even happened if you hadn't left me behind, which is one reason I had that pointed conversation with you earlier. If you're going to be mad at someone, you should stare at your reflection."

The jolt of our connection grounded me, but the need for violence still lingered in the back of my mind. "No other man should touch you," I rasped. "You're *mine*."

"That won't be a problem if you stick with our agreement." She arched a brow. "And of course I'm yours. The whole time, both Struan and I were ready for the situation to be over." She shuddered like the memory was a nightmare.

Somehow, that made me feel better.

THE KINGDOM OF FLAMES AND ASH

"I didn't enjoy it at all." Struan placed a hand over his chest. "I swear, and I hope to never touch her again."

His words thawed my anger, but the urge to stab him on principle clung to me, making me feel more like the man I'd been before Lira and I completed our bond. I exhaled, trying to center myself, and sheathed the sword.

Struan's shoulders sagged, and he leaned his head against the wall.

"This is your one pass." I spoke the words through clenched teeth.

Excuse you. Lira dropped her hands to her sides and arched a brow.

Of course, she'd be here to bind my wings if I stepped out of line. I should've known that I wouldn't get anything past her. "Because there won't be a need to do something like that again." For the past twelve years of my life, I'd refused to allow anyone to speak to me the way Lira did, but with her, everything was different. She was my other half. And blighted abyss, she held me accountable for everything. I wouldn't change that for the realm, though sometimes it was tiring.

Lira smiled, and I could sense how proud she was of me.

"Yes, Your Majesty." Struan rolled his shoulders, and his wings relaxed.

Now that the tension was resolved, Lira began swaying. I wanted to lecture her, but it wouldn't accomplish anything. I hated how she always risked her own well-being for others, but in this instance, I understood completely. She wanted to retrieve Eiric, and I refused to allow Pyralis to capture Lira, so we needed strong fae behind us.

Still, I couldn't let Struan get away with touching my mate. As I took her hand, preparing to carry her to our room, I shifted in front of Struan and punched him in the chin. I didn't use all my strength, but I needed to leave a mark so no one else believed they could go unpunished for touching Lira.

His head jerked back, and black blood trickled from the corner of his mouth. He rubbed his jaw and winced but didn't say a thing.

Lira cut her eyes at me and frowned. *I thought we agreed.*

We did. I kissed her cheek, hating the look she'd given me. *I didn't stab or kill him.*

Are you going to punch me then? She pursed her lips.

Fate, no. You were worried about me, so even though I'm not thrilled about what you did, I understand why you did it. I bent down and picked her up gently, treating her like the precious gift that she was.

I looked at Struan. "It's over now. You don't need to hide from me anymore."

"Good to know, My King." Struan smirked. "I wouldn't expect anything less. This actually brings comfort to me."

Lira turned her body toward me, the side of her face touching my chest and heightening the buzz of our connection. She grumbled, *I'll never understand Unseelie.*

The corners of my mouth tilted upward. *We're actually quite simple, sprite. And sometimes, a punch is what's needed to put the issue behind us.*

I left the bedchamber and took flight in the hallway, heading back to our room. Our bond cooled slightly, informing me even before her breathing leveled that she'd fallen asleep.

Today, my wings had strengthened more than I expected, and I was able to make it back to our room in seconds. I wasn't surprised when I entered the room and found Nightbane lying at the bottom of the bed. That seemed to be the spot the cù-sìth had claimed in the castle, and I wouldn't shoo him out because of his loyalty to Lira. He would die to protect her. I'd never dreamed a beast could care about a fae even half as much as he did her.

THE KINGDOM OF FLAMES AND ASH

I placed her gently on the bed, making sure that her injured wings didn't get crushed underneath her. She needed her rest to recover and heal her own body. I didn't want to contemplate what would happen if Pyralis came back and tried to take her again. She was too weak to fight him. That was one reason that I'd provided her with the sword that lay against her hip as she slept.

My lungs expanded uncomfortably, my heart feeling as if it were too big for my chest. I'd never understood the stories of how much fated mates cared for each other. Some claimed that love was the greatest and most painful experience of all, and that hadn't made sense until she'd walked back into my existence.

The love I felt for her was so powerful that even my magic paled in comparison.

I tucked a piece of hair behind her pointed ear and knew that seeing her like this every day for the rest of eternity wouldn't be enough. I'd do anything for her, even lose my magic or wings, as long as she remained by my side. Her touch, smell, and taste were the only things I required to be truly happy.

A fluttering sounded outside the open door to the bedchamber, and Nightbane leapt to the floor and growled. I lifted my head to find Queen Sylphia leaning against the doorframe, watching me.

She tilted her head. "You truly care for her."

"Of course I do." I straightened and quietly strolled to the queen. "She's my fated mate... my everything."

"That's what she kept insisting, but I didn't believe it was true." She exhaled slowly and looked over my shoulder. "Yet, I've seen the way you two are with one another, and that tenderness I saw on your face just now can't be faked."

Her acknowledgment kindled something akin to hope in my chest—a dangerous feeling after living the way we had for

100

the past twelve years. "But you vowed her to an ashbreath when she was intended to be mine from the very start." As a child, I'd known the two of us would be together, but then she'd vanished from this realm.

"I understand you're frustrated and upset with us." She stood straighter, looking every inch a royal. "However, at the time, we weren't sure what else to do. And the dragons came to us, offering a solution. Our crops were dying; we couldn't hover idly in the sky and allow it to continue."

Unfortunately, I understood. That had been one of the main reasons I'd spent the last twelve years hunting through dreams to locate Lira. We'd been starving, and I hadn't hesitated to consider taking someone's life if it would help my people survive. In fact, if Lira hadn't been my fated mate, I would've killed her without remorse. "You could've tried to have a discussion with my father. Given him a chance to correct his ways."

"We did, Tavish." She wrung her hands. "And he laughed at us and returned to the Unseelie. That was when we knew we had to act for the good of our people. Our guards attacked a couple of weeks later."

My father had come back from the Seelie land acting strange, and Mother feared leaving him alone. Unfortunately, some things that hadn't made sense to me before were becoming clear the more I learned. "He never made me aware of blanketing the entire realm in darkness." And a selfish part of me was thankful because I wasn't sure what I would've done. I'd like to believe that I would've tried to stop my father, but I couldn't be sure. The Unseelie loved the darkness and thrived in it, and we'd been used to it in Cuil Dorcha.

"Your guards put me into a holding cell and didn't allow any sort of healing. They left me to sleep on the floor." That was what Eldrin had told me over the years, and Lira had confirmed that portion of the story.

I wondered what would've happened if she hadn't healed me back then.

"The healer said you'd recover, and we wanted you to remain weak so we wouldn't have to bind your wings. Our goal was to allow you to live and spend time with us."

"As your prisoner," I spat. A foul taste filled my mouth. I wasn't foolish. I understood they'd needed me alive only to keep the balance of magic in this realm.

She sighed. "We can rehash all of this if you want, but I think at this point, we can agree that we've all done things that were unwise. You kidnapped our daughter to kill her."

I winced, and my wings drooped. She was right, and she didn't even know the worst part—the gauntlet. All things I wished I could take back and not have put Lira through. "What do you propose then?"

"That we move forward and determine a way to get Lira out of that vow with the ashbreath." She tensed and ran a hand down the front of her dress. "And then I'll influence my husband to bless the union between the two of you."

I wrinkled my nose. "We don't need his blessing. We're fated mates, and the bond has been consummated."

"True, but it would be good for it to happen for Lira's sake. She's still reacclimating to Ardanos, but I know my daughter's spirit, and she'll want us in her life. Besides, she's our only heir. She'll take the crown if the time ever comes."

Both valid reasons, though I didn't have to be happy about it. But I would do anything to make sure Lira didn't feel as if she had to choose between her parents and me. I also understood that Eiric, Hestia, and Brenin were people she'd want to spend time with.

Being with her meant I had to find a way to move past my resentment of the Seelie, but I wasn't sure how to do that, given the bitterness and hatred I'd harbored for them for the past twelve years. Understanding my father's role was the first step, but I struggled to understand how he covered all of Ardanos in darkness, let alone why. That didn't sound anything like the man I'd known my entire fourteen years before that.

"It'd be easier to get past the chasm between us if our people hadn't been cast out of our magical land, starved, and forced to live on this decimated, dragon-ruined island." I paused, taking a moment to ensure my voice remained level despite the pounding in my ears. "A lot has been taken from us, many have died, and that's something that I, along with my people, need to process. The only reason you're allowed in my land now is Lira and my need to keep her safe. Don't be fooled that my love for Lira means I'll accept your presence in the Unseelie kingdom permanently."

She blanched slightly but nodded.

"And the only reason I allowed my people's weapons to be confiscated was that I didn't want any more of them to die. It had nothing to do with us submitting to you." I needed that to also be clear.

"Understood." She took a step back and glanced in the direction of the prison cell. "I will say that I worry what will happen if we don't get your cousin to speak. Hestia, Brenin, and Lira won't wait much longer before they leave to retrieve Eiric."

In this instance, we had the same worry. Lira draining her magic hadn't been just for Finnian's and Lorne's sake. She would've pushed herself, but maybe not to the point she had today if Eiric weren't at risk. "My cousin is vain and needs to feel important. In chess, Eldrin gloated that he beat me most of the time because I couldn't see the big picture. He's counting on us being desperate for his knowledge because he knows Lira is our weakness. We can't allow him to believe that's the case, which means we must ignore him." Saying those words hurt, because I

THE KINGDOM OF FLAMES AND ASH

wanted the answers as well. But I needed her to understand that having us going to him and demanding answers was exactly what he desired.

"This is a dangerous game with more than Eiric's life at stake." Queen Sylphia crossed her arms, her sparkly blue wings unfurling behind her. "However, you know Eldrin better than I, and he's Unseelie."

I bit the side of my mouth, trying to keep myself from speaking. Six months ago, I'd have agreed that I knew him best, but now I knew better. Eldrin had revealed to me only the parts of himself he'd wanted me to see. In fact, I hadn't known him well at all until the past few days, and now I hated him more than the Seelie. "If we want to free Lira from the betrothal," I growled, "then we need to make him suffer. We still have a little time before Lira loses her patience and demands we save Eiric. We need him to believe that we might not want the information he's trying to bargain with."

Wings flapped toward us, and the queen took a step back.

The frantic pace had me turning and looking out the window. I half expected to see a crimson dragon winging his way back, but instead, I noted the mix of Seelie and Unseelie guards calmly watching the island perimeter. They didn't look worried, which meant something else was happening.

Caelan appeared around the corner, followed by two other Unseelie guards.

"Thank Fate you're here." Caelan sighed as he landed beside the queen. "We have a huge problem."

CHAPTER ELEVEN

TAVISH

My body coiled, and I glanced at Lira sleeping peacefully on her side. She needed her rest; I couldn't allow anyone to wake her. The Seelie queen was right. Lira wouldn't wait long before going after her sister, which meant I needed her to heal to reduce the risk of the dragon prince catching her.

"The—" Caelan started, and I lifted a hand, wordlessly telling him to stop.

I eased into the hallway and shut the door behind me.

Caelan's jaw dropped. "You're worried about waking her when I just informed you that we have a serious problem?"

My wings spasmed, but with the two other Unseelie guards here, I needed to maintain my calm. "Of course. Lira is injured, and her healing is a priority for me. The dragon will be back sooner rather than later, and I need her at full strength. Besides, two seconds won't make a drastic change with whatever you have to alert me of."

He scowled, clearly disliking the answer. But then he shook his head. "The cave. It was damaged in the attack."

Now I understood his concern. Our food supply was already limited, and the mushrooms from the cave were the one thing that provided us with what fae truly needed to survive. The fish only helped us feel fuller and held off the pangs of starvation. "How bad?"

THE KINGDOM OF FLAMES AND ASH

Buidhean, the guard with dark-yellow hair, flinched, giving me the answer I didn't want. Caelan gulped at the question.

"How much of the food supply was impacted?" The walls seemed to close in on me, but I forced myself to remain upright without shaking. A king's fear or desperation had to stay hidden because if the people saw their leader reacting negatively, the situation would grow worse exponentially.

"The majority of it." Buidhean placed a hand on his sword as if his weapon would help solve the issue. "We have a two- or three-day food reserve, tops, with the number of Seelie here with us. After that, we're all going to starve."

Queen Sylphia gasped. "How is that possible? There have to be other places where mushrooms grow. Some of our guards can help you retrieve more if it's a difficult location."

I arched a brow. "The cave Caelan mentioned is the only place where the mushrooms grow, and it took twelve years to produce enough that we could eat two meals a day. For a long time, we ate one, which is why over half of my people perished. There's no getting them back unless your Earth Seelie are willing to regenerate the land."

"But how can that be?" The queen's brows furrowed. "We instructed our guards to ensure you had the means to grow them before they left you here. They should've become more abundant."

"They regenerated the land just enough for us to have half a meal each day." The memories of starvation and parents sacrificing their own needs for their children sprang into my head. So many had starved so that their children could survive. People had stolen from each other, blaming me for my role in how they wound up here. It had hardened my heart and turned my focus toward vengeance. Yet, here the Seelie were, encroaching on our land, and I was allowing it because of one woman.

Though I had no regrets about completing the bond with Lira, the part of me that blamed the Seelie for *everything* surged inside me again.

I pushed it away because if I did anything to the Seelie, Lira could be injured in the cross fire. Harming my mate was the one line I refused to cross ever again. "A lot of us died to make sure the survivors lived."

Sylphia grimaced and bit her bottom lip. "That wasn't the plan."

I lifted a brow, unsure whether to believe her or not. "If you'd ever come back to check on us, we would have told you."

She rocked back on her wooden heels. "You'd have fought us if we'd appeared in front of you. Even with my daughter in your midst, your people rose against us, ignoring your command to end the attack."

"You forced us to live on a ruined dragon island after you tore us from our home and the source of our magic!" Maybe they hadn't murdered my parents, but they'd still taken away everything that was mine, including Lira, and caused thousands of my people to die. "Would you expect us to welcome you here?" I wanted to say more, but I closed my mouth for Lira's sake. Even though she wasn't awake, she'd learn of the disagreement if it went too far.

Arguing wouldn't change anything. I turned to Caelan. "Cut everyone's meals back to one and a half." I ran my fingers through my hair, trying to keep my frustration and anger from becoming too intense.

"No need." The Seelie queen flapped her wings, rising into the air. "Let me locate Erdan—we will have a few of our guards replenish the health of the cave and grow what was lost and then some. None of us can afford to go without nourishment."

"It would be a blasting shame if you and your people were forced to starve like the Unseelie have for years." Caelan

THE KINGDOM OF FLAMES AND ASH

wrinkled his nose.

I understood the sentiment far too well.

The queen tossed her long, light-blonde hair over her shoulder. "We didn't have to come, and yet, here we are, assisting in protecting your land."

"Only because Lira freed Tavish and returned here with him," Caelan spat.

"Are you going to allow him to talk to me with such disdain?" Sylphia's wings beat the air choppily, conveying her frustration.

I wouldn't scold Caelan for speaking the truth, and right then, we had more important matters at hand. Unfortunately, the Seelie were the only ones who could assist with our immediate needs. "I agree there's no reason to argue, and we're wasting precious time. Please see if there are earth fae who can aid us in healing the cave, but let's not make this information common knowledge... not yet. I fear it would throw the entire kingdom into turmoil."

With Lira unwell, Finnian and Lorne severely injured, and me unable to tell which guards I could rely on, I couldn't stop a war. But if we didn't address the food problem, we might as well hand Lira over to the dragon prince because when the dragons returned, we wouldn't be able to withstand their attack.

"Fair point." Sylphia nodded and flew out the closest window into our village, leaving me alone with Caelan and the guards.

Wanting to return to Lira, I placed a hand on the door handle and said, "For now, take stock of the food inventory for the village. Pay careful attention that no one takes more than their allocated rations. If the Seelie don't agree to help replenish the land, there will be trouble when I address the need for the reduction in food."

Buidhean and the other guard turned and headed toward

the castle kitchen.

Once the two were far enough away, I rejoined Lira in the bedroom. Right now, there wasn't a guard watching over our room since Finola and Struan were splitting their time watching Eldrin.

"Are you sure all of this is wise?" Caelan exhaled loudly. "You've handed the Seelie our village weapons and allowed the same king and queen who forced us to move here to stay under the roof of this castle. I worry that you aren't thinking clearly because of—"

My patience snapped. I spun around, grabbing his neck and slamming him into the wall. A little piece of stone fell onto his head.

"I've allowed you to question and disrespect my *mate* for far too long." I bared my teeth. "This ends now. I'm not sure how much clearer I can be, but I'll try one last time out of respect for our friendship."

His eyes widened, and I tightened my grip on his windpipe. I needed him to realize that nothing would ever change between Lira and me, no matter how desperately he wanted it to. "Lira is my fated mate, my future wife, and your future *queen*. You will respect our relationship and her place within our court, or you will be named a traitor."

A hand touched my shoulder, and a jolt shot down my arm and into my chest. That was when I noticed the love and concern floating from Lira to me.

I jerked my head to see her standing beside me with a sad smile on her face. She said, "I love that you want to protect me, but I also appreciate Caelan. Every concern he's ever had has come from a place of loyalty to you. It's okay for him to be hesitant about me. The Seelie did force this horrible situation on you, and at first, you resented me so much that you tried to fight our connection." She kissed my cheek and placed her free hand on my wrist. She then linked, *Release him before you do something you'll regret.*

My chest clenched as every fiber in my being wanted to continue to hold Caelan in my grip to ensure that he understood this was more than a threat... It was a promise. Yet, I found myself relieved when I released him and dropped my hand back to my side.

Lira swayed on her feet, her exhaustion still within her.

Caelan gasped. He wasn't used to me turning my wrath on him; I almost always targeted Finnian. Yet, ever since I'd kidnapped Lira, Finnian and I had grown closer because of his acceptance of her.

Lira moved between Caelan and me and faced him. "I do appreciate that you're trying to protect my mate from me, but let *me* be clear." She pressed her back to my chest, and the thrum of our connection hummed between us. "Tavish and I have completed our bond, and I only want what's best for him. Why would I have broken him out of the Seelie prison if I weren't loyal to him? If you don't accept our relationship, I can't promise I'll be around to stop Tavish next time. So please, accept me. I love him and will be by his side no matter what."

Unable to stop myself, especially after everything she'd just said, I slipped my arms around her waist, careful of the wounds in her wings. After my parents' deaths, I'd believed I'd never experience joy again, but Lira had changed that for me in just the small amount of time she'd been here.

As the food shortage problem pressed on me, terror seized my lungs. I couldn't imagine losing her, not now. If the Seelie refused to help, I wasn't sure how I would protect Lira from the dragon prince.

"You're right," Caelan croaked. He cleared his throat and rubbed the handprint I'd left behind. "I struggle because his instinct is to protect you over his people."

"And that won't blasting change," I growled. "She comes first, and then my people. My need to protect them hasn't vanished, and Lira protects them the same as I do." Even when I'd wanted to punish everyone for turning their wings on us, Lira had encouraged me to give them a second chance like she'd given me. "You need to accept that."

"Believe me." He coughed uncomfortably. "I do, and I won't continue to question it any longer. Your friendship and happiness are important to me."

The uncomfortable temperature of my blood eased, and I took a deep breath, inhaling Lira's moonlight-mist-and-rose scent.

"That doesn't change our need to rely on the Seelie to solve this problem." Caelan shook his head. "I'm not comfortable with that."

Lira's head tilted back. "How long have I been asleep?" She glanced out the window. "What have I missed?"

"You've been asleep for thirty minutes at most." Despite Caelan making the correct decision to locate me and inform me of the problem, I hated that, ultimately, it was me who had woken her up. Now that she was aware that there was a problem, there was no chance she'd fall back asleep. And if I didn't update her, she'd be upset with me. My shoulders sagged as I filled her in on what we'd learned and what her mother planned to do.

She turned so that she could see both Caelan and me. "How long until someone figures out what you've learned?"

"Not long." Caelan rolled his shoulders back and spread his wings. "The rocks that fell have been cleared. That was one reason it took us so long to assess the damage—the cave had almost completely collapsed."

Lira's worry merged with mine, making every limb feel heavy.

We need to find Father so we can talk with him as well. Lira's cobalt eyes glistened with unshed tears. *He needs to hear this from you.*

She was right, but there had been no chance I was going to leave Lira in our bedchamber alone and unguarded. I lifted her into my arms and moved toward the open window. "Lira and I are going to find the Seelie king. Please make sure things are handled."

Caelan nodded. "I'll head down with the others to ensure the rations are distributed appropriately."

Without another word, I flew out the window, enjoying the way Lira melted into my arms.

I know fae don't apologize, but don't you think you and Caelan need to discuss what just happened?

I smirked and kissed the top of her head. *We said everything that needed to be said. We're fine now.* In fact, it was Lira who'd made Caelan understand the issue. She had no clue how influential she was.

Men here make as much sense as the ones on Earth. It has to be due to testosterone.

I had no idea what she was referring to.

My gaze landed on the Seelie king and queen, Brenin, and Hestia, at the bottom of the castle stairs. I headed in their direction, and the four of them took flight our way.

We met halfway, and I could sense Lira's heart racing with mine.

The king's face tightened. "Can you take us to the cave?"

I hadn't expected that, but I nodded. The king had earth power, and he was the strongest of the fae. "Follow us."

I turned and led them the long way around the castle toward the cave, flying under the jagged mountain peak like the Unseelie who'd headed the attack yesterday. We flew behind the village to where the cave was built into the peak.

The cave had collapsed, and the stone had been piled up on one side. Mushrooms lay crushed or ripped into small pieces all over the ground. The cavern now had only about half the growing space it did before.

"Brenin and I should have enough magic to restore the cave," Erdan said and gestured for Brenin to follow him.

I landed at the opening and placed Lira gently on the rocky ground. The queen and Hestia landed beside us.

The king and Brenin raised their hands and spread them out wide. The cave took on a faint, sparkly brown glow, but nothing else happened.

"Something isn't right." Hestia wrung her hands as the two men continued to channel their magic.

"We aren't on Seelie land, so maybe their power isn't as strong." The queen placed her hands on her hips.

Lira took my hand and kept her focus on her father and dad.

More brown swirls filled the cave floor, and I noticed sweat beading both men's foreheads. The cave started to shake.

The king gripped his head and stumbled back just as the top of the cave crumbled.

"Father, no!" Lira shouted, flying toward him.

CHAPTER TWELVE

LIRA

The world seemed to come into sharper focus as I flapped my wings, ignoring the ache that shot through them as I raced toward Father and Dad. I couldn't just sit here and let both of them get injured.

A strong gust of wind pushed past, helping me move faster, as Mother used her wind magic, tossing chunks of debris away from both men.

Dad dropped on top of Father, protecting the king, but his face twisted in agony.

Is someone using illusion magic on them? I linked with Tavish, remembering the way illusion magic had worked on me during the gauntlet. Illusions weren't just visual cues—Unseelie were able to manipulate others into feeling fear by making them hear the voices of people and see things that weren't there.

I landed beside them, my back spasming.

Tavish was beside me within a second, his own concern mounting within him.

No, I don't sense any Unseelie magic here, he replied and scanned the area.

I stared at the cave, waiting to see if anything else fell, but as the brown magic dissipated, nothing else seemed to be a threat.

Mom and Mother joined us as Dad straightened and

helped Father to stand. Both men were drenched in sweat, and their chests heaved.

"I can't locate a threat," Mom gritted out as she searched the entire space for enemies.

"If you're looking for an Unseelie, they didn't do this," Tavish reiterated again. "There is no Unseelie magic out here."

"And besides, they don't have earth magic." There hadn't been anything that indicated frost, and if the falling rock had been an illusion, I doubted the wind would've made a difference.

"It wasn't magic attacking us." Father rubbed his temples like he had some sort of headache. "I was the one who made the cave fall, though I'm not sure how or why. It was like something hindered my magic."

Dad nodded. "Yes. It was like our magic couldn't penetrate the ground, no matter how hard we tried."

I pulled in a shaky breath as the realization of what that meant weighed on me. When Tavish's wings sagged and our bond constricted, I knew that he'd come to the same conclusion.

Since they weren't able to restore the mushrooms, more Unseelie would starve. How could we unify the Unseelie under Tavish after the division Eldrin had caused? They'd blame both Tavish and me for the Seelie being here in the first place, prompting the Unseelie attack that caused the cave-in.

Even though it wasn't our fault, a large portion of the population would see it that way. People always needed someone to blame.

However, we had to face one problem at a time. "Are you both injured?"

"I... I'm unsure." Father's forehead wrinkled. "I felt a sharp pain in my head, though it's fading now. For a moment, I was certain death was upon me."

Dad chuckled but then cleared his throat, trying to hide it. "It's called a headache, Your Majesty. I experienced it too—it's a physical ailment that happened from time to time when I lived on Earth. It's nothing dire; we just strained ourselves in a way that wasn't familiar."

In other words, they didn't have direct access to Seelie magic.

"It's horrid." Father tugged on his golden tunic. "I hope to never experience such a thing again."

"I'm just glad this isn't another attack on us." Mother sighed and lowered her hands.

Mom still had her hands raised, the tips of her fingers red with fire, ready to sprout at any sign of an attack on the Seelie royals.

"There will be more attacks once my people discover that our food supply is severely limited once again." Tavish paced in front of the cave. "Our resources will be strained, and we'll be weak when the dragons return to try to take Lira from me." His hands clenched.

A lump formed in my throat. I hated seeing him revert to the broody Tavish he'd been before we'd given in to our bond.

I couldn't allow responsibility to steal the lightness from him again.

"The Seelie are here, so—" I started.

He spun toward me, his eyes dark slate once more. "The Seelie being here will make things worse. With the strain on the food supply, all of us will weaken. The dragons won't need to fight us because we'll barely have the strength to stand."

A sour taste filled my mouth, and bile churned in my stomach.

"Then the answer is simple." Father stood tall, spreading his wings behind him. "Lira must return home with us so we can protect her from the dragons."

My head jerked in his direction. He'd lost his mind if he thought that I would go anywhere without Tavish. "Like *hell* I will. Neither Tavish nor I will stand for it."

"King Erdan, if you'd just—" Tavish rasped.

"Don't you dare. All I'm concerned about is the safety of my daughter." Father puffed out his chest. "I understand that part of this is my fault for promising her to Prince Pyralis, but that doesn't mean I don't care about keeping her safe for as long as I can."

Dad and Mom flanked the royals, keeping their gazes on Tavish like he was the threat. The thought of them trying to force me to leave had my blood boiling. I wouldn't be going anywhere without my fated mate. Never again.

"It's because of the fated-mate marks." Mother gestured to our hands. "It's made Pyralis obsessed with taking Lira, so she can't be near Tavish."

"Which was why I was going to say that I agree with King Erdan." Tavish's expression became strained. "Lira will be safer there than here with me."

My head swiveled in his direction, and I gritted my teeth. "You've got to be joking right now."

"Clearly, I'm not." Tavish ran a hand down his face. "Because there is *nothing* humorous about this. You don't deserve to starve. And I refuse to selfishly keep you here, knowing that I can't protect you. I'd rather you go back to Seelie where you can be happy and safe."

Out of the corner of my eye, I saw shock on the faces of all four of my parents.

My own surprise changed into fierce determination. I wouldn't leave. "We are stronger together. You *know* this."

Tavish's sadness and regret panged through our bond. "Yes, you're right, but not when we're both starving and unable to fight. Sprite, this isn't something I want. The selfish part of me wants to tell your father he can go choke on dirt."

"Then that's what we do because I don't want to be

anywhere you aren't." I pushed my heartbreak toward him. The fact that he could fathom me not remaining by his side shattered my heart into pieces.

He took my hands in his. The buzz of the connection sprang to life, but this time, it wasn't comforting. This time, it felt like a taunt.

"Ripping my heart from my chest would be less painful than even considering you leaving here." He cupped my face, his eyes turning a bright light gray. "But the only thing that hurts worse than that is imagining the dragons coming and taking you *from* me. I love you too much for you to suffer such a fate, so I'm willing to let you go temporarily while I force Eldrin to inform me how to get you out of the blasted vow with Pyralis."

My eyes burned as tears filled them, clouding my vision. I understood his point, but he'd failed to mention one thing. "Pyralis tried to take me from Gleann Solas already. And what if he comes here and is unable to locate me—who's to say the dragons won't harm you, especially if he's determined to keep our bond from interfering? I might as well stay here."

"Lira... Pyralis wasn't able to take you from our home. He managed to take Eiric from here." Mom moved beside me and placed a hand on my shoulder. "Besides, you being here could make things worse for King Tavish. If Pyralis sees the way you two fight for each other, he'll no doubt try to take him prisoner. If you two aren't together, he won't feel nearly as threatened by your mate."

Blighted abyss. Mom knew all too well how to reason with me. Still, it didn't feel natural to be away from Tavish.

Even though my pain didn't lessen, my determination did ease. If leaving Tavish would protect him from the cruelty of the dragons, who was I to be selfish and stay? Yet, my heart and soul screamed that separating from him was a bad idea. "It doesn't feel right, and the Unseelie will still starve. Tavish is my fated mate, and I don't want to leave him. Being away from him hurts, and it won't fix the real problem."

Mother and Father glanced at one another with unreadable expressions as Dad strolled closer to me.

"Neither will doing nothing to retrieve Eiric right this moment, but we're waiting so we have a better chance of being successful when the time comes," he argued.

Screams rose from the village, causing my heart to drop into my stomach. Seelie guards flew from the edge of the land in that direction in case of trouble.

Our group glanced at each other, and before I even registered what was happening, Tavish had me in his arms and was flying that way.

I wrapped my arms around his neck, holding tight to him, needing him more than ever. The threat of us separating, even if it was temporary, made panic claw deep into my chest. Still, I didn't want the little bit of time we had left to be full of dread. *You didn't leave me behind this time.*

I made a promise to you. He arched a brow. *Taking you toward danger doesn't come naturally to me, but I knew you'd fly after me if I didn't take you.*

I probably would've begged Dad to carry me instead. But the point was made. I would've refused to be left behind and would've flown if I had to.

More screams rose as we flew over the roofs of the village. A group of about a hundred Unseelie were on the castle steps, banging on the double doors.

It reminded me of riots I'd seen on TV back on Earth. The Seelie guards closed in on the crowd, ready to use their magic and weapons, but the people's focus wasn't on them.

The doors opened, revealing Caelan, Struan, and several other guards.

"What is the meaning of this?" Caelan demanded, a few

pieces of his dark-blond hair falling from his bun.

A man with skin as pale as snow lifted a fist. "We want to know why the news of the food shortage is being kept from us. Where is King Tavish?"

Tavish tensed. *How do they know already? I told both guards to keep this information quiet.*

Do you think they're both trustworthy? I didn't know either guard well. One of them might have purposely let it slip or perhaps had been asked a direct question and hadn't been able to find a way to answer it without lying.

He sighed. *I don't know. Eldrin has me doubting everything, which is what he wants—for me to become paranoid and distrustful.*

I couldn't wait for the horrible man to die. I hoped I would be able to witness his demise, something I never would've thought two months ago, but now I wanted to see the bastard gasp for his last breath.

"Where the king is and what he decides is none of your concern." Caelan flapped his wings, rising over their heads. "All of you should turn around and focus on your jobs."

My parents flew next to us as more Unseelie poured from their homes, joining the protest.

"We deserve to know how he plans to provide for us and when these sunscorched will go home, seeing as they're eating our few remaining resources."

More people joined in, voicing their agreement.

Tavish turned toward Dad, and I knew immediately what his plan was.

If you're going down there, you better be taking me. I arched a brow, holding on to his shoulders tighter. *If you want them to ever see me as their queen, I need to be right by your side.*

The corner of his mouth tipped upward for a second, but then he nodded. *Fine, but don't go rushing into the crowd to fight.*

Sometimes, you're unpredictable. He began the descent, heading straight toward Caelan and the guards at the open door.

I snorted. *I've been told being impulsive isn't necessarily a good attribute, but I'm not sure I agree. I like keeping you with your wings prepared to fly.*

"There he is," a woman shouted from below. "And he's with her."

People grumbled underneath us, and a few threw sneers my way.

Once Tavish landed between Struan and Caelan, he placed me next to the guard. He glared and said, "*I* will carry her if things go awry."

"Understood, Your Majesty." Struan swallowed and placed his hand on the pommel of his sword.

Standing tall, Tavish took a step forward, extending his wings as far as they could go.

My body warmed at the breadth, an indication of the size of another of his body parts that I loved. I tore my gaze away from him and looked toward my parents, who'd remained behind. Mother and Father engaged in conversation as if there weren't a threat right before us.

"I learned of the shortage not too long ago. Lira and I just came from the cave because we were assessing the damage. It is true that our food supply was impacted, and we'll be forced to make hard decisions to ensure our survival."

A man with yellow eyes wrinkled his nose. "It's because of the Seelie. They should've never been allowed to stay."

Of course the people wouldn't take responsibility.

Something inside me snapped. I stepped forward, leveling my gaze on the nightfiend. My body swayed a little as fatigue tried to hit, but I refused to show additional weakness in front of them. "The Seelie weren't the ones throwing the explosive rocks that caused the cave to crumble."

Tavish's wings stiffened. *Don't make yourself a target.*

I've never stopped being one, thorn. That's part of the problem. Ever since I came to the island, everyone had hated me. Their hatred had bred more hatred, but at some point, it had to end. They'd blame everything on the Seelie if we let this sort of malice consume our hearts. "Yes, the Seelie were wrong to banish you here, but this latest disaster was due to the actions of your own people. Don't let fear make you lose logic and cast blame where it isn't warranted. If you're to be mad at anyone, then it should be the ones who attacked the Seelie without regard for your safety."

"This is the issue," the pale man spat out. "The king is weak due to his connection with the Seelie princess. Eldrin was right. He'll allow us to starve as long as she's alive and messing with his mind. He doesn't care about us, and now more of us will die."

More people joined the chanting, adding to the mob mentality.

I was chilled to the bone, and it had nothing to do with the snow around us. We needed to kill Eldrin for the mere fact that he continued to divide the Unseelie by still breathing.

For every person out here, there was an Unseelie back in their house, watching from the windows with a frown on their face.

The crowd surged forward, mobbing the door, and Struan grabbed my hand and dragged me back into the castle.

"Get Lira out of here," Tavish shouted as he raised his father's sword. "They won't risk killing me, or they'll lose even more magic."

Blast that. I wasn't going anywhere.

I yanked my hand from Struan's and clutched my own sword. Maybe I'd be forced to leave Tavish soon, but right now, I was here, and I'd damn well fight by his side. I wouldn't run and leave him to face this alone.

A pale man flapped his cream wings, barreling right toward me. He soared past Tavish just as my mate swung his blade clean through the man's wings. Blood splashed all over me as the man continued his forward motion despite wailing in pain.

I jabbed my sword forward, the blade stabbing the man straight in the heart. His black eyes widened, and his body shook from the impact.

I lifted my foot and shoved his body off my blade, making a sickening sucking noise, and was prepared to strike once more when Father yelled, "Stop," and landed in front of me.

I glanced upward and saw Mom, Dad, and five other Seelie guards preparing to use magic on everyone.

No. What had I done?

Chapter Thirteen

Lira

Despite my father's command, the Unseelie attacked even more aggressively. Dad dropped in front of Father, protecting both his king and me. With two gigantic men protecting me, Struan and the other Unseelie guards who had stayed behind at the door flew into the crowd, using their frost and illusion magic to force people back.

Yet, more pressed forward to take their places.

Caelan grabbed my arm, forcing me to stay back. "Don't make Tavish lose his focus. He needs to get the people under control, or more will rise against him."

I opened my mouth to tell him where he could go, but my lungs seized. My skin crawled, and the pressure in my chest built like I might implode. The sensation didn't feel like my own, and the memory of how I'd felt during the final part of the gauntlet resurfaced. One of the competitors had made me feel complete terror inside, and I'd struggled to function.

The common people didn't have weapons because the Seelie guards had confiscated them, but their magic wasn't hindered.

A creepy, lime-eyed woman near me grinned.

Something brushed against my side and leg, and a familiar warmth spread through me.

Nightbane.

His presence eased some of the influence the woman had to be pushing toward me.

Father and Dad grunted and fell to their knees. They weren't using their magic, which meant they had to be dry from the ordeal back at the cave.

"Erdan, no!" Mother exclaimed.

Flames shot from Mom's hands and hit the edge of the crowd. A man stumbled back, and both Dad and Father seemed to breathe easier. Mother mixed wind magic with her fire, creating a blazing tornado that swirled above the Unseelies' heads.

People's heads jerked upward, and they shrieked as the funnel descended toward them.

Frustration and rage slammed into me from Tavish, and then I sensed the sluggish sensation of his nightmare illusion.

The ground shook as Seelie used earth magic, and flames landed on Unseelie, causing more screams. Water slammed into some of the people at the back. A breeze picked up as if it was trying to push the frost, snow, and illusion magic away from us.

Terror had my blood freezing as the illusion intensified, and the urge to flee took hold, causing me to dig my fingers into the cù-sìth's fur.

I gritted my teeth, fighting the unwanted feelings. Two men charged Father and Dad, and I stumbled forward. The chaos seemed to only get worse.

Caelan caught my forearm and yanked me back just as Nightbane ran in front of me and shoved me, helping Caelan out. Nightbane snarled and ran past both Father and Dad and attacked the men threatening us.

His teeth sank into one man's throat while his long, thick claws ripped through the other man's chest. Black blood coated the greenish-tinged ends of Nightbane's fur.

The unwanted sensation in my chest lessened, and Tavish

THE KINGDOM OF FLAMES AND ASH

connected with me, *Lira, get inside. You've already been attacked once, and I sense my people using magic.*

I'm done with people—including you—telling me I should leave you. Everywhere I turned, another situation stacked up against Tavish and me, with people trying to keep us apart. *I'm not going anywhere.* Thankfully, both Father and Dad stood and removed their swords from their sheaths.

Both Unseelie and Seelie guards darted downward as the chaos intensified. Tavish's magic strengthened along with his frustration. *Sprite, I swear. You're going to be the death of me.*

A chill mixed with the ickiness of the nightmare magic blanketed my body.

Tavish cloaked me, hiding me from the others, and thanks to the cloudy skies, the sun's light wouldn't reveal my location. I growled faintly, frustrated that he was resolved for them not to see me out here with him.

The fire tornado touched ground, dividing the crowd, and Mother and Mom worked together to make a straight line of fire that held most of the Unseelie back except for the thirty in front of it who could still fight against us.

The clash of all the different types of magic had the ground shaking and sparks flying. If I were back on Earth, I would've sworn that we were either getting bombed or experiencing an earthquake during the Fourth of July.

All of a sudden, the front line of the group, still trying to attack us, fell to their knees and clutched their heads as Tavish's magic wrapped around each one of them.

"This ends *now*," Tavish shouted, his face gray from the flush of his black blood. "Fighting against one another accomplishes *nothing* and only uses energy that needs to be conserved. We should be limiting strenuous activities that don't assist in keeping our community running."

The fire tornado vanished, and the Unseelie at the front

whimpered in agony. Whatever Tavish was forcing them to experience left each of them completely immobile.

Silence spread.

Nightbane snarled, drool dripping from his teeth as he trotted back to the spot next to me. Even though Tavish had hidden me, the beast knew exactly where I was.

"This will *not* be tolerated." Tavish lifted his sword, his wings expanded and taut. "The people who led this attack will be placed in prison *immediately*. They will get the least amount of food for rising against their king and future queen. As for all of you—" He pointed the sword toward the people who'd been separated by the fire but would've attacked if they'd had the ability. "You won't be placed in prison, but my guards will take note of each and every one of you. If you go against me one more time, you'll be killed on the spot. I will not tolerate any of this anymore. I am your *king*, and Lira is my fated mate. I don't blasting care what you think because Fate decided it for the two of us. And I tell you, the Seelie are here to help protect us when the dragons return—because they will."

Struan flew over the crowd, taking note of each person.

The woman with the strange lime eyes took several steps back, scanning the area like she was searching for something.

Was it me?

There was one way to find out. *Tavish, uncloak me. The imminent danger is gone, and I need them to see that I wasn't afraid. I need them to know I'm not a coward.*

I need to make sure they don't try something again. He didn't even glance over his shoulder at me, pretending I wasn't even here.

I fisted my hands, my nails cutting into my palms. *We talked about this earlier.*

Blighted abyss, sprite. You're not a coward, but you're injured, and your magic is drained. You're struggling to stand. I hid you because I couldn't be there to protect you and you aren't strong enough to fight on your own. If I can't trust you to know when to fight and when not to, then I have to make the decision for you. His chest rose and fell rapidly.

His worry and fear choked me, causing me to hang my head in shame.

You're right. I was exhausted, had no magic, and my wings burned from my effort to protect Father and Dad. *It's just hard to sit back and watch you and my parents risk your lives while I hide in the darkness... literally. I should be fighting alongside you.* And that was my pride speaking.

I'll uncloak you, but I need to know that you won't act irrationally and get yourself hurt. He pulled back on the darkness, the chill leaving my body and ebbing from our bond.

Remember that when Pyralis returns to take me, I countered, wanting him to realize that his words would come back to haunt him.

The creepy-eyed woman's gaze immediately landed back on me.

That's different, and you know it. Tavish lifted his chin and cleared his throat. "Every person outside has been noted."

Father folded his wings as he moved around Dad to stand in front of the crowd next to Tavish.

"And every one of you should be ashamed of what you've done because your king has accomplished something Eldrin would never have been able to." Father wrinkled his nose and spat.

Neck cording, Tavish tried not to fidget, but I could see the way his head tilted back slightly and feel the suspicion that churned inside him.

My head spun, and I leaned on Nightbane, needing his support. I wasn't sure what Father had hidden under his wings.

"You have no need to worry about food because tomorrow,

you will be returning to the true Unseelie land, Cuil Dorcha, where you can once again live—albeit with certain precautions now that you all fought against us again."

A collective gasp broke from the Unseelie. Hope bloomed in my chest, and my gaze went to Mother to find her beaming.

Did you know about this? Tavish connected, turning toward me. His brow furrowed as if he were attempting to solve a complex equation.

I shook my head, unable to form words even telepathically. I wasn't sure what made Father change his mind, but I was so damn thankful he had.

My heart quickened with the wondrous feeling coming from Tavish. The thought of returning home had alleviated part of the resentment within him, but then his relief disappeared as if a light had been smothered.

He pulled back his nightmare magic, giving the petrified men relief from their worst fears. "Upon our return, these men will be chained, so they still can't access Unseelie magic." Even though he sounded almost normal, I heard a growl in his tone. I could sense Tavish's concern about whether to believe Father.

"Excellent decision." Father steepled his hands. "But for now, everyone should eat up to ensure they have the strength for the half-day flight tomorrow."

My knees almost gave out thinking about Finnian and Lorne. I needed to heal them so they could make the journey, which meant I had to find a way to get my healing magic up to full strength.

Most of the people who'd rioted crossed their arms and narrowed their eyes, but a handful seemed thrilled without reservation.

"The Seelie king and I have several things to discuss, and once all has been settled, you will be alerted of our decisions." Tavish sheathed his sword and moved to my other side, placing me between him and Caelan.

"Until then, stay in your homes. If anyone leaves the land without permission, they'll join the others in prison." Tavish then waved at the men who had caused the riot. "Take them to the cells immediately and keep them away from Eldrin."

"Yes, Your Majesty." Struan bowed his head and then gave orders to the guards.

Tavish wrapped an arm around my waist and guided me through the castle entryway once again. Caelan and Father followed close behind us.

Something isn't right. Tavish clenched his jaw. *I don't understand why your father did that. He didn't discuss our return with me. In fact, he seemed adamant that we should stay here. Will he find a way to take it back so more of my people will turn against me? Or does he want the Unseelie to believe I'm even more Seelie-friendly, which would have the same end result—more people turning against me?*

I grimaced, trying to work out my own uncertainty. None of it made sense to me. Father was a man of his word, but he understood well how to play the political game and was adept at dancing around the truth without lying.

As soon as Mother, Dad, and Mom joined us in the entryway, Struan closed the doors.

"I thought they were taking the people prisoner?" Mom scowled.

"They are." Tavish turned to face my parents, keeping his arm solidly around me. "Prisoners don't travel through the castle. They'll be brought in through the window nearest the prison cells."

The night Tavish had taken me from Earth and brought me here, he had brought me in the same way.

"No one without a personal invite from the Unseelie king enters the castle," Caelan added, remaining on my other side as if we were facing an enemy. "It may not be the real Dunscaith, but we uphold our fae traditions even in barren land."

My stomach roiled. I'd hoped that we'd be beyond this by now, but the distrust between the two species made it hard to bridge the gap between us. Instead of posturing, I'd rather get to the point. "What was that out there?"

Father smirked. "Always direct, my little sprout. Maybe your bond with the frosty fae influenced you even as a young child."

A muscle ticced in Tavish's jaw, and I leaned into him, hoping to ease his trepidation.

"That's not helpful. You just declared that all the Unseelie will return to their land without mentioning it to Tavish beforehand. What's your real plan? Haven't the Unseelie suffered enough?" If he wanted me to feel ashamed of my fated-mate bond with Tavish, he'd soon realize it wouldn't work.

"Oh, Lira." Mother placed a hand on her chest. "That offer was sincere. Your father and I discussed it briefly, and when it became clear that you would fight us on taking you back to Gleann Solas and that the Unseelie wouldn't have enough to eat, we agreed to allow them back home."

Tavish scoffed. "I should have made the announcement after we discussed a strategy. This isn't your kingdom or your people, though clearly, you decided otherwise twelve years ago."

I winced at the resentment in Tavish's tone, but he had every right to feel that way. The Unseelie never should've been banished to begin with. "A discussion would've been the diplomatic way to go about it."

Father's face flushed a faint yellow. "There wasn't time, and I don't appreciate being questioned about my intentions or how I decided to handle the matter. Your people were out of hand, and Sylphia and I had agreed moments before the riot to take down the veil. I was assisting in calming the crisis."

So, that was what the anxious discussions and looks they'd been exchanging before the revolt started had been about. Even though I appreciated the sentiment, I understood the outrage Tavish felt.

"A crisis *I* needed to handle." Tavish's fingers dug into my side. "And you even decided that we'd leave tomorrow while Lira is still recovering and can't safely fly, and two of my men are severely injured. The three of them can't leave tomorrow."

Unless I can determine what's hindering my magic from coming back. I'd had no issue healing during the gauntlet, and I'd been this drained then, too.

"We will assist them in traveling." Dad tapped the hilt of his sword.

"The Unseelie aren't in a situation where they can defend themselves." Mother bit her bottom lip. "Not if they're starving and fighting among each other. And Lira won't stay away from you long. Erdan and I have come to accept that, and it's best if you return to your traditional home and get stronger so we can fight the dragons together. They'll never expect that."

My throat closed. I couldn't believe all the anger and disgust I'd felt for these two people when I'd awoken in Gleann Solas when they were now doing all they could to keep me safe. They had been misguided, but maybe there was hope for peace between us.

"We'll also be able to get your cousin to speak sooner if Tavish, Sylphia, and I are at full power, so we can get Lira out of this blazing vow." Father rubbed the spot over his chest where his magic lay underneath his heart. "Trying to repair that cave drained my magic. I barely feel a hint of it left." His expression crumpled. "I've never experienced it depleted like this. In fact, all the Seelie are growing weaker. And I fear we're going to need all our strength to retrieve Eiric and keep Lira away from Pyralis."

Mom winked at me, essentially telling me *I told you so*. She'd told me that my parents loved me and that eventually everything would work out between us. Too bad it had taken so dire a situation to get us to this point. We most definitely weren't in a place to win against the dragons.

If the cave hadn't collapsed...

The volcanic rock had caused the collapse, and the stones that had crushed the mushrooms had been a dark, smooth gray. The same type of stone that the arrow that had pierced my wings and injured them so badly had been made of.

My geology classes from college came rushing back to me, and the world stopped. "I think I know what's going on."

Chapter Fourteen

Lira

Tavish turned toward me, sensing my dismay.

I swallowed, not wanting to speak the words out loud, but that was foolish. Not informing them wouldn't make the situation vanish or change.

"You have our attention, Lira," Caelan said gruffly with his head tilted.

Nose wrinkling, Tavish flicked his gaze at Caelan, giving him a stern warning.

"Fae don't have exploding rocks in our kingdoms." I didn't want any more tension and disagreements between our group, so it was best to move this conversation along. "The rocks were created by dragons—they're tied to their magic. Right?"

"Yes. Their magic isn't the same as that of the fae." Father steepled his hands. "It isn't tied to their land—it comes from within them. That's why they eventually ruin any land they live on. It isn't able to tolerate their magic."

That bit of information confirmed my suspicion. "The exploding rocks the Unseelie were throwing caused the cave to collapse, and now bits of those rocks are embedded in it. When people moved the debris out of the way to get back inside, the dust from those rocks must have gotten on the mushrooms and killed them. The residual dragon magic is now all over the cave."

Both sets of parents took in a shaky inhale while Mother asked, "So even though the dragons haven't lived here for years, their magic is still impacting the land? How is that possible?"

"On Earth, many people believe that gemstones and rocks harness energy and promote different types of things, such as claiming amethyst channels balance, black onyx blocks negativity, and hematite helps with courage, like the minerals themselves carry a type of magic, though it's not the same as here." None of my classes ever confirmed the theories, but Eiric and I had always felt a connection to earth and water, which made sense now. We were fae and had an affinity for the elements. "But the logic still holds here. This island clearly had volcanic eruptions, which spread the leftover dragon-magic residue throughout the island. That could be why the mushrooms struggled to grow outside the cave and why more things don't grow here, even after all this time."

Tavish froze, resembling a statue.

"Which means living here isn't a viable option for anyone long term." Caelan shook his head. "Yet we were forced to suffer through the entire situation." Bitterness hung heavy on each word.

"Our intent wasn't for you to lose half your people." Father ran his fingers through his beard. "We thought the earth would heal itself easily with the dragons gone and you could survive. But now we have an even larger problem. If the dragons kill the land they live on, they'll eventually need to find yet another place to settle, and Aetherglen will be the next place they'll want to take over.

"That must be why Pyralis is determined to marry Lira, and if he's aware that Eldrin knows something that would free her from the vow, then he won't want to wait." Tavish's features twisted. "That way, they'll be set when they need to relocate again"—he turned to me—"and all the dragons would need to do is kill your parents. Then you'd reign over the island, and he'd be—" He didn't finish that sentence.

Father's nostrils flared. "The dragons approached us about the alliance. They pressured us for the betrothal, which we agreed to so we could eliminate the threat of darkness quicker because our land had already begun dying. That isn't enough to void the agreement, so there has to be more."

"We must focus on one issue at a time, or we'll be overwhelmed." Mother pursed her lips. "Right now, we need to get off this cursed island and back to Aetherglen. We have three injured fae who we assume won't be able to fly tomorrow, so we need to find a solution for how to get them to our land without straining others too much."

A part of me wants to resist returning to Aetherglen merely because your father was the one to decide it on our behalf, but it would be a death sentence to my people if I let my pride get in the way. Tavish closed his eyes. *If it weren't for you and the safety of my people, I'd harm him right now.* He exhaled and braced himself. "We'll leave at first light."

I forced my mouth closed, though I wanted to scold him for still wanting to hurt Father. I understood why Tavish still harbored resentment, but my father was trying to make things right. However, I'd need to discuss that with my mate later, not now.

My wings fluttered, causing my back to spasm. After flying to Father and Dad, my wings were in just as bad of shape as yesterday, despite my healing magic. "I fear I won't be able to fly." I let it hang there because only Caelan and Tavish knew about my healing magic. Even though I trusted both sets of parents, I also trusted Tavish when he'd said we should limit the number of people we told. If it got back to Pyralis, there was no telling how he'd react to the news.

You used your magic to quicken Finnian's and Lorne's

healing instead of using it on yourself. Tavish leaned his head against mine. *Maybe you shouldn't do that and let yourself heal.*

My magic still wasn't working despite the rest I'd gotten last night. I was barely at a quarter strength, and I hadn't even healed myself that much. Something had changed, but I had no clue what it could be.

"We'll figure it out." Dad rocked back on his heels, using his wings to balance himself. "Don't worry. We're not going to risk losing you, too. Once we arrive back in Aetherglen, we'll have the resources to focus on keeping you safe and retrieving Eiric."

Eiric.

My heart squeezed. Once again, she'd sacrificed herself for me... and this time, it could quite possibly cost Eiric her life.

"She's alive." Tavish kissed my forehead and continued, "He won't risk her because he knows how much she means to you."

"I agree with the Unseelie king, which is the only reason I haven't raced off to save her yet. We'll get her back, you'll heal, and we'll figure out how to handle the dragon prince." Mom smiled. "Trust us. When have we ever steered you wrong?"

They hadn't, but there was always a first time. However, I kept my mouth shut, knowing that she hadn't said it only for my benefit but also her own.

"All I know is if we're leaving that early, Lira needs her rest." Tavish placed his hand at the center of my back. "And just to be clear, if Lira isn't able to fly on her own, then I will be the only person carrying her tomorrow. I don't blasting care who handles Lorne and Finnian, but my sprite is all mine."

Head jerking back, Dad frowned. "I'm more than capable of carrying her as well. After all, I'm responsible for her protection."

"Protection, yes, but she's my mate." Tavish lifted a brow.

THE KINGDOM OF FLAMES AND ASH

"And I expect everyone, Seelie and Unseelie, to assist in her protection."

I leaned into his side, trying to ease his aggravation. *You going to kill my dad if he tries to carry me once you get tired?*

No, but I still don't like the thought of anyone but me touching you. He lifted a brow.

Fair enough. It wasn't as if I wanted anyone but Tavish to carry me. Still, I'd rather be able to fly and not be a hindrance to anyone.

"Let's inform the guards so we can ensure everyone gets adequate sleep to make the journey tomorrow." Father flapped his wings, ready to execute the plan. "King Tavish is right. Lira should get some rest, and I'm sure he has matters to attend to."

"Since we're leaving, we should have plenty to eat for dinner, so we'll regroup then." Tavish lifted his chin, authority ringing from his voice. "In the meantime, if you need anything, please let Caelan know."

I lifted a brow. *Caelan? Where are you going to be?* I didn't like the thought of him being in the village when people were eager to attack him. I understood that they wouldn't kill him since that would result in the Unseelie losing their magic, but that didn't mean they wouldn't hurt him.

With you. He guided me toward the hallway that led to our bedchamber. *There is no other place I need to be with you injured and a sadistic ashbreath desperate to take you.* The sluggish sensation of jealousy bled through our bond.

I wanted to reassure him that there was no reason to be jealous, but the words died on my tongue. Technically, the dragon prince was my fiancé, even though he'd never proposed to me. It was more than an arrangement, it was a vow, unbreakable without significant consequences.

Both sets of my parents left the castle, and Tavish said sternly, "Caelan, come with us."

138

"Is something wrong?" Caelan asked, taking the spot on my other side.

"I want to know how the entire kingdom discovered that the cave was destroyed."

I flinched. In all the turmoil, I'd forgotten the true issue that had caused the problem in the first place.

"I'm unsure. The two guards got to the food distribution site a few minutes before I did. Nothing seemed amiss when I arrived, but someone alerted the village to the problem. Did anyone fly by the cave while the six of you were attempting to heal the ground?"

I thought back. I'd been focused on Dad and Father. "Not that I noticed, but then again, I had reinjured my wings, so I wasn't very alert."

Tavish's guilt filtered through our bond. "We can't be certain, but I never sensed anyone else's presence."

Since neither of us was certain no one else had been there, we couldn't even assume it was the two guards. They could be on Tavish's side.

The Unseelie were going to return to their land, but they were more divided than ever. Returning home and becoming stronger only meant the fighting would be more deadly if they didn't unify.

"I wish I could heal Finnian and Lorne. It would be helpful to have two more people we trust in our midst, assisting in determining who's loyal."

"Wait." Caelan paused.

Tavish and I took another step before realizing he'd stopped. I glanced over my shoulder at him.

"Your wings aren't healing where the arrow hit them, right?" Caelan turned his attention to one of my wings and reached out a hand like he was going to touch it.

On instinct, I folded my wings in, the pain searing me.

"What the blast?" Tavish seethed, moving quickly between Caelan and me and shoving him away. "Do not touch her."

"Fine." Caelan brushed a piece of hair out of his face. "I was only going to look at the wound. Remember, the arrow was a Seelie weapon, but the tip felt slightly porous and rough, and not like the wood from the trees back home, despite the rest of it being made of that."

My breath caught. "Like lava rock after it's exploded." If the rocks could hinder Seelie magic from restoring the ground, it made sense that the substance would also impact my healing magic. "But I took a bath."

Tavish scoffed. "That doesn't mean traces of it didn't remain behind. I should examine your wings."

Knowing that he'd be the one doing it and not Caelan, I extended them again, pushing through the pain.

Tavish stroked the edge of one wing, and my body warmed at the intimate touch. He stepped directly behind me and examined where the arrow had pierced one wing and lodged in the other.

"I see small pieces in several places." Tavish's unhappiness inundated the bond between us. "That thornling was mine to kill. I hate that she didn't die slowly by my own blade."

I suddenly understood the point of killing the woman who'd shot me. Eldrin must have known what the arrow was made of and that I wouldn't be able to heal. He'd want to make sure Tavish hadn't achieved justice for me, thus making him feel not in control.

I should go in there and punish Eldrin. Tavish's rage boiled over again, but his fingers remained gentle.

That's what he wants. I spun around and cupped his face with my hands. I needed to get through to him before Eldrin had Tavish playing right into his nightfiend hands. *This has to be part of his plan. The best way to punish him is for him to see me healed and flying once again.*

His anger didn't ease, but he hung his head. "You're right. I can't wait to watch him bleed out, but for now, let's get you to our room so we can take care of your wings."

"In the meantime, I'll give notice that we're leaving and make a plan with Struan and Finola." Caelan spread his wings, ready to take action.

"Excellent. Let me know if you need me for anything," Tavish replied, taking my hand and leading me toward our bedchambers once again.

We walked the rest of the way in silence, the throbbing in my wings worsening.

As soon as we made it into the room, Tavish went to the table where his chessboard used to sit and picked up the mending kit. I turned my back to him so he could easily access the wounds.

I felt him settle behind me, and he gently touched my shoulder. *I'm sorry. This is going to hurt, but I'll be as careful as I can.* And then he began working.

Each time the needle prodded at the small pieces, pain almost as bad as during the gauntlet rocketed through me. Tears streamed down my face as he worked, each spot worse than the last, as if he was ripping the skin from my bones.

After what felt like hours, the agony was over. My knees gave out, and I landed on the bed. Tavish lay down beside me just as unconsciousness descended.

A blowing horn woke me from my slumber. I opened my eyes to a hint of sunlight streaming through the windows. Tavish's chest pressed against my wings and back.

When I'd last awoken, after several hours of sleep, my wings had greatly improved, and both my water and healing

THE KINGDOM OF FLAMES AND ASH

magic had recovered to about half strength. Against Tavish's protests, I'd healed Finnian and Lorne as much as I could before I'd grown fatigued again and headed back to bed.

This morning, my magic spun within me once again, and my wings felt like they were back to normal.

Nightbane whimpered and lifted his head, his green eyes focusing on me.

My blood turned to ice, and Tavish jolted upright and reached for his sword.

"Are the dragons here?" he rasped as his chest heaved.

"No." I winced, regretting that I'd worried him, but we had a different problem I hadn't fathomed. "Nightbane. We can't leave him here." The thought of leaving him alone to starve had me ready to carry the beast myself.

Tavish chuckled. "Don't worry, love." He leaned over and kissed me. "I already discussed him with Caelan. He'll have a solution. I knew you wouldn't leave him behind."

The sounds of flapping wings and busy villagers reverberated, even through the glass windows of our chamber. Everyone was brimming with excitement about returning home, so at least today, there shouldn't be any fighting.

"We need to hurry." Tavish threw off the covers, his excitement flickering through our bond. "I don't want the dragons showing up right when we're trying to leave."

The two of us dressed and hurried to the door. I paused for a moment to take in the place. Even though the island never should've been home to the Unseelie, this room was where Tavish and I had completed our fated-mate bond.

He wrapped his arms around my waist and connected, *We can come back here from time to time, and we'll make memories in our new place.*

Right. Leaving today didn't mean we couldn't ever visit. But while I'd never forget our bonding, this place was also full

142

of memories of threats and attacks. Hopefully, our new home will have better memories.

A knock came on the door a second before it opened, and Finnian strolled in.

My breath caught, and a smile spread across my face. His complexion was still slightly gray, but he looked significantly improved.

"The prisoners are in the hallway, surrounded and ready to go. We don't want to move them until the two of you have left." Finnian pulled me into a hug. "Thanks for making it not hurt to be alive."

Tavish scowled, but Finnian let me go before he could make any threats.

My jaw dropped. "Did you just thank me?"

"I did because that's how much of a difference you made for me." He held the door open. "But we can talk on the way. Right now, everyone is waiting on you two."

Tavish took my hand and led me into the hallway. All the prisoners stood to our right with at least fifty Unseelie guards.

My gaze landed immediately on Eldrin, who wore a massive smirk. Anger jolted from Tavish into me.

Don't let him know he upset us, I linked, needing our plan to make him feel unimportant to work. Wanting to knock him down a peg, I spread my wings, revealing that I was healed.

Eldrin's face paled, and he frowned.

"What's wrong, Eldy?" Finnian asked, exiting our room with Nightbane in his arms.

I smiled. The cù-sìth was almost the same size as he was.

"That's not my name." Eldrin seethed, his face darkening.

I pressed my lips together, trying not to laugh.

Then Finnian whispered in my ear, "Oh, wait. It's about to get better."

CHAPTER FIFTEEN

TAVISH

Between the way Finnian whispered in Lira's ear and the proximity of Eldrin, something dark and sinister churned inside me, eager to spill blood. Once upon a time, this sort of rage was reserved solely for any injustice done to my people, but now Lira was the main trigger that made me want to kill anyone who dared get close to her.

Even my best friends.

Caelan wasn't nearly as huge of a threat, but Finnian adored Lira, which made him way too attentive to her for my comfort.

I swallowed my ire, watching as Finnian picked up the large animal, making Lira's joy flash through our bond.

For her, I could tame my bloodlust because she hadn't felt this lighthearted since we'd cemented our bond. Her delight radiated like the sun, melting the snow that I'd laid with my power.

Eldrin glowered at my mate. His displeasure at her no longer being injured was obvious, confirming that the thornling who'd shot the deadly arrow at Lira had meant to disable her wings for as long as possible.

Eldrin had known that Pyralis would come for her, but how was that possible? We'd never been in communication with the dragons.

Finola stood close by my cousin, her hand on the hilt of her sword. She watched his every reaction, knowing the exact type of threat he was.

Hey, don't let him get to you. Lira turned in my direction, though her eyes remained on Finnian's back. *Eldrin wants us to be miserable. We need to make sure we don't seem that way when he's nearby.*

The jolt that thrummed between us increased as we touched, and my body warmed in a less-than-ideal way, given the circumstances.

I'd barely gotten any sleep since the night Pyralis came, too consumed with staring out the windows to ensure the dragons weren't attempting to sneak up on us. Even though I didn't doubt the Seelie would protect their princess with all their might, I'd burn the entire realm down for Lira if that was the only way to keep her safe.

Finnian headed straight to Eldrin and, when he got close, said, "Eldy, Caelan and I talked and decided it makes sense for you to carry Nightbane to Cuil Dorcha."

Laughter built in my chest, but I managed to hold it in. Eldrin always refused menial tasks, and carrying the animal he'd always detested would infuriate him. He would feel as if we didn't view him as important, something Finnian likely knew. He was better at understanding people than Caelan and me.

"Absolutely not." Eldrin took a few steps back, the chains restricting his wings. His feet tangled in them, causing him to stumble, but he caught himself. "I will not carry anything."

Other than his stumbling, he didn't look any worse than usual, except for the scruff on his face. He didn't look malnourished, but he'd been without food for only a day, so that wasn't a surprise.

"If you don't carry Nightbane, then you will remain here with the beast." I stretched out my wings, trying to seem unconcerned even as adrenaline pumped through my body.

Eldrin bared his teeth and glared. "You wouldn't dare risk leaving me."

He had no clue how much I wanted him dead. If I left him here, I could come back and interrogate him after he'd had a few days here all alone.

"You overestimate your worth." Lira placed a hand on my chest and continued, "You claim you have information we need, but we have no reason to believe you."

Eldrin laughed bitterly. "Though your memories and magic have returned, speaking like that invalidates your position among Seelie royalty."

The edges of my vision darkened, but Lira kissed my cheek and pushed some of her calm toward me.

If it weren't for her, I'd have already allowed Eldrin to manipulate me into ruining the ruse that he was unimportant.

"Says the man chained and imprisoned." Lira didn't miss a beat, and instead of becoming angry, she laughed. "I'm still upset that what you know isn't important, especially considering how you're trying to get a reaction from Tavish."

Even though Lira embodied a strong, confident woman, I could feel the impact Eldrin had made on her soul when he'd attacked her in the bathroom. I'd give anything to go back in time and prevent that happening. It was yet another regret and something I needed to make up to her for the rest of our lives.

"Don't play coy with me." Eldrin lifted his chin. "I know what you're doing. All of you are dying to learn what I know. Otherwise, you're stuck marrying an ashbreath sooner rather than later."

My body coiled for an attack, but Lira just rubbed her hand over my chest. She connected, *Thorn, remember the plan. He knows threatening me is the way to get a reaction from you.*

And he wasn't wrong. Still, if I wanted the knowledge he

had, I needed to remember the overall strategy. Thank Fate Lira was here. "This is your last chance." I straightened my shoulders, spreading my wings wide and wrapping the edges around Lira's body, making sure everyone saw the intimate gesture. "Carry the cù-sìth and ensure he isn't harmed or get left behind. Those are your only options."

Eldrin's jaw clenched, and his eyes flashed with anger. I sensed he was bordering on losing control, which I enjoyed immensely.

"Fine, but you're going to regret it," he vowed.

Despite his threat, the benefit of his carrying Nightbane was that the beast would keep him in line. And he'd be so worn out from carrying him, his magic being drained, that he wouldn't be able to cause trouble before we locked up his wings again.

The *whooshing* of wingbeats sounded from behind me, and I turned to find Hestia by the window we would be vacating from.

"Are we ready to leave?" She surveyed the thirty or so prisoners standing in the hallway. "The villagers are waiting."

The last thing I wanted to do was release the chains from the prisoners' wings, but I didn't have a choice. They had to fly with us. Hating what I needed to say next, I inhaled. "I'd like to have twenty Seelie guards help mine keep an eye on the prisoners. We need to ensure that they don't try to fly away or do something asinine, resulting in injuries."

"I'll make the arrangements now, but the king and queen want Lira to fly in the middle of the group with them where they're protected on all sides. Of course, you're welcome to join her."

"I want her in the safest place as well," I agreed easily. For now, the Seelie and I were aligned in wanting Lira safe and away from dragons.

Only if you're with me, she connected, moving in front of me. Her long, wavy blonde hair hung over her light-gray dress. Aside from her vibrant blue eyes, she could easily be an Unseelie. *Remember, we stay side by side.*

My plan had been to keep an eye on Eldrin. However, I'd made a promise to my mate, one I never wanted to attempt to break even if I were able. *I'll join you, but I'll need to take a few breaks to check on the prisoners.*

She frowned but nodded, knowing what I meant.

Some of the tension ebbed from my shoulders and wings. It was time to return home after so long. "Remove the prisoners' chains, and if any of them do anything that poses a threat, do not hesitate to kill them." I tapped into my magic just enough that my words echoed against the walls, making sure that every guard and prisoner heard.

The Unseelie guards sprang into action, pulling out keys and unlocking chains while Finola handled Eldrin. She kept his chains in her left hand, ensuring her right was free. And then Finnian shoved Nightbane to Eldrin.

Nightbane huffed and shook his fur, his drool hitting Eldrin's strained face.

I'd always tolerated the beast, making sure I trained him to be vicious enough to keep the prisoners in line. Since Lira had come, I'd felt guilty for my treatment of the cù-sìth, and in this moment, I found myself warming to the creature. Anything that could irritate Eldrin made me reconsider my stance about it.

Concern pulsed through Lira. "Finola, I need you to stab Eldrin in the heart if he so much as looks like he's contemplating letting go of Nightbane."

"Don't fret, Your Highness." Finola bowed her head slightly. "It would be my honor to end his life for any reason."

Lira's breath caught, and surprise pulsed from her. *She just called me Your Highness.*

I did make it clear I plan to marry you and make you their queen, and you're Seelie royalty. My people would bestow upon her the respect she deserved, like it or not. I'd kill anyone who insulted her from here on out.

"Nightbane is larger than Eldrin." Finnian rocked back on his heels, watching my cousin struggle. "I bet the beast's penis is also bigger than his. No wonder neither men nor women were interested in him."

Eldrin huffed, and Nightbane growled. The animal turned his gaze on Lira, his green eyes pleading.

Don't even consider it. You just healed yourself, and I can sense that you aren't completely better. Lira would no doubt try to carry him otherwise.

She cut her eyes at me in warning, but she didn't argue.

Struan stepped forward, holding a set of chains at his side. "All the prisoners are ready to fly."

Excellent. The urge to leave this entire island behind took hold.

Taking Lira's hand, I guided her past the guard and the fifteen prisoners who had attacked us the day before. We flew out the window, the chill of the air brushing over my skin. Down below, the Unseelie villagers were gathered in the center of the town. Most carried small bags of their possessions. For myself, I had no desire to bring anything back from here. I wanted to start afresh back in my rightful kingdom with Lira by my side.

The Seelie guards lined the edge of the village while about thirty Unseelie guards instructed the villagers on the ground.

As soon as we flew overhead, a few of the children pointed upward, and Isla yelled, "It's time to leave!"

We met up with Lira's parents at the edge of the sea, and my focus turned in the direction of the new dragon kingdom. I half expected to see dragons rushing in our direction.

THE KINGDOM OF FLAMES AND ASH

After what felt like hours but had to be mere minutes, our massive group of six thousand fae began the journey over the ocean. Hestia, the king, the queen, Lira, me, Finnian, Caelan, and Brenin hung back, allowing a third of the Seelie and Unseelie guards and half of our people to head out first.

Soon, our group of eight moved forward in the heart of the group, and we started across the water.

With each flap of wings, my excitement increased, but so did my concern. I glanced over my shoulder at the prisoners, who were close behind us, surrounded by guards. The rest of the villagers were behind them, and the remaining soldiers brought up the rear.

The memory of how we'd been herded to this island within a day of Eldrin freeing me from the Seelie castle sprang into my mind. I'd used glamour to hide between Caelan and Finnian. Dragons had circled us, ready to shoot fire, and the Seelie guards had been prepared to use magic and weapons on us if we flew an inch out of line.

Unlike the prisoners now, we hadn't deserved mistreatment.

As my attention split between watching the prisoners and keeping an eye on the skyline, something deep inside me became unsettled.

Is something wrong? Lira asked, her irises darkening with concern.

I could sense her worry about flying over the open sea, which had to be adding to my trepidation. *I'm not sure what we're heading back to. Did the Seelie ruin our land, or will they be the same as when I left as a young man? When we escaped and hid in the underground lair, we didn't see much of the kingdom.* Our magic naturally charged the land and made them darker and colder, but not one Unseelie had been there for years. I feared that, just as we hadn't been at full strength living on the ruined island, our natural land would have been hindered by our absence.

There's only one way to find out. Lira looked left and addressed her parents. "What is the state of the Unseelie land now? What can they expect when they arrive?"

The royals glanced at each other before the king cleared his throat. "If you're asking if we tried to infuse our magic into their land, the answer is no. We also never tore down their houses. Some of our guards were stationed there with their families to ensure nothing strange happened. It's not the same, but it shouldn't be hard to restore the land. We didn't risk disturbing the magic."

Hearing that they hadn't deliberately ruined our land gave me some relief, but it didn't stop the nagging sensation deep within me.

The group fell silent as we continued to push toward Aetherglen. Even Finnian and Caelan were unusually quiet.

Lira flew closer to me and took my hand, alleviating some of my discomfort. *When we return, we'll get the people set up and the land back to normal,* she reassured me.

The wind warmed, and the water gently crashed underneath us. My anticipation grew. Would our kingdom be what we remembered, and would it still feel like home?

Either way, I knew that, as long as Lira was by my side, everything would be all right.

When the border of Aetherglen came into view, my wings beat a little bit faster. I remembered the impact on the strength of my magic when we'd stayed here just one night, and all of us needed to recharge.

Suddenly, there was a commotion in front of us.

At least one hundred people in golden armor flew from the island directly at us, their wings flapping hard.

My stomach sank, and Lira's hand tightened on mine.

I had worried that the Seelie lured us here under false

THE KINGDOM OF FLAMES AND ASH

pretenses, but I'd hoped that, for Lira's sake, they wouldn't manipulate us.

"What is the meaning of this?" Lira's eyes cut toward her parents.

"We had no way to inform the guards on duty here that we were bringing the Unseelie home. It's nothing to be concerned about." The king glanced at Hestia. "Order them to stand down and inform them that the Unseelie are returning."

"Yes, Your Majesty." Hestia darted out of the group and headed toward the oncoming Seelie guards. However, when she glanced back at Brenin, she hesitated.

Something was wrong.

When I followed her gaze, my entire world shifted. Terror froze my heart, and I yanked Lira behind me.

Five figures soared in a slithering fashion high in the sky.

Dragons were coming to Aetherglen, somewhere they shouldn't have known we'd be.

Chapter Sixteen

Lira

My body jerked as Tavish slung me behind him. I found myself with my chest plastered against his back, the jolt of our connection springing to life as his terror clawed inside me.

Alarm rang through me. Only one thing would put him on edge like that.

Dragons.

Needing to know what was going on, I flew an inch higher to see over his shoulder.

The world seemed to tilt. Of course, they'd arrive as soon as we reached the kingdom. We couldn't have even a few minutes to get settled before the next threat materialized.

"We need to hide Lira," Finnian said and turned in our direction. "There's no telling who is part of the party or what they're going to demand once they arrive."

Our group moved forward once more, Tavish keeping a firm grip on my wrist to keep me behind him.

"I'm not hiding." I'd sneak away from everyone if I had to. The dragons had Eiric, and I needed to know how she was doing. I wouldn't turn my back and let my sister suffer because she'd gotten into this whole mess by protecting me.

You're not going anywhere with them, Lira. Tavish's body coiled, bracing for attack. *I'm not losing you again. I'll kill them all if that's what it takes.*

THE KINGDOM OF FLAMES AND ASH

I believed him, but even if he could follow through on that promise, that wouldn't fix the entire problem. My sister was being held by the enemy, and she'd already been there for several days, far longer than any of us intended.

Yet I understood that handing myself over wouldn't get her back. They'd have no reason to let her go. Dragons loved to hoard, and they were angry with my parents for the choices they'd made in sending me to Earth and not notifying the dragons upon my return, as well as from learning that I had a fated-mate bond with the Unseelie king.

They wanted retribution, and I had no doubt they would use Eiric to get it.

There were only two ways we could get her back safely— either by making an exchange where I was handed over at the same time she was given back or starting a war. Because, at the end of the day, the dragons were determined to solidify a union between their prince and me.

With the injuries we'd sustained and the chaos of the Unseelie rebellion, we hadn't gotten a chance to address the problem. And now we faced a decision we might not be prepared to make.

The five dragons drew closer, and I noticed their scales were black, iridescent, hunter green, royal blue, and silver. Not the crimson of the prince, the gold of the king, or the jade of the queen.

"I doubt that's the royals. They wouldn't come here with so few guards," Mom said before I could inform everyone.

"That means the dragons fear we might challenge them or fight to ensure that Lira remains here." Father rubbed a hand over his beard as our entire group continued to move.

Dad drew his sword, preparing to defend my parents and me, just as we reached the edge of the island where the Aelwen River flowed between the border of the Seelie and Unseelie

154

kingdoms. The leader of the guards who'd been flying toward us finally stopped in front of Father and Mother. The moment I noted the auburn hair flying out of the helmet, I knew exactly who it was.

Sorcha.

The female guard who'd given me a hard time when Tavish had been captured. She hadn't trusted me not to do anything foolish.

"Your Majesties," she said, bowing her head and then narrowing eyes that reminded me of flames under a midnight sky. "We were concerned when we saw the large group flying toward us and then the dragons. I needed to check that you weren't under attack or being threatened."

"None of that. The Unseelie are here with my blessing, but not the dragons. Nonetheless, our group should stay on course." Father flapped his brown wings harder, picking up our pace. "Head to Dunscaith as we originally planned. They can follow us there if they have a message to deliver from their royals."

I expected some of the stress to ease from Tavish, but instead, his body coiled tighter. Our group flew over the trees in the direction of the Unseelie castle, located close to the center of the true Cuil Dorcha. We followed the river embankment, knowing it would lead directly there.

Sorcha flinched. "You're taking them back to Cuil Dorcha, not to Gleann Solas as prisoners?" She glared in my direction, and I had no doubt she thought that I'd caused all these problems.

I hadn't been the actual cause... just the catalyst for everything to come to fruition.

"Since Tavish needs to remain here with the Unseelie, should Finnian leave with Lira and take her someplace else?" Caelan's jaw clenched as he kept glancing in the direction of the dragons.

THE KINGDOM OF FLAMES AND ASH

A strangled gasp left Sorcha, and Caelan finally looked at the newcomer. They both gaped at one another.

I had no clue what was going on, but that didn't matter. I moved to Tavish's side, refusing to remain hidden behind him. The dragons would overtake us, so they would eventually see me. Trying to hide would only make me look like a coward. "Eldrin would rat us out as soon as the dragons asked questions, so we need to get him away from them." I had no doubt that Eldrin would do anything to gain favor with the dragons since our goodwill was exhausted.

"Rat us out?" Mother's forehead wrinkled. "What does rat mean?"

Dad pressed his lips together for a moment. "She means Eldrin would inform the dragons of what happened to Lira. It's an Earth saying."

"Another one." Finnian tapped his forehead. "Locked and loaded." He raised both hands, mimicking guns. "See! I'm learning."

When Eiric and I escaped Caisteal Solais with Finnian and Tavish, Eiric had given Finnian a crash course in Earth vernacular and symbols, which he had clearly taken to heart. I smiled, but I could feel the frustration in Tavish.

"That's not helping right now," Tavish bit out, glaring at his friend. "But Lira is right. Eldrin won't hesitate to inform the dragons that we're hiding her from them."

"And they're already upset about me being hidden on Earth; the last thing we need to do is upset them more by hiding me in this realm." I took Tavish's hand and squeezed, needing him to see reason. "The best thing we can do is face them as a united fae front with me beside both my parents."

Hurt snapped through our connection, and Tavish's nostrils flared. "And me," he rasped, making it clear he wasn't happy with what I'd said.

Finnian rolled his eyes. "Yes, because Lira standing by her fated mate—the very man who threatens any who so much as touch her—would improve matters. We might as well invite Pyralis to stay with you two for a couple of days so he can see how you hover over each other."

"She is *my* mate." Tavish pounded his chest.

"We all are quite aware." Caelan finally pulled his focus away from Sorcha and sighed. "But we don't need to antagonize the dragons more than they already are."

Father nodded. "Everyone here agrees, so that's how it should be. If she is standing between her mother and me, rather than beside Tavish, it'll help the dragons feel more comfortable with her remaining in Gleann Solas, which will permit all of us more time to get answers from the nightfiend who claims he has information that will void the vow. So that's what we're going to do."

Hot anger and cold fear blended together in Tavish, and I flew closer to him, letting our wings brush.

Thorn, it has nothing to do with me not being proud of you. I just need to make sure we don't make things worse, in case they take it out on E. I hated making him feel this way, but at the same time, I needed to protect my sister the best way I knew how.

He started. *I know. I just despise how much influence these dragons have on our relationship. I want to kill the ashbreath, so this whole ruse can be done. I'm tired of someone else believing they have any sort of claim on you.*

I feel the same way. Love isn't enough to describe what I feel for you. In fact, I wasn't sure what came close. Nothing seemed adequate.

The trees thickened on both sides of the river as we traveled deeper into Cuil Dorcha. Soon, we turned another bend, and in the distance, I could see the top of the Unseelie castle. The

THE KINGDOM OF FLAMES AND ASH

sun shone down on the land, and grass, trees, and flowers grew thick. This place was the opposite of the ruined dragon land.

The river ran toward the castle, curving around one side before vanishing. The castle wasn't as dark as the one in the ruined land, but it looked gray from a distance. Murmurs from the Unseelie above and behind us grew louder, most probably unaware that dragons were approaching.

"Sorcha, return to Gleann Solas and retrieve more guards in case the dragons attempt to cause problems," Mother commanded. I suspected that the directive came from her so that Father could deny that he called for reinforcements.

Finnian's brows rose as if he were surprised by Mother's sternness. "Now I see where Lira gets it."

I smirked, enjoying the fact that so many people underestimated her. Mother ruled just as strongly as Father, but she had a quieter way and worked more behind the scenes. When called for, her fierceness showed without hesitation.

"Yes, Your Majesty." Sorcha bowed and stole one last glance at Caelan before turning and flying back toward the Seelie kingdom.

The Seelie guards in the front directed people toward the villages they used to live in while the group of prisoners, the guards monitoring them, and our group headed to the grassy fields between the river and Dunscaith. The others spread out, making room for us to land at the double wooden doors that led inside.

The eight of us turned—our backs to the castle—as Eldrin and the other prisoners landed in front of us. Eldrin released Nightbane, whose fur seemed to be more of a matted mess than ever, and he ran straight to my side, squeezing between me and Tavish.

As soon as the guards landed, the Seelie surrounded the prisoners, and the Unseelie guards locked up the prisoners' wings again. The entire time, Eldrin's arms hung limply at his sides. Sweat had soaked through his gray tunic and covered his brow, but the vile man wore a humongous smile.

Acid burned my throat. I couldn't wait for this man to die, and I could only hope that it happened at my hands.

He was thrilled about the dragons because he knew they threatened Tavish's and my happiness. The very issue he proclaimed to know how to get me free of... for a price. His eternal freedom was potentially too huge of a price to pay.

I won't let the dragons take you, sprite, Tavish reassured me as he reached behind me, brushing his fingers along my wing.

The sensation caused a shiver to race through me. *That's not what I'm worried about. It's Eldrin gloating. He looks as if the dragons coming here are an answer to his prayers.*

It probably is because, if giving him his freedom keeps you by my side, I will gladly make the sacrifice. His irises darkened as he stared into my soul. *Because not having you as my mate, my wife, and by my side can't ever happen.*

My heart skipped a beat, seeing how much he loved me.

The sound of flapping wings had me looking straight ahead. The dragons would be here momentarily.

Eldrin doesn't need to listen to our conversation with the dragons. None of the prisoners do. Tavish pointed to the right around the castle. "Someone fly ahead and check the prison cells while the rest of the guards follow and watch the prisoners until they're secured once more."

Finola, Lorne, and Struan tensed, but Tavish bit out, "Now. I need you three to handle this." He didn't have to tell them why. They knew he trusted only them.

Obliging, the three of them commanded the guards, and the prisoners began moving just as the five dragons landed.

The ashbreaths were at least eight times my size and were careful to land at the edge of the water, but not so much that they touched the liquid.

Water was their one weakness, which was why I was puzzled that they wanted me so desperately.

The black dragon stepped forward, its body shrinking right in front of my eyes. My jaw dropped. I'd never seen a dragon shift into human form. Its legs grew shorter and thinner, and its wings disappeared into its middle, which then elongated into a human form. The black scales faded, and long dark hair sprouted from its head. The body slowly transitioned into a breathtaking woman whose skin reminded me of the night sky and whose eyes were the color of stars. Thankfully, she wasn't naked when she took non-beast form.

Finnian inhaled sharply as the woman scanned us, pausing a little longer on Finnian, then Nightbane, and lastly, me before sliding over to Father. "King Erdan," she said, bowing her head slightly. The four dragons behind her remained in beast form as they watched us.

"I'd greet you, but I'm not sure of your name and rank." Father puffed out his chest despite being two inches shorter than the woman.

"Zyndara." She straightened, oozing confidence in her flowy golden dress.

Mother clasped her hands in front of her chest. "Lovely name. Sorry for not already being here to greet you, but we weren't notified you intended to visit."

"Just as we weren't aware that the Unseelie were being allowed to return to their homeland when our peoples made the decision to banish them together."

I already hated the bitch. "This is a fae matter, so I'm sure your royals will understand." I placed a hand on my hip, refusing to play with words. I wanted to get to the heart of the matter. "And I doubt they're the reason you're here."

She smirked. "You're right. They're not. We came to inform

the king and queen that you were in the former Tìr na Dràgon, but clearly, they already knew and decided to bring back not just you but the Unseelie as well."

"Their food source was ruined. Had we not brought them here, the Unseelie would face extinction, which would hinder our magic." Father spread out his wings. "We didn't have time to travel to Tìr na Dràgon and have a discussion."

"Always an excuse, which my king and queen grow tired of."

Tavish arched a brow. "Your prince came to my kingdom and tried to kidnap Lira. I doubt he informed King Ignathor and Queen Sintara of that information."

"The Seelie princess is betrothed to Pyralis. It's his right to spend time with her before they marry. He was merely exercising that right after he learned of a fated-mate connection formed between her and another. The vow bound by the realm takes precedence over everything, including fated-mate connections, as we're all aware. But I didn't come here to have this discussion. I came for another reason altogether."

Mom and Dad tensed, and Nightbane stepped closer to my legs. The Seelie guards remained around us, each one alert.

"Well, forgive us if we aren't available right now." Mother smiled, putting on her Seelie charm. "We've had a long journey, and we would like to rest before discussing anything."

"Don't fret. It's not a conversation. It's very simple." Zyndara looked right at me. "I came here to retrieve the princess and bring her back home with me."

"Not even if my existence ends," Tavish snarled, retrieving his sword from the sheath. "Lira isn't going anywhere with you or near Pyralis."

She threw her head back and laughed. "Don't be foolish enough to believe that you are part of this." She turned back to my parents. "There's no decision for any of you to make.

THE KINGDOM OF FLAMES AND ASH

You excluded the dragon royals from all your recent decisions about Pyralis's betrothed. They aren't requesting anything unreasonable. She's old enough to wed, but they're still willing to wait until she's twenty-five, provided she leaves with me."

"We do not agree." Father lifted both hands, his fingertips brown with his own magic. "So, you should leave."

"That won't be happening," Zyndara scoffed. "Don't make us use force."

Smoke trickled from the four dragons' noses as they prepared to drench us in flames.

Oh, hell no. I wouldn't stand for that.

I yanked on my water magic, ready to unleash it.

CHAPTER SEVENTEEN

LIRA

Straightening my spine, I lifted my hands, allowing my refreshing, cool water magic to pulse from my palms and raise the water from the river behind the dragons. I could also shoot water from my palms if needed, but I wanted to make a stand. Attacking them would no doubt cause this situation to escalate further, which wasn't my intent. Though a part of me would like to douse the ashbreaths in water and relish watching them squirm, that wasn't in my best interest. "Let me be clear; I won't allow you to take me. My magic is strong enough to drench you all with water if needed."

The water rippled behind them, causing Zyndara to look over her shoulder and take a large gulp.

A few other Seelie stepped forward with their hands raised, and I had no doubt they could also bend water and would be stronger since they weren't half drained.

Tavish tilted his head back and jutted out his chin. "And though my people don't control water, they can use ice."

The dragon sneered, her eyes brightening like a star flashing. "We came in peace, asking for the princess betrothed to our prince to come with us, and this is the response we receive?"

"Let's be clear." Mother lifted a brow. "You just proclaimed that our daughter *would* be leaving with you three years before

THE KINGDOM OF FLAMES AND ASH

the agreed-upon date. If anything, your royals are abusing our agreement terms to fit their needs, which won't be tolerated."

I sighed, ready for this all to be over. I wanted to get out of the asinine agreement with Pyralis, kill Eldrin, and live happily ever after with Tavish. Was that really too much to ask? "In other words, I'm not going anywhere."

"Very well." Zyndara moved her feet shoulder-width apart. "I didn't want this meeting to come to this as we were hoping it would be amicable, but if you refused to have Princess Lira return with us, we were to deliver a message."

My stomach tightened, and Nightbane growled, the fur around his neck rising.

"Princess Lira is to come to Tìr na Dràgon of her own free will within three days, or there will be dire consequences."

My breath caught, and heat slammed through our bond as Tavish's face flushed.

We both knew exactly what they were going to dangle in front of me.

Eiric.

"And what exactly are those consequences?" Father asked curtly while both Mom and Dad stood frozen like statues.

Zyndara steepled her fingers, and her pupils elongated. "Her friend perishes slowly and brutally."

My heart squeezed. Mom's wings twitched, ready to fly forward, but Caelan snagged her wrists and held her back.

I couldn't believe they were threatening someone so important to me, but it was the only way they would get the desired outcome.

Tavish unleashed his magic, causing snow to fall and the sky to be shrouded in darkness. "Not only does the ashbreath keep claiming my mate, but he's willing to kill someone she cares about just to get her to come to him? He is either ignorant or suicidal."

164

"It's obviously the first one." Finnian scoffed and wrinkled his nose. "I'd heard the rumors that dragon's penises were large, but the sacrifice was a lack of intellect. Most of the energy rushed to the penis and testicles, leaving only leftovers for the brain."

I coughed a laugh as both Mother's and Father's eyes widened. That was one thing about Finnian; he didn't act cold and broody like most of the Unseelie fae. If I hadn't known better, I would've believed he was Seelie.

The royal-blue dragon huffed, a trickle of flames coming from his mouth. I readied to toss water in his face, but he didn't actually attack. He must have reacted in disgust.

"Insult us all you want." Zyndara smirked. "But these are our demands, and we aren't asking for anything truly unreasonable. Prince Pyralis simply wants to ensure that his future wife doesn't breed with a nightfiend. He wants his wife's bloodline to continue only from him."

Tavish unsheathed his sword and darted toward the dragons. Zyndara's skin thickened, her dark scales returning.

My heart hammered, and I prepared to do whatever was necessary to protect my mate.

I couldn't lose him.

Not like this.

Not when his goal was to save me.

"Blighted abyss," Caelan rasped, flying after Tavish with Finnian on his wings.

Heavier smoke trickled from the dragons' snouts, and I smelled brimstone. It made me want to gag.

They all pivoted, readying for Tavish to strike Zyndara, but instead, Tavish cloaked himself in darkness and stabbed the pearl-colored dragon on the end through the neck. Crimson blood sprayed as it tossed its head and roared.

Both Finnian and Caelan paused about ten feet away as

the other dragons opened their mouths to let loose their flames on Tavish, so I didn't hold back. I directed the stream so the water crashed into their faces, pushing liquid up their noses and down their throats.

Both Seelie and Unseelie guards sprang forward as the earth shook under the dragons' feet. Between that and the way they thrashed, I suspected that Tavish, if not more Unseelie, was using his illusion magic on the dragons.

"Stop," Zyndara shouted, gripping the sides of her head as a snout began to form on her face. She growled, "We don't mean you any harm. If we don't arrive back in Tìr na Dràgon by the end of the day, your friend will die."

I stopped calling the water, but I kept my hands upright.

"Stop the attack," Dad bellowed, voice rife with panic.

As the pearl dragon dropped to the ground, succumbing to death, Tavish pushed the darkness away, revealing himself right in front of Zyndara. The blood from the pearl dragon splattered all over his face. He could've killed her too, if he'd desired.

"Inform Pyralis and the other royals that their message was received and that if he sends anyone else here to threaten my mate or her friends, I won't stop at one death. I'll kill them all." His wings spread out behind him, blocking my view. "This is our land once more, and I won't tolerate my enemy treating it like it's their home. Do I make myself clear?"

Zyndara's face smoothed into its human form, and her chest heaved. "I'll inform the royals. I'm sure they'll be very interested in the turn of events here."

"Excellent." Tavish slid his sword back into its sheath, unafraid that the other dragons would attack.

In fairness, it would be foolish if they did. They were grossly outnumbered, and our magic was stronger here.

"Three days, *Princess*." Zyndara focused on me once again

and curled the side of her mouth. "I hope you take this time to get your affairs in order and come to us so your friend might live."

"How do I know they'll truly hand her over?" None of the royals were here making the vow, and I needed to make sure they weren't trying to skirt around the law of the realm.

She snarled, "The girl's parents can come with you. When you arrive at the border, we'll release her. You can watch her return to them before handing yourself over." Then she allowed a sinister smile. "And if you try something foolish, we'll wage war. It's that simple. Either way, the Unseelie king will pay for killing Pyralis's cousin."

I hated the way my knees wanted to give out. Tavish killing a royal family member had made the situation worse.

He didn't miss a beat. "I look forward to it." Tavish folded his wings back and gestured to the castle. "I invite Pyralis to come any time and take this issue up with me. In fact, tomorrow works perfectly."

Did you know that dragon was related to Pyralis? A sour taste filled my mouth because I hoped that my nagging suspicion was wrong.

"I'll alert him," Zyndara gritted out through clenched teeth, making the disdain she felt for him clear. "Now we'll take our dead and leave."

"Please." Tavish brushed at the blood that stained his sleeves. "I'd rather not have dragon remains left behind to poison our soil. If you don't, I'll be forced to toss him into the water."

The hunter-green dragon breathed heavily, but with water still dripping from him, he could barely make a trickle of smoke escape his nose. I took a step forward like I might use my magic on him once more, causing the dragon's eyes to widen marginally.

THE KINGDOM OF FLAMES AND ASH

At least they had reservations about my abilities. Granted, on dragon land, who knew how strong I'd be, but this close to Gleann Solas, I could feel my power intensify.

The royal-blue dragon lifted the pearl dragon in its talons while the green and silver dragons watched and Zyndara transitioned into her dragon form.

The silence surrounding us seemed deafening as the four of them flew away.

As their figures grew smaller and smaller, I clenched my hands together and repeated the question. I suspected that his continued silence validated my thoughts. *Tavish, did you know?*

The pearl scales are a sign of a higher-caste dragon. He crossed his arms and stepped backward to Nightbane's side. *But they came onto my land, demanding that my mate hand herself over, threatening her sister, and then flaunting all the heirs the prince wants to have with you in my face. Killing just one was me showing restraint, so I decided I would eliminate the one that would mean the most to them. It's common sense.*

I placed a hand on my chest, trying to keep it from aching more. *I hope that they don't take their anger out on E.*

They won't, he assured me and took my hand. *They know if they don't hand Eiric over, the Seelie will declare war. They want Eiric here, so both sets of your parents acknowledge that they had to give you up in order to get her back. It would be a daily reminder that they lost control to the dragons.*

I should've known it would come down to that.

Control. Power. Two things the dragons cherished most. It must have driven them crazy when we'd told them I wouldn't be going home with Pyralis as soon as he demanded it.

My entire future had just been stolen because the choice before me had been made perfectly clear.

Father cursed. "Blasted abyss. I can't fathom how their timing was so perfect. Have they been watching our kingdom,

168

waiting for us to return?"

"Not possible, Your Majesty." Dad kept his sword in his hand, searching the horizon. "The guards we left behind kept watch. They would've noticed if dragons had been lurking, and there isn't anywhere for them to land and rest between our kingdom and theirs."

"Then how did this happen?" Mother hung her head. "It seems too coincidental."

Finnian pursed his lips. "I'd say someone alerted them, but we took a head count of everyone before we left. All were accounted for."

"Even though we need to have this discussion, right now, we should prioritize helping the Unseelie return to their homes." Caelan pushed a stray lock of hair out of his face. "And we probably want to discuss this inside the palace."

Despite him being right, two things kept running through my mind. In three days, I had to hand myself over to the dragons, or Eiric would die. A war with the dragons wasn't far off if I didn't go willingly.

"You two handle the housing situation and establish shifts with the guards so that someone is always watching the perimeter," Tavish said stiffly, tugging me to his side.

Nightbane huffed and moved out from between us. He hovered in front of me like he was waiting for another attack.

"I'll leave some Seelie guards to assist in covering the area since it's so large. The others will return home to alert the rest of our forces of what happened." Dad flew over to a group of guards, leaving the five of us alone.

I turned to see Mom looking paler than I ever remembered seeing her. My heart lurched in my chest, and even though the one place I wanted to be was at Tavish's side, I needed to comfort her. I could only imagine how she felt. I risked losing a sister, but she risked a daughter.

THE KINGDOM OF FLAMES AND ASH

I untangled myself from Tavish and hurried to Mom. As I hugged her, her body shook, and she returned the embrace even tighter.

My lungs screamed, but I refused to move or complain.

"Don't worry. It's all going to be okay." A sob began in my chest, but I tried to hold it back. I hated how hopeless I felt right now. I couldn't allow Eiric to die because of my selfishness.

"Sprite," Tavish growled menacingly. "I can feel what you're thinking, and I won't allow it." His anger hadn't ebbed, and now determination fueled it.

He had no intention of letting me go, even if it meant Eiric's life.

"You don't get to make that call, Tavish." I ran my fingers through Mom's hair, trying not to snag any curls. "If it's between me being a captive or E being killed, I know which one I'm going to pick. Look at what this is doing to everyone."

Hestia jerked upright, tears trailing down her cheeks. "This isn't just about Eiric. You should know better than that. This is about you, too. Either way, I lose a daughter. Yes, Eiric could die, but a life with the dragons might be a harsher fate than death."

"Unfortunately, Lira's biological parents didn't agree with you since they're the ones who got everyone into this situation." Tavish turned his steely eyes on my parents and continued, "They promised their daughter to someone more vile and power-hungry than my father ever was."

"I resent that accusation, and your father was going to allow the rest of us to die by killing our crops." Father brandished his finger like a sword and jabbed it at Tavish as he continued, "So the Unseelie are the real reason we are in this mess. King Dunach disrespected the balance of power."

"Which is impossible." Tavish chopped the air with his hand. "He wasn't capable of that sort of strength!"

170

Dad rejoined us, eyes widening at the obvious tension.

Fighting among ourselves wouldn't accomplish anything. "We're wasting time. We need to deal with this situation; what happened before is irrelevant. The Unseelie king blanketing the sky in darkness and me being promised to the dragon prince are in the past. We can't undo any of that."

Mother nodded. "We need to channel all this turmoil into determining a solution."

"Yes, and right now, I can think of only one." I bit the inside of my cheek, wondering if I had the strength to do what was necessary. I would lose a piece of myself, and I could only hope that the end would be worth the sacrifice.

"You are *not* handing yourself over to that ashbreath." Tavish's chest heaved, and darkness curled around his body as his temper took control. He marched over and clutched my arm. "I won't allow you to do it. Your sister purposely took your place, and you'd dishonor her sacrifice? Do you have any idea of what that would do to *me*? Knowing you're with him would kill me. And if our places were reversed, would you let me leave? We will fix this or go to war with the ashbreaths. You're worth fighting for, and I vow I will strike down anyone who stands in our way until my last breath."

I didn't like him telling me what to do, but even as I tried to hang on to the anger, the buzz of our fated-mate connection had it slipping away.

"He's right, sprout." Father winced as if agreeing with Tavish hurt him. "We have two full days to find a solution that doesn't involve handing you over."

I snorted bitterly. "It's either that or a war." If we wanted Eiric alive, we couldn't just do nothing. Still, I lifted my chin. "For the record, I wasn't talking about handing myself over. I meant we need to talk to Eldrin, and now."

Tavish smirked, though I could feel his surprise. "Now

THE KINGDOM OF FLAMES AND ASH

that's a good plan. Let's go." He immediately set off, leading us around the side of the castle. However, instead of flying upward to the castle windows, he stopped at a stone door that had been left open.

"The prison is this way," he said, flying into an underground setup that was nothing like the cells in the castle at the ruined land or the prison in Caisteal Solais.

Lorne, Finola, and Struan stood in the center of a huge dark space with cement rooms on either side, each with a solid metal door.

"Your Majesty, the other guards left a few minutes after we got the prisoners secured in their cells." Finola bowed her head, taking in both sets of parents behind me.

"Where's Eldrin?" Tavish barked.

Lorne pointed at the door closest to us on the left.

"Open it."

Not hesitating, Lorne did what Tavish commanded.

When the door opened, what I saw made me want to kill Eldrin even more.

Chapter Eighteen

Tavish

I gritted my teeth, trying to come off as impartial as I could, but the way Eldrin leaned against the stone wall, wearing a smirk, had the nightmare illusion magic swirling inside me, wanting to release and cause him agony.

I couldn't react impulsively. He had been strategic and calculating over the years, focusing on the end result—like I must now.

Next to me, Lira quivered, her rage spilling through our bond and making my bloodthirsty instinct surge to life. I'd been able to control it better, but ever since the Seelie arrived, my thirst for blood had grown harder to ignore.

With desperation causing sharp aches in my chest from the threat of Lira giving herself up to Pyralis to protect her sister, my sanity was blasting close to being lost forever. The only thing holding me together was the need for answers from Eldrin on how Lira could get out of this blighted vow that had been forced upon her.

With dirt smudged on his face, wrinkled garments, and white hair hanging limp with grease, he shouldn't appear so confident, but he knew why we were there.

"Ah... you've ignored me, starved me, and forced me to carry that animal, but as soon as the dragons arrive, you're back." The lantern above his head flickered, providing the

THE KINGDOM OF FLAMES AND ASH

illusion that he'd called shadows to cloak him.

Too bad his wings were bound by the chains that kept him from using magic.

The Seelie royals and Lira's second parents were behind us, and I needed to take control before the Seelie king did. I needed Eldrin to believe that no bad blood remained between us despite nothing truly being resolved.

"You aren't our priority. In fact, I'd rather you not be here at all, but it seems Fate keeps granting you favors." I kept my hand tight in Lira's, needing to know she was at my side and not trying to sneak away.

"Fate?" Eldrin laughed and wrinkled his nose. "Fate has nothing to do with this. I set everything in motion. It was all *me*. And now I'm in a position to get out of this place and continue with my life without hindrance."

"Like *hell* you are," Lira spat, moving to stand shoulder-to-shoulder with me. "You're going to stay in here and be the miserable piece of shit you are."

He shrugged. "That's fine with me. Go marry the dragon. I don't blasting care. I think you don't realize that either way, I win. I tell you, and I'm free to do as I wish. I don't, and Tavish has the most important thing stripped from him. He'll live in misery the same way I have for the majority of my life, not even considered worthy of being a spare, despite the king treating me like one of his sons."

The hatred I'd nurtured for the past twelve years ignited. The edges of my vision hazed as I channeled all that hate toward the man I'd considered a second father. "You weren't the heir. There wasn't anything he could do. It's not how our magic works. You *know* this." I released Lira's hand and placed mine on the hilt of my sword, ready to slay him now.

Nightbane snarled, hunkering closer to Lira, sensing the threat before us. He'd always detested Eldrin even more than he did me, and I'd never thought anything of it. I'd grown up believing he was a stupid beast, but now things made more sense. Eldrin had always been despicable. He had no redeeming qualities, caring for no one but himself. He'd never truly cared about protecting the Unseelie.

I stalked inside the cell, torn about what to do. I wanted to kill the wildling, but if I did, I had a significant risk of losing Lira. My breathing sped up, and the walls seemed to close in on me.

Kill him, Lira connected. *We can't risk him getting free and trying to take over once again. I can't relive the torture he already put us both through.* Her worry constricted our connection, adding to mine.

And I can't kill him, knowing that Pyralis could very well get his talons on you. The two of us were at odds, wanting the same for each other. I needed her safe and free while she wanted to ensure that my cousin didn't take me captive and beat me. *I'd rather be a prisoner, knowing that you're safe in Aetherglen. That's what's important to me. Blast Eldrin and the Unseelie people. They can all burn as long as you're safe.*

Her eyes narrowed, and I could tell that she disagreed with everything I'd just said.

"It's best if you're forthcoming, nightfiend," King Erdan said loudly from his spot behind us. "This isn't a chess match between you and us. This impacts my daughter's life, and I refuse to barter with criminals."

"I disagree. Any sort of political maneuvering is exactly that—a game of strategy." Eldrin waved one hand toward Lira and added, "And your daughter is rather good at it, seeing as she managed to manipulate Tavish and Lorne and survive the deadly gauntlet. She never should've lived."

I removed my sword from its sheath and stabbed Eldrin in the leg, pushing so that it pierced through muscle to the other side, ensuring the wound would heal slowly, especially without the help of his fae magic.

He grunted, hunching over, as black blood seeped through his pants and onto the ground.

"What is he talking about?" the queen asked, her voice rising.

At the question, Eldrin looked up, beaming.

Lira took in a ragged breath and shook her head. "It's not going to work, Eldrin. I know what you're trying to do, and the past is the past. That's where it's going to stay. I survived the horrors, and I know you were behind each one of them. But your game's not going to work this time. You'll see."

She strolled past me, and I wanted to reach out and pull her back. I didn't trust him, nor did I want her anywhere around him, but Nightbane remained at her side, giving me reassurance.

Gripping his chin in her hand, she cut into his skin. Blood oozed under her fingernails, but she didn't flinch.

Eldrin's forehead wrinkled just enough for me to register his shock before he forced his expression back into that smug smile.

"We're going to break you," she whispered, her normally bright cobalt eyes darkening to navy.

My dick twitched, causing my pants to feel too tight. I rarely saw this side of Lira. Watching her threaten the man who'd terrorized her had me ready to slam her against the wall and claim her.

"And when we do, I'll be the one to slowly slide a blade into your heart and watch the life leave your body. Not because of what you did to me but for everything you've done to Tavish."

A vein bulged in his neck, but Eldrin chuckled darkly. "We'll see about that. I told you my terms. If you want to know how to free yourself from your binding agreement with the ashbreaths, then I need a vow from every royal in this room that they will ensure no harm ever comes to me. That includes you, *Princess*."

She released him, dropping her hand to her side. His blood dripped from her fingers to the floor, and she turned her back to him. In fairness, he wasn't a threat, not with his injured leg and chained wings. But I also didn't want to underestimate him.

"I've grown bored with him." Lira yawned. "I say we head into the castle and get some rest. It has been a long day of travel."

If I didn't feel her anxiety through the bond, I'd believe that she could go to sleep.

We're not going to get anything out of him, she linked, her gaze locked on me. *We need to come off like we aren't desperate until we can find a way to hurt him.*

I hated that she was right, but I sheathed my sword.

Eldrin straightened, seeming to become more confident. Maybe he knew we'd given up.

When Lira and Nightbane left the cell, I spun around to find the king, the queen, Brenin, and Hestia scowling. The way their attention flickered between Lira and Eldrin turned my stomach leaden with dread. "Lock him back up. Don't feed him or allow anyone to check on his wounds. I want him miserable and uncomfortable."

Lorne shut the door, locking it once again. "Of course, Your Majesty. It will be my honor."

Hestia and Brenin led the way back outside, followed by the king and the queen, with Lira, Nightbane, and me at the rear.

Each step away from Eldrin felt harder than the last. I hated that my life continued to be influenced by him when I was ready to cut him out of it forever.

We'll figure something out, Lira connected as she looped her arm through mine.

THE KINGDOM OF FLAMES AND ASH

The jolt of her touch eased some of my anxiety, but frozen tendrils of terror clawed deeper into my heart. I hadn't felt this feral since the gauntlet. Watching her come so close to death all those times had been unbearable, making me borderline insane, but nothing compared to *this*. The thought of her leaving in three days to be with another man... an ashbreath, determined to marry her and force her to carry his babies...

We have three days. A lot can change in that time, she continued, trying to offer me comfort.

But three days was a blink in Seelie time. It took me twelve *years* to learn that Eldrin had been plotting against me.

When we stepped outside, I took a deep breath, enjoying the dark sky, the snow falling once more, and the scent of mist and vanilla that I hadn't experienced since I was a child. But even that didn't bring peace to my restless heart.

As soon as we shut the doors that led into the dungeon, King Erdan cleared his throat. "What is this gauntlet Eldrin referred to?"

"Nothing we need to discuss," Lira answered, placing her head on my shoulder. "It doesn't help us with our current problem."

"If we're trying to mend the relationship between us and the Unseelie, then we need to be honest with each other." Queen Sylphia pushed a piece of hair behind her shoulder. "Clearly, this trial isn't something you want us to learn of, which makes me hesitant to work with the Unseelie."

Even though I suspected it would cause more problems between her parents and me, I understood. If I were in their place, I'd want to know the same thing. The more Lira tried to evade the question, the more determined the four of them would be to learn the answer. "As you're aware, I kidnapped Lira from Earth. My intention was to bring her to the Seelie veil and kill her once her magic returned, allowing the Unseelie to return to our land. I was resolved to fight our bond at first because how could I ever accept a fated mate from the people who'd murdered my parents, kept me prisoner, and then cast us from our homelands into a dragon-ruined kingdom to perish?"

The queen placed a hand over her heart while the king scowled. Hestia's and Brenin's faces were twisted in anger, probably as they decided how I should die.

"But it clearly didn't happen." Lira stepped closer. *Are you trying to get them to hate you again?*

They've been suspicious of us and doubted my intentions almost the entire time. The only way we're going to move forward is by being honest with each other, especially since Eldrin is going to continue to pit us against one another. I was willing to do any blasting thing if it helped keep Lira by my side. Even be completely up front with the Seelie.

"That's the only reason the Unseelie king still has his wings attached right now." Hestia's body remained rigid. "But I still want to know about the gauntlet."

"Hestia," Brenin warned.

The two guards were better than Lira and Eiric at hiding their time on Earth, but Hestia speaking out of turn was one of the sure signs she'd lived elsewhere for a while.

I opened my mouth to continue, but Lira interjected, "One night, I had the opportunity to escape, but some of the villagers found me. They tried to detain me, and I fought to get away. Since I was technically a prisoner and I'd tried to escape, I precipitated something that had been created to keep the Unseelie in line—the gauntlet. A competition in which every prisoner has a chance to survive three days of trials."

"It was something I instituted to stop my people from rising against me." I didn't want them to believe I'd created it just because of Lira. "I didn't want Lira to take part, but my wings were tied."

"You put the Seelie princess into battle with Unseelie prisoners?" The king's eyes narrowed.

"He protected me." Lira moved between her family and me. "I would've died if it hadn't been for Tavish intervening, which allowed Eldrin to convince more of the Unseelie to turn away from him. He made mistakes the same way you did by betrothing me to an ashbreath."

King Erdan's nostrils flared. "We did what we thought was right at the time."

"So did he." She spread her wings, blocking me from her parents.

Once again, Lira was ready to fight to protect me. My heart warmed toward her even more. I couldn't lose her. I'd come too close so many times already, and I refused for it to happen again.

I needed to kill the dragon prince.

"She's right, Your Majesties." Brenin pivoted so he could see both sides of the group. "We don't need to argue over these things—we need to focus on finding a way to retrieve Eiric and keep Lira from being forced to go to Tìr na Dràgon."

Lira's wings lowered slightly, allowing me to see the king and queen exchange a look while Hestia closed her eyes.

"We need to find something that will hurt Eldrin." Hestia looked skyward like she was searching for answers.

I groaned. "That might be impossible. He only cares about himself."

"It's getting late, and we haven't rested or eaten." Lira moved between Nightbane and me again and continued, "We should take a moment to clear our heads, and Tavish and I need to settle in here. How about we reconvene first thing in the morning?"

I agreed. Rest would help us think clearer, and we did need to survey the castle. It had been unoccupied for too long.

"That's a good plan. I can return to the study and review all the information on dragons we have on hand." King Erdan sighed. "And catch up with our people. We'll come back with fresh breakfast for everyone in the morning."

Eating food from home sounded too good to be true, but I'd give it all up if that would guarantee Lira would be with me for the rest of eternity.

She hugged both sets of her parents and then turned to me as the royals flew off.

Having her in my childhood home like I'd imagined as a little boy let a smile break through my worry. "Let me find some clothes to change into, and then we'll check in with Caelan and Finnian."

"I kind of like you covered in enemy blood." She winked.

"When I'm done with the ashbreaths, I'll be soaked in it."

Her face fell a little, so I kissed her, enjoying her sweet taste.

"Come on," I rasped, taking her hand. The two of us flew up to the window that led to the royal chambers.

Nightbane whined below at being left behind, but the cù-sìth would find us within minutes.

As we reached the glassless window the Seelie had smashed the night of the attack all those years ago, memories came crashing back.

And suddenly, I landed, but my legs weren't there to support me.

Chapter Nineteen

Lira

I flew close behind Tavish, needing time away from everyone else to clear my head. Between Eldrin's arrogant demeanor, the delicate relationship between my parents and Tavish, and everything the dragons' visit had brought, I wanted to burn the entire realm. Every time we turned around, something else stacked up against us.

Even coming back to the true Cuil Dorcha wasn't a full win. The Seelie guards were still surrounding us under the ruse of offering protection, but I had no doubt that they had orders to watch us in addition to watching for dragons.

As Tavish flew through the window, I tried to focus on releasing some of my anger. The two of us were feeding off each other, and one of us needed to calm down so we could achieve some sort of rest.

But then agony shot through our connection, and he sank onto a cream-colored rug lying on the smooth brown floor.

My heart hammered, and my stomach turned as I landed beside him. I placed a hand between his wings on his back, sensing heartbreak through our connection. *Thorn, what's wrong?*

I scanned the room, but I didn't find any answers. The only thing that stood out to me was that the room wasn't anything like the castle we'd just left. In fact, it could easily have been a night chamber in Caisteal Solais, the Seelie castle, with the gigantic space and flower-shaped chairs in the corner.

Even though it had been abandoned, there wasn't dust or dirt in sight with the candles lit. How long had we been out there, or had the castle servants focused on the royal rooms first?

The floor reminded me of tree bark, and the sheets on the king-size bed were a shade of evergreen, reminding me of the woods between the Seelie and Unseelie border.

I... I haven't been back here since I was a boy. He straightened but remained on his knees, breathing slowly. *I didn't mean to worry you, but the emotions took me by surprise. Knowing my father was responsible for their deaths has made returning here harder than I imagined.*

I wanted to kick myself. In all the drama and turmoil, Tavish hadn't been graced with the time to come to terms with everything he'd learned. I should've foreseen this issue, but I'd been wrapped up in freeing Eiric and myself. *What can I do to help you?* I knew words wouldn't provide comfort, and I didn't want to give him false pleasantries. At the end of the day, his father had murdered both his wife and himself, and nothing was ever going to make that better.

Wrapping my arms around my mate's shoulders, I pulled him tight to my chest. I'd do anything to take away his pain.

You being here is all I need, he replied and turned toward me, placing his forehead against mine.

Our connection sprang to life. He ran his fingers through my hair and then pulled back. *I love you, sprite.*

My heart swelled, and some of my worry dissipated because he was right. We could get through this together. I just hoped we could figure out the dragon issue so we never had to be apart.

"Do you want to tell me about your mother?" I figured that

THE KINGDOM OF FLAMES AND ASH

talking about his mother would be easier. "I don't remember much about her other than seeing her watching you and smiling when we spent time together."

His eyes glistened. *She was a good mother, and I do want to tell you all about her. But not yet. I'm not ready. I hope that doesn't upset you.*

Of course not. I cupped his face with my hands. *You just learned the truth, and if you need to process it on your own, I understand.*

He kissed my lips softly. *I don't deserve you, but I'm never letting you go.* His irises darkened to the color of stormy clouds. *Never. Do you understand?*

I do. He had no intention of letting me go, even if we weren't able to find a solution. However, I couldn't live with myself if I just let my sister die. This wasn't her burden, and she shouldn't have to pay for being close to me.

I kept my mouth shut because I didn't want to confirm what he already knew. He was declaring this to me because he knew my intentions.

"Good. I just want to be clear where I stand on the matter." He climbed to his feet then helped me to mine.

He scanned the room one last time, and pain struck through the bond once more.

I hadn't been sure what we were going to walk into, but the room was clean, and I would've never known there had been a struggle.

Intertwining our hands, he led me out of the chambers and into a long, lantern-lit hallway. We took the next set of wooden double doors that led into another bedchamber. As soon as we entered, I knew that this was his room. To the right, there was a thick wooden bed with frost-blue sheets similar to Tavish's room in the island castle. Navy-blue curtains draped the sides of the bed, and directly across from it sat a square wooden table with a chessboard. The pieces were positioned strategically, indicating he'd been in the middle of a game when the attack happened.

"You played chess even back then?" I didn't know why, but I'd assumed it was something he'd begun when they relocated to the ruined land.

"With Eldrin, a few months before the Seelie attacked." He shook his head as he unfastened his sheath and placed the sword on the navy chair at the side of the bed. "I was so flattered that he finally wanted to get to know me, so I eagerly accepted his invitation. He told me the chessboard had belonged to my grandfather, who'd given it to him, and that he felt the time had come to pass it along to me. He said our grandfather said it was a gift for becoming the spare."

My breath caught because something about that story didn't feel right. Why would Eldrin give the chess set to Tavish when Tavish was the rightful heir? Was it Eldrin's way of hinting what was to come? Questions clamored in my head, and the world seemed to tilt under my feet.

"Sprite, I'm okay." He placed his hands on my shoulders and smiled sadly. "I promise. I can feel all your worry, and I'm fine. We're back on Unseelie land, and you're in my room like I always imagined you'd be when I was a young man. In some ways, this moment is a dream come true, and I have you to thank for that."

A little bit of happiness radiated through our bond, making the decision for me. For now, I wouldn't tell him my worry because it was completely unfounded.

"Now I want to take a bath with my mate so I can get this ashbreath blood off me and forget about the dreadful things that lie before us for a little while." He removed the tunic from his body, revealing his six-pack abs and sculpted chest. I loved the way his muscles bunched with each movement he made and everything but him left my mind.

His wings expanded, emphasizing his substantial size.

I couldn't tear my gaze away from Tavish's captivating form as he stood before me, his eyes filled with a mixture of desire and affection. Tension thickened, the undeniable pull between us growing stronger with each passing moment.

That sounds like an excellent idea. I let out a shaky breath as heat bloomed deep in my stomach.

He smirked while his hands trailed down my arms in a featherlight touch that sent shivers down my spine.

He placed a hand around my waist and led me across the room to the bathroom. When we entered, I gasped at the sight of light-bluish-green walls. They could easily be the color of frozen water, making me feel immediately at home.

Two steps led to the large, ornate bathtub across from us, and the glowing lanterns hanging everywhere gave the room a more welcoming feel than the dim bathroom in Tavish's chamber back at the ruined land. I hadn't realized how differently they'd been forced to live, assuming that with Tavish's affinity for darkness, he'd preferred it.

Removing his arm, he turned the golden lever of the tub and it began filling with water.

He turned to me and removed his pants, allowing me to see his entire naked form. He arched a brow. "I thought we were taking a bath together."

"Yes, but I'm enjoying the view." My legs moved toward him of their own accord, and when I stood before him, he gripped the neckline of my gown.

With a playful smirk, Tavish ripped the fabric and let it fall to the floor. He linked, *Now it's fair. I'm getting to enjoy the same sort of view.*

He reached out, his touch sending a spark of electricity through my body as his fingers traced the curve of my spine. I shivered, need building inside me.

He kissed me, slowly climbing the steps and guiding us into the warm water. My body tingled as we submerged, and both of us relaxed as the realm outside ceased to exist.

Once settled, he held his breath, going underwater. I followed his lead, allowing the water to surround me and clean me of all the filth after traveling and being in the prison.

I stayed under, enjoying my connection to the water until my lungs threatened to burst. When I surfaced, I found Tavish resting against the back of the tub, watching me with eyes dark with desire.

"You're so gorgeous," he murmured and stood, his dick already hard and on full display. "If you're finished, I'd like to make love with you now."

As if that's even a question. I smirked, desperate for him. With the threats pressing in on us, the two of us needed time to reconnect... for our souls to merge.

He lifted me in his arms and carried me back into the bedchamber, then tossed me on the bed, causing me to giggle as he hurried and locked the door. I enjoyed the rare times like this that we had together.

Within seconds, he lay next to me, our bodies already dry, his lips on mine. The buzzing from his touch overwhelmed me, and I opened my mouth eagerly. Our tongues collided as he slipped his hand between my legs.

The urgency picked up between us, and he circled my sensitive spot and slid two fingers inside me.

Wanting to make him feel the same crazed desire, I reached down and stroked his cock.

He groaned, his body shuddering, and ripped his mouth from mine.

"No," I whimpered, but then he lowered his head, using his tongue to caress my nipple.

THE KINGDOM OF FLAMES AND ASH

Between his hands and mouth, my breath hitched, and I quickened the pace of my hand as a wave of pleasure consumed me. I arched my back, moaning when he moved, so I couldn't reach him any longer.

As the ecstasy ebbed, I panted. *Why did you move away?*

Because I'm not ready to finish. He smirked, removing his hand from between my legs. *I want to be inside you.*

I spread my legs, welcoming him in, but instead of positioning himself between them, he trailed kisses from my neck to my ear, his lips gently caressing the lobe. "Do you trust me, sprite?"

"Always," I breathed.

He gripped my hips and tossed me onto my stomach, then lifted my backside into the air. He then positioned himself behind me.

I gasped as the tip of him pressed against my entrance, and he leaned forward, wrapping his arm around my hips and placing his fingers between my folds once again.

Is this okay? he asked, kissing my wings, causing a painful need like I'd never experienced before thrumming inside me.

More than okay. I pushed back, needing more of him inside me.

He chuckled softly, the sound vibrating against my skin, and began to enter me. He moved slowly, methodically, and when I thought he was completely in, he continued to fill me.

When he was seated to the hilt, his fingers circled quicker, and with a groan, he began thrusting in and out of me.

My eyes fluttered shut as the intensity of the moment overwhelmed me. His hips rocked into me in a perfect rhythm, driving us both closer to the edge.

I moved with him, sensations like never before crashing over me. His mouth continued to caress my wings, and his fingers pressed a little harder, causing friction to build even

188

stronger than before. When his wings extended behind me, gently brushing against my skin, I was damn near imploding.

"You're mine. No one else's. Forever," he grated, and with one last thrust, he released within me, his wings surrounding us both as we tumbled over the edge together.

An orgasm engulfed me, and our bond connected, so we were feeling each other's pleasure. Something so powerful and indescribable that my legs gave out and I fell flat on the bed once again.

Tavish dropped to his side and scooped me into his arms, cradling me against his chest.

You're so blasting perfect, and I love you so much, he linked, kissing my bare shoulder. *And I refuse to let anything ever happen to you.*

I wanted to tell him that it wasn't his choice, but I didn't have the energy. Between exhaustion, being completely satiated, and knowing I was safe in his arms, my eyelids grew heavy. And before I even realized what had happened, I fell fast asleep.

A loud huff followed by bad breath hitting my nose caused my eyes to open to find Nightbane standing at the edge of the bed. His eyes glowed a light lime color, suggesting he wasn't completely happy.

I shook my head, trying to get my bearings, and then I remembered why things looked so different.

We were in the real Cuil Dorcha, in Tavish's childhood bedroom. I patted the spot on the bed where Nightbane normally lay, not wanting to move out of Tavish's embrace, but the beast huffed even louder.

I glanced down and realized I was completely naked. "Is it because I'm naked that you don't want to come up?"

He gave a sharp nod, confirming what I'd always thought.

THE KINGDOM OF FLAMES AND ASH

He understood me.

"Well, okay." I chuckled, moving slowly and trying not to wake Tavish.

When my feet touched the cold floor, I sucked in a breath. Shit. Tavish had ruined my gown, which meant I didn't have anything to wear.

I'd just have to wear one of Tavish's tunics until I could find something else. It would be sort of like a dress on me.

I went across the room to the walk-in closet and found an emerald-green tunic I'd never seen him wear before.

I'd just slipped it over my head and entered the room again when there was a frantic knock on the door.

"Tavish," Finnian yelled. "I've got a key, and I'm coming in."

"What?" Tavish blinked and shifted when there was a click of the lock.

My pulse raced. "Don't open—" But before I could finish, the door opened, and Finnian rushed inside.

Tavish sat up, completely naked, and his eyes widened as he took in that I was across the room and Nightbane was standing at the edge of the bed.

"Get *out*," he shouted.

Finnian froze. His head tilted back, and then he belted out laughter. "Now *this* is a surprise. Nightbane watching and without Lira. What would she—" He followed Tavish's gaze and saw me standing in front of the closet.

Even though I had my bits covered, the tunic hit midway down my thighs.

Finnian scratched his head. "Okay, with Nightbane *and* Lira watching. I don't understand."

Face flushed, Tavish rolled from the bed and landed on his feet. His nostrils flared. "Get the blast out of here before I kill you."

190

"I mean, that's not going to end the entire list of questions I have." Finnian smirked, rocking back on his heels. "In fact, it might give me even more. Like, what else are you trying to hide here?"

When Tavish's rage slammed through the bond, I had to do something. I hurried toward Finnian, which caused Tavish to snatch his sword from the floor and aim it at Finnian's neck. "Get out of here, or I will kill you. Lira isn't fully dressed. Be glad she's covered, or you would already be dead."

"Whoa." Finnian lifted both hands. "No need to be harsh here." He smirked like he truly had a death wish.

Wings flapped, and before I could reach the door, Caelan dashed in. "Finnian, what's taking—" His words died, taking in the situation, now even worse, with a naked Tavish holding a sword at Finnian's throat.

"Get out of here and shut the blighted door," Tavish yelled.

Caelan clutched Finnian's arm, dragging him back into the hallway. Tavish slammed the door. I hurried over to him, needing to calm him. I wouldn't be surprised if he got dressed and tried to finish killing Finnian.

"Tavish, Finnian was supposed to come get you. We have a problem," Caelan called from the other side of the door. "One that requires both of you immediately."

My heart sank. *No. Not something else. Not again.*

Chapter Twenty

Lira

Tavish's jaw clenched, and I could feel the frustration coming through. "Is it the dragons?"

"No," Caelan responded.

"Then it can wait." Tavish resheathed his sword. "It's early, and I need more time with Lira before the day officially begins." His gaze landed on me, and he linked, *You look blasting sexy wearing my shirt. I think when we do sleep with clothes on, you should wear this and not a nightgown.*

Need knotted in my stomach, and I closed the distance between us.

"It can't, Tav," Finnian answered. "We just learned how the dragons knew that we would be here."

My feet stilled, and the floor seemed to tilt underneath me. "What do you mean?"

"At least I have Lira's attention," Finnian grumbled. "Tavish has been a slave to her—"

"Are you wanting death?" Tavish bit, his head jerking to the door. "Because if you finish that statement, even our friendship won't save you. You won't disrespect Lira that way."

Something akin to a smack sounded from the other side of the door, followed by Caelan gritting out, "If he doesn't kill you, I will. Now isn't the time for your mouth to run rampant. Be quiet." His voice then grew louder. "We found someone trying to sneak into Aetherglen on the Cuil Dorcha side. We thought the two of you would want to interrogate him before we put him into prison."

I could read between the lines. They meant before they put him in the same place as Eldrin, who this person must be loyal to.

Must everything disturb our time alone together? Tavish rubbed his forehead and rolled his shoulders. "Finnian, be useful and go find Lira a gown to wear from Mother's closet. Hurry, and when you return, knock on the door, and *I'll* open it wide enough to retrieve it."

If we hadn't learned that a traitor had returned to our land, I would've found this moment comical, but not right now. We needed to know what this person told Pyralis and everything else that he knew before Eldrin could fill his mind with more propaganda or have him killed.

Tavish flew past me toward the closet, and I took the time to appreciate his naked form. My feet shuffled to get into position to watch him longer, but Nightbane cut in front of me, huffing. The cù-sìth lowered his head as if he were pouting.

Realizing that I hadn't given him as much attention as normal, I scratched behind his ears and kissed his forehead. He whimpered, leaning into me, and I wrapped my arms around his neck just as Tavish rejoined us.

He wore his typical black tunic and pants, giving me comfort that some things hadn't changed.

He smiled tenderly. *I'm glad that the beast is loyal to you. Many fae are petrified of cù-sìth because some believe they're an omen of death.*

"There's not a malicious bone in his body," I cooed, giving him another good scratch just as a knock sounded.

Tavish barreled to the door and cracked it open. He reached through the small gap, snagged the gown, then slammed the door.

"Ouch," Finnian whined. "That was my nose you hit."

"Then you were way too close."

Pressing my lips together to fight a grin, I removed the tunic and took the silver gown. Just like all the other ones I'd borrowed, the dress hugged my curves a little too tightly. I hoped my parents would bring me some of my own gowns upon their return later, but for now, this would do.

Once I was sufficiently covered, Tavish opened the door, and the two of us joined Finnian and Caelan in the hallway.

Black blood trickled from one of Finnian's nostrils, but he wiped it away and flew down the hall deeper into the castle. Tavish and I followed, and I tried not to get distracted by the pictures on the wall of Tavish with his parents.

Lanterns glowed every few feet, making it easier to see things here than back in the ruined dragon land. The hallway was long and bright, and soon, we came to a spiral staircase that curved the entire way down to the first floor.

The three of us flew over the railing to where Lorne and Finola stood with Buidhean, who'd informed Tavish of the mushrooms being destroyed.

My mouth dried, and Tavish's anger rose once more. The captive had his wings chained already, and Lorne and Finola flanked him, each gripping an arm.

Tavish growled. "So, you were the one who informed the village of the destruction of our food supply." He glanced at Lorne and then Finola. "How did we not realize he was gone?"

"Various guards reported numbers since we didn't have the time or capacity to count everyone personally." Lorne winced. I noticed his skin was back to its normal complexion, no longer tinged black from dragon fire. "Clearly, that was a mistake, but we were trying to relocate all of our people at one time."

And he and Finnian weren't back to full health, I added,

wanting to ensure that Tavish remembered that we were still down two of our most trusted people. None of this was the fault of our allies.

I landed in front of Lorne, knowing that Tavish needed to be the one who addressed the captive.

"Your Majesty, if we had even suspected—" Finola started.

Tavish lifted a hand as his feet hit the floor. "It's not anyone's fault except this guard, Eldrin, and whoever else is conspiring with them. They will be the ones to take the blame and die." He unsheathed his sword, ready to follow through on his words... or at least give the illusion of that intent.

"Right." The captive's voice deepened with hatred. "I'm going to die because I did what was best for our people. Why should I be punished for doing what needed to be done?"

Shaking his head, Caelan moved closer to Lorne and me and said, "The dragons don't care about our people."

"Who said I went to the dragons?" Buidhean lifted his chin, oozing defiance.

"Fair." Finnian steepled his hands. "Then what was the last mass of land you flew over before this one?"

I grinned, noting how specifically Finnian had worded his question. If this man had gone to the dragons, he wouldn't be able to say the true Cuil Dorcha unless he accounted for that question.

"Cuil Dorcha." The captive smirked, knowing he'd won this round.

"Then did you stray from traveling straight from the former Cuil Dorcha to here?" I straightened my back, wanting him to address me as well as the others. I didn't know why, but it seemed important.

He wrinkled his nose. "I don't have to answer to a blasting Seelie."

In a blur, Tavish had the tip of his blade to the prisoner's throat. "Yes, you do. She is my fated mate and the Unseelie's future queen."

Buidhean threw his head back and laughed, causing both Lorne and Finnian to jerk at the unexpected movement. Still, they tightened their hold, keeping the captive in place.

"What's so humorous?" Tavish rasped, digging the tip of the white blade into the man's throat. Blood trickled down the man's neck and hit the edge of his dark armor. "You don't think that I'll kill you?"

"It's funny that you think you'll continue to rule when Eldrin got us back to our rightful land."

I flinched, but before I could question what he meant by that, he continued, "The sunscorched will never be yours to wed. She's going to be Pyralis's bride, and there's nothing you can do about it. You'll be forced to watch as a prisoner while—"

Tavish rammed the blade through the man's throat, cutting off his words. Buidhean's eyes widened, and Tavish slid the sword in deeper, though he didn't need to. Tavish quivered with unbridled rage as he snarled, "She is *mine*. No one else's. I'll kill anyone who tries to come between us, including the ashbreath."

His emotions swirled through our bond with an intensity I'd never experienced before, making my mind race. Tavish was so close to losing every ounce of his self-control, all because the prisoner had just played on his biggest fear.

We had two days to find an answer before our world fell apart.

I placed a hand on his shoulder, allowing our connection to spring to life. A bit of his craze ebbed, but not nearly enough. Something had to give, and I feared what it might be if we didn't come up with a solution. I loved Tavish, but I couldn't live with myself if I allowed my sister to die on my behalf.

Tavish kept his eyes locked on the captive as the man

died. Finnian and Caelan glanced at each other. Even without a fated-mate bond, the strain on their faces informed me that they realized the same thing I had.

Their king, my mate, was completely volatile.

"Tav, I'm quite certain he's dead," Finnian said, leaning in front of Tavish and poking the captive in the chest.

The man didn't grunt, flinch, or move in any way except from the momentum of the jab.

"I wish I could bring him back to life so I could kill the thornling again." Tavish bared his teeth and placed his foot on Buidhean's chest. "Release him," he commanded.

As soon as Lorne and Finola obeyed and stood to the side, Tavish shoved the man off his blade, allowing him to fall in a heap on the floor. His blood covered the blade, but Tavish didn't hesitate to put the sword back into its sheath.

He reminded me of the man he'd been when he'd kidnapped me, but with an even darker edge.

Stepping over the dead man's body, he held out his hand to me and said, "Let's go find something to eat. You must be starving." His eyes lightened as they focused on me, revealing the kindhearted man who still resided there.

Food was the last thing on my mind after what I'd just seen. Still, I nodded, wanting to get both of us away from the body.

"We'll stay here and clean up this mess and meet you after you've had time to calm down." Finnian folded his wings tightly behind him, though he forced a small smile.

"That would be wise." Tavish nodded, intertwining our hands and leading me deeper into the first floor. A gigantic rectangular table sat to our left in a room lit by vine chandeliers glowing with candles. The table was made of the dark wood that grew in the Unseelie land and with sizable chairs made of leaves at each place. The floor-to-ceiling windows behind and to the side of the table were all open air, similar to the dining room in the castle back in Gleann Solas, giving us a view of the village at the foot of the castle.

On the table sat a large bowl full of water, which Tavish headed to and placed both hands in to wash off the blood.

As soon as we sat down, Sine hurried in with lemon bursts, honey, and bread. She placed plates in front of Tavish and me and then returned a few seconds later with glasses of water.

I took a bite of the bread and honey and glanced out the window, noticing the villagers already leaving their houses, working on getting the village put back together once again. The cottages resembled the ones back home but were made with the darker wood and the evergreen bristles of the Unseelie land.

We sat in silence as tension continued to radiate from Tavish, so I reached across, touching his arm. *You killed him. The deed is done. You can calm down now.*

But I can't. His face twisted in agony. *Because we have two days, and we're no closer to freeing you from this blasted vow. I know you're going to demand to go and free your sister, but Lira, I'm not joking when I say I couldn't survive it. Knowing you were with him, married to him, and having—* He closed his eyes, and sharp anguish shot between us.

A vise tightened around my heart, making it hard to breathe. *Thorn, I...* I wasn't sure what to say. I couldn't promise him what he needed because I couldn't lie. *I don't want to turn myself over either, but we can't risk a war while Eiric is their prisoner. I have to hand myself over to save her, but that doesn't mean I'll remain. However, if the vow isn't dissolved, then—*

There was a chance I'd be forced to remain with Pyralis. I couldn't say those words, but I didn't have to. He knew exactly what I meant.

The crazed sensation grew once again, his emotions taking

my breath away when I heard Father ask from the other room, "What blasting happened? Is the dead man out front the captive my guard alerted us about?"

My stomach tightened, making the few bites of bread sit heavier than before.

"It is," Caelan answered simply.

"Why is he dead?" Mother pressed. "He needed to be questioned."

"Well, your royal Seelieness, I assure you he didn't stab himself in the neck. That was done by our fearless king himself," Finnian deadpanned.

After a pause, Mom broke the silence. "Without allowing us to question him ourselves? Did he at least provide valuable information?"

More awkward silence.

Tavish flew from his seat in the direction of the foyer.

Not wanting to be left behind, I followed, and as soon as he entered the room with the others, he said, "He was my responsibility, and I took care of him."

"That is one way of putting it." Finnian rolled his eyes. "But it might have been beneficial to not kill him within the first five minutes."

Tavish's wings expanded. "Are you questioning my judgment?"

I couldn't stand back and let Tavish's fear control him once more.

I pushed around his wings so that the others could see me. "He's dead. Arguing won't bring him back to life. We need to turn our focus forward and not argue over something that can't be changed."

Dad turned toward me, lifting both his hands. "Lira, I understand your point, but have you noticed how many times you've had to say that very thing about him?"

Now rage spiked inside me, boiling my blood. "And about you all, too. Don't forget, you aren't innocent in this either. Maybe you didn't kill Tavish's parents, but *none* of this is Tavish's or my fault. We were children when all this happened, and we're handling each situation the best we can. Casting judgment is easy, but taking responsibility for your own actions takes a strong person, which, right now, none of you seem to be doing *except* Tavish. He isn't blaming someone else for making him kill the traitor, so maybe you all should take a hard look at yourselves!"

All four of them recoiled, and the comforting warmth of love floated through our connection from Tavish. The sense of fury disappeared, and some of the stress left my body.

Chuckling, Caelan bowed his head. "Lira is right. We need to discuss strategy. The four of us have been up all night, trying to devise a plan that will work against Eldrin. We couldn't think of anything. All Eldrin cares about is himself. Hurting someone else won't break him, and if we injure him, he'll enjoy it, knowing we're doing it because we need information."

Father stroked his beard. "Does he have any children? A lover?"

"The only lover he's ever had is himself." Finnian snorted. "I mean, he's fornicated with men and women, but he doesn't care for anyone. He wouldn't blink if you killed them."

"We haven't eaten this morning, and our people delivered food to the castle last night." Mother curtseyed. "Why don't we all move into the dining hall where we can have breakfast and strategize? I'd prefer to get away from the blood on the floor."

I could hug Mother for giving Tavish the respect he deserved as the ruler here, but I didn't want to make her feel more uncomfortable than she already was.

Tavish placed his hand on my shoulder, the buzz springing up between us. "Yes, we can move it in there and continue this conversation."

"Perfect," Father said and patted my shoulder.

Finnian cleared his throat, and when I looked in his direction, he mouthed, *Need to talk to you alone.*

Taking my wrist, Tavish tugged, wanting me to walk beside him to the dining area.

I need to check on Nightbane and run to the bathroom. At that moment, I realized I would have to make a pit stop, so I wasn't lying. *Go on, and I'll join you in a minute.*

Let me know if you need me, he replied, releasing me and leading my parents to the dining hall.

I moved to the stairwell and headed upstairs to follow through on my promise.

Caelan and Finnian followed me, and I flew into our bedchamber to lower the risk of being overheard. I opened the door to find Nightbane lying on the bed, snoring, and turned to face Tavish's best friends.

"What's going on? Why do you want to talk to me without Tavish?" I leaned back on my heels and crossed my arms.

"We're worried about him." Finnian bit his bottom lip. "The way he acted this morning at the mention of you and the dragon prince—it's only going to get worse if we don't get answers from Eldrin about how to break that vow."

"You calmed him down, but the closer we get to the deadline, the harder that will be." Caelan rubbed his hands together. "We need to figure out a plan quickly because you're the only thing that grounds him."

No pressure. "And you're concerned about how my parents might react if they knew." The last unhinged Unseelie king had killed himself and his wife.

Fuck.

But then the answer hit me. I knew what to do to get Eldrin to come clean. Something Buidhean had said earlier had given

THE KINGDOM OF FLAMES AND ASH

me the answer.

I surged forward, swiping Finnian's sword, and flew over their heads and out the nearest window.

With determination like nothing I'd ever felt before, I flew to the dungeon and pounded on the door. It cracked open, and Struan tilted his head back. "Lira?"

"Let me in," I commanded, not wanting to be questioned.

He narrowed his eyes and then shrugged, allowing me in. Then I gestured to Eldrin's cell. "I need to go in there."

"Alone?" He looked over my shoulder, obviously expecting Tavish to be with me.

I unfolded my wings and raised the sword. "Do you have a problem with that?"

"Fate, no." He stumbled back a few steps and unlocked the cell. "I just don't want you or Tavish to kill me."

I shoved past him, entering the cell. Eldrin smirked, and I chuckled darkly then lunged right at him.

Chapter Twenty-One

Lira

I didn't hesitate, choosing to stab him in the shoulder. The blade was so sharp I didn't even realize it had gone in until his face twisted in agony.

He hissed between clenched teeth, and my stomach didn't revolt. The act of brutality didn't even cause me to flinch. This bastard deserved every ounce of pain he got.

"I'm not falling for your brave facade." Eldrin's chest heaved. "You aren't strong enough to do anything to me."

Dark laughter caught in my throat, sounding like someone else. A bitter taste filled my mouth, and I fought the urge to spit. I didn't want him to know how much he'd gotten to me.

Refusing to react to his words and grant him any sort of power, I lifted my chin so I could stare down my nose at him. "You're going to tell me everything I want to know."

He laughed. "I'm not." He smirked. "Though I applaud Tavish for considering a different tactic than I expected."

Of course he'd believe Tavish had sent me here. Since I was Seelie, I couldn't think of anything original on my own. I dug the blade in deeper until I felt something stop the point from continuing —I'd hit bone. "Tavish doesn't even know I'm here." I yanked the sword out, making sure that it came out roughly so the skin wouldn't be able to heal easily.

He groaned, his face flushing as his blood poured down

his arm and hit the floor.

"I'm only going to say this one more time. You're going to tell me everything you know, or your future is going to be the one you fear." I had to latch on to the one thing he cared about most. The Unseelie people and the need he had for them to obey his commands.

"I don't fear death. Not that *you* would be able to deliver that fate to me." He straightened his shoulders, trying to appear unaffected, but he winced.

"Death isn't what I have in store for you." I smiled sweetly, though adrenaline made my heart race in anticipation. "I've given it a lot of thought, and you do have one weakness. A weakness I will use because, frankly, I don't give a blast about you."

Sprite, is something the matter? Tavish linked.

Eldrin bared his teeth, though his white eyes widened. "I don't have a weakness. That's why I'll win, either by death and you becoming Pyralis's wife or by guaranteeing my own life and doing as I please. Either way, it's enough for me to have peace."

I'm fine. I hated that I hadn't kept my emotions in check. I should've known Tavish would notice the spike.

Turning my attention back to Eldrin, I said, "I have no intention of killing you." I placed the flat part of the blade on my shoulder, allowing the blood to run down the end and splatter on me. "Nor of giving you immunity. I merely plan to remove *a* wing... or both your wings. It depends on how difficult you want to be."

"You wouldn't." He laughed, though his Adam's apple bobbed as he swallowed.

"That's where you're wrong." Hope kindled in my chest, but I pushed the sensation away. I didn't need to get too excited until I knew this would work. If it didn't, my gut was completely wrong. Eiric would tell me to think things through instead of reacting, but I was already here, and it was too late. "Harming you will be retribution for what you've done to Tavish and to me. I've noticed you hold your sword in your right hand, so I'm thinking the left wing should be first. That way, if I only get to slice off one before you sing, it'll be the one that will most hinder your fighting."

His expression shifted into one of indifference, but his neck corded.

Where are you? Tavish asked. *I just left to check on you in our bedchambers, and Finnian said you aren't there.*

Blighted abyss. Finnian had a big mouth. If I didn't tell Tavish where I was, he'd fly off the deep end. Worse, I wasn't sure if I meant that literally or figuratively. It could be both. *I'm with Eldrin.*

Knowing I was making Eldrin nervous, I took another moment, ignoring my racing pulse, and tapped my free hand's index finger against my chin. "I wonder how the Unseelie would feel about you then? Do you think they would want to follow someone who had their wing removed by a Seelie?"

Eye twitching, Eldrin laughed. "So what if you kill me?"

I threw my head back and laughed, not even needing to pretend near insanity. The pure hatred I felt for this man caused my hand to itch to kill him. But that was a tolerable fate to him, which meant I couldn't. "That's the thing, *Eldrin.* I plan on removing your wings and then letting you go. Yes, I might be forced to marry Pyralis." Those words caused a deep ache to pierce my heart. "But you'll have to live among *your people* unable to fly. I'm thinking that sort of fate for you would be the same as mine if I can't remain with Tavish." Which was sad. I'd give up one wing or both if it meant I could remain at Tavish's side. The only reason I wasn't willing to break the vow my parents had forced upon me was because of the consequences—the Seelie would lose their magic. That would

THE KINGDOM OF FLAMES AND ASH

make the fae magic unstable, which would hurt Tavish.

He shook his head hard. "You wouldn't—"

Time was precious, and I didn't want to be near him more than required. With no other choice, I pivoted the sword, placed it at the top of his wing, and pressed down, increasing the pressure inch by inch. I wanted the removal of his wing to be slow and agonizing.

Jerking, he tried to retreat, but all that did was allow the blade to slide a little bit deeper.

Blood flowed like water, the dark color barely noticeable against his black wings. I was about halfway through the base muscle that connected his left wing to his back.

"Stop!" Eldrin's bottom lip quivered. "I'll tell you something. Just stop."

Against my better judgment, I lifted the sword, admiring how the wing hung haphazardly from the top of his back. "Yes?"

His face was strained as his eyes glistened with unshed tears. "If I tell you this, I risk my own safety. What guarantees—"

Not amused, I lifted the sword and moved so that it was back in place. "You get no assurances of anything other than not losing your wing. I won't stop—"

"All right," he shouted. "I'll tell you how you can get out of the deal with the dragon prince."

My heart lurched, but I tried to keep my emotions steady. However, I heard the sound of the basement doors slamming open and the sound of wings flying inside.

No doubt Tavish and the others.

Static electricity hit my back, indicating that Tavish now stood behind me.

Eldrin's head tilted back as a tear tracked down his face.

"What's going on here?" Dad asked in a voice an octave higher than normal.

I didn't have to turn around to know that his mouth was

206

hanging open. I'd never had a malicious bone in my body. He'd never witnessed me being forced to fight.

"We're about to learn how I can get out of the vow with Pyralis." I tilted my head, keeping the sword ready to slice Eldrin's wing once again.

You're blasting sexy like this, Tavish linked, his arousal floating through the bond and into me.

We can handle that when I'm done here. Besides, we'll need to celebrate if he actually tells us something. I tried pushing away the heat flooding me. I couldn't deal with a distraction when we were so close to answers.

Eldrin closed his eyes, and I moved to finish what I'd started.

"Time's up." I slid the sword back into the section.

He inhaled deeply and said quickly, "The dragons set everything up."

I froze. That didn't make sense. "What do you mean?"

Eldrin lifted a shaky hand. "Remove the sword, and I'll tell you."

"I won't stop next time." I lifted a brow. "Do you understand?"

"Yes." He winced as his eyes narrowed.

If I'd thought he hated me before, I'd been so wrong. One side of the face of the man standing before me now curved with ultimate disgust.

Still, I removed the sword, eagerly awaiting answers.

"Out with it," Father commanded behind me, making me want to roll my eyes.

"The dragons want Lira to be Pyralis's wife, so they found a way to make it happen." Eldrin glanced at the dirty floor puddled with his blood. "If it weren't for them, my uncle never would've gone mad and tried to blanket the realm in darkness."

Anger flashed through the bond from Tavish.

THE KINGDOM OF FLAMES AND ASH

I still struggled to make sense of what he'd said. "This all happened because of *me*?"

"I'm sure there are a ton of dragons who would be suitable as Pyralis's mate." Mother scoffed. "He has to have his story mixed up."

My hand tightened on the sword hilt, and Eldrin lifted both hands, unable to hold his right hand as high as the left, thanks to where I'd cut his shoulder. "Yes, the prince has a ton of options, but why marry another dragon when he can breed with a fae that controls water?"

"But why does that—" Finnian started, but Caelan cut him off.

"Because any children they have together could be immune to the effects of water. It would be a breed of dragons, *royal* at that, who would have no weaknesses."

Bile inched up my throat, and I removed the blade from Eldrin's back. The thought of having children with Pyralis had been horrible enough, but understanding the reasoning— "They want to control the realm, which could be possible if—" I stopped, unable to finish the sentence.

"They've been behind all of this. Manipulating us into a vow to cause the very fate we joined forces with them to prevent? Ardanos isn't meant to be led by one species. That would cause an imbalance of power," Father growled so deeply the ground quaked as his earth magic bled out.

"Wait." Mom cleared her throat. "How did they manage to get the Unseelie king to cloak the realm in darkness and kill himself?"

Eldrin shook his head. "I've told you that the dragons tricked you, which voids the agreement. In our realm, no agreement withstands if there is knowledge of manipulation. The rest—"

"You will tell us *now*," Tavish commanded, stepping beside

me with his sword in his hand and swinging his blade so it slid right where I'd already begun severing the muscle. He went an inch deeper, blood rushing even faster.

"They gave me a sword to give him." Eldrin's voice cracked. He leaned back toward his wing as if that would reattach it. "A sword made of dragon materials, and I glamoured it with Unseelie magic so he couldn't feel the dragon's power coming off it." His gaze landed on Tavish's sword.

"The sword Tavish has now?" I needed to hear him say the words.

He paused and exhaled. "Yes. Since it holds dragon magic, it amplifies their magic when we're at our strongest on Unseelie land."

Tavish took a step back. "Is that why Father began acting strange?"

"The dragon king said it would make him unstable and he wouldn't be fit to lead." Sweat beaded Eldrin's brow. "I didn't know it would drive him to kill the queen and himself."

Even though I was certain Father had stopped shaking the ground, it still seemed to move under my feet. "Was that the compensation you received? You made the king unable to lead his people so you could take over?"

"Yes! I should've been king, but my father passed before the power transfer, which made King Dunach the next to inherit the crown." He smacked his chest, his irises darkening. "If Father had just remained alive for ten more years, the crown would've been mine. Now it's Tavish's when I should be the one in power and taking care of our people."

"You thornling. Father brought you into our castle and treated you like one of his sons. He protected you, clothed you, and trained you. Everything you wanted or desired, he provided," Tavish snarled, cutting through the rest of Eldrin's left wing.

THE KINGDOM OF FLAMES AND ASH

The dark wing dropped, and Eldrin screamed. Blood spurted from the muscle, hitting the wall behind him and coating the floor. Through his cries, he shouted, "I should've been the one to care for him. It wasn't supposed to be that way!"

Tavish's rage blazed through him, and he lifted the sword to cut off the other wing. However, I caught his arm. There was still one question I needed answered, and slicing off the other wing would prevent him from telling us anything else.

He turned his stormy irises on me, and I linked, *Give me one second.*

Not waiting for the answer, I looked at Eldrin once again. The agony on his face didn't stir my empathy. If he died, I wouldn't shed a tear. "If the sword caused King Dunach to kill himself, why did you give it to Tavish? That makes no sense. If Tavish dies, the magic will go with him."

"I watched him closely to ensure he didn't show the same signs as his father." Eldrin's body shook. "Tavish never showed signs of losing his mind the same way. In fact, the sword seemed to help him become the type of leader we needed. That is until you came along."

And that was the last bit of information I needed. Instead of allowing Tavish to take the life of his kin, something that I knew for certain would haunt him eventually, I lunged forward and stabbed Eldrin in the heart.

His eyes widened. "But you said—"

"I never vowed immunity. And I want you to die knowing that I won't be Pyralis's and that Tavish and I will rule together with me as queen by his side." I stared him in the eye, wanting to be the last thing he ever saw. A ruthlessness I never knew I had surged inside me.

You are so sexy, Tavish connected, looping his arm around me. We both watched Eldrin take his last breath.

The moment seemed to stretch, but the life drained from

Eldrin's eyes. When his heart stopped, I didn't even bother to remove the sword. Instead, I released my hold, allowing Eldrin to fall forward, the hilt splashing into his blood on the floor. He then dropped to one side, his tunic soaked in it.

When Tavish and I turned to exit, I found Finnian, Caelan, Lorne, and both sets of my parents staring.

Tavish took my hand and led me out the door.

"It appears our little Seelie princess has become more entertaining." Finnian beamed. "Something I didn't think was possible."

Even though Eldrin's death didn't bother me, I hadn't relished it. "I merely did what was necessary. He couldn't be trusted, and I refused to allow him to breathe when he had every intention of harming Tavish and myself."

"You did the right thing, Lira." Father smiled proudly. "Considering how human you've been acting, I just didn't expect that."

"My upbringing on Earth will always have an impact on me, but I *am* fae." Even as I spoke the words, I realized how much I'd changed in the last month. Still, I wouldn't have done anything differently in the gauntlet because the prisoners had been doing what was expected of them. Eldrin had wanted to hurt the person I loved most. "No one attacks my mate. Everyone should be aware of that."

"Sprout, we all came to that realization when you escaped with two of our prisoners." Father pressed his lips together, but the anger that would've been in his tone was missing. "And hearing that the dragons were behind the realm being cloaked in darkness proves that I should've listened to you from the start."

With those words alone, all the reservations I had about my biological parents disappeared. They also had to protect our people, but they truly did care for me. Those two things would

THE KINGDOM OF FLAMES AND ASH

be in conflict at times, but that was something I understood now, being fated mates with Tavish. "We're here now with each other, which means we need to determine a way out of this mess together."

"What do you propose?" Finnian scowled. "Pyralis has Eiric. He's not going to allow her to leave just because we know the truth. If they're that desperate for Lira to be his wife, then he'll still insist on the exchange."

He was right. That would still be their plan, but at least I wasn't obligated now that we knew the secret.

"Well, Lira doesn't have to hand herself over." Tavish placed his arm around my waist. "The Seelie won't lose their magic now."

"But Eiric will lose her life." Mom's voice cracked.

I was more concerned about Tavish's words. I couldn't tolerate Eiric's death, so I had to change their mind. And I knew of something that might help with that.

I spun around, ready to do what had to be done.

CHAPTER TWENTY-TWO

TAVISH

The feral glint in Lira's eye startled me despite the determination that powered through our connection. Her hand darted to my side and removed my sword from its sheath. She jerked it behind her and arched a brow. "I'm taking this."

My brows furrowed, and I shrugged. "Anything of mine is yours. You know this."

"No. I mean permanently." She lifted the sword, the weapon too large for her small stature. She shook a little as she held it. "I can sense the magic now, but it's so faint I never would've noticed if I hadn't been searching for it. It has the chill of frost and darkness magic."

"This is my father's sword... the last thing he wielded." Then my bones grew heavy, and my head jerked toward Hestia. I grated, "Is that the weapon Father used to kill Mother and himself?" Each word hurt my throat worse than the last.

Hestia nodded. The walls seemed to close in on me.

The stench of Eldrin's blood added to the nausea that settled hard in my stomach. For the last twelve years, I'd been carrying that dragon-born sword around like a prize. And even now, the thought of replacing the weapon with another sword had anger bubbling inside me.

"Which is an even better reason for you not to carry it any longer." Lira's expression softened. "If this will drive you mad—

THE KINGDOM OF FLAMES AND ASH

" She cut off the rest.

Her concern swirled through my chest, helping ease the ache and the irrational anger. If taking the sword away would keep her safe, I'd give it up. Nothing was more important to me than Lira... not even my people. "I understand and agree, but can I hold it one last time? After learning that it contains dragon magic, I need to sense it at least once more."

Her eyes darkened, searching deep within me for something. After a second, she nodded and handed it back to me.

"It's very faint, so I'm not quite sure how it holds the dragon magic." She bit her bottom lip, watching me.

The sword somehow felt different in my hand. More like a threat, and the solace of it being my father's sword didn't comfort me anymore. It felt heavier than before, but the weight hadn't increased. It was the burden it now represented.

Concentrating on the hilt, I searched for any hint of magic to confirm Eldrin's words. With the weapon once again on me, I wanted to bring Eldrin back to life so I could kill the wildling myself. The bloodthirsty desire slammed into me and stole my breath.

If the sword caused such intense feelings, no wonder Hestia hadn't wanted to relinquish it to me.

I inhaled, pushing the urge away, and focused on the magic pulsing from the weapon.

At first, all I could feel was the strong essence of Unseelie magic. The frigidness of the frost, the chill of the shadows, and the sluggish feeling of the illusion magic that permeated our land. The magic twined around me, taking my focus away, until I homed in on a faint magical pulse full of volatility... like the volcano of the ruined island.

"How is that possible?" I whispered, narrowing my eyes. None of the porous rocks we'd found on the former dragon

214

land felt anything like this hilt.

Lira tilted her head, examining the stone. "I never paid attention until now since I assumed the sword was made of Unseelie materials, but this looks like the obsidian rock back on Earth. It's made by rapidly cooling lava, which would be a water source. The quick cooling has to be what kept residual dragon magic within the rock, allowing it to be used as such a weapon. Think about the lava rocks and how they killed the mushrooms in the cave. The rocks were formed by the dragon's magic."

"How in Ardanos do you know this?" The queen's eyes widened. "We don't have any volcanoes in our land."

Brenin smiled. "On Earth, Lira was in her senior year at college, majoring in geology. She knows more about Earth rocks than any normal person does."

"As I mentioned before, many humans believe that rocks and gemstones can hold different energies... things that we would call magic here. It's not nearly on the same scale on Earth as here, but this is further proof that humans aren't as daft as some fae would like to believe. Anyway, the idea has merit here. The obsidian is made from lava... the very thing that would ruin the land, like where the Unseelie were living. And if lava is a product of their power source, then it makes sense that their dragon flames are so potent." Lira's attention landed back on me. "There's no telling what this has been doing to you. We need to destroy it."

Anger rippled through me once again, but I gritted my teeth. The emotion didn't make sense, especially since I didn't want to carry this weapon anymore. "I agree. And the extra boost of power was how Father managed to cloak the realm in darkness. Now that feat makes more sense. His power couldn't have been strengthened that much by fae magic."

"Maybe we shouldn't be so rash." Caelan lifted a hand. "If this sword contains dragon magic, then it might be helpful for

THE KINGDOM OF FLAMES AND ASH

when we attack the dragons to retrieve Eiric."

The thought of getting close to the dragons, knowing how desperate they were to get Lira to breed with Pyralis, made me clench my free hand. My chest thudded. "But then we'd risk Lira."

Lira lifted her chin, the skin around her eyes tightening. "I love you, but I need to be clear. I refuse to allow my sister to die. She put herself in that situation to *protect* me, and I won't be able to live with myself if I allow her to die."

I gritted my teeth, trying to contain the crazed emotions taking over. "The thought of you in danger doesn't sit well with me. I can't risk you. You're too important."

"So is Eiric." She gestured to her father and mother. "She's important to *me*, and I refuse to allow her to die because she loves me."

Lira's parents cringed and glanced at each other, and Hestia and Brenin's expressions became strained.

My shoulders relaxed. The Seelie royals agreed with me.

"Sprout, Eiric is important to all of us, but—" the king started.

"With no disrespect," Finnian interrupted, bowing slightly with a wink at my mate.

The eye he left open would be the one I'd remove in a moment. I could leave it behind with Eldrin's body so the guards could clean it up with my cousin's remains.

"Not going to retrieve Eiric won't accomplish what we desire." Finnian steepled his hands in a grand gesture. "If the dragons are that desperate for Lira, then they'll come straight here to fight us as soon as they realize that Lira won't be handing herself over."

In my haze to protect her, I hadn't thought beyond the deadline. Unfortunately, Finnian was right, so maybe I wouldn't remove the eye completely. Just damage it enough that he'd spend the rest of his life with some sort of patch.

Lira placed a hand on my shoulder, and the jolt of our connection eased more of my discomfort. "And we'd be fighting on Seelie and Unseelie lands, which they won't hesitate to destroy. It's best to take our fight to them, especially if we can catch them off guard."

I didn't like the sound of that.

At all.

If I didn't settle my emotions, I feared my wings would get in a bind and make Lira more resolute. As much as I loved how she thought for herself, at times like this, I wished she'd be more pliable to my way of thinking.

We could still have a betrayer among us, and I refused to risk Lira more than necessary. "Why don't we head inside the castle to discuss this instead of talking in the prison cell?"

"Agreed." King Erdan took a few steps back, giving us an opening. "It's best if we discuss things in private, away from prying ears. Not taking a stance may be something we should consider." He scanned the room coyly, indicating that we should join his ruse.

My wings tensed. I'd assumed Eldrin had been the only one discussing such things with the dragons, but we didn't know who was loyal to Eldrin and might want to take his place. They'd want to prove their worth to the dragons. "Clearly, that's what I would prefer to do. And if all the royals are for it, then we should set up precautions if we allow the dragons to even come into our land. I agree; let's take this conversation elsewhere."

Lira's nostrils flared, but she nodded. *I'm remaining quiet but not out of agreement. I just don't want anyone who shouldn't to overhear my ideas and plans.*

I closed my eyes. *Sprite, you've made your stance clear. This is all a performance in case there's still a traitor among us.*

"I'll head out first to ensure nothing has been set in motion

THE KINGDOM OF FLAMES AND ASH

by Eldrin's death." Brenin flew out with King Erdan and Queen Sylphia strolling after him, giving him time to scout the area.

Lira reached across my body, placing her hand right above mine on the sword's hilt. Her voice popped into my head. *I worry about you carrying it on you at all times after learning what it did to your father. However, we need to put the sword away in case we do need it.* She didn't yank at the sword; she was merely making the request.

Hestia placed her hand on her own weapon, watching the exchange. She was another who'd gained my favor for the way she protected and loved Lira.

The fact that Lira gave me a choice made removing my hand and allowing her to carry the sword easier.

Our bond expanded, indicating that she'd been worried, and I hated that I'd put her through undue stress. I'd caused her enough grief.

Dropping her hand from the weapon, Hestia rolled her shoulders while Lira held the sword at her side, blasting stunning with Eldrin's blood spattered across his gown, her face flushed still from the adrenaline that coursed through her, and with the sword at her hip. She was the epitome of royal, swordsfae, and perfection. Add in the way she loved those close to her, the concern she had for others, her fierce personality, and she had to be the most perfect being in Ardanos.

Some of the anger receded, and I took her hand and led her back outside. I commanded, "Lorne, get someone to clean all this up and relieve you down here. Now that Eldrin is eliminated, I'm not as worried about someone doing something foolish." I needed to pretend we didn't have anything else to worry about. I hoped that we didn't, but with everything that had transpired, there was no way to be certain.

When we stepped back outside, the sun shone faintly through the dark clouds I allowed to hover. The Unseelie preferred darkness, but now that we had returned home, some light helped aid nature with growth and, most importantly, Lira needed it. Seelie fae weren't made to be without the light.

Flying back toward the front of the castle to enter through the window, I looked at Lira and asked, *A geologist? You went somewhere to learn about that?*

She smiled sadly, causing my breath to catch and our bond to constrict slightly. *On Earth, children attend school to learn, and once they master the basics, some continue their education in a subject that interests them. Water and earth always spoke to me in a way that didn't make sense to humans. It made me want to learn more about the planet so I could understand why the elements brought me such peace. It wasn't until I returned here and remembered my heritage and my royal blood that I finally knew why.*

I couldn't imagine what it was like growing up as a human with no recollection of fae life. It must have been confusing, something I hadn't considered... until she had an explanation as to how the rocks made of dragon lava could hamper the land even after they left. Though the explosive lava rocks didn't contain dragon magic but rather the poison that affected the land.

Soon, the eight of us returned to the dining area, where our food remained as it had been when we'd rushed out, fearing Lira was in danger. Lira placed the sword against the wall in the corner of the room while the Seelie king took the seat across from me once more, the queen next to him and across from Lira.

"Despite what was said in the prison, I'm assuming we're retrieving Eiric from the ashbreath?" Finnian asked, sitting next to Lira.

I hated to consider going to war, but I'd do anything to ensure the dragons never touched Lira again. "You're right.

They would come here to fight for Lira, which is unacceptable. However, we have to plan this perfectly."

"If they come here, they'll want to make us weak, which would require destroying our land as much as possible." The king took a bite of his bread and honey. "We need to take the fight to them."

"Your Majesty, I do like the thought of the fight not happening on our land." Hestia stood at the end of the table, pacing in front of the window. "But we know *nothing* about the land there or how they're organized."

Lira leaned into my side and said, "And won't their magic be strongest on their own land?"

"The dragons' magic is internal and manifests through their flames, which affect the air and ground around them, making it harsh and barren and creating the lava that produces the volcanoes where it spills out." The queen took a sip of water. "That's why they're able to move locations—their magic travels with them, unlike ours, which flows through the land we live on."

Another reason that dragons were so untrustworthy. Their magic killed nature, the very thing the fae respected and clung to. The image of the ruined land and the suffering that my people had to endure crashed over me once more. Living like that had been horrific.

"Didn't the fae visit the island the dragons relocated to and document the area?" Caelan propped himself on the seat of one of the windows, stretching out his leg. "Shouldn't the information be in the Seelie library somewhere?"

Sighing, Brenin stretched out his wings. "Yes, the four of us stayed up late, researching dragons, and we had details about the island, but they've lived there for over fifty years now, and it will have already started to react to their magic."

"And we have no idea how the dragons populated the

place. Where they placed their castle, where their villages are, nothing," Hestia added.

The more we discussed, the more I realized we were still at a major disadvantage. Yes, we'd learned the dragons had manipulated us into the contract, which made it void, but that didn't extinguish the real threat. The dragons wanted Lira, and they'd do whatever it took to take her from me. The idea of losing her had my mind racing and desperation sinking its claws into my chest.

Lira fidgeted. "Didn't you get any information when you promised my hand to the dragon prince? Shouldn't you at least have answers to some of those questions?"

King Erdan hung his head. "Our land was dying, and we thought we had a common enemy that needed to be contained fast. The dragons pushed for the agreement before they'd aid us, so no. We didn't obtain any information or even think to ask many questions at the time. We believed we'd learn it when the time came."

She laughed bitterly. "Well, that's worked out well for us, hasn't it?"

I placed my hand on her thigh, trying to provide comfort. "We'll do the best that we can."

"We can do better than that." Lira lifted her chin in defiance, her one tell when she knew whatever she said was going to upset someone. "I'll hand myself over, see the dragon land, and relay all that information to Tavish. Eiric will be safe, and you'll know exactly where I am."

My vision turned black, and I jumped to my feet, spreading out my wings behind me. "The blast you will!"

Chapter Twenty-Three

Lira

Eyes, the color of storm clouds, locked with mine while Tavish's determination and fear pounded into me like a tidal wave.

Even though I understood that his first priority was to keep me safe, that didn't mean I would bend to his will. Eiric had protected me her entire life, even when we didn't remember our fae blood, and I wouldn't abandon her now. My hand chopped the air between us. "It's the only plan that makes sense, Tavish, and you *know* it. It will free Eiric, and she'll inform you of everything she knows while I try to fill in the rest of the details." I feared she wouldn't be able to tell us much, given she'd been a prisoner the entire time, but I kept that to myself.

"Do you even hear what you're saying?" He slammed a hand on the table, and bits of frost crept from his fingertips onto the wood while edges of darkness surrounded his arms. "You want us to hand you over to *spend the night with him*?"

"I'm in agreement with Tavish." Father shook his head like he couldn't believe what he'd said. "You handing yourself over is too risky. If they were to find a way to keep you, knowing that breeding with you—"

"First off, if I did stay overnight, it wouldn't be *with* him." I rolled my eyes. Even though Tavish didn't like my plan, he didn't have to be so dramatic. Worse, he was getting Father riled up. I had to de-escalate the situation. "So there would be no chance of *breeding*. I'd demand my own room."

"How would that have gone if you'd done that when you were held prisoner by me? And dragons are ruthless. Who said you have to be willing?" Tavish's jaw clenched, and a dangerous glint reflected in his irises.

All that accomplished was me straightening my back and refusing to back down. Yes, there were risks to my plan, but the biggest positive was that Eiric would be handed over safely.

"In truth, you never treated Lira like a true prisoner. She's spent less time in prison than I have." Finnian leaned forward, placing his elbows on the table. "In fact, I've come closer to death at your hand more often than she ever did."

Tavish looked at Finnian and snarled, "Much like at this moment."

"Everyone is flying with their wings clipped right now." Caelan turned so his back was to the open window with both of his feet firmly on the floor. "Both Tavish and Lira have valid points, but I suspect there's a way to utilize both ideas."

"What do you suggest?" Mother ran a finger along the top of her glass.

"If Tavish is up for the challenge and at all full strength, a group of us go to Tìr na Dràgon and he cloaks us in darkness so no one can see us. If we leave now, we'll arrive there an hour or so before the sun goes down. Tavish can cover the sun so none of the group will be noticed, and we'd have time to scout the area. Lira wouldn't be forced to stay overnight but could safely make the exchange to free Eiric."

Even though I didn't like the idea of Tavish being involved, I understood his staying behind wasn't an option, especially if I planned on handing myself over.

"That still means Lira hands herself over." Tavish crossed his arms. "I'm not willing to risk it."

I stood, shoving my seat back and pivoting in his direction. Frustration and annoyance burned in my chest. "You don't get to make that decision, Tavish. I'm going because my not being part of the plan is as asinine as you being left out of it. You can hide people, and I can use my water magic, which is their weakness. Not only that, but I can get Eiric out of there. I have to because the dragons won't hesitate to kill her when they realize I have no intention of remaining or marrying Pyralis. I've proven that I can handle any battle thrown my way, and I find it insulting that you make it seem as if I'm not capable of protecting myself."

"I understand I'm not a royal, but Hestia and I have known Lira longer than anyone else here." Dad stood at the end of the table between Tavish and Father and continued, "And Lira is more than capable of handling herself. She's trained her entire life. Believe me, I wouldn't risk her if I had any doubt. She's like a daughter to me, and I couldn't handle losing both of my children, especially not to ashbreaths."

His pride warmed my chest until I noticed the way Mom frowned... like she didn't agree with him.

"There's no question that Lira can handle herself." Tavish's expression softened, and he touched my arm.

If it hadn't been for the comforting buzz of his touch and the love and concern weaving through our bond, I would've pulled away. Instead, I found myself craving the support I needed from him.

"She's proven it over and over, much to my chagrin." He moved closer to me, our entire arms now touching, and continued, "I just don't want her to have to do that anymore. I want to protect her from anything that risks her well-being, whether emotionally or physically."

Then you need to let me go because not going will cause problems between us, and I have to be there for my sister. Imagine if it were Caelan or Finnian. He needed to put himself in my place and imagine if one of the two people who had truly become family in the last twelve years had been taken. *Would you be willing to stay behind while I went off in search of them?*

Fair, but would you be as keen for me to go with you if another woman was determined that I marry and impregnate her? He arched a brow. *Would you be thrilled at the prospect of me flying into her during the exchange?*

The mere suggestion of it had me wanting to stab their eyes out. I'd kill someone for even hinting at that. I hadn't realized that I'd dug my nails into my palms until he smirked. *See. You're enraged, and it's merely an idea that isn't true, unlike the ashbreath adamant that you are his.*

Father cleared his throat, pulling our attention from each other to him. He said, "I still struggle with putting our only heir in harm's way, especially after only recently getting her back."

We were wasting energy and time arguing. If I wanted all of them to consider my involvement, I couldn't continue to get upset. I needed to list my reasons and stop being reactive and impulsive. All it was doing was making the situation spiral. We needed to move on. "Just listen, please. And if you still don't agree, I promise to give you the same respect until we find a way to settle the matter." At the end of the day, I wasn't the Seelie leader, nor had Tavish and I gotten married. Technically, the three of them would make the decision—not that I would obey. Still, it would be easier if we could all get on the same page.

"I'm in agreement." Mother nodded, leaning forward in her chair.

I cut my gaze to Tavish.

He sighed. "I don't truly have much choice in the matter, so I agree."

"Smart man," Finnian coughed.

Tavish sneered. "Why are you still alive? Times like these,

I struggle to remember."

"Because *you* need me. I do what Caelan and you don't want to. Who was the one who helped Lira remember how to fight with a sword?" He placed his hands behind his head, allowing his wings to unfold. "For that, you will be forever in debt to me."

"Don't forget about what I walked in on that night when you had Lira on the bed," Tavish hissed. "That removes any misgivings you've misdirected my way."

This bickering ended now. None of us had time for that. "Father?"

"Please proceed." He stroked his beard, nodding.

"I agree with Caelan." I wanted to give him credit because I might need his support to get Tavish on board with my idea. "Tavish and a group of people leave now to watch the area and learn as much as they can about the kingdom. Then, they return and relay the information. Then they'll rest so we can prepare for tomorrow evening when I'll hand myself over to the dragons. Once Eiric is released, we attack. I won't be taken far within the island, and I won't need to stay overnight." I believed this was the most likely common ground we could find.

"Tomorrow?" Father dropped his hand. "We have two days before anything has to be done."

Mom paused her pacing at the other end of the table. "If Lira hands herself over early, they'll believe she's truly desperate to save Eiric. They won't suspect that we'll attack then because she came *early*. If she hands herself over on the exact deadline, they'll expect a plan."

My pulse thudded. "Exactly." If Mom had followed my train of thought, then it had to be a solid idea.

"I'm fine with everything up to Lira giving herself up." Tavish exhaled sharply. "But unfortunately, I understand the merit of the plan. If she hands herself over, and I cloak the army, the dragons will be none the wiser."

Agony ripped through our bond, proving how hard it had been for him to say those words. "That's the point. To save Eiric and eliminate the dragon threat by having as much of an advantage as possible. We won't be on our land, so it won't be destroyed, but our magic will be weaker. If we can fight hard and fast, then maybe we'll still have the advantage."

"Won't the dragons sense Tavish using his magic?" Finnian pursed his lips. "Remember how the Seelie guards were able to track us while you were hiding us after we escaped from the holding cell?"

Father grimaced but then smoothed out his expression. "The fae are more attuned to fae magic, but theoretically, the dragons could sense it if they were actively searching for it."

"If we fly high over the land so we aren't cloaked nearby, then we should be able to eliminate that risk." Tavish rubbed the back of his neck. "We might not know details, but we can see enough to get an idea of how things are laid out, and Eiric can likely give us details about the prison area. She should've gleaned something from her time there. Also, Lira won't get far enough away for getting her back to be a problem."

"Then I believe it's time for Tavish to select his group and leave." Dad chewed on his bottom lip. "And see what information can be noted. We can meet in the morning to see what has been learned and decide the best way to proceed."

Right. We could sit here and talk generalities all day. However, the more information we could learn without risking exposure, the more we could fine-tune everything.

"I'd like for a few Seelie to be part of the group." Father stretched his wings. "And since you're unsure who can be trusted in Cuil Dorcha, Lira should return with us to Caisteal Solais tonight since the number of trusted guards at hand will be further reduced and Tavish won't be by her side."

THE KINGDOM OF FLAMES AND ASH

My breath caught. I hadn't considered leaving. "I have Nightbane. I can't leave him here alone. Not again." He was already upset with how little attention I'd given him. This would be an excellent opportunity for us to bond.

"The cù-sìth?" Mother's nose wrinkled.

"She and the beast have a unique connection." Caelan shrugged. "I don't think any of us understand it."

"Then bring him back with us." Mother shrugged. "Having extra protection is never a bad thing, especially since I know Hestia and Brenin will want to be part of the group to examine the dragon land."

"We would like to, but if—" Mom started.

Father waved a hand. "Of course you two will be part of it." Her shoulders relaxed.

"Well, if we're going to do this, it's best we leave now to have more time to watch from afar." Tavish placed an arm around my waist, pulling me closer to him as he continued, "Caelan, you can stay here and keep an eye on things. Finnian, Finola, and Struan can join me and leave Lorne here to rest after his night of watching the prison cells. He's trustworthy if anything happens."

"Sounds good to me." Caelan nodded. "I can keep the other guards busy cleaning up the village, so no one should notice you're gone. I'll even stow the sword so no one notices it here."

Finnian flew out of his seat. "I'll grab the others and Nightbane."

Even though I hadn't expected to return to my childhood room, a part of me was excited. I could wear my own clothes instead of the former queen's gowns.

Within minutes, everyone gathered in the foyer. Nightbane stood at my side, glaring at my parents. My heart ached, realizing that Tavish and I would be separated, if only for a few hours. But I didn't want to push going with them tonight. Tomorrow was going to be hard enough on him. Not only that, but it would be best if I returned to Gleann Solas to recharge my magic for the inevitable fight.

Tavish kissed me, his tongue slipping into my mouth.

I'm going to miss you, sprite.

I wrapped my arms around his neck, eagerly responding. *Don't be gone too long. I'd like to have some time alone with you before the fight.*

Now that is something that I won't disagree with you on. He pulled away, his silver eyes shining bright. *Be safe and enjoy your last night in your childhood room. When this is over, you'll be mine in every way and living permanently in Dunscaith with me. We'll never be separated like this again.*

That sounded more than perfect. *Agreed.*

"If we don't want people to see you leave, you should go now." Caelan gestured to the hallway. "Maybe cloak yourself, Finola, Struan, Finnian, Nightbane, and Lira until you're away from Aetherglen so no one says anything to the Unseelie."

"Good idea." Tavish's magic churned through our bond, stronger than ever before.

The chill of the darkness covered my skin, the sensation now as comforting as my own magic. Tavish took my hand and flew upward while Struan grunted, picking up Nightbane, and Finola flew behind us.

My parents followed closely, and we headed toward Gleann Solas.

We flew over the forest that divided our land, the trees changing from evergreens to Silathair trees that resembled cherry blossoms. Soon, silvery bark and leaves twinkled below, reminding me of starlight. The silver contrasted with the Ironbark trees, whose trunks and leaves were rusty like metal.

As we passed the waterfall, the towering Seelie castle

appeared.

Father and Mother flew ahead while Dad said, "Take Lira to her room, and we'll wait for you where the dragons approached us when we returned."

Hiding from other people was more than okay with me.

We flew around the side of the castle, passing the place where we'd escaped through the hidden passage in the walls and came to the large, open window of my childhood room. Tavish landed beside me right at the opening of the wall-sized window underneath a Silathair, and Struan placed Nightbane on the ground next to me.

I can't stay long. A Seelie could sense my magic. Tavish frowned but quickly kissed me one last time. *If you need anything—*

I'll let you know. I cupped his cheeks, needing to reassure him once again. *You're the one heading to the dragon land. Be careful. Don't let them know you're there.*

We won't. He released me and frowned. *I just want the next two days to be over so we can finally spend time alone without a constant threat.*

Me too. And I'll be able to relax once I know that Eiric is safe and home. I love you, thorn.

I love you, sprite. His face strained as he turned his back to me.

I glanced at Finola and Struan before Tavish withdrew his magic from me. "Keep him and yourselves safe." I cared deeply for all three of them.

Struan smiled. "We will. I promise."

"Please, I'll have to be the one who keeps all four of us safe." Finnian winked, trying to make me laugh. "Don't you worry, Princess." He bowed and headed off.

I stood there, unable to see the four of them fly away, yet knowing that they were as the chill of the darkness faded from me. Knowing I needed to be in the room in case someone flew by, I stepped inside with Nightbane by my side.

Something shifted in my closet, causing Nightbane to snarl.

My mouth dried. "Who's there?"

And then there was a loud crash.

Chapter Twenty-Four

Lira

My heart hammered in my chest. Who would be in my room, especially since no one expected me to be back at the castle?

We moved past the tree that grew through the open window, causing a few of the pink flowers of the Silathair to fall to the floor. Normally, I enjoyed the scent and view, but right now, it kept me from being able to see clearly inside.

Nightbane barreled deeper into my room in the direction of the closet. A whimper sounded, and I flapped my wings, trying to reach the person at the same time as he did.

When we entered the closet, I found wide aquamarine eyes staring at the beast. Gaelle, the high fae assigned to work as a luxury castle maiden, dropped the gowns she'd gathered in her arms and lifted her hands as Nightbane hunkered down.

I gritted my teeth. I wasn't going to allow her to use her wind magic on Nightbane. "Put your hands down, Gaelle." I landed between her and the cù-sìth, not wanting the situation to escalate.

She pushed her dark-blonde hair out of her face. "Me? The monster is trying to kill me! Do you despise me so much that you're commanding me to stand here and die?"

Nightbane growled, and I could sense his rising alarm at her tone. Knowing that I had to calm him before he attacked,

I turned my back to her, spreading my wings to block her from Nightbane's view. My closet was sizable, with garments hanging on both sides, but the tips of my wings still brushed the clothes. "It's okay, boy." I tangled my fingers in the fur on top of his head. "She doesn't mean us harm."

At my touch, he calmed, and soon he stopped growling, though his hackles remained up.

Moving so my right side brushed the gowns, I positioned myself so that my other side pressed against him. That was when I noticed that my closet didn't seem as full as the last time I was here, and my gaze homed in on the gorgeous gowns in sky blue, forest green, and sunray yellow that Gaelle had dropped on the floor.

She hastily bent and picked up the dresses and placed them back on the tree branches that had grown from the wall. She avoided my gaze.

"What are you doing in here?" Something felt off, and the sense of warning returned.

"I... I was..." She tucked a piece of hair behind her ear and then spun toward me, placing her hands on her hips before asking, "Wait. Why are *you* here?"

She was deflecting. However, I'd play her game for now. "I decided to return home. Besides, all my things are here. Is there a problem with that?"

"Fate, no." She laughed, a little high-pitched. "I'm sure your parents are thrilled about your return. They just didn't inform any of us of those plans. That's all."

"It was a very last-minute decision." I smiled, wanting to ease the tension between us.

As expected, she exhaled, and her wings relaxed.

"I'm sure if they'd had ample notice, they would've alerted you. Which brings me back to my first question. If you weren't aware of my return, then why are you in my closet?"

THE KINGDOM OF FLAMES AND ASH

Once again, her body stiffened, though this time, it was from my question and not from Nightbane. "Oh... well... I just wanted to check on some things."

"I noticed that you were holding three of my gowns, and several more appear to be missing." In fairness, I wouldn't be able to point out which because I still missed jeans and T-shirts and wore gowns only because they were the only clothes provided. But she didn't know that which meant I could potentially trick her. "I'd love for you to locate a gown I have that looks similar to yours. It should be in here somewhere."

Her breathing turned ragged.

That confirmed my suspicion. "Is it a problem if I wear a dress similar to yours?"

Dropping her arms, she pivoted toward me. She swallowed. "You are clearly already aware this is your dress, or you wouldn't be making such comments."

"So, you've been taking my clothes?" I crossed my arms. "You weren't in here to check on my wardrobe but to take more pieces for yourself?"

"And why not?" She huffed, not even bothering to pretend any longer. "Someone might as well. You ran off with a nightfiend, leaving behind your parents and your people. You shouldn't have been allowed to come back, and yet you convinced your parents to not only permit you back here but to let the nightfiends reinhabit their world. When the sky is filled with darkness once more, the Seelie will have only *you* to blame."

Not only did she have the audacity to steal my clothes, but she believed she could speak to me so rudely. I narrowed my eyes, stepping into her space. "And when peace is actually bridged between our two species and Tavish and I are united as one, I'll make sure your high fae title is stripped from you and you can go live with the common Seelie working the gardens."

234

Her face flushed, and she took a step back, trying to counter my move. However, she'd already backed up almost to the wall when Nightbane entered and chased her.

"By tonight, I expect every piece of my clothing to be returned. If it's not, I will alert my parents to what you've done." The two of us were similar in age, but we'd never liked each other. Mainly because I didn't trust her, and I'd watched the way she'd tried to elevate her status. This moment proved everything I'd believed as a child. "And if you ever speak to me that way again, there will be dire consequences. I doubt my parents will stand in the way of your punishment."

She swallowed loudly and then huffed. "Fine. I'll return everything."

"You'll return everything what?" I arched a brow and smirked.

"*Princess*," she hissed.

I didn't care if she hated me, but I did care if she treated me with respect. "Then you may leave and focus on whatever else requires your attention."

"My pleasure," she said curtly, taking a step toward me.

Nightbane snarled once again at her proximity, his mouth open wide and drool dripping from his teeth. His lime eyes were bright, even though we weren't cloaked in darkness.

Her bottom lip quivered, and she looked at me.

I paused before touching Nightbane's neck, wanting her to sweat another moment. He quieted, and she flew over him and rushed out the door.

Guiding Nightbane back into the bedroom, we entered the main room again, just as the door to the hallway shut, indicating we were once again alone.

I shook my head, trying to come to terms with what had just happened. I shouldn't have been shocked; Gaelle took advantage of any situation that would gain her favor.

THE KINGDOM OF FLAMES AND ASH

Exhaustion from the past few days settled hard within my bones, and my bed looked inviting. The emerald sheets reminded me of Eiric's eyes, and the fluffy pillows called to me.

I locked the door and hurried to my bed, then lay down and patted the side next to me where Tavish would normally be. Nightbane didn't hesitate, lunging onto the mattress, and I turned onto my back, our sides touching. I drifted off to sleep, welcoming the much-needed rest.

Hunger pains shooting through my stomach woke me. Groggily, I opened my eyes and saw that the sun was getting close to setting. I'd slept longer than I intended, which meant that Tavish had to be close to Tìr na Dràgon.

The warmth in my chest comforted me, though the bond contracted.

Did you arrive all right? I asked, needing to check in.

Yes, sprite. We're fine. We're watching from far away, waiting for darkness to settle. I've been slowly covering the sun so it doesn't seem completely out of the ordinary. Right now, there isn't much activity other than their guards watching the boundaries of the kingdom.

They were there, and he hadn't let rage take over. I feared that if I were there, he wouldn't be as levelheaded—another reason I hadn't pushed to go with them tonight. *Any sign of Eiric?*

He paused before replying. *No. But none of us expected to see her. She'll be locked in a prison cell.*

My heart ached, my hunger forgotten. Once again, the dragons were affecting me in ways that I would never want to admit. *Do dragons hate the Seelie like the Unseelie hated me?* The night Tavish had taken me from Earth back to the ruined dragon land, an Unseelie guard, Malikor, had attempted to scar

236

my face like my people had done his. Before he could, Tavish had intervened, thanks to our fated-mate bond coming into play.

Eiric didn't have that luxury.

There was no one there to protect her.

No, they don't hate the Seelie the same way, he reassured me. *They may not favor them because they tend to stick to their own kind, but the dragons that were involved with the relocation of Unseelie from Cuil Dorcha to their former land—their hatred was focused on us.*

Though that wasn't the best answer, it did give me a little peace of mind concerning Eiric. And better, he wouldn't have been able to say it if it weren't true. *I need her back home, thorn.* A sob built in my chest, and I held it down, not wanting to alarm Nightbane.

Still, the beast lifted his huge head and whimpered, curling tighter into my side. I turned, wrapping my arm around him, enjoying the warmth he provided. I couldn't imagine how I'd be doing if he wasn't here, especially with Tavish's absence.

Affection spread from Tavish's side of the bond. *We're going to get her back. We'll make sure of that tomorrow.*

His words released some of the apprehension in my stomach. I feared that he would still try to talk me out of the plan tomorrow, but I could feel his intention behind the words. He wouldn't stop me.

I love you. I'd spoken those words right before he left, but I needed him to know the magnitude of my feelings and how much I appreciated him.

That may be true, but I love you more. The sun is setting, so I need to concentrate. Make sure you get something to eat. Don't think I didn't notice you not eating this morning. If you're going to hand yourself over to Pyralis, you need to be at full strength because there will be war. Eat and rest, and I'll inform you when we're returning.

I almost replied *Yes, Dad,* but I doubted he'd understand the joke. Sarcasm didn't land as well in Ardanos as it had back on Earth. The only person besides Dad, Mom, and Eiric who even somewhat understood it was Finnian.

My stomach grumbled just as I heard a knock on my door.

"Princess Lira, your parents have requested your presence at dinner," Sorcha called.

Of course it'd be her, especially since Mom and Dad had left with Tavish. "I'll be there in a minute." I glanced down at Tavish's mother's gown, which I still wore, knowing I wanted to change into something that fit better.

"I'll wait for you out here," she replied, sounding bored.

I rolled my eyes. She always had to be difficult. "I can go to the dining room alone."

"I think it's better if I escort you."

Not wanting to argue, I quickly changed into a light-pink gown that hugged my curves without being uncomfortable. I glamoured my face to make it appear like I wore natural makeup and ensured I left my fated-mate markings on full display. Petting Nightbane, I asked him to stay then headed to the door.

When Sorcha saw me, her attention immediately went to my markings, and her face twisted with disgust. She disliked my bond with Tavish.

"You know, you should glamour those." She pointed to them before turning down the hallway that led to the dining hall.

I had no intention of hiding anything, especially the sacred connection Tavish and I shared. "Noted."

She shrugged. "Fine. You can't say I didn't try."

We flew the rest of the way in silence, though every fae I passed either avoided my gaze or glared at me with hatred.

Two reactions I had gotten to know quite well during my time as Tavish's prisoner. Blast, even some of the Unseelie still tried to keep their distance from me, but most had come around to accepting that my presence was permanent.

After making the turns, I found the opening to the dining room and slowed, not wanting to appear hurried.

As I breezed over the threshold, I found Father sitting at one end of the table, seeming too big for the chair made of roots and the leaf he was perched on. Mother sat on his left, wearing a sparkling blue gown, her legs crossed.

Servants stood in one corner of the room. Seeing them looking down at me had my knees growing weak. Not wanting to risk tripping, I flew to the spot across from Mother where a third place had been set. From this position, I could look across the massive balcony to an absolutely gorgeous view of the village below.

The three of us took the chance to get reacquainted with each other. They asked about my time on Earth, and I asked about what had happened the past twelve years in Gleann Solas. We enjoyed each other's company, something we all needed to feel like family once again. Though it would take more effort than just now, it was a beginning.

By the time we finished, the moon had risen high in the sky, indicating that it was time for me to return to my room to rest. We had a war to fight tomorrow.

I gave my parents big hugs and grabbed some food for Nightbane. Sorcha escorted me back to my room, and I noticed how quiet the entire castle was.

When we reached my bedroom door once more, Sorcha opened it, preparing to go inside.

"Nightbane is in there. He won't have let anyone enter." The cù-sìth would protect me with his life.

"Princess—" she started, but I lifted my hand.

"It's fine." Even though I believed those words, there was more to my story. "If you go in there, he'll feel threatened, and I won't be able to protect you. It's best if I enter alone."

She scowled but nodded, moving out of the way.

Wanting to get away from the moody guard, I slipped into the room and shut the door behind me. I locked it for good measure, at least ensuring a warning if someone tried to get inside.

That was when I heard Nightbane snoring.

I laughed. With all the chaos, he must have been more tired than any of us realized. I set the food on one of the pink rose petal cushions by the wall. He could eat later.

Yawning, I strolled back into the closet and changed into an orange petal nightgown. I was exhausted.

As I stepped back into the room, a shadow fell across me, coming from the direction of my bathroom.

A scream lodged in my throat, and I spun and kicked the man in the stomach. His sword missed me, and familiar red eyes widened as he crouched, protecting his stomach. Taking the opportunity, I slammed my elbow on the back of his head. His sword clanked to the floor, and he crumpled after it.

I kicked him in the head, making sure that he'd completely passed out. As I bent to retrieve the sword, a key slid into the lock of the door.

Shit.

Chapter Twenty-Five

Lira

I clutched the hilt of the sword and flew over the downed man, who groaned and lifted his head. His thin lips pressed together as he wrinkled his nose.

Sprite, what's going on? Tavish asked, but I didn't have time to answer.

The knob turned, and the door began opening. There was no telling how many were coming for me. All I knew was that I had to fight.

Someone's in my room. Landing next to Nightbane, I shook his body. I'd never seen him sleep this hard, but he'd have to catch up on his rest later. We needed to leave to survive—but even shaking him didn't make him stir.

A lump formed in my throat. *And something's wrong with Nightbane.*

I lifted my head as Sorcha darted into the room, her sword raised.

Of course, she'd be the one behind the attempt on my life. It was probably why she'd wanted to enter first.

Are you in danger? Tavish's fear strangled our bond. *I knew I shouldn't have left you!*

Sorcha stopped directly over my attacker with her sword at the back of his neck. "Why are you here, Greason? You know you've been banished from the castle."

THE KINGDOM OF FLAMES AND ASH

Exhaling, I leaned over Nightbane, checking his breathing. I tried to slow my racing heart, but I struggled. The last time I'd seen Greason, I'd given him sunberry tarts, distracting him so I could steal the key that would allow me to free Tavish and Finnian from their chains. My actions had cost this man his job, so there was clearly resentment. *I'm not in danger anymore. An ally guard is here, but Tavish, the man who attacked me, is the guard who must have been blamed for your escape.*

At least I know what he looks like so I can kill him upon my return. His hatred pulsed through our bond. *What did he do to you?*

Nothing. I didn't want to answer that for so many reasons. *I stopped him before he could even get his hands on me. He's laid out on the floor.*

I rubbed Nightbane's fur, and my hand hit some sort of narrow object. I yanked it from his skin and saw that it was a dart. He must have been drugged with something similar to what the Seelie guards had used on me when they'd taken me back to Gleann Solas right after Tavish and I had completed our fated-mate bond.

Sorcha moved the edge of her blade under Greason's chin, forcing him to lift his head.

He wore a tattered dark tunic and holey pants, a sharp contrast to the golden armor he'd donned as a guard.

"Answer me," she growled. "How did you even know she was here?"

That was the real question, but I suspected the answer to that was clear. "Gaelle was in my room when Nightbane and I first arrived. She could have informed others." It wasn't that we were purposely trying to keep my presence here a secret, but the fewer people who were aware, the less hysteria it would cause while Tavish and the others were away. Even though I hoped no one here would betray us, some Seelie might feel loyalty to the dragons since the details of what had truly happened hadn't been circulated yet. We had to be careful and hide our plans until Eiric got back here safely.

She glanced over her shoulder at me before refocusing on the enemy. She lifted the sword higher, and I noted honey-colored blood welling from where his skin must have gotten cut.

"You're already in enough trouble. Don't make it worse. What were you doing here?"

"Getting vengeance for what the princess did to me," he answered and sneered at me like I didn't deserve to breathe the same air as him. "If it weren't for her, I wouldn't have been shamed and forced to work the fields."

"Nightbane hadn't done anything to you, yet you hurt him." I lifted the dart so both he and Sorcha could see. "And Tavish and Finnian being imprisoned was foolish. They deserved to be free, and we didn't harm you when we could have."

"You didn't *harm* me?" He scoffed and stumbled to his feet. "I got demoted from high fae. Generations of my heritage and loyalty to the king gone because of *your* blazing loyalty to the worst of the nightfiends. Seeing how easily he managed to manipulate you, it's best if we rid the realm of your existence. You're a threat to my king and queen. Eliminating you will prove my worth to them once more."

My head jerked back, and I swallowed a laugh. He believed every word he spoke and didn't realize that none of it made sense.

Sorcha shook her head and yelled, "Someone call the king and queen and bring them to the princess's room. Quickly!"

Even though most of the fae would be retiring for the night, guards were positioned throughout the castle, and someone would hear Sorcha's message.

Greason shook his head. "Sorcha, don't do this. Just let

THE KINGDOM OF FLAMES AND ASH

me go. You must agree that she's a threat to our kingdom and survival. If she continues to choose the Unseelie nightfiend over her own people, the dragons will attack us, and we could lose our magic!"

That made more sense. Losing one's magic was essentially the same as losing one's wings. Both of those things defined who we were, how strong we were, and what our position among our people would be. "You aren't at risk of losing your magic." I understood that I couldn't tell him how or why, but he did deserve that. After all, I had tricked him in order to free the two prisoners under his watch.

His brows furrowed. "So, you're marrying the dragon prince?" His red eyes lightened, reminding me of flames. He doubtless had fire magic.

"He's not a guard or part of the royals' inner circle," Sorcha warned, placing the heel of her boot against his chest and shoving. "He's not allowed to know anything."

Greason slammed against the wall. The back of his head hit the stone surface, and blood rolled down his neck into the collar of his tunic.

Several sets of wings flapped from the direction of my parents' room. Their chambers weren't far from mine, and as expected, a guard had managed to reach them quickly.

Nightbane whimpered, and I turned my attention back to him. My knees weakened in relief. If I hadn't already been touching Nightbane, I would've fallen over, but instead, I gripped him tighter.

My healing magic pulsed faintly, but it was mainly in vain. Nightbane hadn't been wounded but rather medicated, which meant my magic didn't have anything to latch on to and heal.

Father barreled into the room, his gaze landing on me first. When he realized I wasn't injured, his head snapped in Greason's direction. He spat, "What are you doing here?"

Not wanting to have the conversation multiple times, I repeated the information when Mother joined us. The guard who'd retrieved them remained in the hallway, keeping watch, and the sound of more guards fluttering sounded outside my gigantic, glassless window.

"You came here to *kill* our daughter?" Mother's hand shook as she placed it on her chest. "And believed we would appreciate it. Is that what our people think of us?"

"We don't have to explain ourselves to a thornling." Father rocked back on his heels while spreading out his wings, quite an intimidating sight. "He entered not only our castle but our daughter's room without permission, which is unforgivable. I shudder to even consider what he'd planned to do with her if Sorcha hadn't intervened."

My mouth dropped open. He hadn't even considered the possibility that I'd manage to protect myself. However, before I was able to correct him, Sorcha cleared her throat.

"Your Majesty, it wasn't I who protected her." She folded her wings behind her back. "When I entered, Greason had already been handled."

Father's brows furrowed while Mother grinned.

"I guess what Hestia, Brenin, and Tavish mentioned earlier is true." Mother smiled and dropped her hand back to her side. "You seem to be a worthy warrior yourself."

"Tavish?" Greason spat out. "You've been spending time with the nightfiend as well? There have been whispers, but none of us in Gleann Solas believed it."

That sparked anger deep within me. It was one thing to question my loyalties—Tavish was my fated mate, so I could understand the concern—but to question my parents, who'd sacrificed so much for their people, was insulting. "Speak like that to them again, and you won't be able to so much as whisper once I remove your tongue. We may have had a misunderstanding upon my return, but know that they are my family, and I won't tolerate them being disrespected."

Nightbane rumbled pitifully, lifting his head and trying to face the threat. His head bobbed around like he was dizzy, which only fueled my rage even more.

Lira, I'm heading back. I can't handle feeling all your emotions without knowing what's going on. I—

We're fine. I promise. Stay so we can handle the dragon threat and start our new life free and together tomorrow night. My parents are here, and the problem has been dealt with. He's just accusing my parents of potential treason.

"Lira, I appreciate your enthusiasm, but I can handle punishment on my own." Father smirked, pride gleaming in his eyes despite his words. He turned back to Greason. "But before anything else happens, I want to know who alerted you to Lira's presence here so you knew to hide in her room for her return."

"And how you knew that Nightbane was with me." I pointed at the beast, who flopped back on the mattress, whimpering.

Even though I knew the answer, I kept my mouth shut, knowing that Father would want to hear the answer from him alone.

Greason stayed silent.

Holding out his hand, Father said, "Sorcha, take him to the holding cell so we can prepare him for torture. I want to know who informed him, who's been whispering about us, and anything else that might be beneficial."

Greason's face flushed, and the trickle of blood down his neck congealed as the wound clotted. "I won't inform you of anything. I dedicated my life to you, and all of you have abandoned me."

"You were stationed at the cell to ensure no prisoners escaped. Not only did Lira steal a key from you, but she managed to free two Unseelie fae in the process. You were trained to evaluate threats, and you were aware of the connection my daughter had to the Unseelie king. You failed at your job, and I won't risk anything like that happening again, not even if my own daughter is involved."

Those few words were the equivalent of a punch in the gut, but I understood why he had to say them. I needed to remove my emotions from the equation and think like a royal. If his people were concerned, he needed to make it clear to everyone, including Sorcha, that our magic came first. And the truth was, I agreed it should come before me. But that didn't make hearing it any easier.

"That's good to hear, Your Majesty." Sorcha bowed her head. "And, of course, I'd be honored to take him to the holding cell. Is there anything I should prepare?"

Father nodded. "The thorn whips, the short swords that won't go too deep, and don't forget the mistveil blossoms because he *will* tell us everything he knows before his death."

Even though it wasn't the norm in Gleann Solas, unlike what Tavish had made the standard in Cuil Dorcha, an attack on the royal family meant death.

Sorcha grabbed Greason's arm and yanked him upright. The male guard standing in the hallway hurried into the room and took the other side.

Father handed back her sword and stood tall and regal despite wearing his thin night tunic and lounge pants. "I'll be there momentarily."

"No," Greason shouted, trying to dig his feet into the floor to stop the forward movement.

Still, the guards flew, the sound of them carrying him off heavy on my heart. I knew asking Father to spare him would be foolish. These were the rules, and most importantly, if he began making exceptions, more people would ask for them.

With the guards and my attacker gone, I hugged Nightbane,

THE KINGDOM OF FLAMES AND ASH

hating that he'd been caught in the cross fire.

"Are you okay, sprout?" Mother asked quietly, as if she were afraid that I'd be scared away like a mouse.

Well, if mice lived in Ardanos.

"I'm fine." I straightened, begrudgingly letting go of Nightbane. "It just caught me off guard."

"Do you have any speculation about who might have informed people?" Father pursed his lips. "I hate to think we have the same sort of traitors here that Tavish has to contend with in Cuil Dorcha."

His calling Tavish by name instead of an Unseelie slur had me fighting a smile. I didn't want Father to notice and become uncomfortable. I wanted everyone to get along because I had no intention of ever giving Tavish up.

"I have an idea." I hadn't yet checked to see if Gaelle had returned my clothes.

As I leapt across my bed and into my closet, both Father's and Mother's eyebrows rose comically. But there was nothing funny about this moment.

None of my clothes had been returned as instructed. Gaelle had thought I would die tonight.

Mother's light footsteps entered the closet behind me as she said, "Honey, what's—" Her voice cut off before she exclaimed, "Where are all your clothes?"

"Gaelle took them. I caught her taking more when I arrived here earlier. I told her to bring them back by tonight, and as you can see, she didn't bother to do so."

Folding her wings tightly behind her, she frowned. "Greason lives next door to her in the high fae village. They sometimes traveled to work together, and I suspect that they're lovers, so it makes sense she'd be involved."

"What has come over our people?" Father stepped through the doorway with his wings hanging at his sides.

248

That one was easy. "Fear and self-interest. Twelve years ago, because of the actions of Tavish's father, you created a veil so the Unseelie couldn't enter. Then, I was betrothed to the dragon prince. My being fated to Tavish made things worse upon my return. They're scared they'll lose their magic and wings. Greason pretty much told me that before you arrived."

"The fear needs to be contained." Father rolled his shoulders. "When we're free of the dragons and have Eiric back, we'll need to reunite the land and inform everyone what has transpired. The lack of understanding as to why the Unseelie are back must have affected our people more than I realized. I'd hoped they would trust your mother and me as their rulers, but maybe we've been unfair to them by keeping the knowledge from them."

"Don't be too hard on yourself, love." Mother patted his arm. "We haven't even had time to sleep well since we returned a day ago. This is a trying time, but I assure you we and our people will overcome it."

I smiled, seeing the type of leader I wanted to become. I knew Tavish wouldn't be as understanding as Father. He'd led a different life than he should have for the past twelve years. But that didn't mean that we couldn't figure out how to be more like my parents and not lose a piece of ourselves in the process.

"Either way, Gaelle and Greason will be punished for acting against a royal." Father closed his eyes like he was preparing for what would come next. "Four guards are stationed outside your door now, and I'll assign another two outside your window. They're aware that if anything happens to you under their watch, their fates will be the same as the attackers. Get some rest; you're going to need it for tomorrow." He took Mother's hand and then kissed the top of my head. "Your mother and I need to get to the holding cell."

"Let me know if you need anything." I wanted to go with

them, but I couldn't leave Nightbane like this.

Mother patted my cheek, and then they left. When my door shut, I hurried back to Nightbane, whose dark-green eyes were open and focused on me.

Like earlier, I crawled into bed and turned so I could hold him. "I'm sorry, Nightbane. That should've never happened."

He sighed, his misty breath hitting my face, but then his eyes closed as he fell back asleep.

Knowing I needed to tell Tavish what had happened, I reached for our connection. But before I could yank at it, his magic swirled deep inside me like it did when we were under attack and he needed the full strength of both our powers.

My heart screamed with fear.

Chapter Twenty-Six

Tavish

My skin crawled, the urge to turn around and fly back to Gleann Solas so strong that I struggled to breathe despite the pure air all around us. Once again, desperation clung to every inch of me at the knowledge that Lira had been attacked and I hadn't been able to protect her.

I remained in place only because the threat had already been thwarted. However, it should've been thwarted by *me*.

Starting deep within me, my darkness hung even closer to my skin. I wanted to fly back and be the one to kill the thornling who dared threaten my mate, but right now, it was best if I remained here as we'd planned. After all, Lira was determined to hand herself over to the dragons tomorrow night, and we needed as much information about them as possible before the exchange for her sister took place.

Cold dread sank into my body at the thought of letting her do what she planned. However, I knew Lira. She would do *anything* to get Eiric back, and not even I could stop her. The only reason I'd given in to the awful plan was that I knew she'd resent me for the rest of eternity otherwise. And I couldn't fathom taking her warmth away... the warmth I'd come to cherish and crave.

On my left, Struan turned his head toward me, and my wings stiffened. In my moment of turmoil, I hadn't been paying

THE KINGDOM OF FLAMES AND ASH

attention to Tìr na Dràgon in front of us.

"My king, do you see something?" he asked.

My brows furrowed, and I narrowed my eyes, staring through the mountains of the island that the dragons now claimed as theirs to Caisteal an Dràgon, the dragon castle.

The gigantic castle nestled between all the mountains. The dark stone was the same color as the one we'd been forced to live in for twelve years, but this one had a gigantic dragon statue towering over the top of the double doors in front.

All we'd seen today were common dragons. None of the royals had come out. It was as if they were hiding inside.

"I don't. Do you?" I didn't understand why he'd ask that, so I glanced at Finola, who had her hand on the hilt of her sword as if she'd sensed the same urgency that I had. Yet, she didn't move forward, instead remaining rigid beside me.

"No, but from the way you're antsy, I thought I missed something. What's worrying you?"

Blighted abyss. Even my own guards could tell that I was distracted. I needed to brush away my frustration because, if I didn't, then Lira could be in even more danger than I wanted to consider.

"Don't be a fool." Finnian snorted from the other side of Struan. "We know what's causing our dear king to be distracted. It begins with LI- and ends with -RA."

Annoyance flared inside me, and I clasped my hands to keep from punching the thornling. We had to be careful. We were about five thousand feet over the surface of the water that hit the dragon border. I'd rolled darkness in over the past few hours, making it appear like clouds until we were finally able to get this close. We also made sure that we stayed where the wind blew at us, not risking our scent drifting below.

The dragons had excellent senses of hearing, smell, and sight, so we had to be careful to not alert them to our presence, and I had to keep my magic steady so they wouldn't sense fae magic either. Any aggravation I wanted to take out on Finnian would have to happen later.

Hestia and Brenin ignored us. They stayed close together on the other side of Finola while they watched not only the castle but also the surrounding areas, trying to discern where Eiric might be. I hoped that maybe we could locate Eiric and retrieve her so Lira wouldn't have to be put at risk.

As if Fate wanted to answer my unspoken wish, one of the double doors opened, and Pyralis stepped out of the castle and hurried down the stairs.

My chest tightened and every cell in my body blazed. My illusion magic spun inside me, and the darkness clung to me more.

This was the man who wanted to take my mate away from me. He wanted to impregnate her and use her as a means to make the dragons indestructible. There was one way to ensure it never happened—killing the ashbreath.

Wind hit my face as my wings pumped, pushing me toward him. I hadn't even realized I'd started moving.

This wasn't a thought-out plan, which meant that if I did this, Eiric could get hurt. Lira would never forgive me.

I gritted my teeth and stopped, though it went against every instinct. The last twelve years had taught me to kill any threats, and he posed a great risk to the most important person in my life.

Hands gripped my arms, yanking me back.

"I understand you're upset, but we can't be rash," Brenin gritted out from my right side.

Hestia squeezed my other side tightly as she arched a stern brow. "Our eldest daughter is down there in Fate knows what sort of condition. Don't you think we're struggling just as much as you are, staying up here and hiding when she's so close?"

THE KINGDOM OF FLAMES AND ASH

Although I understood they loved Lira, what they felt for her didn't even come close to my love for her. Lira had thawed my heart after twelve years of it being frozen, and I wouldn't want to survive in a realm that didn't have her in it. "I stopped myself." I hated that I'd lost control, but when something risked Lira, I saw black. "I didn't realize what I was doing at first, but I barely flew ten feet."

"We have to be sure." Brenin kept his hold firm. "If we release you, are you going to do anything reckless that could compromise one or both of our daughters?"

For some reason, his calling Lira his daughter eased some of my disquiet. Despite returning to Ardanos and the four of them regaining their memories, they still loved Lira as their own. They wouldn't risk her for Eiric. They wanted both of them safe.

Pyralis headed around the castle, taking his time. He held a plate in his hands, and he kept stopping and turning around before continuing. If I didn't know better, I'd say he was trying to decide on something.

Is everything okay? Lira's voice entered my head, her fear pronounced within me.

Eyes locked on the ashbreath, I took a deep breath, trying to settle my anger and magic. I didn't need her to get worried and then do something foolish, like fly out here to check on us. The thought of her getting close to this island had the edges of my vision darkening. *Yes, the ashbreath just exited the castle, and the urge to kill him nearly took over.*

Tavish! she exclaimed, her emotions constricting our connection. *If you do that—*

I know. I said nearly *took over. I caught myself in time. Besides, your parents were right on my wings the entire time.* I exhaled, but still, the anger the dragon bestirred in me stole my breath. I had only hated one person as much as him, and Lira

254

had taken care of his death.

To be clear, it's not only Eiric I'm worried about. I'm sure the dragons wouldn't mind making you their prisoner either if the opportunity presents itself. I can't lose you, not now... not ever. However, I can't stay safe and allow Eiric to die for protecting me either.

Caring about others made Lira different and had drawn me to her in the first place. *I understand. That's why I'm keeping watch and going along with this plan. If you're going to hand yourself over, I'm going to do my best to ensure that you remain safe and that I will always be able to locate you.*

I know, and I love you for it. Her end of the connection began cooling like she was getting sleepy. *Will you be coming here when you're done or heading straight back to Cuil Dorcha?*

That question had one side of my mouth lifting. *Sprite, wherever you are, is where my first stop will be. I plan to gather you in my arms and take you home... right where you should be.* The image of her in my arms once more had my wings feeling lighter.

Sounds perfect, she murmured. *I love you.*

I love you, too. Words I never imagined I'd say after the death of my parents. Yet, I would never tire of saying them to her. *Get some rest.*

Pyralis had made it halfway around the castle when he stopped in his tracks once again. This time, when he spun around, he continued to the stairs. As soon as he took a step up like he was heading back inside, he stopped once more.

Finola, Struan, and Finnian flew to the right of Brenin, where we were all hovering in a line once again.

"What the blast is he doing?" Finnian muttered. "Maybe killing the dragons won't be a problem after all. They can't even decide where they want to go. We could just fly around them in circles, and they could make themselves dizzy before succumbing to unconsciousness."

Out of the corner of my eye, I saw Hestia smirk. She wasn't nearly as annoyed as the Unseelie guards and me.

All of a sudden, the breeze shifted, hitting our wings and backs and blowing toward Tìr na Dràgon. The six of us tensed before flying to the right, trying to get out of line with the castle before the dragon had a chance to smell us.

My gaze remained on Pyralis, who had frozen in place.

Pulse hammering, I pushed farther to the side where one of the mountains had become a volcano due to the dragon magic.

Waiting to see if he alerted any guards, I continued to move so I could see every expression and gesture as we positioned ourselves so that the wind hit us more on the right side, blowing toward the ocean instead of straight down to the island.

Pyralis didn't even glance in our direction. Instead, with a steady gait, he walked around the castle once more... to whatever destination he'd been originally heading.

"That was too blazing close." Brenin huffed. "I was certain the ashbreath sensed us."

I had been too, but for once, maybe Fate was on our side. "I didn't even feel the warning of the wind shift."

"We didn't bring anyone with wind magic." Hestia shook her head. "We should've considered it and taken the time to locate someone."

"If the wind were usually that volatile, it would've crossed our minds, but that change wasn't typical." Brenin bit his bottom lip. "It must be tied to the volatility of the land with the dragon magic."

He was right. In every land we'd lived on, changes in wind direction were rare and usually happened around the solstices. We were nowhere close to the June solstice.

"The castle is surrounded by mountains, so maybe they blocked our scents." Finnian lifted both hands as the six of us hovered, waiting to see what happened now that we weren't upwind of them again. He continued, "I doubt Pyralis would've carried a plate of food around if he planned on summoning an army."

"We should stay here and make sure that nothing happens." Finola's hair blew into her face. "And if they do something aggressive, we can race to alert the other fae."

From our position, we would be able to see any dragons that tried to fly toward Aetherglen. "Agreed. Let's wait."

Something settled hard in my stomach as we waited for what had to be a couple more hours. Though flying was second nature to us, the amount of time we had to hover in the sky made my muscles grow tired... yet we still had to endure for a while longer.

The six of us remained silent, scanning the land, taking in every indication of movement... waiting for dragons to take to the sky and search for us. The dragon village to the right was situated similarly to the one in the former dragon land, the houses stacked on each other with large windows so they could easily fly in and out. They were at the bottom of a range of mountains on the east side of the island, with one of the mountains smoking from the top like it was transitioning into a volcano.

A few dragons in human form hung out at both edges of the village. I assumed there were guards within the castle, which had my wings moving a little easier. If they knew we were here, they'd no doubt have come out and already be attacking.

Eventually, Pyralis returned. His expression was strained, and he carried the now-empty plate at his side. He didn't glance around, entirely focused on the double doors as he jogged up the stairs four at a time. He hadn't scanned the area like he sensed danger.

"I think we're good to leave," Struan whispered. "And fly

THE KINGDOM OF FLAMES AND ASH

around the entire island to see if we missed anything."

Right. The night would end in a couple of hours, and it would be best if we were already halfway home so our scents wouldn't still be in the air if the dragons decided to fly anywhere. "My magic is getting low, so I won't be able to hold on to the darkness much longer. I agree. We need to do a quick fly-by and head back."

The others nodded, and we banked to the right, paying attention to the wind so it wouldn't blow our scents back inland.

As we flew around the rest of the island, we noticed dense copses of trees at each section of the mountains. We found two more additional villages built in the same style with dragons posted on each side, watching for danger. The second one, in the north, was set against mountains like the other, while the village on the western side was nestled between a lake and the ocean that separated this kingdom from our own.

Satisfied that we'd gotten a feel for the land, the six of us headed for home. My magic was drained dangerously low, but I kept tugging on the connection until the dragon land faded from sight. Then I released it.

Hestia shook her arms. "I thought I'd never feel warm again."

"Be glad we didn't use our frost powers." Finnian waggled his brows.

"If you look at my wife that way again, you'll never have another opportunity to use your magic." Brenin glowered.

Immediately, I liked the Seelie guard better. "He does the same blighted thing with Lira. It makes me furious. One day, he's going to die, and he'll be the only person to blame."

"You could never kill me." Finnian wrinkled his nose derisively.

"I'm concerned." Finola flew slightly ahead, the skin around her eyes tight. "The last island was huge, but the only village they had was located where we all lived. Why would they separate and spread out here?"

Good question. "Maybe to distribute their magic so it doesn't concentrate in one area?"

The sun rose over the water, and we angled ourselves toward Gleann Solas, my wings moving a little faster. Though it'd been mere hours, it felt like an eternity since I'd seen Lira.

"There are many possible reasons." Struan shrugged. "We won't know unless they tell us."

"Either way, the placement is strategic for them. They can't be caught off guard as easily as they could on the other island." Brenin pursed his lips. "We need to have this discussion with our royals as well, so let's wait until we arrive home."

Unfortunately, the *why* didn't matter. We had to account for that advantage in our plans.

Our group fell silent.

An hour or so later, Aetherglen lay before us just as alarm that wasn't mine churned through me.

My mouth dried. *I'm almost there, Lira. I can see the mountains of Gleann Solas.*

Then you should come quick. Father has asked us to meet him on the dining hall balcony, and I don't know why. However, he hopes you are close since he wants you here for this.

"Something is happening. We need to hurry," I barked, pushing myself faster than I thought possible after how tired I'd become.

The others kept up, and I didn't bother attempting to cloak us. My magic was too low, and I didn't have any strength to spare because I needed to reach my mate.

The villages we passed looked empty, the fields of the sunberries devoid of workers. Guards were lined up across the land, watching the edges of the kingdom as if they were expecting a threat.

What could be happening? We hadn't seen a dragon pass by.

We soared over more mountains, and the Aelwen River in front of the castle came into view.

Every fae we hadn't seen stood in the opening of the village under the castle, looking up where Lira, King Erdan, and Queen Sylphia hovered above the balcony in front of the dining hall.

Fae only gathered around the castle for one thing, and I hoped that I wasn't wrong.

CHAPTER TWENTY-SEVEN

Lira

My heart pounded against my rib cage as I flew slowly down the hallway toward the dining area. Sorcha had knocked on my door about twenty minutes ago. She informed me that my parents wanted me in the dining hall as quickly as possible, and to dress like a princess.

I'd selected a pale-blue dress, wanting a color that could pass as both Seelie and Unseelie. Though frost blue was a tad lighter, this blue wasn't quite as bright as the sky, landing somewhere in the middle. I'd glamoured my face with subtle makeup, not wanting to take too long preparing. I wanted to know what was so important that they'd woken me this early.

Nightbane kept pace at my side, staring at each person we flew past. Unlike last night, the Seelie castle workers didn't glare at me but rushed past, trying to get away from my beast.

"Why have you brought the nightmare with you?" Sorcha scowled over her shoulder. "He's causing chaos."

I landed next to Nightbane, tangling my fingers in the nape of his neck. "I'm not leaving him in my room alone after what happened last night."

When we turned into the dining room, both of my parents were standing at the opening to the balcony. The sun rose over the mountaintops, declaring a new day. This was the day that everything changed.

THE KINGDOM OF FLAMES AND ASH

By tomorrow, Eiric would be back, no longer a captive, and I hoped like hell that I would be in Cuil Dorcha with Tavish.

Nightbane huffed, and Mother turned, her sparkly blue wings fluttering. "Oh, sprout. Did you sleep well after the attack?"

I smiled at the tenderness etched on her face. "I slept fine. I hope it's okay that I brought Nightbane. It's just, after last night—"

"Of course he's welcome." Father half smiled. "The cù-sìth is loyal to you, so I have no objection to him being here. Besides, the whole castle learned about your return and the huge animal staying with you after the guards retrieved Gaelle and brought her in for questioning."

My shoulders relaxed. Once again, I'd been ready for Father to reprimand me as he had when I'd first returned to Gleann Solas. Instead, he'd shown how far our relationship had come. He had begun accepting me for who I was now.

"You called for me very early." Anticipation churned through me. Between what was to come and not having Tavish beside me, I didn't feel right in my skin. "Is everything all right?"

"We've called an assembly of the people." Father steepled his hands. "Is Tavish near? I'd like him to be here for the announcement."

My cheeks ached from how wide I smiled. I never thought I'd hear anything remotely close to those words spoken by either of my parents. "I haven't heard from him, but he should be here soon."

"Don't bother him yet. We need to bring Greason and Gaelle from the holding cells first. We aren't quite ready." Father nodded at Sorcha and continued, "Go retrieve them now."

Throat drying, I tried to swallow but failed. I didn't like the sound of that.

I'm almost there, Lira. I can see the mountains of Gleann

262

Solas, Tavish mind-linked.

Knowing he was close had the lump in my throat shrinking. The only thing that kept me sane was the fact that his magic and emotions seemed to stay level on the other side of our connection. Nothing seemed awry. Otherwise, I would've gone searching for him. Still, knowing that something would most likely happen to Greason had the walls feeling as if they would close in on me. *Then you should come quick. Father has asked us to meet him on the dining hall balcony, and I don't know why. However, he hopes you are close since he wants you here for this.*

Determination flooded our bond, and I wasn't surprised that he didn't answer. Tavish had one goal—to return quicker, as requested—and I wouldn't distract him. I needed him by my side. "Tavish just told me that they're almost back."

"Excellent." Father tugged on his golden tunic, topped with his earth-brown royal coat the exact color of his wings, giving the illusion that they were larger than they truly were. "We shall begin so that, when he arrives, there won't be an outcry."

My chest swelled with hope.

Mother held out an arm toward me, her pink gown hugging her every curve, and I hurried to her side with Nightbane close to my hip and looped my arm through hers, Father flanking her other side. Standing on the edge of the balcony, I could see the thousands of people gathered below.

There was a time I remembered during my lifetime that all of the fae had been called to gather... the day my parents had announced that the Unseelie were officially the enemy when they had pointed to the darkened sky that had plagued us for weeks.

Uneasy expressions strained each Seelie's face as they waited. More people flew toward us as the villagers who lived farthest away arrived.

A woman near the front scowled and pointed at me then

turned her head to the person beside her. One by one, people noticed me standing next to Mother and aimed looks of mistrust or disgust my way. Unease coiled inside me. I hated that my people viewed me as a traitor.

Those who weren't directing their attention to me seemed to have homed in on Nightbane. The cù-sìth hunkered down and growled. Even I could feel the animosity wafting from the crowd, and I didn't have animal senses.

"Erdan, how have we allowed our people to hold our daughter in such disdain?" Mother rasped.

"I'm unsure, dear, but it ends now." Father looked at me and continued, "It's time to unite our land."

The three of us flew up above the edge of the balcony so that everyone could see us, even those far in the back. Mother and Father held hands while Mother and I kept our arms interlocked, a symbol of unity as we hovered together.

People stood below us, looking up as they waited to hear what we had to say. The sheer magnitude of our numbers overwhelmed me. There were easily over ten thousand, proving that the Seelie population was now more than three times that of the Unseelie fae.

No wonder Tavish had wanted to drain my blood so they could catch the Seelie off guard. That would have been the only chance the Unseelie would have to win.

Father cleared his throat, and the crowd became quiet.

"Something happened last night that has made it abundantly clear to both the queen and me that we need to make an announcement." Father's voice boomed, similar to Tavish's, as he addressed the crowd below. "Last night, our daughter, your princess, returned home."

A few brows creased while others shook their heads in disbelief.

A brave young woman shouted from the back. "After she

freed the nightfiends? She's a traitor."

Mother's arm tensed. "Say that one more time, and you'll be punished." Her normally sweet voice held a ruthless edge as she stared at the young woman who had dared to speak such words about me. "She is our daughter, and we won't tolerate any disrespect toward her."

The woman jerked back, and a few of the people who'd been glaring at me gasped.

Six figures appeared in the distance, flying in our direction. The yank in my chest informed me who was heading our way— Tavish. I wanted to race to him and bury myself in his arms, but I couldn't leave. Not now. Not when Father was informing everyone of what had happened and showing his alliance with the Unseelie.

The rest of the world faded as my entire being called out to my mate. It'd been way too long since I'd last seen him.

As Tavish and the other five approached and flew over the gathered Seelie, heading straight to us, the people below us shrieked.

"Unseelie!" one yelled. "Where are the guards to protect us?"

"Be quiet," Father thundered. "They are our guests here."

Tavish didn't hesitate as he flew directly to me. He took my hand and hovered next to me with our arms pressed together.

Finnian and Struan fell in behind us, flanking Nightbane, as Mom flew to the other side of Tavish and Dad to the king, making it clear they were guarding the four of us.

That Tavish was essentially family.

Unshed tears burned my eyes. I'd never expected a moment like this to happen for Tavish and me.

I never imagined coming back to a moment like this, Tavish linked as if he'd heard me, his shock and happiness running through me. However, I sensed a little bit of worry underneath.

"Each one of you should remember what I just said because a reminder is coming for what happens if you go against the queen's and my command."

Father lifted a hand, and Sorcha yelled, "Bring in the prisoners."

Both Gaelle and Greason were in the dining hall, and guards dragged them past the table. Greason's face bore yellow bruising, and Gaelle's pale-yellow nightgown was torn to one hip.

"Oh... I'm so glad we got back for this," Finnian whispered. "I hope the coward guard dies."

The four guards forced them onto the balcony underneath us, where Father held out his hand to Dad. Dad didn't hesitate, removing his sword from the sheath and handing it to him.

Lowering himself to the balcony floor, he first moved to Gaelle.

Tears rolled down her cheeks. "My King—I didn't—"

"Be quiet," he spat. "You stole royal clothes and alerted people that my daughter had returned, knowing it would put her in danger. You are no longer employed in the castle and instead assigned to manual labor in the fields."

Her bottom lip quivered, but she shook her head. "Yes. I'll gladly take that and not death."

"You won't die." He raised his sword, stepping now in front of Greason. "But you will live knowing that you were the cause of his death."

"I—I didn't know the full story. Had I—" Greason started.

Father cut him off. "I never denounced my daughter. You attacked a royal. Therefore, your sentence is death."

My stomach roiled as Father jabbed the blade into Greason's heart. I hated that this had to happen, but it was how things were done in this realm... even if I didn't like it.

Tavish squeezed my hand and linked, *Sprite, if your father didn't do it, I would. That couldn't go unpunished, or more people would try to kill you.*

That doesn't mean that if he'd known everything, he would've still made the same mistake. That was what bothered me, but the rules were the rules in Ardanos.

The guards released Greason's arms, allowing him to fall as everyone watched the life drain from him. Gaelle sobbed, clutching her chest. And when it was over, the guards dragged each of them out while the Seelie people watched.

"Let this serve as a reminder." Mother straightened her shoulders. "Those rules aren't to be broken unless the king or I command it."

No one spoke as the silence hung over all of us.

"This brings us no joy." Father lifted his chin, his royal power emanating from him. "The unnecessary loss of an individual is a burden that our magic and land have to bear. Our daughter's actions may be construed as traitorous, but we understand why Lira made the decision that she did. Not only is the Unseelie king her fated mate, but he and his people are no longer our enemies." He paused, allowing the crowd to gasp and glance at each other, absorbing the information.

"But they cloaked the sky in darkness, killing our plants," a man near the middle called out, though not with malice. He scratched the back of his neck as if he were trying to make sense of it.

Father informed everyone of what the dragons had done and how an Unseelie had aided in the chaos. "There was no reason not to let the Unseelie return to their land. Any attack on them or my daughter will be punished the same as if it were an attack on our own kind." Father gazed slowly across the masses as if he were looking at each person. "It is time for fae to truly unite with each other once again, and there's no better way than the union of my daughter and King Tavish." He gestured to the two of us.

I thought we weren't going to alert everyone in case someone else was working with the dragons, Tavish linked with me, rigid.

I swallowed, knowing he was right. *They didn't discuss this with me.*

A few people in the back cheered, but most didn't react. It would take time to mend the twelve years of hatred that had brewed between the two species. Still, that didn't mean it wasn't salvageable.

"But even though this is part of a new chapter to our story, it isn't free of issues." Father frowned and patted Brenin's shoulder. "The dragons intended to capture Lira, but Eiric glamoured herself and took my daughter's place like a true royal guard. Because of this, the dragons are demanding that we hand Lira over to them to free Eiric. However, I refuse to bend to the will of the dragons and allow them to use my daughter to create heirs that could one day take over all of Ardanos!"

Even though this hadn't been the plan, my parents had already gone down the course. Before I realized what I was doing, I said, "And allowing Eiric to die in my place isn't right. But there are more reasons than just her death." The fae wouldn't understand why it wasn't right. I was the royal; her life wasn't supposed to be as valuable as mine. I hated that line of thought and believed that Earth's way of caring for each other should be what we strived for here. "At the end of the day, the dragons need me to create future heirs that could withstand all elements. Even if they kill Eiric, they will bring war to our land. They already expressed their intentions when they delivered their message."

"They'll ruin our land with their magic," someone cried.

"Which is their intent." Tavish spread out his wings as he hovered, wanting his strength and presence to be felt.

I could feel exactly how tired he was, though I wouldn't

have known by looking at him.

"But you expect us to just suddenly trust the Unseelie?" a man called out.

"No, I don't." Father rubbed his hands together. "Time will be required to heal from the twelve years of misinformation the dragons caused. However, right now, our kingdom and royals are being threatened, which will not be tolerated. All of our resources must be focused on the dragons and their threats. The discord between the fae must end now, and we need to help the Unseelie rebuild their food supply in Cuil Dorcha once again. Otherwise, it's going to put a strain on ours."

The crowd glanced around, staring at one another. Not only was Father telling them we had a new enemy—the dragons—but he was throwing additional work their way.

"So, who can I count on to help restore Cuil Dorcha?"

Several beats passed, and not one person lifted a hand.

My heart sank. How were we going to win a war and live in peace if we faced resistance everywhere?

CHAPTER TWENTY-EIGHT

LIRA

Concern swirled from Tavish, mixing with mine. During the entire conversation, I'd sensed conflicting emotions within him, but there was too much going on to even attempt to talk via our fated-mate bond.

However, the tightness of the bond reflected our emotions perfectly. This seemingly simple question spoke volumes about what sort of future the two of us would have—one leading toward peace for both our people or one where they would always be at odds.

I already knew my choice. I would always choose him, no matter the consequences.

Still... it'd be easier if our people could learn to at least accept one another.

Father's wings lowered marginally, the only sign of his own disappointment in our people, which caused me to release Mother's arm and tug Tavish forward with me.

He didn't resist, though his confusion wafted through the connection.

"I understand your hesitation." I straightened, now hovering in front of both of my parents. I could see Father's raised eyebrows, but he didn't intervene.

He was going to let me say what I wanted.

My heart swelled, causing my chest to feel like it might

explode. Father trusted me. Something I hadn't even realized that I wanted.

"For over twelve years now, you've viewed the Unseelie as a threat to our realm, our safety, and most importantly, to our land and magic." Even though both Seelie and Unseelie were fae, Unseelie magic could thrive in the darkness and frost because that was part of what made them, whereas Seelie magic couldn't. We had to have a balance of day and night and warmth for our magic and land to remain at their strongest. "And even before that, there was mistrust because our magic can be at odds."

A few nodded, encouraging me to continue. I tried to ignore the butterflies soaring inside my stomach and the urge to vomit. Somehow, fighting for my life in the gauntlet had been easier than standing up here, trying to plead for the Seelie to not view the Unseelie as their enemy. "But although the moon and sun are opposites, they complement each other. Without the light, our crops can't grow, and without the night, the heat would scorch our land." The island where the Unseelie had lived was an anomaly. The dragons had ruined it, and nothing could grow outside the cave, so Tavish cloaking the land in constant darkness and snow had been a tactic to discourage the Seelie and dragons from coming back.

"Why did King Dunach cover the entire realm in darkness if their food supply was at risk as well?" someone shouted from the back.

Fair question. One I wasn't certain Tavish would want answered. I turned to him, knowing Father had alluded to the fact that the dragons had used their magic to influence the Unseelie. He hadn't gone into detail, which I'd appreciated. That wasn't our story to tell.

Tavish smiled sadly at me and then stared back at the people. "As King Erdan referenced, my father was influenced by dragon magic and wasn't in his right state of mind. People in our court noticed, and he was being watched constantly. He shouldn't have been able to blanket the realm in darkness; no one is meant to be capable of that. Everyone is aware of how our magics work together in Ardanos to balance our world. None of us had even considered the possibility of my father doing that, but recently, we exposed a traitor close to the royal family who was working with the dragons. All I can say is that neither my father nor my mother ever intended to take control of the realm. In fact, prior to the dragons' influence, my father was convinced that Lira and I should be married to unite the fae." His regret filled our bond, causing a deep ache in my chest.

The past twelve years had been so hard for him, and I wished I could go back and prevent the chaos that had consumed our realm. I couldn't do that, but what I could do was stand beside my mate. "Yes, his father was wrong, but haven't the Unseelie paid enough for their former king's mistake of trusting the wrong person? The Unseelie lost their king and queen as a result, and a fourteen-year-old young man was tossed into a leadership role, unable to mourn the death of his parents. His people were kicked out of their rightful home and banished to a land ruined by the dragons, where he had to witness almost two-thirds of them starving to death and try to keep the ones who remained alive from fighting one another for resources. Don't you think they've suffered enough? Especially when the dragons are the ones who caused all of this?"

I needed the people to redirect their hatred to the *right* species. They had to realize that the Unseelie were just as much, if not more, victims as we were. The Unseelie were just as important to me as the Seelie, and I needed the two to get along because both were now *my* people. In my heart, there wasn't a divide anymore. "Working together will allow us to be strong and face the bigger threat."

"We aren't asking for instant trust or friendship." Tavish placed a hand across his chest. "All I ask is that we not fight or live in fear of each other. You are Lira's people, and I love her with my entire being, which means that I bear you no ill will—unless you threaten Lira. If you threaten her, you'll wish that I handled you as nicely as King Erdan did that blasting wildling."

"And he was doing so well," Finnian whispered loudly.

Finola chuckled quietly. "He's still Tavish. That will never change."

"True. Thank Fate for that."

Remind me to stab him when we're away from here. Tavish's jaw clenched. *He's been driving everyone insane, including Brenin.*

Father and Mother flew forward, and once again, the four of us hovered in a line.

"I support King Tavish and my daughter's message. It is time to begin repairing the rift between our peoples." Father arched a brow. "I will ask once more—are there any volunteers who will help the Unseelie harvest their land once again? They are down significant numbers, and this is a way we can show our support since it was us who forced them from their land."

There was another pause, and my heart dropped. Tavish and I had both tried to connect with the Seelie, but it hadn't been enough. I wasn't sure how we were supposed to have the Unseelie and Seelie come together if they wouldn't even try at the request of their king.

I deflated, though I tried to give off the impression I was unaffected.

Sprite, this doesn't change anything between us. Tavish turned and kissed my cheek. *I will not give you up for anything—dragons, betrothals, or even if the Unseelie and the Seelie remain enemies.*

Why can't Fate just give us— I started.

THE KINGDOM OF FLAMES AND ASH

"I'll help the Unseelie," a woman called out from the back of the crowd. "I'm ahead of my numbers for the week."

Both of our heads jerked back toward the people. Someone had finally spoken up. It wasn't much, but at least it was *somebody.*

A man near the front raised a hand. "I can help as well."

One by one, more people volunteered. And each time someone new offered, the surprise in Tavish remained the same. He truly hadn't expected anyone to help.

When it was all over, one hundred Seelie had volunteered. Even though that was a fraction of the Seelie numbers, it was a huge start.

"Excellent." Father beamed. "The one hundred volunteers should leave once this meeting concludes and will be rewarded for their contribution."

My breath stopped. I hadn't expected Father to reward anyone who helped. I had merely been thankful for him doing what he had today.

A few hushed sounds came from the crowd, but Father and Mother turned and flew back into the dining hall. I followed suit, a sour taste filling my mouth when we flew over blood.

Greason's fate would haunt me because my betrayal had led to his death.

His death isn't your fault. Tavish landed on the smooth floor a few steps away. *You didn't make him attack you.*

I did disgrace him, and his guard role was taken away. Castle guard was a coveted position since most guards were stationed outside to watch the borders. Even though the dragons were supposedly our allies and the Unseelie had been kept out by the veil, my parents believed in keeping watch.

A server hurried past me, calling her water magic to wash the blood off the floor.

Father took a seat at the head of the table and gestured for the rest of us to join him. "Please sit. Let's eat so we can discuss what you've learned before you head back and rest."

Sorcha flew around the table, but Finnian chased after her, catching her arm. Her breath caught as she turned and faced him.

"What are you doing?" she gritted out, though I noticed she didn't remove her arm from his grasp.

"Just wondering where you might be later." He winked. "I thought before I head out to battle that maybe we could spend a little time together."

"Thanks, but I'll pass." She jerked her arm away and spun around, retreating.

That was strange. She never acted that way around me.

Placing an arm around my shoulders, Tavish led me to the seat to the right of my father. Our connection sprang to life, generating the soothing buzz between us. As I sat, Nightbane lay at the end of the table between Father and me and huffed.

"Finnian, what have I told you about always flirting?" Tavish rolled his eyes as he sat next to me. "We don't have time for distractions."

"Says the man who was grumpy the entire time we were away, all because of a certain somebody." Finnian's gaze landed on me. "Though I'm not naming names."

"Do you think we might not know who you're referring to?" Struan rolled his eyes as he took his spot behind me while Finola stood behind Tavish. Mom and Dad positioned themselves behind my parents.

Mother sat across from me and patted the seat next to her. "Finnian, why don't you sit here, and Struan, Finola, Hestia, and Brenin, do join us. I know it's unorthodox, but you all were out the entire night and need to eat before the battle tonight."

The four guards froze.

"You heard the queen." Father leaned back in his seat and

leveled his gaze at each of them. "Join us. She's right. You are all exhausted."

Finola sat next to Tavish with Struan on her other side as Dad took the seat between Mom and Finnian, whom he scowled at.

Did something happen between Finnian and Dad? I'd never known Dad to dislike anyone who didn't deserve it. He was gentle, stern, and even-keeled unless someone mistreated Mom, Eiric, or me.

He kept winking at Hestia. Tavish shook his head and yawned. *I hope Brenin will stab him so he'll learn because anytime I harm him, it seems to encourage him.* Scooting closer to me, Tavish turned his attention to my parents. "I appreciate the speech you gave out there, but I thought we agreed that we weren't going to inform anyone what we'd learned about the dragons. We have no idea if anyone else is compromised on either side."

The server who'd cleaned up the blood hurried back across the room as five more servers entered, carrying two plates each, and set one in front of each of us, including Nightbane.

Father picked up a yellow sunberry. "We did, but after Lira was attacked last night, Sylphia and I discussed matters. Gaelle had informed more people of Lira's return to the castle, and we feared one of them would try to retaliate since word of the Unseelie return had spread. We hadn't realized that our people would hurt our daughter, but after she aided in your escape, they equated her with the Unseelie. It was a tactical decision and the best one we could determine to allow Lira to move back and forth between the two kingdoms as she wishes."

"Before the speech, we deployed half our guards to survey Aetherglen. They'll keep watch overnight while the more seasoned warriors sleep to prepare for tonight." Mother placed both hands on the table. "That was the other reason we had to make the announcement this morning. There won't be many guards patrolling the border between our two kingdoms because we'll be stretched thin."

My head swam. There were so many moving parts that this plan felt like it was ever-changing.

Tavish took a large gulp of water, frazzled as much as I was. When he set the clear glass back on the table, his expression settled into indifference. "I understand and appreciate you including Cuil Dorcha in the watch."

"Even if we manage to surprise the dragons, they could retaliate by attacking us while we're preoccupied." Father ran a hand over his beard. "There are so many possible scenarios, and every time we run through the plans, I think of something new."

"Ah... expect the unexpected." Finnian stuffed his mouth with bread. "That's been my personal mantra ever since Lira arrived."

"That doesn't help matters." Dad rubbed his temples like he had a headache.

I tried to hide my smile. Finnian had that effect on people.

"Did you learn anything valuable?" Father asked.

The six of them took turns updating us on what they'd discovered, and we discussed the strategies we could employ.

"Our best strategy is the one Lira has suggested all along." Struan winced like it pained him to say the words.

Tavish's hold on me tightened. He hadn't moved his arm from my shoulders. His emotions were swinging between fear, anger, and frustration, and I hated what all of this was doing to him.

"The island is set up so we can watch her hand herself over without risking losing her. The castle is visible from the sky as long as Tavish has time to recharge and cloak us," Finola said. "We'll need the warriors split into three groups to cover the villages once they can fly inward and engage in battle. Struan and I will decide who we believe we can trust on the Unseelie side to join the war."

"Noted, and yes, we need those we are certain are trustworthy." Father finished his last bite and pushed his plate away. "The six of you should go rest and recharge. Tonight will be long for all of us."

I quickly stood, eager to spend time alone with Tavish. The two of us needed each other.

"We'll meet two hours before darkness at our kingdom's border on the side closest to the dragon land." Tavish got to his feet, sliding his hand around my waist and pulling me close to him. "That should give us enough time to get into position before—" He closed his eyes, unable to finish that sentence.

He didn't have to. Everyone knew what he meant.

"We shall see you then." Father nodded and smiled at me. "Until tonight."

Finnian, Finola, Struan, Tavish, and I turned to face the balcony. It was time to return to Cuil Dorcha. I bent to carry Nightbane, but Tavish pulled me away.

"Finnian, bring the beast," he commanded.

Head tilting back, Finnian pointed at himself. "Me?"

"Yes, since you annoyed everyone else, this is the consequence." Tavish rocked back on his feet.

I chuckled, knowing how the two of them could be. "I got rest last night. I can carry him."

But before I could bend, my feet suddenly lifted out from underneath me.

Chapter Twenty-Nine

Lira

I yelped. I hadn't expected Tavish to carry me, especially since he was exhausted from being out all night.

"You are most definitely carrying Nightbane because Lira and I aren't heading back to Dunscaith with the rest of you." He lifted his chin toward Finnian. "And I fear I might kill you if I am forced to be around you a moment longer."

Even though I enjoyed the thought of alone time with my mate, I knew Tavish needed rest. The three leading emotions soaring through our bond were fear, anger, and exhaustion. *We should go with them. You need sleep.*

If we go back there, our time will be stolen by battle plans and constant interruptions. His eyes turned dark silver. *I need quality time alone with you.*

He clasped me to his chest, causing the buzz between us to turn electric.

"You wouldn't kill me." Finnian wrinkled his nose. "You haven't yet, which speaks volumes."

I pressed my lips together, trying not to laugh, though Tavish's eyes lightened. He could sense that I was trying to hide my laughter, so I might as well say what I thought. "We don't need a second chessboard ruined." I wrapped my arms around my mate's neck and smiled. "So, it's clearly in Tavish's interests for us to go somewhere you aren't."

Somewhere nobody can disturb us. Even him. He fidgeted as his desire slammed into me.

Need knotted in my stomach. *I really like the sound of that.*

"Your Majesty, you need your rest, and we need to discuss our strategy." Finola lowered her head, making it clear that she wasn't attempting to be disrespectful.

"No one cares more about me getting enough rest than I do. I understand that my magic needs to replenish so I can ensure that my mate returns to me." His heartbeat quickened. "I trust you, Struan, Caelan, Lorne, and Finnian to handle strategy. We will return two hours before we are to meet the Seelie at the border."

"What our king is trying to say is that he and Lira have some needs to handle." Finnian smirked, rubbing his hands together. "A pressing situation that only she can relieve. A meeting of the mind and body, if you will."

I inhaled deeply and shook my head at Finnian. He needed to stop. He was taking his own uncertainty out on Tavish.

Tavish snarled. "Say another thing that disrespects what Lira and I share, and I *will kill* you. You are alive because you are one of the best swordsfae in the lands, but I can train someone to become just as good."

Finnian rolled his eyes. "I'm not being disrespectful." He picked up Nightbane as the animal groaned. "But I do need to get going if I'm taking him. I'm fairly certain he weighs at least twice as much as Lira. I'd know." He winked and then dashed out the window.

The way Tavish's teeth ground together told me that I needed to intervene before the two fought one another. I planted a soft kiss on his cheek then linked, *Are you taking me somewhere or wasting more of our time allowing Finnian to pester you?*

He exhaled and relaxed marginally. *Nope. Not any longer.*

Then he soared from the balcony, heading toward Cuil Dorcha. The land blurred beneath us, and all I could do was keep my gaze on his strong face.

Even though we didn't speak, I could feel the tumult of his emotions. They blended with mine, and I wanted to ease his concern, but that would result in the two of us having the same conversation over and over again. I had to save Eiric; there was no other choice. Besides, the dragons weren't going to just let me go. We had to fight them.

When we reached the trees that covered the land at the border, he angled downward, and I felt the coolness of his darkness magic cover me. He was cloaking us, and I got a strong suspicion about where he was taking us.

We landed in a thick section of trees where the evergreens of Cuil Dorcha and the colorful trees of Gleann Solas merged and framed a thick patch of brush... the very place where the Unseelie underground quarters were.

You weren't joking when you said you wanted no disruptions. I grinned, rocking back on my heels.

I never joke when it comes to spending time with you, sprite. He squatted and stuck his hand under the brush. I had no doubt he touched some sort of mechanism that would recognize his blood, and after a second, the brush lifted, revealing the secret passage into our former hiding spot.

When he stood once again, I slid my arms around his waist and looked up at him. *Now this is perfect.*

It'll be even better once I get you inside. He kissed my forehead and then detangled himself, snagging the torch inside the door. He raked it against the stone wall, lighting the end, and led me down the stairs.

When we reached the bottom, he flew to the center of the gigantic room and lit the candles of the huge silver chandelier, his wings moving gracefully.

I moved to the center of the four oversized, dark-gray, oval couches and enjoyed the view from below. He scurried to the large rectangular wooden table and placed the torch against the side before coming back toward me.

"How many people can access this shelter?" I ran my fingers through my hair, trying to get some of the knots out of it. "Will Finnian figure it out and come here to torment us?"

"If he could, he would." He laughed deeply. "But only I can open the door. It's meant to be a safe haven for the royals, and it can sense Unseelie royal magic. Now that Eldrin is gone, it will work only for me."

We were truly alone. No one could interrupt us. Desire swam through me. "Oh, really now? For once, we don't have to be quiet or be careful where we *cuddle*?" I didn't want to assume we'd make love... at least, not until he got some rest. He'd had a long night.

"Cuddle?" he choked, stalking toward me. "That *is* on the agenda, but I was hoping for something else before we got to that."

When he stood in front of me, I placed my hands on his chest and stood on my tiptoes. "Hmmm. And what might that be?"

Heat flooded our bond, and he hoisted me up against him, so I wrapped my legs around his waist. Wind hit my back for a second before I was pressed gently into a solid wall.

He grabbed my wrists and pinned them above my head, causing my breath to catch. When he leaned forward and captured my bottom lip between his teeth, I felt like I could explode.

I whimpered, needing more, and he slipped his tongue inside my mouth, his wintery taste teasing my senses.

Leaning to the side, he kept my wrists restrained with one hand as his other slipped under the top of my gown and cupped one of my breasts. When he gently rolled my nipple between his fingers, I leaned my head back. He didn't miss a beat, moving in tandem with me.

Thorn, I linked and arched my back.

Blighted abyss, sprite. I blasting love the way you respond to my touches. He released my wrists and placed my feet on the floor before bending down and raising the hem of my gown. He slowly peeled it away, leaving me completely naked in front of him.

His eyes traced every inch of my body, and he reached down and adjusted his visible bulge. "You're so beautiful," he murmured, his hand gently trailing down my side and cupping my ass. "And perfect in every way for me."

Knowing we were both desperate and didn't have much time, I reached for his clothes, eager to see him the same way. His irises lightened to my favorite color as I removed his shirt and pants. Once he was naked in front of me, I took in every delicious inch that I needed to feel inside me.

Not waiting for him to take the lead, I wrapped my hand around his dick and stroked him. He shuddered, crowding me against the wall and slipping his hand between my legs. With his mouth on my breast, his tongue teased the tip as his fingers entered me.

I love you. He brushed his teeth gently against my nipple, and I shuddered. *And I can't wait to make you my wife.*

I quickened the pace, his words pushing me even closer than his touches. *Is that your way of asking me to marry you?* My other hand threaded through his dark hair and pulled gently.

As long as you say yes, he replied, his thumb rubbing between my lips as his fingers surged deeper.

The friction inside me built, causing my head to spin. "Tavish," I breathed, his name the only thing that made sense to me. Just as I was about to fall over the edge, he stilled.

THE KINGDOM OF FLAMES AND ASH

My body hummed, waiting for him to continue, but nothing happened.

I opened my eyes to find him staring right at me.

"Why'd you stop?" I asked through ragged breaths.

"You didn't answer me," he said simply.

I shook my head, trying to clear the fog. "What are you talking about? You never asked me a question."

"Fine." His hand cupped my face as his other one brushed against my lips again. "Will you marry me, sprite?"

If he wanted to play, two could do that. "I don't know. I might need convincing." I tilted my head.

He grinned. *Oh, really?* Gripping my ass, he hoisted me against him again, his dick hitting right at my entrance. I tried to push down so he could enter me, but he moved, so all I got was the tip.

"I need an answer," he breathed against my lips as he slid a tad bit more inside me.

I spread my legs out more. "Maybe." I licked his mouth, wanting to do to him what he was doing to me.

Sliding in a little bit more, he connected, *I need an answer, or this is all you get. I want you to be my wife more than anything in this realm.*

His warmth and vulnerability flashed through our bond, and I realized our game was over. I leaned back so I could stare into his eyes. "Yes, Tavish. I want to be your wife."

He beamed. "Right answer." He then thrust deep inside me.

I moaned as his mouth devoured mine and our bodies moved together. Each time he entered me, he somehow went deeper, and the friction took hold once more.

Fate, I love you, I linked and pushed my love toward him. My chest felt so full that I wasn't sure that I could stay this happy for long.

284

He opened to me, our emotions melding together. We felt the same for each other, and one day soon, we'd be husband and wife.

The orgasms ripped through both of us, the high more intense than ever before. Our bodies were slick with sweat as we continued to ravish each other, and after Fate knew how long, the pleasure subsided.

Scooping me into his arms, he carried me to one of the bedrooms we shared the last time, where we cuddled with each other. Soon, sleep took us both.

This was it. The moment we'd been dreading. Even though I felt no hesitation in handing myself over, uncertainty about what would happen next set in.

Tavish and I'd had sex one more time after waking before returning to Dunscaith and meeting with everyone. The little bit of time we'd had was sweet and desperate, both of us wanting tonight to be over but afraid of what could happen once it was. I had no intention of remaining with the dragons, but the plan wasn't without risks.

Now Tìr na Dràgon lay in front of us with the moon high in the sky. We had to make sure that Tavish's darkness magic couldn't be detected.

We planned to split into four groups that had already been assigned. Both sets of my parents would fly with me to the dragon land. Once the dragons gave Eiric back, my parents would notify them that we knew the vow was not valid and that I wasn't obligated to hand myself over. Then, if the dragons insisted, there would be war, and the fifteen hundred guards we'd brought would attack.

It was a simple plan but one that should be extremely effective.

THE KINGDOM OF FLAMES AND ASH

Tavish was adamant that he be with us, but everyone had agreed it would make the dragons suspicious. No fated mate would willingly hand over half their soul to another.

Tavish's emotions were volatile through the bond, and the world seemed to close in around us. I had to believe that Fate wouldn't have put us together only to force us apart.

Even Finnian was quiet, which seemed abnormal.

From the front, next to my parents, Finola raised a hand. Tìr na Dràgon would come into view in moments, which meant it was time for us to split apart.

Tavish took my hand and pulled me against his body. Then his mouth was on mine, his desperation slamming inside our bond.

Sprite, I swear to Fate, if something happens—

I hadn't realized how hard this moment would be for us. If everything went wrong, this would be the last time we got to see, touch, and smell each other. *I have to believe we'll be fine.* I cupped his face, pressing my forehead to his. *After all, I agreed to be your wife. That's a vow that can't be broken.*

He smiled, but it didn't meet his eyes. *I swear to you, I will kill anyone who stands in the way of us being together. You have to come back to me, or I won't survive.*

I won't tolerate being apart from you either. I opened myself to him so he could feel my resolve. *We'll both eliminate any threat to our relationship.*

"Come on, Lira." Father placed a hand on my shoulder. "We need to go before a dragon flies by and sees us."

Right. Tavish couldn't cloak all of us, or he wouldn't have any magic for the attack.

You are *coming back to me.* Tavish's eyes flashed with determination.

I nodded, unable to say anything mentally or physically, as my eyes burned.

286

Turning my back to him was the hardest thing I'd ever had to do, but I swallowed and envisioned Eiric's face, which strengthened me.

Mom and Dad flanked me, flying ahead of Mother and Father. I needed to be in front to make it clear that I was leading the charge—that *I* was handing myself over.

Tavish's magic thrummed through our connection, indicating that he was cloaking the five hundred guards he was staying with a hundred yards behind us. The other two groups had moved so that they were out of sight but could hear the cry of battle and attack the other two villages if the time came. We didn't want to expend too much fae magic at one time.

"Just know that we aren't happy about you doing this," Mom said from my left side. "Losing you would be just as painful as Eiric. You're both our children."

My chest expanded at knowing how lucky I was to have two sets of parents. I placed a hand on her arm and smiled as we continued to fly toward Tìr na Dràgon. "I know that, and I never thought you wanted me to do this. But we're going to get Eiric home and take the dragons down."

I had to believe that.

"We need you to know that we wouldn't be upset with you at all if you decide not to do this," Dad added from my other side. "It'll be okay."

"I'm doing this for me." I placed a hand over my heart and glanced at both my parents. "The dragons took her because she protected me. I can't let anything happen to my sister."

Both of them nodded, though I couldn't help but notice a tear trailing down Mom's cheek before she quickly wiped it away.

Land appeared in front of us, and my stomach hardened. This was it.

Out of the corner of my eye, I saw one of the volcanoes

nestled in the mountains spilling smoke, almost like a warning.

A chill shot down my neck.

Something wasn't right. I couldn't explain it, but something felt off.

I opened my mouth to tell Mom and Dad, but then a dragon flew from behind one of the mountaintops and roared.

Chapter Thirty

Lira

Every cell in my body sizzled.

We were still twenty-five yards from Tìr na Dràgon. Tavish was struggling for control, and I started sweating.

I was thankful that my emotions didn't alarm him more because if he knew why I felt uneasy, he would've already grabbed me and whisked me away.

The burnt-orange dragon roared once more, causing four more in their person forms at the edge of the village closest to us to turn in our direction. Luckily, the dragon guards didn't seem extremely alarmed, probably because they saw only the five of us approaching.

Shouts from the castle could be heard as the dragon circled behind us, the stench of brimstone filling my nose as another gust of smoke billowed from the top of the volcano.

A shiver ran down my spine as my chest seized. Mom and Dad glanced at me, and I could sense their concern. I needed to calm down, or I would do something foolish and wind up getting Eiric harmed. I had made the decision to do this, and I had to deal with the consequences.

The double doors to the front of the castle opened, and two men armed with swords came out, followed by a man and woman I'd never seen before. There was no doubt who they were since they both wore a crown. The dragon king and queen.

THE KINGDOM OF FLAMES AND ASH

Pyralis strolled out right behind his parents.

The royals stood at the bottom of the stairs, and King Ignathor lifted a hand, beckoning us toward them.

Sprite, if he so much as touches you, I will slit his throat in front of everyone, Tavish connected, his rage so hot that it blazed uncomfortably through our bond.

All I need is for Eiric to be free, then I won't even try to stop you. I understood how hard this situation was for him, but it would all be in vain if we weren't able to free Eiric. And there was no way in hell I'd leave here without her in tow.

Mom and Dad waited for me to make the first move, so I inhaled deeply and flew toward the royals. As I passed over the land, a dry heat hit my face, no doubt from dragon magic.

Mother and Father remained about ten feet behind us, and the whooshing of the dragon's wings informed me it was flying directly behind us.

Though we passed by many trees, we were flying so high that the villagers could keep their gazes on us. I tried to ignore the way my skin crawled.

With every flap of my wings, the strain from Tavish increased.

Do you know how blasting hard this is for me? he linked.

I'm sorry. I didn't care if this meant I owed him because this whole situation wasn't fair. Eiric should've never been taken in the first place. *But the fact that you understand why I have to do this means more to me than you'll ever know.*

Be glad you're already far away, or I'd be carrying you away right now, no matter that you'd wind up resenting me.

I flew closer to the ground, the breeze picking up. Maybe Fate was trying to issue me another warning. King Ignathor's shoulder-length, mocha-brown hair, the same color as that of Pyralis, blew into his face, and he pushed it behind his ears. Queen Sintara stood next to him, tendrils of her almost-white

290

hair falling from her braid. She wore a white dress trimmed with golden lace and a jade gemstone pendant.

As I landed before them, King Ignathor arched a brow and gestured for Pyralis to stand on his other side. His beady brown eyes homed in on me. "Princess Lira, you've grown far more enchanting than we could have hoped for. This bodes well for your and my son's future children."

Bile inched up my throat, but I remained silent, not trusting myself to speak.

Lira, please open our bond. I want to see if I can hear what's going on because all I want to do is fly next to you and protect you.

I didn't want to consider how I'd feel right now if I were in his wings. Doing what he asked, I tugged at our connection. Rage blasted into me, but underneath the heat, cold tendrils of fear nearly froze me in place. He was an even mixture of emotions that compounded each other, increasing in strength.

Knowing I had to keep it together, I absorbed them and pushed away the extreme sensations, focusing on my task.

Father cleared his throat. "I want to be clear that I don't appreciate what you've done. Your attempt to kidnap our daughter was not part of our agreement. She's not yet twenty-five, the age upon which we decided she would come to this land."

I glanced at Pyralis, prepared for him to rant about why I had to come here. But I didn't see the arrogant man who'd been at Gleann Solas. Instead, he kept his amber eyes on the yellowing grass at his feet.

"And Pyralis wouldn't have been forced to take such extreme actions if you hadn't allowed the nightfiend to locate her on Earth and bring her back here." The king straightened and smoothed down his jade shirt with golden lace accents that matched his wife's dress. "Not only did you fail to inform us of

THE KINGDOM OF FLAMES AND ASH

her return, but you initiated an offensive to retrieve her without informing us that she was in danger."

Queen Sintara clasped her hands in front of her stomach. Tilting her head, she scanned me. "And she completed a fated-mate bond with someone else and didn't even attempt to hide it."

Between Tavish's rage and now my own, I couldn't stop the words from leaping from my mouth. "Because hiding the fated-mate markings would have made it all better?"

I'm not sure which one I'm willing to keep alive, Tavish's voice popped into my mind. *I think I hate the king and queen equally.*

At least, this confirmed that he could hear the conversation.... A neat little trick we might need to use again.

The queen's jade eyes widened. "Pyralis mentioned that you spoke your mind, but I'd hoped being around the Unseelie had inspired that unflattering attribute. Such disrespect won't be tolerated here."

And there's my answer. The queen it is, so you can visit her in the dungeon and disrespect her every day for the rest of her existence.

I gritted my teeth, wanting to tell her exactly what she could expect, but I had to blasting play nice until Eiric was safe. Swallowing my bitterness, I inhaled, trying to keep my voice level. "Understood. But as requested, I'm here to trade places with my—" I cut off my words, not wanting to say *sister.* If they realized she was family to me, there was no telling what they might do with that information. "Guard."

Queen Sintara smirked while King Ignathor steepled his fingers.

"Very well, but first, there is something we want to discuss since King Erdan and Queen Sylphia decided to join you today." Faint ruby scales spread across King Ignathor's face as if he might shift. "Why did you allow the Unseelie back in their land? Not only are they free once again, but that nightfiend killed one of our family members. Why weren't we consulted?"

Mom and Dad placed their hands on the hilts of their swords as Father moved next to me, standing tall.

"Why would I consult you when no one informed me that Pyralis planned to kidnap my daughter?" Father clenched his hands and spread his earth-brown wings behind him. "We went to the former Tìr na Dràgon to retrieve my daughter, only to find the entire kingdom in chaos. The Unseelie were fighting among themselves, and my daughter was distraught because her guard sacrificed herself to keep her from being taken. As far as the Unseelie king killing one of your family members, be thankful it was just the one. They came onto fae land uninvited and demanded my daughter go with them."

Smoke wafted from the king's nose. "If you'd allowed Pyralis to bring the princess with him as he requested, then none of this would've happened, including the spilling of dragon blood. So you see, the problems arose from you and your decisions."

Queen Sintara nodded, placing her hand on the king's arm, and added, "You sent her to Earth to protect her, yet the nightfiend found her. Now you've allowed him to not only form a connection with the princess but to reinhabit land where he can become strong once more. Have you already forgotten what happened twelve years ago?"

Mother laughed bitterly. "Believe me, we have not. But we're doing the best that we can with the information we've been given."

Even though I couldn't see Mother's face, I had no doubt she was wrinkling her nose in contempt. We needed to stop talking because nothing good could result from this. "This conversation isn't helping matters, just rehashing information

THE KINGDOM OF FLAMES AND ASH

both sides already know. I'm here as requested. I'd rather make the exchange and resolve some of the conflict between us."

Pyralis straightened, reminding me of the arrogant prince I'd seen in Gleann Solas. He lowered his head. "I agree with Princess Lira. This conversation is futile."

"Well." Queen Sintara placed a hand on her chest and smiled. "That just melts my heart. The two of them are already making progress in their relationship."

I wanted to puke. In fact, my stomach gurgled at the words while Tavish's rage swept through me.

Mom glanced at me, scowling. I didn't need a connection with her to know she was torn at this moment. She wanted Eiric back, but not at the risk of me.

Lira, I— Tavish sounded broken even in my mind.

It's almost over, and then we can put this whole night behind us. I felt helpless, but there wasn't any way to comfort him.

The dragon king lifted a hand and looked over my head at the dragon that had herded us in. "Get the prisoner and bring her here."

Wings flapped behind us, and a dragon banked to the left side of the castle.

That's the direction Pyralis went last night, Tavish informed me. *He took food to someone.*

My mouth dried. I hoped he'd taken care of Eiric. There was no telling what state she'd be in. I wanted to ask if she was well, but the dragons already knew she meant something to me. I didn't need to reveal how much.

"I hate that things have gotten so hostile between our species of late." King Ignathor pressed his lips together, though the concern didn't reach his eyes. "I'm hoping we can move beyond that, especially since your daughter will now be living with us."

I tensed, realizing that his dead expression reminded me

of Eldrin.

Father smiled, sincerity thick in his warm voice. "Oh, I'm quite certain we will move on from this."

They were goading each other, and my stomach knotted even more. I wanted this entire night to be over.

The sound of returning wings had me glancing up to see Eiric on the back of the dragon. Her long, curly hair looked frizzy, like she hadn't bathed since Gleann Solas and her bronze skin was coated in thick patches of ash that could be seen from here. When her huge emerald eyes locked on me, they widened, and she shook her head.

My heart leapt in my chest. She might be dirty, but she didn't appear to be injured. Still, it was clear that she hadn't expected to see me here.

Mom and Dad sighed softly, no doubt taking note of the same thing I had.

I see her, I linked, needing Tavish to be ready and to know that the end was truly in sight for this horrid situation.

Within seconds, the dragon landed and lay on the ground. Pyralis hurried over and helped Eiric off its back. She turned her attention to him, and I noticed that his face twisted in what could only be perceived as agony.

What was going on?

Once Eiric was settled on her feet, he removed a key from his pocket and unlocked the chains on her wrists and wings.

The same chains we used in Aetherglen.

He held her wrists tight as his gaze bored into me.

"There's another decision that my husband and I made moments before you five arrived." Queen Sintara stepped forward, regarding her son. "Something that we haven't gotten a chance to tell Pyralis, though he'll be *thrilled* to know what we've decided."

Pyralis's forehead wrinkled, and his jaw clenched.

THE KINGDOM OF FLAMES AND ASH

His concern had my mouth drying.

"And what might that be?" Father said through gritted teeth.

"We understand that our agreement was for the two of them to wed when she turns twenty-five, but we hadn't settled on when they could have children." The queen laid her head on the king's shoulder and said, "Once the exchange is made and all of this is settled, Pyralis and the princess will consummate their relationship and produce heirs as soon as possible."

I burst out laughing. "That's absurd. We don't even know each other, and you expect me to just—"

Do not *finish that sentence, or I won't be able to control myself any longer. Make the exchange so I can kill the ashbreath now.*

"Lira," Father said sternly, placing his hand on my arm. "There's no reason to argue over this."

My head snapped toward him, but then I understood the look in his eyes. None of this mattered. I wouldn't be staying. Fighting them would only make the situation more volatile and drag this out longer.

"Yes, My King." I lowered my head, though it was the last thing I wanted to do. I wanted to hold my middle fingers high, but they wouldn't understand what the gesture meant.

"Ah, firebreath," King Ignathor cooed, kissing his wife on the forehead. "She does understand respect. That will make training her easier."

His condescending attitude had my own ire boiling. *I want to stab the king before you kill him.*

Then you shall get your wish, sprite. But Pyralis is mine.

Fine with me. I lifted my chin and spoke out loud. "Are we ready to make the exchange?"

"Of course. We're thrilled you decided to come tonight instead of pushing the deadline." King Ignathor pointed at

Mom and said, "Hand the prisoner over to this woman."

Pyralis didn't move for a moment, but when his parents turned in his direction, he tugged Eiric along.

My heart raced, knowing that the battle could begin at any moment. There was only one technicality. I would be forced to hand myself over as agreed.

When Pyralis and Eiric reached us, Mom grabbed Eiric's wrist at the same time that Pyralis snagged mine. He then tugged me to his side.

The exchange was complete.

"Was that so hard?" King Ignathor placed a hand on my shoulder, the heat of his magic nearly burning me.

"Yes, it was." I made myself stand still, though I wanted to recoil. "But I won't be staying."

Mom yanked Eiric behind her, spreading her wings, as Tavish's magic slowed and dropped away. The five hundred fae soared toward us, bearing arms.

King Ignathor tossed his head back and laughed. "That's where you're wrong."

Fire shot through the sky from the village to our left, heading directly at my mate.

Chapter Thirty-One

Lira

My heart hammered against my ribs, and my knees wanted to give out, but thankfully, my refreshing magic swirled inside me.

"You are surrounded, King Ignathor," Father rasped, not yet noticing the chaos behind him.

All I could focus on was Tavish's eyes locked on me as he led the attack, unaware of the flame streaming directly toward him.

"We're being attacked," I yelped, and I lifted water from below the group of dragons over the sea. I linked, *Tavish, watch out!*

The flame had almost reached him as it arced through the night sky.

Tavish jerked his head around just as the water I'd called splashed up and doused the flame that had come within feet of hitting my mate. Now that it was extinguished, I could make out what it was.

An arrow.

Father, Mother, Mom, Dad, and Eiric spun around just as twenty more flames soared from the village toward them, aimed at different sections of the group.

"They're shooting arrows at us," Tavish shouted, alerting the masses that might not have seen. "Be careful."

King Ignathor gripped my upper arm and yanked me backward. The heat from his touch almost burned my skin, and at the back of my mind, I wondered if my touch felt like that to Tavish.

"I'm assuming that was you, seeing as everyone else is focused on charging us," King Ignathor spat as he created distance between me and the others. Pyralis remained stuck in his spot in front of Eiric and our parents. "Pyralis, come."

I dug my wooden heels into the uneven ground and pumped my wings, trying to break free, as Dad pivoted toward us and saw the dragon king and queen pulling me away.

Shaking his head, Pyralis rushed to catch up to us as Dad unsheathed his sword and raised it just as the dragon behind him opened his mouth and expelled flames.

Mother spun around and redirected the air so the flames hit the dragon in his own face instead.

"Don't do this, King Ignathor," Father yelled as more arrows arched toward the fae.

Every time Tavish tried to break away, more arrows were loosed, derailing his advance without anyone getting severely injured. The Seelie fae, with affinity to water and wind, tapped into their magic, but more arrows were released every few seconds.

"Me?" King Ignathor snickered. "You set every bit of this in motion. You vowed your daughter to us yet didn't respect us enough to include us in any conversations where her future was concerned. My son had to request that she come live with us early because she completed a sacred bond with another man. And yet, you still turned your wings on us! And now you come here with every intention of attacking us—as if we didn't sense that nightfiend last night watching us. We thought the attack might have come last night, but when nothing happened, we prepared for it. You think we're buffoons, and I'm tired of the constant insults. Leave now, or your kingdom will pay the price."

My stomach dropped. Something had to have happened to alert them to Tavish and the scouting group's presence.

"I won't tolerate my daughter being taken prisoner," Father gritted out, and the ground underneath our feet began to shake.

I glanced up and saw Tavish freeze an arrow that had been heading for him. Finnian and Struan stood beside him, and my mate's eyes met mine.

Deep roars came from behind us, and my parents' faces blanched in terror. With the loud flapping of wings, I didn't have to question what was going on.

Dragons in animal form had arrived.

Dad joined Father in making the ground shake, and I knew I had to do something.

Ten dragons flew over my head, with more following. I could only hope that the guards who'd been attacking the other two villages would gain the upper hand.

I couldn't believe we'd been so foolish.

"Kill the Seelie king and queen," King Ignathor commanded nonchalantly as the dragons continued past us.

The dragons opened their mouths, ready to cover my family in flames. My breath caught as the dragons opened fire, and I yanked at my water magic once again as Mother used her wind magic. Our two magics merged, and the soothing wind mixed with the refreshing pulse of water, forming a massive water tornado that whirled around them.

My body steadied as Father, Dad, and Mom used their own magic against the dragons. Dad and Father flung pieces of the volcanic mountain rocks at the dragons while Mom used her own fire magic. Eiric had dropped to her knees, her eyes focused between Pyralis and me.

"Take her inside the castle," Queen Sintara shouted. "So

we can end this foolish fight."

I laughed, unable to stop myself. "Do you think they're going to forget about me if they can't see me? And you question why others view you as ignorant." The last thing I would do was go inside with them. I had to get out of this situation.

The king yanked me around, scales covering his face and hands. Smoke curled from his nose. "It's best if you don't insult us, Princess. We could make your life very uncomfortable."

"I won't be living here, *Your Majesty*." I kneed him in the stomach, but it felt as if I'd hit steel. My knee popped, followed by a sharp pain, and I gritted my teeth as agony rolled through me.

He smirked, his pupils turning into slits. "And you called *us* ignorant. You just kicked a partially shifted dragon. Our scales protect us."

I wanted to smack the smirk off his face, but his scales were still there.

Lira, I'm coming, Tavish linked, his desperation and fear spiraling inside me. *What did they do to you?*

Of course he'd felt my pain, which would distract him even more. *Focus on your own fight. I'll be fine.*

The blast you will, sprite. Which one harmed you?

I did it to myself. I didn't need him sidetracking me either.

I was certain there was one place the king didn't scale over, so I focused, wanting him to feel a portion of my pain. This time, I moved forward, pretending to be in agony, and then jerked up my injured leg, striking his balls with the top of my thigh. More pain radiated from my knee, but the king released me and hunched over. His body began to increase in size, shifting more fully.

Queen Sintara slapped my face. My ears rang, and my cheek throbbed, but I called my healing magic forward to help heal my knee and then pulled on my water magic. Water from

THE KINGDOM OF FLAMES AND ASH

the sea drenched the queen and the king.

The king sputtered, and his body grew larger. Queen Sintara huffed as her gown and hair matted to her skin.

I was preparing for whatever they'd do next when someone grabbed me around the waist and pulled me away from the king. When my skin didn't buzz, I knew exactly who it wasn't—Tavish. Instead, I found myself being carried by none other than Pyralis.

"Princess, this isn't the way to handle things." His amber eyes darkened as his own crimson scales began to appear on his skin.

"Take her inside and teach her some manners!" Queen Sintara heaved herself up from the spot where I'd been moments ago, beside the king, now in beast form. The crown hung on one of his spikes as if he'd placed it there on purpose. "We can't lose her. You *know* that."

If it weren't such a horrible situation, I'd laugh. Thankfully, my healing magic had already started working on my knee, which meant that I should be able to walk on it soon without draining myself too much. I wouldn't be able to recharge as quickly here on dragon land though, so I had to be careful how much I used.

Pyralis glanced over his shoulder in the direction of my parents and Eiric. He sighed, faced forward once more, and headed to the double doors that led inside the castle.

I swallowed, knowing that I needed to get back to Tavish and my people.

I whimpered, trying to sound helpless. The dragons underestimating me would be my greatest advantage now.

"Don't worry. You won't be mistreated." Pyralis grimaced, and the heat of his arms made me even more uncomfortable than his touch. "I'll make my parents understand why you're reacting this way. I'll make sure you're safe here."

The fact that he felt compelled to reassure me of such things proved that I wouldn't be an equal here. This was just another prison sentence.

We'd gotten halfway up the stairs when the sound of swords clanging, roars, and screams echoed all around us. On top of that was the stench of fire and magic.

This was pure chaos.

I flapped my wings fast and hard, catching Pyralis off guard. I opened them wide, placed the tips of my wings around his face to block his view of everything...and then headbutted his forehead.

My ears rang once again, and the world seemed to tilt around me, but his arms loosened, allowing me to break free of his hold. I pumped my wings hard, flying high, when huge hands gripped my ankles.

"For Fate's sake, Lira, why do the Seelie have to make things so complicated?" Pyralis growled. "I'm trying to get you away from the fighting so you're safe."

"I won't be safe in there!" I kicked, trying to break free, but his hands were like a vise. "We know everything. My people aren't going to give up as long as you keep me captive here."

He didn't respond, but his grip didn't slacken.

I needed to reevaluate. This wasn't working.

Acid crept up my throat. High in the night sky, I could see flames in the direction of one of the villages. They truly had prepared for us.

Between all the dragons, flames, and magic, I couldn't make out where anyone was. The only thing that kept me sane was the fact that I could feel my connection with Tavish.

Where are you? he linked.

The castle stairs. I hated to tell him, knowing it might make him more desperate, but lying wouldn't fix anything.

"We don't have time to waste, Lira." Pyralis huffed. He

THE KINGDOM OF FLAMES AND ASH

began climbing the steps once more, no longer bothering to try to pull me down to his arms again. "I need to get you inside so you can be guarded. You'll be safe in there."

Like hell I would be. I didn't want to be the kind of safe arranged by blazing dragons. Deciding on a different tactic, I stilled my wings and dropped on him suddenly. I made sure to land on his head and then flapped my wings, forcing him to fall backward.

Even as he fell, he kept his grip on me. His body hit the stone as we tumbled together. A scream pierced my ears, and the sound brought a lump to my throat.

Eiric.

The double doors creaked open behind me, and heavy footsteps charged out.

"It's the prince. He's injured and with the Seelie princess," a woman called.

This was getting worse and worse. I had to get out of here. I reached for Pyralis's side, hoping he had a weapon, and grabbed a warm hilt that felt like the dragon sword Tavish had carried. I held on tight, but a woman fisted my hair, pulling me up.

Of course, *now* Pyralis let me go.

However, his eyes widened when he felt the sword leave his side with me.

Stunned, he said, "She's got a—"

But I swung the sword across my body, stabbing the woman in the side. Her grip on me slackened, and I flew upward as Pyralis clambered to his feet. I pumped my wings, trying to get back to my people.

I needed to aid them in the fight.

I heard scuffling behind me, followed by the sound of dragon wings.

"Don't hurt her," Pyralis cried out, and I foolishly glanced over my shoulder to find the prince stumbling in my direction.

304

He just wouldn't give up. What was up with these dragons?

Just as I was about halfway back, a cream-colored dragon flew over my head, talons descending. I called my magic and sent a stream of water from the palm of my free hand into the dragon's underbelly. I didn't know what I expected, but clearly the only thing water hindered was their fire. Not their large, strong bodies.

The dragon shook itself, reminding me of Nightbane, and lowered toward the ground. I swung the sword, aiming for the tips of its talons. All I needed was to make them bleed.

Then, suddenly, the dragon moved a few inches behind me, and I realized its intent.

It wanted to damage my wings, so I couldn't fly.

Jerking downward, I spun around and swung the blade at the talons. The dragon threw its head back and roared. Crimson blood shot from the wounds, covering my face and chest. The stench of fire grew even stronger, as if their blood smelled of it as well. I spun around, allowing it to splash my backside, and began flying once more.

My whole world stopped when I noticed Eiric running toward me out of the chaos. Her hair was tangled and her eyes bloodshot as she took me in.

"Lira, you're safe." She hurried to me.

I landed before her, looking over my shoulder to find five more dragons racing our way.

"You need to fly home." I didn't understand why she was still here. "They threatened to kill you—it's not safe for you here."

She shook her head. "I'm not strong enough to fly, and I'm not leaving you or Pyralis here."

My head jerked back. *"Pyralis?" Holy crap. Please don't tell me she has Stockholm syndrome.*

What does that even mean? Tavish replied, making me

realize that I had unintentionally spoken to him.

I didn't want to bring up what she'd said, so I changed the subject. *I'm with Eiric. She's too weak to fly.* I glanced up through the dragons to see Tavish fighting alongside Father and Mother. Mother was using her wind magic to knock dragons back while Father kept bending the earth to his will. Impressive though it was, they wouldn't be able to continue this much longer because we weren't on Seelie land.

We had to get leverage, but how? The dragons had clearly been prepared.

"Here, I'll carry you." I held out my arms, hoping that I'd still be able to fight while holding Eiric's weight. "I'll just need you to hold on to me tight."

"Listen to me—the only way we're going to get out of this is Pyralis. We need him." Eiric stared into my eyes, the emerald in hers darkening as she pleaded.

I shook my head. "E, that's heading toward more dragons. We need to get away."

"Lira, listen—" she started, but the roar of the dragon behind me had me spinning around to face my enemy.

All five of them were descending upon me, the injured dragon flying to the right, glaring at me.

Knowing that I couldn't carry Eiric and move fast enough, I stood there, feet shoulder-width apart, prepared to fight once more. I couldn't allow them to pin me down.

Then I took off, the adrenaline coursing through my body, helping take the edge off my pain. The first dragon was smaller, which I hoped meant that it wasn't as tough of a fighter. I'd never fought a dragon before, but I would have to figure it out on the fly. Remembering how Tavish had killed the dragon in Cuil Dorcha, I decided to start by aiming for its neck.

The first dragon was on me, its pale-yellow scales reflecting the moonlight. I pretended to fly downward like I was going underneath it to get it to move along with me. As soon as I watched it dive toward the yellowing grass, I tilted my wings and flew up, stabbing the blade through its neck. At first, the sword met resistance, but I strained and pushed it in farther and out the other side, blood squirting all over me, even into my mouth.

The blood tasted like ash. I spat, trying to get the nasty taste out of my mouth, just as the second and third dragons attacked me from both sides. Their eyes were wide with rage. I tried to yank the sword from the other dragon's neck, but it was stuck.

I wasn't going to get it out in time. If they didn't tear me apart, there was still no way I would get free. My heart sank.

I needed help.

Chapter Thirty-Two

Tavish

My heart had never felt so frigid before. Being so far away that I couldn't protect Lira once again made me feel entirely helpless.

Every time I tried to fly toward her, another blasted dragon got in the way. The only redeeming thing was that she'd gotten away from Pyralis, but five shifted dragons flew after her.

She'd just stuck a sword through the one dragon's neck, completely unaware that the other four were ready to attack. They'd be on her in seconds, and I was still too far away.

I had to help her.

I held my sword tighter. It wasn't the one that had belonged to my father. I'd told someone else to bring that one because I couldn't get past the fact that the weapon alone had changed my entire world.

A dark-green dragon soared before me, opening its mouth. Thick smoke hit my face, searing my skin with its heat.

I tugged at my magic and lunged forward, thrusting the sword inside the dragon's mouth. I let go of it at the same time flames erupted from the back of the dragon's throat, burning my arm. As the blade pierced its neck from the inside, the dragon's eyes widened, and I jerked my arm out just before its teeth clanked shut.

The dragon jerked back, choking, its talons reaching for its throat as I pushed my illusion magic toward the four dragons attacking Lira. The dark-green dragon in front of me opened its mouth, a trickle of smoke emerging.

I couldn't retrieve my sword. I'd have to use my quickly weakening magic.

The dragons attacking Lira crashed below her. She turned her head in my direction. Blood painted her face, hair, and body, making her look like a warrior goddess. The warmth I felt through our bond sealed it.

I'd do and risk anything for my fated mate.

I can't funnel this much magic for long. Illusions took the most control. The darkness and frost didn't require as much unless I was cloaking others or the entire sky as I had been. *I need you to kill them.*

On it. She spun around with the sword back in her hand.

I glanced up at the green dragon, hoping to get my weapon back, but it hadn't died yet.

"Your Majesty, you're bleeding," Lorne said as he flew to my side. His face and hair were soaked in blood, same as the rest of us, almost to the point that I couldn't see the light blue in it anymore.

"I'm fine," I rasped, needing to reach Lira. My attention homed in on the sword sheathed on his left side. My father's sword. The one I hadn't wanted to carry but had asked Lorne to bring, just in case. "I need that sword."

Lorne paused like he was deciding something.

"*Now!* Lira needs me," I commanded, my attention heading back to my mate. The power still churned inside me, and I got the view of her slitting one of the dragon's throats. The other three roared and screamed at whatever nightmare I'd forced them to see.

"Just be careful." He handed me the sword.

As soon as my fingers brushed the hilt, my bloodlust

intensified, but not by much. It didn't make me feel like a different person, but I still hated everything that it had taken from me. I held on to it and flew toward my fated mate once more, Lorne keeping pace beside me.

I landed beside my mate and pulled back my illusion magic because I wanted the dragon to know that I was the one who killed him. The dragon moved its wing, readying to fly, when I swung my blade and cut through its neck.

I spun around to find Lorne using his magic against another dragon, causing it to lie down and whimper. He stabbed it in its head, and when I turned to Lira, she'd slit yet another dragon's throat.

The sound of more wings had me lifting my head once again. This time, eleven dragons were heading toward us... ones that hadn't been in battle yet.

"We need to get Lira and Eiric out of here," I shouted to Lorne. "They're determined to capture Lira."

Lira shook her head. "I'm not leaving without you. You're just as much at risk as me."

I stepped toward her, cupping her face. "Sprite, they won't kill me. Otherwise, they risk the magic in this realm being imbalanced. They are desperate to have you, and they won't hesitate to kill Eiric as punishment. You two need to leave now so everyone else can focus on fighting and not on trying to protect you."

Her bottom lip trembled, but I could feel the moment she relented. The bond tightened, but it wasn't from anger.

She was putting my wishes above her own.

I have a problem. E doesn't want to leave. She keeps saying we need to get Pyralis.

My head tilted back. Out of all the scenarios, I hadn't expected that. Dropping my hand, I noticed that I'd smudged blood on her sun-kissed cheek. *She won't have a choice.* I spun to see Eiric staring in the direction of the castle, and I glanced over my shoulder to see crimson scales.

Pyralis was one of the dragons barreling toward us.

"Leave. Lorne and I will hold the dragons off." I pointed in the direction of Aetherglen in case Eiric had forgotten.

"If we wait for Pyralis—" Eiric started.

My patience snapped. With clenched jaws, I bared my teeth at her. "Do you want Lira to be kidnapped and forced to breed with the dragon prince? Because just saying the words is bad enough for me... to be expected to live through it—"

Eiric lifted both hands in surrender. "Okay. I don't want it either."

I exhaled, relief flowing through me. I personally cared about Eiric only because Lira did, but I also knew there was no chance of Lira leaving if her sister remained behind. "Good. Go before I make you."

"I... I can try to fly. I'm just weak." Eiric chewed on her bottom lip.

Lira walked past me, taking her hand. She said, "I'll be there and help you."

"The dragons are almost here," Lorne gritted out, and I looked at Lira one last time and linked, *Get somewhere safe. Avoid the fighting and stay toward the sky. I can cloak you.*

She nodded, knowing better than to argue. *I love you, Tavish. I swear to Fate, if something happens, I will come back. I can't live without you either.*

I moved forward, kissing her quickly and pulling back. *Leave before we distract each other and both of us get into trouble.*

Blowing out a breath, she turned her back to me. Still, I could feel the agony of her leaving me behind, heavy in our bond.

She and her sister flew away. I spun back around to find the eleven dragons twenty feet away. I linked, *Hurry, get out of here.*

THE KINGDOM OF FLAMES AND ASH

I allowed my magic to funnel toward the two of them.

Pyralis was in the middle, flanked by five guards on either side. I raised my sword, my hand throbbing from the dragon flames, and prepared to fight off at least five. I wasn't sure how this was going to work, but I had to believe they had enough sense not to kill me. Either way, I wasn't turning my back on the species that threatened my fated mate.

The sword hilt vibrated in my hand, reminding me it was full of dragon magic. I tried to push away the odd sensation and soared into the sky. We couldn't just stand here and expect to take them. We were going to need to fly around and divert them.

Knowing Lira was hidden from sight, I was able to move more easily. Lorne followed my lead, the two of us breaking apart, causing five to peel off in my direction and the others to follow Lorne. Pyralis kept flying straight, no doubt searching for Lira. Something he'd eventually realize would be futile because I had her and Eiric cloaked tightly. I refused to chance anyone seeing them.

I flew straight up, pushing as hard as I could into the sky. The dry air made it hurt to breathe, and my hand throbbed. There was no way that I would be able to fight with my right hand, so I begrudgingly switched the sword to my left.

The dragons were gaining on me, and I hated how their larger bodies didn't hinder them. Instead, it was all muscle, allowing them to move faster than us. But we were more agile. I paused midflap, allowing my body to plummet toward the earth. The five dragons took more time to change course, and I dropped past them, catching them off guard.

One spun around, trying to hit me with its tail, so I adjusted my weight, caught a little air, and landed on top of it. The dragon jerked his tail to the side, trying to knock me away, but I wrapped my legs around it and swung the sword down.

312

The blade sliced through half the tail without even requiring me to use all my strength. The pale-yellow dragon groaned and jerked to shake me off as the dark-orange dragon on its right flew beside me. The orange dragon opened its mouth, so I cloaked myself and dropped back toward the ground. Flames exploded where I'd been moments ago, and the dragon whose tail was almost cut off thrashed, hitting the navy-blue dragon on the other side of him.

Knowing that the orange dragon was in attack mode, I twisted to the right, avoiding the flames. I kept myself cloaked and flew toward the dragon. I needed to end all these ashbreaths once and for all and get back to Lira.

I moved right behind the dragon when it stopped spewing flames and looked around to see if it had hit its mark. Not waiting, I sliced through its neck, causing the other four dragons to stare toward me. The beheaded dragon dropped, and the indigo one roared, spewing flames at me.

I lifted my hand, allowing ice to fly from my palm and collide with the flames. My magic showed the other three dragons exactly where I was.

My magic dwindled, and my body throbbed. I pulled back the darkness, needing to conserve my strength for Lira and Eiric since I was now getting dangerously low.

More fae flew past, but I could use the distraction. The pale-yellow dragon's wings weren't moving quite as steadily, evidence that the injury had affected him more than I'd expected. However, the pupils of the indigo one on my right and the violet one on my left slitted more as they locked in on me.

Tavish, I'm coming back, Lira connected, her panic flowing into me.

My heart raced harder, and the indigo dragon lunged at me. Swinging the sword, I aimed for its snout, but the indigo dragon jerked back, and the violet dragon snapped at my already injured arm. I kicked its nose, pushing myself away, and angled my wings so that I sailed past them and had time to recenter myself.

I'm all right. Don't come back here. Just keep going. That's the only thing that's going to help end this battle. I firmly believed that when the dragons realized Lira wasn't here, they'd fall back and regroup to attack another time. But we'd have time to create a better plan than this, which would include hiding Lira in the Unseelie underground shelter.

I could feel her hesitation, but then she said, *If you get hurt again, there won't be any talking me out of it.*

Despite my horrible pain, I felt my cheeks lift. She was my rain on a warm sunny day. I spun around to find both the indigo and the violet dragon slithering toward me. Their smoking nostrils indicated their plan. Worse, my magic was almost depleted, and I had no clue how far away Lira was. She still felt close.

I readied my sword. I couldn't risk using more magic to hide myself. Yet, I couldn't get hurt again, or Lira would come rushing back.

I had to do something they wouldn't expect. I sheathed my sword and ignored the stinging, burning sensation in my arm every time I moved. Flicking my gaze between them both, I flew toward them as fast as I could. The violet dragon's eyes widened. I held out my hands and shot ice just as the two dragons expelled their flames at me.

The flames met my ice, a collision of their magic and mine, neither one taking over for a long moment. Then, the dragons' fire began to push through my ice toward me.

As if that weren't bad enough, I could feel Lira's fear spike through our connection. My heart turned cold as I reached a spot between the dragons and their heads turned to face one another. I could feel the flames lick my hands, their power almost completely overtaking mine, and I pushed my wings to fly me higher.

They raised their heads, following me. So, like before, I dropped. The dragons didn't expect it, and I free-fell as I swung my sword toward the violet dragon. The blade plunged through its head.

The violet dragon's eyes rolled back, and I yanked out the blade just as the indigo dragon's flames warmed my body. I closed my eyes, waiting for pain to engulf me, but suddenly, the heat stopped, followed by a sickening splat.

I opened my eyes to find Caelan, Sorcha, Lorne, and Finnian glaring at me.

"You took on five dragons by yourself?" Finnian snapped and rolled his eyes. "Why am I not surprised?"

"Now isn't the time." Caelan shook his head. "We need to end this battle before even more people die on both sides."

I was focused on one thing. My breath caught. *Sprite, are you okay?*

It's Eiric. She's slowing down, and I don't know what to do.

I didn't understand what was going on, but I knew I needed to reach her. *Where are you? I'll come to you.*

Relief emanated from her. *We're behind the fighting, about thirty feet out.*

I moved forward when Sorcha got in my way. "Where do you think you're going? I was told to ensure that your wings don't get burned since you're the last living Unseelie royal."

"Finding my mate," I snarled, harnessing all the hatred I had building deep inside me. "And if you try to stop me, I'll kill you myself. She needs help."

Sorcha's brows lifted. "How do you know that?"

"Because she mind-linked and told me." I shoved past her, not allowing her to waste more time, when my power suddenly

THE KINGDOM OF FLAMES AND ASH

depleted so low that I could feel the cloak I had around Lira give out.

No.

Take Eiric and leave. My magic isn't covering you anymore. My heart pounded as fear took over. *I'm on my way, but don't wait for me. I'll catch up.*

Okay, I'll try. I could sense her desperation.

I dodged through the fighting, trying to fly a straight line to her. A dragon lunged into my way, forcing me to stop. Its beige scales glistened as it prepared to envelop me in flames.

I gripped my sword, prepared to battle, when Struan appeared by my side, covered in blood. He rasped, "Go, save Lira. I'll take care of this one."

Before I could respond, Lira connected, *Tavish, Pyralis caught us.*

The realm tilted.

The dragon prince had already located her.

I was done fighting defense. It was time to force the dragons to their knees.

Chapter Thirty-Three

Lira

Even as the cold tendrils of the cloak Tavish had wrapped around us faded away, I didn't understand how Pyralis had tracked us. He was like Nightbane when he hunted for me, almost as if he could feel the pulse of our magic, but that would be impossible with the number of fae fighting all around us.

Maybe he'd been able to smell us. That was the only thing that made sense, but how, when there was so much chaos, scents, and blood?

He flew in front of us, cutting off our path. His amber eyes looked freaky in dragon form, contrasting with his scales, and I had the urge to scream, though all that would do was alert more dragons to our location.

"Thank Fate," Eiric sighed. "We need your help."

I stared at her. She had truly lost her marbles. Why would she believe that the dragon who planned to wed me would help us? I couldn't fathom what she must have experienced during her time as his prisoner to derange her so badly.

Pyralis rose above us, and his talons reached toward us. I lifted my sword, ready to fight him, when Eiric screamed, "Don't." She flew in front of the blade.

Fear coiled in my chest. I could fight and protect myself, but then he'd have Eiric to use against me... to punish me. The whole point of this mission was to save her and prevent the dragons from attacking Aetherglen.

With my left hand, I shoved Eiric out of the way and swung my sword once more.

She grabbed my wrist and jerked me back, causing my weapon to fall short. Before I could try again, his talons wrapped around my body tightly, crushing my wings and squeezing the breath out of me. He jerked me to him, and the sword slipped from my hand and fell into the water.

A sob built in my chest, and I twisted around to tell Eiric to get away just in time to watch her fly willingly into his free talon.

Tavish, Pyralis caught us, I linked, knowing I had to inform him.

Immediately, our bond changed from pure rage to pure terror, adding to the tension in my lungs.

Where are you?

Wind scraped at my face as Pyralis flew to the right of the fighting. He continued to move past the other dragons, but he let out a strange series of growls like he was somehow communicating.

We're behind all the fighting, northeast of the island. I couldn't help but glance at the chaos. The battle seemed to be even—the fae were holding their own, but the dragons refused to disengage. So much blood splattered everywhere, and there were bodies of both fae and dragons floating facedown in the water. My stomach churned, and I realized this would all be in vain if I didn't free myself from Pyralis.

Knowing my options were limited, I did the only thing I could think of—I called my water magic, hoping it would force him to release us. It was hard to control it without the use of my hands, but I could manage.

Pyralis flew strong and steady, his attention held firm straight ahead of him while I concentrated and directed water to splash all over him.

He huffed and shook his head, but the water didn't cause him to falter *at all.*

Water was supposed to be the dragons' weakness, and I'd seen that for myself when I'd attacked the dragons who'd issued the warning about Eiric's future if I didn't hand myself over, but Pyralis didn't seem bothered.

"Lira, what are you doing?" Eiric screamed. "He's taking us to safety like I told you he would. Why are you trying to dissuade him?"

The careful and methodical person I knew was gone. Eiric never would've said something so ridiculous before.

A bitter laugh built in my chest. "Oh, I don't know. I'm trying not to be forced to marry someone I don't love and have his babies. Remember that?"

Eiric recoiled, and her face twisted in agony, but she didn't say anything.

Good. At least she hadn't lost all reason.

Suddenly, Pyralis loosened his grip on me, and I could move and breathe a little more easily. He banked toward the mountains, and the sound of fighting ebbed on our right side but grew louder on the left.

I leaned forward and spotted another battle occurring over one of the other villages.

How had the dragons known we were coming?

I linked with Tavish, giving him an update.

Blighted abyss, sprite. His rage bled through his fear, and I breathed a little more easily. He continued, *I'm on my way. Keep me apprised of the situation until I can locate you.*

I hated feeling helpless. There had to be a way out of this; I merely had to figure out *something.*

When I glanced over, Eiric had paled even more and was nibbling on her bottom lip. Now, she was nervous. Maybe she should've thought of that before. There was no doubt she'd be in trouble if we didn't get out of this.

Then it hit me. There was something I could try.

I leaned forward and bit into Pyralis's top talon. My teeth hit what felt like a cement wall back home, and he barely flinched. Still, he tilted his head down and glared at me, a wisp of smoke leaving his nose.

At least I'd bothered him. Wanting to capitalize on his distraction, I splashed water into his face. This time, his eyes widened, and he lifted his head and made a choking noise.

I squirmed, trying to get free of his grasp, which caused him to tighten his hold once more. Now we were flying over land with sparse trees down below, barreling toward the mountains. He coughed some more, so I called more water and shoved it in his face like I'd done before.

All of a sudden, he descended straight toward the ground. The wind clawed past my face, and the earth raced toward us. For a moment, it reminded me of how Tavish had flown when he'd brought me back from Earth, but this time, there was no sense of attraction or safety.

At the last second, Pyralis flipped over, allowing his back to take the brunt of the impact. Still, my body jostled, causing the pain in my knee to flare up once more.

Pyralis's hold loosened, setting us free. Stunned, I looked around. We were at the edge of the woods by a mountain. One that was smoking from the peak.

I surged forward, flapping my wings, but my back ached with discomfort. I could still fly, but I worried about Eiric.

"Pyralis," she said urgently.

She slid from his talons and landed next to his face. He choked, and she pressed her hand to his cheek.

"We need to leave," I whispered, afraid that others might be around. He'd brought us this way for a reason. *We landed at the base of the volcano,* I linked Tavish.

I'll be there as quickly as I'm able, he answered, his frustration coursing through me. *Struan, no!* His panic heightened, swirling through me.

My stomach dropped. *What's wrong?*

He... he died protecting me. Tavish's heartbreak coursed through the connection. *He did it so I could get to you. I'm on my way.*

My heart shattered, thinking about Isla. It felt as if Ardanos itself was determined to keep us apart and slowly make everyone I care about suffer.

Not only that, but I didn't understand why Fate would make us mates if she was just going to allow us to continually get torn apart.

I flew to Eiric and tugged her to her feet as Pyralis's body began shrinking. I couldn't let Struan's sacrifice be in vain.

Pyralis was shifting back to his human form.

I didn't care to find out why. I clutched Eiric's hands, dragging her back. "Do you want to die? Because that's what's going to happen if we don't get the blast out of here."

"Lira, he's on our side. If anyone should give someone a chance to explain their actions, it should be *you*." Her bottom lip trembled, and she didn't look anything like the strong sister I'd always known.

Pyralis finished his shift, thankfully with his clothes on. His finger dripped a little blood, and he groaned, "Lira's right. You need to leave immediately and protect yourself. If my parents locate you, they'll kill you now. It's written in your fate." His attention flicked back to me. "Water is our weakness, but to wield it, you have to do what you just did to me—force it into our throats when we're about to use our flames. If you douse the flames within us, it makes us weak."

I blinked, grappling with what I'd just heard. He'd clearly

been messing with my sister's mind, the twatwaffle ashbreath, and now he wanted to mess with mine as well.

I wouldn't fall for it. "Says the dragon who communicated something to all the other dragons when you caught us. Did you tell them to follow us? E, I don't know what happened during your time here, but we need to leave before you're taken prisoner again." I glared at Pyralis. "I don't believe your lies for a second."

"He's not what—" Eiric started.

But Pyralis cut her off. "I didn't alert them that I'd captured you. I informed them that you got away, hoping to divert attention from us. I was taking you to the volcano, someplace no dragon would think to find you because no fae can withstand the heat."

I laughed bitterly, my parched throat aching. "If you don't want to marry me, you don't have to kill me. We already know the truth."

His pupils turned into their dragon-like slits. "What are you talking about?"

"That you dragons manipulated the Unseelie king and drove him to madness so that the Seelie would be forced to enter an alliance with you." I gritted my teeth, wishing I still had my sword. I could easily kill him. "The agreement is void, Pyralis. We were misled. I am under no obligation to marry you."

His shoulders sagged, which caught me off guard, but then he tensed again.

That was when I heard the beat of sizable wings, and I glanced up and saw a pearl-white dragon and the scarlet scales of the king flying toward us. I remembered Tavish alluding to the white color signifying the royal family and guessed the other dragon was the queen.

Scales pebbling along his skin again, Pyralis focused on Eiric and growled, "Go."

However, the four dragons that had visited Cuil Dorcha land appeared from other directions and surrounded us.

We were captured once again.

I'm surrounded—

Tavish interjected, *By the dragons that visited our land. I see them, and I'm trying to get there.* Pain coursed through our bond like he'd been injured.

A lump formed in my throat. His worry for me must be distracting him. He was being harmed *because* of me.

The king and the queen landed on my right side, and their bodies began to morph smaller. The other four dragons stood behind us, hemming us in. If we attempted to fly away, the four of them could take us down easily.

"Pyralis, what are you doing?" Queen Sintara spat. "Your father and I have been growing suspicious, but we never imagined you'd be capable of *this.* Were you going to let *both* of them go?"

My head tilted back before I could stop it. Something had created a rift between him and his parents... but what?

Pyralis tugged Eiric behind him. "It doesn't matter anymore. The fae know what you did."

King Ignathor smirked. "It doesn't matter. None of that changes that the princess is on our land, and I declare we shall keep her. She will be your wife and breed your heirs. Everything before that merely served to get her here."

"I will *never* marry him." The idea of being with someone besides Tavish made me want to vomit. "There's nothing in this world that could make me do that."

"Nothing?" The queen tilted her head and arched a brow.

A chill raced down my spine just as a dragon flew over the side of the mountain with Tavish in its grasp. His arm and side of his face were burned, and his shirt was tattered. His body hung limp.

Fate no.

My heart ached so hard that my chest wanted to explode. *Tavish?*

Despite our bond feeling warm, he didn't respond. I clutched my chest.

"You have a choice, Princess. Either we torment your mate every day for the rest of his existence, or you agree to marry Pyralis and birth his heirs. We'll allow the Unseelie king to go back to his miserable existence—without his wings. That will keep the Unseelie royal magic alive so it doesn't threaten the balance of our world, and he can live out a semi-healthy life in Cuil Dorcha."

Tavish lifted his head and linked, *Lira, I'd rather be tortured forever than have you marry him.*

No. The dragons couldn't win, not like this. They didn't deserve to breathe the same air as us. Something had to give.

"Pyralis, do something," Eiric wailed.

He shook his head. "I can't. There's too much at risk."

Her face paled, and I realized that he was a prisoner to his parents, the same way they intended me to be. I hadn't gotten that impression before, but something had fundamentally changed.

Eiric.

Could they be fated mates? No. They weren't even the same species.

That's when I realized the dragons' biggest mistake. They didn't know how strong Tavish and I were together. Digging deep, I yanked at my healing magic. The comforting thrum soared through me, and I pushed the magic through our bond the way I'd done before.

Lira, no! You need your strength to get free of them. Tavish locked gazes with me.

We aren't doing this choose one or the other business

anymore. It was always me trying to protect Tavish or him trying to protect me. One of us sacrificing everything for the other. *This time, we save each other. We truly work as one.*

His brows furrowed, but he nodded faintly. Then he opened the bond on his end, allowing my magic to flow into him with ease, the sensation similar to when we had sex and merged our souls.

The strain on my magic slackened, and my water magic sang inside us.

"Are you done fighting us, Princess?" The queen lifted a hand, and I realized she was the one in charge and not the king, as had been portrayed when we first arrived. "Or do we need to torture your *fated mate* to get the message across?"

I could feel Tavish's strength returning, and my own knee was healing again in the process. The storm-gray color returned to his eyes, and I knew this had to be it.

"You know we could live in peace. It's not too late, but you need to stand down now and stop more blood from spilling," I stalled, wanting to give him a little more time to recover.

Out of the corner of my eye, I noticed Finnian, Caelan, Sorcha, Mom, Dad, and Lorne hovering in the trees nearby. They'd no doubt chased after Tavish when he'd been captured. They must have heard my offer and wanted to see if the dragons took it.

"Peace doesn't work for dragons. It's conquer or die." The queen lifted a hand. "But remember, we gave you a chance." To the other dragons, she said, "Grab the princess and hold her captive. If she tries to help her fated mate, kill her." White scales covered her face, though she remained in non-beast form. "Maybe next time you won't waste it." She dropped her hand, and the dragon holding Tavish opened its mouth, smoke billowing out.

The black-scaled dragon, Zyndara, reached for me as I

yanked on my water magic, letting it rage through my body. It was time for the dragon king and queen to die.

Chapter Thirty-Four

Lira

Knowing that I had to act fast, especially with the threat to Eiric, I lifted both hands and pushed water into the faces of Zyndara and the dragon who held my mate captive, aiming for their nose and mouth. Both dragons jerked back, and Tavish managed to use the momentum to break free from his captor's grasp.

"He shouldn't be able to move like that!" the violet dragon shouted as if that would change anything.

The remaining three dragons closed in on Eiric.

I had to reach her. She was in the most danger.

One of the dragons roared, and I prepared to splash the three in the face when King Ignathor's large arms circled around me and shoved me to the rocky ground.

Sprite! Tavish linked.

My injured knee flared and bits of stone cut into my knees, palms, elbows, and face. The king's weight covered me, making it hurt to even breathe, and my lungs screamed for oxygen.

I gritted my teeth and tried to roll him off me, but I wasn't able to budge him an inch. Instead, all I managed to do was expend more energy and deplete what little oxygen I had left.

My head spun, and I realized that if I didn't get free soon, I'd black out. Maybe that was the king's plan. My instinct was to call out to Tavish for help, but I swallowed the words, knowing

THE KINGDOM OF FLAMES AND ASH

he was engaged in his own battle.

Just as I felt myself fading, King Ignathor's weight lifted from me.

I raised my head and dragged in a deep breath, then saw Sorcha standing with her back to me just as Zyndara charged at the Seelie guard.

Finnian flew over the dragon's head, ice shooting from his hands and onto the dragon. Sorcha flew up, swinging her blade at the dragon's neck. At the last second, Zyndara flipped around and slammed her tail into Sorcha's side, sending the guard flying several feet away and leaving me wide open to attack.

I tried to climb to my feet, but my knee gave out, and I dropped back onto the rocky ground. Pain jolted through me again, stealing my breath.

Turning my head, I saw Pyralis fighting two of the dragon guards and protecting Eiric, causing some of my worry about her well-being to dissipate.

Flapping my wings, I rose so I didn't need to stand, and I found Tavish fighting King Ignathor while Mom, Dad, and Lorne fought Tavish's captor and the emerald-green dragon.

I tapped into my water magic to help aid the fight but realized that both of my magics were depleted. Blazing abyss. I had to find a way to help without my innate weapons.

Looking around, I realized there was one thing I could use for defense.

Rocks.

I grabbed a huge round rock and glanced up to choose my target.

A small, strong hand clutched one of my wings and yanked me backward. I landed against a tree trunk, which knocked the wind out of me. My lungs couldn't work, but I held on to the rock as my only line of defense.

Queen Sintara stepped in front of me, wearing a deep

328

scowl. "It didn't have to be this complicated, Lira. All you had to do was marry my son." She gripped my arm, not acknowledging the rock I had in my hand, and jerked me up. I stumbled, and agony shot through my knee again. I went down, the rock rolling a few feet in front of me.

Lira, I'm coming, Tavish linked, fear for me taking hold.

I swallowed a whimper, but not soon enough. The corners of the queen's lips tipped upward. The fighting continued around us, and then the queen jerked on me once more. My eyes burned with unshed tears. *Focus on your battle. Both Ardanos and I need you to live.*

"My knee. I think it's broken," I wheezed. "I can't walk."

Huffing, the queen bent down to lift me, and I realized that *this* was my chance. Gritting my teeth, I rolled forward, startling the queen, and managed to grab the rock. The queen bent toward my other side then clutched my left wrist. With all the strength I had left, I lifted the huge rock with my right hand and smashed it into her head, knocking off her crown.

I heard a sickening *crack*, and her hand released my wrist.

She wobbled, reaching up to touch the top of her head. Crimson tracked down the side, and her pupils slitted. White scales showed faintly on her skin, but her body glistened.

I reached for the rock again, shifting both knees for balance. Blinding pain slid through me, and the queen reached out to stop me. However, I swung the rock at the side of her head once more, and the impact made her collapse to the ground.

She didn't stir. My gut twisted as blood pooled under her head. I hadn't expected it to work that well since dragons were so strong, but clearly, in their smaller form, they were similar to us.

"Lira," Eiric cried, and I rolled onto my ass, unable to stand the weight on my knee. I turned to find Eiric running toward me with Pyralis right behind her.

THE KINGDOM OF FLAMES AND ASH

She dropped beside me, her face strained. "Where are you hurt?"

"I don't—"

Pyralis fell forward, causing both Eiric and me to jerk up. The dragon prince rolled onto his back while Tavish flew over him.

Raising the dragon sword over his head with the white jagged blade facing downward, Tavish snarled, "You'll die knowing you never had my mate. That she is mine, always and forever. And I'll enjoy killing you for everything you've done to her and to my people."

"No," Eiric shouted, jumping to her feet. "Tavish—"

But my mate didn't even acknowledge Eiric. Rage and hatred churned in him, making my insides feel gross.

He swung downward just as Eiric jumped on top of Pyralis, covering him with her body.

My heart skipped a beat. *Don't hurt Eiric!* I wanted to intercept the sword, but I was at the mercy of my wounds. All I could manage was to scoot over to them, hiking my dress way too high for comfort or being ladylike.

Tavish lurched to the side, barely missing Eiric. He breathed erratically. "What the blast are you doing?"

She stared straight at him. "He's my fated mate. You can't injure him."

"Eiric, get off me," Pyralis commanded. "You're going to get hurt, and this is my punishment to bear."

"Even he agrees," Tavish sneered. "He keeps trying to claim my mate."

Pyralis rolled over Eiric and stood, his scales splotching his face. "However, I'm not going to just lie here and die. I will protect myself and most definitely Eiric."

Sinking into a fighter's stance, Tavish prepared to advance. rapidly to us: "Tavish, you can't kill him," Caelan shouted as he flew

330

Instead of listening, Tavish lunged. Pyralis jumped back and changed partially into his dragon form. Tavish didn't pause and stabbed the prince in the arm. Blood spurted, and my mate smirked and yanked back his sword.

"Stop!" Eiric screamed, but Mom and Dad landed behind her and grabbed her arms just as Caelan landed between Pyralis and Tavish.

"You can't kill him, Tavish." Caelan lifted his own sword with a shaky hand, the tip of his blade coated in red. Black blood oozed down his arm.

Snarling, Tavish growled, "People keep saying that, but I can and will."

"The dragon king and queen are dead. He's the last living dragon royal." Caelan lifted a brow. "If you kill him, then our world will become unstable, which will impact the fae and maybe even your relationship with Lira. Is that what you want?"

Pyralis gasped and hung his head. He glanced at his mother, who lay bloodied not far from him, and his face twisted in agony.

Tavish lowered his weapon just as Lorne, Sorcha, and Finnian landed between Tavish and me. I glanced behind them and noted that the dragons we'd been fighting had all been slain. Everyone was dead except Pyralis.

Some of the pressure lifted from my chest. At least none of us had been killed.

"He's the one person I want dead." Tavish wrinkled his nose.

I didn't know what to say because I didn't want to add to his turmoil. If someone had tried to stop me from killing Eldrin, I might have lost control. I didn't want Tavish to feel like I was choosing the dragon prince over his needs, but...

"Maybe he's willing to do what's right." I had to hope he could be a decent guy and a potential ally, given what I'd feared was true—he was indeed Eiric's mate.

Pyralis clutched his arm where he'd been stabbed, but he turned to me.

"Don't blasting look at her, ashbreath," Tavish seethed.

"Fine," Pyralis said and faced Tavish. "There's been too much death on both sides. I can end the fighting. This arrangement was my parents' doing, not mine. And they paid the ultimate price with their lives." His eyes glistened, but he straightened his shoulders.

"Yet you tried to kidnap my mate and bring her here." Tavish grimaced. "It wasn't all your parents."

Pyralis's scales reappeared on his face. "I never wanted to marry her. I agreed only to help our people. When I brought Eiric back instead of Lira, everything changed. However, my parents wouldn't listen to me. Maybe if they had, things would be different right now." He growled, "I will return after I call off the fighting."

"Pyralis, you're hurt." Eiric's face twisted in worry.

Mom kissed her forehead and said, "Your dad and I will go with him."

It wasn't just to keep watch over the prince but to make sure he didn't betray us.

Pyralis flew away, blood still seeping from the wound on his arm, and Tavish rushed to me. When he reached my side, he placed an arm gently around me.

I was so worried about you, Tavish linked, kissing my forehead.

"Uh..." Finnian's head tilted back. "Who killed the queen? I've never seen anything so barbaric."

"That would be me." I raised my hand. "I didn't have a sword or dagger, so I had to improvise."

He grinned and placed both hands on his hips. "Why am I not surprised? You've always managed to find a way out of a tough situation. If you weren't fated to Tavish—"

Tavish snarled, "Stop speaking," as Sorcha smacked him on the back of the head.

"We should go and make sure the fighting stops." Caelan pursed his lips. "They may need our help."

"And the princess should really pull her dress down." Lorne cleared his throat uncomfortably.

"Don't look or try to help her." Finnian fluttered his wings. "Otherwise, Tavish will kill you."

Tavish stood and gathered me into his arms, and I yanked my gown back down where it should be. Still, we both flinched at Finnian's choice of words right now. Pyralis was right. There were way too many deaths; even kidding about it right now seemed insensitive.

"Finnian, please, for once, be careful how you speak," I said gently, knowing that he hadn't meant it so inconsiderately. "We've lost a lot of people today."

In fact, I feared the numbers.

Sadness flooded into me from Tavish, and he said, "Yes. Let's not make light of all those we lost."

There was no telling how many graves we'd need to dig. My heart grew heavy.

Caelan moved to pick up Eiric, but she shook her head. "I'm good right here."

"Finnian and I can stay here with her," Sorcha offered.

A dragon roared louder than I'd ever heard before.

Without a moment's hesitation, Tavish took to the air. Now that the battle was over, I began to notice every ache in my body.

As we continued upward, I glanced all around at the fae and dragons. Flames weren't flashing anymore, and the sound of swords and screams had calmed. The dragons that had been fighting over the water were flying back toward the island, leaving the fae with their weapons raised.

Pyralis had come through. The fighting had stopped.

And with that realization, I nestled into the arms of my mate and let darkness overtake me.

Epilogue

Tavish

After my parents died, I thought I'd never find happiness again. Now, each day that I woke with Lira by my side—as my queen, fated mate, and wife—I felt happier and more fulfilled than I could have dreamed.

The past five years had seen tenuous peace, but Ardanos finally seemed to be heading in the direction it was always meant to go... except for right now, with *him* here.

I sat at the end of the table in the dining room, admiring Lira. She stood in front of the huge windows overlooking Cuil Dorcha, one hand on her stomach, which was full with our child. Isla stood next to her, wearing one of her rare smiles, Nightbane on her other side. Nearby, Eiric leaned back against Pyralis's broad chest, his hands on her shoulders, while I glowered at him.

Even Nightbane's lime-green eyes glowed, emphasizing his own distrust of the dragon. It was the second of two things the beast and I had ever agreed on—the first being our love for Lira.

Finnian entered the room and took a seat to my right, across from Caelan.

"You do realize that he never wanted Lira, right?" Finnian took a sip of his drink.

THE KINGDOM OF FLAMES AND ASH

"Doesn't matter. He said he did." I wasn't sure I would ever like the dragon king. His only salvation was that the new dragon queen was Lira's sister and best friend. That was the sole reason I tolerated him. That and because he made sure to always keep Eiric between the two of them and never got close to my mate. "That's something I doubt I'll ever get over."

"Good thing for Caelan that doesn't apply to all the other dragons," Finnian goaded. "Otherwise, he wouldn't be able to have his fated mate live here."

Another future dragon-fae hybrid baby in the making. However, Caelan's fated mate was an ideal citizen. In her dragon form, she'd helped the rebuilding of Cuil Dorcha go that much faster. At first, it had been in repayment for Lira healing so many of the dragons once she came to from unconsciousness, offering her secret gift of healing to everyone, but then her helping turned into something more between her and Caelan.

"Don't pretend like you yourself aren't madly in love." Caelan rolled his eyes just as Sorcha and Emberlyn entered.

Sorcha flew to the seat beside Finnian and arched a brow. "He better be."

Caelan's mate Emberlyn strolled around the table to her spot beside him, her radiant pink hair glowing as the two of them stared into each other's eyes.

The only person who hadn't had it easy since the war ended was Isla. Struan had died handling the dragon for me, leaving her without a father. A role that Lorne quickly stepped in to fill. When everything settled, Lira had asked Isla to be her main handmaiden, allowing the girl to make her own money and have one of the most prestigious jobs in the kingdom.

The moon rose high, and Eiric leaned in to give her a hug. They'd been here for four hours—not that I was counting every excruciating minute of Pyralis's company.

We all said our goodbyes, and after far too long, I managed

to get Lira alone in the royal chambers.

She'd painted the walls green, and combined with the wooden floors, it reminded me of the time we'd spent together in the woods when we were younger. Memories of those happy times helped me get past the fact that my parents had died here, since the two of us had moved into the chambers of the Unseelie king and queen.

"Thank you for being tolerant of them." Lira removed her blue gown, a color I favored because it matched her eyes. She stood naked in front of our bed. She'd always been gorgeous but was even more so now that she was carrying our child.

"I don't need to tolerate her. *He's* the problem." My legs brought me to her without permission, and I cupped her face. "It's not Eiric's fault that Fate cursed her with him."

Lira laughed, the sound making my heart race. That was my favorite sound in the realm.

"Well, we'll be with them all day tomorrow." She placed her arms around my neck, pressing her breasts against my chest.

Blighted abyss. I should've taken my tunic off, but even with the material between us, the jolt that hummed between us coursed to life. My dick twitched, ready for what came next.

"Did you hear what I just said?" She grinned, playing with the hair at the nape of my neck. "I was talking about Eiric and Pyralis's wedding tomorrow at Caisteal Solais."

Though she did live with him, Pyralis had delayed marrying Eiric, wanting to prove to us that he was a true ally. He'd wanted to make things right, which I might have admired if he hadn't tried to claim my mate in the past. In fact, a few weeks after the war, I had married Lira, claiming her in all ways.

"Can we not talk about them tonight?" I placed my hand between her thighs, knowing her weakness.

Her legs automatically opened for me, causing all brain cells to leave my head and go straight to my cock.

THE KINGDOM OF FLAMES AND ASH

Her lashes fluttered, and I kissed her lips, linking, *Sprite, I love the way you respond to me. You're so perfect for me in every way.*

Her tongue slipped into my mouth, and I hoisted her into my arms and carried her to our bed. Nightbane huffed and ran into the bathroom, having long ago learned what to do when it came to this.

Within minutes, we were naked and exploring each other's bodies with our hands and mouths, free of threats, enemies, and anything that could distract us from doing this for the rest of our lives.

Even with Pyralis as part of the family package, I would never want any other life than this.

The life Lira and I had found with each other.

ALSO BY JEN L. GREY

Of Fae and Wolf Trilogy
Bonded to the Fallen Shadow King

Rejected Fate Trilogy
Betrayed Mate

Fated To Darkness
The King of Frost and Shadows
The Court of Thorns and Wings
The Kingdom of Flames and Ash

The Forbidden Mate Trilogy
Wolf Mate
Wolf Bitten
Wolf Touched

Standalone Romantasy
Of Shadows and Fae

Twisted Fate Trilogy
Destined Mate
Eclipsed Heart
Chosen Destiny

The Marked Dragon Prince Trilogy
Ruthless Mate
Marked Dragon
Hidden Fate

Shadow City: Silver Wolf Trilogy
Broken Mate
Rising Darkness
Silver Moon

Shadow City: Royal Vampire Trilogy
Cursed Mate
Shadow Bitten
Demon Blood

Shadow City: Demon Wolf Trilogy
Ruined Mate
Shattered Curse
Fated Souls

Shadow City: Dark Angel Trilogy
Fallen Mate
Demon Marked
Dark Prince
Fatal Secrets

Shadow City: Silver Mate
Shattered Wolf
Fated Hearts
Ruthless Moon

The Wolf Born Trilogy
Hidden Mate
Blood Secrets
Awakened Magic

The Hidden King Trilogy
Dragon Mate
Dragon Heir
Dragon Queen

The Marked Wolf Trilogy
Moon Kissed
Chosen Wolf
Broken Curse

Wolf Moon Academy Trilogy
Shadow Mate
Blood Legacy
Rising Fate

The Royal Heir Trilogy
Wolves' Queen
Wolf Unleashed
Wolf's Claim

Bloodshed Academy Trilogy
Year One
Year Two
Year Three

The Half-Breed Prison Duology
(Same World As Bloodshed Academy)
Hunted
Cursed

The Artifact Reaper Series
Reaper: The Beginning
Reaper of Earth
Reaper of Wings
Reaper of Flames
Reaper of Water

Stones of Amaria (Shared World)
Kingdom of Storms
Kingdom of Shadows
Kingdom of Ruins
Kingdom of Fire

The Pearson Prophecy
Dawning Ascent
Enlightened Ascent
Reigning Ascent

Stand Alones
Death's Angel
Rising Alpha

ABOUT THE AUTHOR

Jen L. Grey is an *USA Today* Bestselling Author of romantasy and paranormal romance. In her stories, you'll find angsty fated mate stories with tons of action.

Jen lives in Tennessee with her husband, two daughters, and three Australian Shepherds. When she isn't writing, you'll find her with a nitro cold brew in hand while chauffeuring her children around town or watching television.

Learn more at: jenlgrey.com

ANYA

PAGEANDVINE.COM